RED LINE

AN INIQUUS ACTION ADVENTURE ROMANCE

CIA COLOR CODE

FIONA QUINN

RED LINE

FIONA QUINN

THE WORLD OF INIQUUS

Ubicumque, Quoties. Quidquid

Iniquus - /i'ni/kwus/ our strength is unequalled, our tactics unfair – we stretch the law to its breaking point. We do whatever is necessary to bring the enemy down.

THE LYNX SERIES

Weakest Lynx

Missing Lynx

Chain Lynx

Cuff Lynx

Gulf Lynx

Hyper Lynx

Marriage Lynx

STRIKE FORCE

In Too DEEP

JACK Be Quick

InstiGATOR

Fear The REAPER

Striker

UNCOMMON ENEMIES

Wasp

Relic

Deadlock

Thorn

FBI JOINT TASK FORCE

Open Secret

Cold Red

Even Odds

KATE HAMILTON MYSTERIES

Mine

Yours

Ours

CERBERUS TACTICAL K9 TEAM ALPHA

Survival Instinct

Protective Instinct

Defender's Instinct

Delta Force Echo

Danger Signs

Danger Zone

Danger Close

Cerberus Tactical K9 Team Bravo

Warrior's Instinct

Rescue Instinct

Hero's Instinct

Cerberus Tactical K9 Team Charlie

Guardian's Instinct

Certified Cerberus Tactical K9

Beowolf

CIA Color Code

Red Line

This list was created in 2024. For an up-to-date list, please visit www.FionaQuinnBooks.com

If you prefer to read the Iniquus World in chronological order you will find a full list at the end

of this book.

Dedicated to my fellow travelers:
We may not have Paris, but we'll always have Casablanca.
Sam, Misa, Peter, Janelle, Abby, Wei, Isaac, Saima, Sonya,
"Here's looking at you, kid."

THE PLAYERS

Iniquus

- Nutsbe – Panther Force, tactical operations coordinator

CIA Color Code

- Anaïs Marie Rousseau AKA Johnna **Red**, Cassandra Kromos
- John Grey
- John Black

Delta Force Echo

- Algernon Leeland Kesling AKA **Nomad,** Nicholi Kromos
- T-Rex
- Ty
- Havoc
- Jeopardy
- Nitro
- Colonel Watts, JSOC
- Asad, DIA

Color Code Assets

- Sophia Abadi Ackerman
- Dr. Wajeeb
- Dr. Klein
- Moussa

PROLOGUE

Hans Klein

WITH THE SLAM OF A CAR DOOR, HANS TURNED HIS ATTENTION toward the towering window bank. The late afternoon sun did its best to shoot light into the dim reception area, but decades of accumulated city grime veiled the glass, creating a privacy curtain.

Another car door banged shut. The reverberations echoed off the stone facades of the Munich city buildings, most of them empty with "for rent" signs displayed on the stoops.

Two car doors, that was typical.

Hans's clients usually showed up with some form of security at their heels, especially in this neighborhood.

This had been a suitable locale in Hans's younger days, vibrant and bustling. But this part of town was now out of fashion. His wife begged him to move somewhere closer to their house or at least to a less run-down area. Somewhere safer. But at seventy years old, the life force necessary to organize such a change had drained away. With forty-five years of collected reference books, equipment, and memories, it was simply easier to stay.

Hans turned to the clock. Six minutes until four.

By the time the client climbed the three flights of stairs, the knock at his office door would be perfectly timed. *Respectful,* Hans thought as he shifted his weight, placing his hands on the arms of his chair, preparing for the process of standing.

Cracked with dry rot, the red leather of his armchair had peeled away in patches, exposing the tan suede underneath. It was an ugly chair. An uncomfortable chair. The cushions sank under the weight of his arthritic hips, sending bright streaks of pain up Hans's spine, where it swirled and pressed against his lower back.

Hans refused to get rid of this chair. Even through the pain, there was a sense of familiarity that he liked. It was polished with a patina of sentimentality, a gift from his wife so many decades ago when he'd set up his business conducting artifact appraisals related to gemology. He was not a local jeweler. He held a Ph.D. in conserving and restoring objects containing precious gemstones. His opinions, when it came to authentication, were authoritative and much sought after.

Through this work, Hans had proudly provided a quiet, comfortable life for himself, his wife, and her cats.

A third, then a fourth, door banged outside.

Four doors? That was unusual, Hans thought as he pressed into the rounded arms to push himself up.

With a glance back at the chair, Hans mused that his wife was now equally lumpy and cracked. Equally, she was a pain in his backside.

At the window, Hans peered out. Through squinted eyes, he could make out the silhouettes of five men advancing toward his entrance.

Five? This had never happened before. What could they be bringing for him to look at?

He rubbed his hands with greedy anticipation and waited for their knock.

Hans didn't know who was mounting the stairs. A stranger with a Slavic accent had called earlier in the morning, saying he needed information about a ring. Hans had rebuffed him, explaining that his role was to work with rare pieces. Pieces, for example, that a museum was interested in having appraised and described. He worked with the private collections of the hyper-wealthy. He'd worked for royals, both European and Asian. Many from the Middle East. Rare artifacts, priceless objects. He didn't look at family jewelry for insurance purposes. His fee was too pricey for the unexceptional.

Hans didn't intend to be elitist or dismissive; he'd explained cordially and then offered the names of three honest appraisers who did good work.

When the man on the phone responded, his voice glimmered with amusement. He simply said, "This is a piece that you'll want to see, Dr. Klein. I'll be there at four this evening." They'd set the appointment even though the man had avoided offering a name.

Curiosity had tickled over Hans's nervous system. A mystery was afoot. Very intriguing. He'd called his wife to tell her not to expect him until late. He'd hung up on her as she complained about his safety. It was always the same from her. Her doomsday fears were without foundation. What did he have that anyone could possibly want? The only thing of value here was the knowledge Hans held between his ears.

The group moved up the steps, their footfalls reverberating in the stairwell. There was no chatter along the way.

With a stir of excitement, Hans pulled the door wide.

Three men, wearing tailored suits with thick-soled black boots, swarmed into the office space.

Hans stuck his head into the hallway, where a fourth man stood at attention just to the side of the door. The fifth man was not to be seen. Hans thought he was probably standing guard at the door downstairs. Towering over Hans's stooped frame, the hallway man reached for the knob and tugged the door shut, forcing Hans to quickly pull his head back out of the way.

Now, one man stood in the center of the reception area, depositing a sleek, black leather briefcase on the small wooden desk where Hans liked to draft his reports. Hans noticed the handcuff that secured the case to the man's wrist. Yet another thing that had never happened in Hans's experience.

His excitement shifted to something wary.

The other two men made themselves welcome, moving throughout the office—into the bathroom, opening the closets, into the laboratory with its specialized equipment—returning to stand like soldiers on the side wall. The shorter one, the one with mean eyes, pronounced, "All clear."

Only then did the man with the briefcase turn to face Hans. "Dr. Klein?"

"That is correct," Hans stammered.

The apparent leader nodded without offering his own name. Retrieving a tiny key from his suit pocket, he slid it into the tiny hole in the handcuffs, and with a twist, he released himself from the handle. As he pressed a code into the case's lock, he said, "I need you to verify the authenticity of a ring. You will create a document, and then we will leave."

The briefcase opened. There was a thick bundle of banded euros and a ring box made of polished ebony. The leader extracted the box and held it in front of Hans's nose.

Slowly, the nameless man lifted the hinged lid, exposing a red stone in a golden setting.

Heart pounding, Hans fingered the cord that dangled his glasses on his chest, opened the earpieces, and slid his readers into place on his nose. Hans didn't need the glasses to know what he was looking at; he was simply buying himself a moment to think.

This was the Fire of the Desert.

Hans reached for the ring, sliding it onto the tip of his pinky finger and bringing it closer for inspection.

There was a forty-million-euro bounty on this ring.

Forty million euros, and here he stood with it wedged onto his pinky finger just above his jagged hangnail.

Hans trembled from head to foot.

"I see you know what this is."

"I do," Hans conceded.

The ring wasn't worth even a tenth of that reward price. In today's market, at auction, it would garner just over three—yes, maybe, *possibly* as much as four—million euros simply because it had a romantic mythology and, of course, because of the rarity of the pure scarlet-colored two-carat diamond. The forty-million-euro reward was merely a way to catch the attention of the right kinds of people.

Zayd Ali Kamal, the man who put up the reward, didn't care about money. Ten million here or fifty million there was unremarkable to him. But to a world filled with treasure hunters? Yes, it was a bounty that would motivate action. Sometimes, by not such nice people.

How had this team of men come upon this ring that had been missing since World War II?

The leader was staring at him; Hans should say something.

"It is the Fire of the Desert, or so it appears." Yes, Hans told himself, since it had been missing for eighty years, it was much more likely that this was a clever counterfeit than the actual artifact.

Hans had a reputation for precision, for being one of the most knowledgeable in the field, and for integrity. His ethics were everything to him. He would be out of business—done—if he said something untrue. Less of a man. His life's work would lie in ruins.

Hans felt the beads of sweat gather on his brow and above his lip.

For the first time in his life, Hans was afraid. Deep down in his core terrified.

These men concealed guns in their clothing, he was sure. They came here like this, with their legs spread wide and their arms crossed over their muscled chests, meaning to leave with what they wanted.

What would it mean if Hans did not give them the papers that they required?

Would they shoot him?

Would they … would they beat him? Torture him?

Why had he answered that phone call?

Hans's glasses steamed in the heat of his distress, obscuring the ring. He tried to thrust it back at the man with the briefcase.

The man didn't lift his hand to receive it. Instead, with a low, steady voice, he demanded, "Tell me what you know of this ring."

Hans stumbled backward until the red leather chair, his old friend, caught him at the back of the knee, and he dropped into the seat.

Hans tugged his glasses down his nose with his free hand, letting them fall with a thump against his chest. A test? Probably not. Well, maybe.

Should he lie and make up a story about a ruby? Hans was honest, as a rule. Since he'd been a boy, a lie would heat his face until he turned red and sweaty, and his words would tumble over themselves as he stammered.

No. Lying to these men would be a mistake.

"The diamond was mined in South Africa in the 1920s," Hans began, his voice just above a whisper. "The coloration is classified as pure scarlet, the rarest of the rare, so red that many thought it was a ruby, but no. At that time, the stone was sold to a prince who was born of the bloodline of not one but three Middle Eastern royal families. He bought it for his betrothed, a very romantic gesture." The story grounded Hans; he felt better for telling it as if repeating a well-worn children's tale. His voice no longer quivered and took on a conversational tone. "It was unusual that a royal marriage was based on passion rather than politics. But that was the case here. The prince sought the perfect representation of his love. As the story goes, the prince, declaring his betrothed to be his life's blood, purchased the pure scarlet diamond, reputed to look like a drop of blood in the light. He had it mounted in a gold filigree setting, offering it to his wife, Haamida, on their wedding night, affirming that each beat of his heart was for her alone." Hans stopped and licked his lips with a dry tongue.

"Continue." The leader's voice was even, but it was a command.

Hans glanced down at the ring still wedged on his pinky and held aloft like it was a lit match that, with any false moves, could burn everything down. "Decades later, during the Second World War, Haamida's sister was in Morocco. When she became dangerously ill, Haamida went to her. At that point, under the order of the French Vichy government, the Nazis in Casablanca captured Haamida and her sister. The prince went to Morrocco, rescued his wife and sister-in-law through bribery, and the couple returned to their homeland to love each other until a very old age. However, when she was taken prisoner, the Nazis stole Haamida's ring, and it was not recovered. The last known documentation says that the Fire of the Desert was stored in a salt mine in Berchtesgaden near Adolf Hitler's retreat."

"As a whole, the ring has a romantic history." The leader nodded.

"Yes," Hans exhaled. Yes, this ring was an object of legend. It was a treasure sought for almost a century with no sign. How had these men found it? Or was this a clever ruse? Hans pulled off his glasses, lifted the ring to eye level, and peered at it.

"A man will go to great lengths to prove his passion to his beloved," Leader-man said. "In this case, Zayd Ali Kamal wished to find the ring and give it to Haamida's great-granddaughter, Sireen, on their wedding night. Hence, the high reward was posted for the recovery of the ring. If," he paused until Hans looked up and held his gaze, "it could be located before the wedding. And the wedding is in three weeks."

Hans gulped.

"You seem very nervous," the leader-man said. "And I can understand why. Let me clarify. Our team thinks we've found The Fire of the Desert. We came to you to verify that we did. It would be death to each of us if we were to try to hand Zayd Ali Kamal a ring and accept the prize money if we were mistaken. That is where you come into the picture. Our lives are literally in your hands. If you lie about the authenticity because you're afraid to tell us an answer we don't want to hear, our lives will be very short."

Hans noted that this man spoke well but with an odd pattern to his words. Though they were both speaking English as a second language, he understood the essential meaning.

"You need to trust that we are here for the truth. And we must trust that you will perform your work with integrity. Yes?" The leader lifted his brows with the question.

"Always." Hans had to sit there for a moment to let the

man's words sink in. This was not what he had imagined. When he saw the ring, Hans believed that he was going to die that day, and it would be a brutal exit. But no, this would be fine. They both wanted to act with honor, each for their own reasons. "Okay. Then I get to work." He slid his hips to the edge of the chair. Holding the ring high with his right hand, he pressed with his left, wobbling a bit as he came to stand.

"And I will go with you," the leader said. "The ring does not leave my sight."

"Certainly. I understand." Hans held out a hand to invite him to enter the lab. "To this day, science does not know what makes a red diamond red," Hans said as he flipped on lights and moved his stool to the counter. "The chemical composition is the same as a colorless diamond." After placing the stone on a velvet cloth, he moved to the sink to wash his hands. "Gemologists speculate that the color has something to do with the plastic deformation in the crystals' lattice structure." He used a hand dryer instead of a cloth to ensure he had no lint on his fingers. "That, and perhaps, the type of atoms gliding along the structure as it underwent the pressure needed to form. Since there is no scientific understanding of the red diamond phenomenon," he turned to catch the leader's gaze, "there is little I can do to verify the red diamond except to ascertain that this was not lab-created and that it conforms to the documentation. I will ensure that it is a singular color with the proper clarity, cut, and carat weight as is listed in my books."

The leader pressed his lips together with a look of dissatis-faction.

"I can show you this, however." Hans went to the cupboard to pull out a light source. "Most red diamonds will demonstrate fluorescence in the presence of a long-wave UV light such as this." He plugged in the lamp. "If you would please turn off the overhead lights." Standing in the sudden darkness of the windowless lab, Hans flipped the switch, holding the light next to the diamond. "You see? This fluorescence is the first of the tests I need to assure myself that this stone was formed naturally and not lab-grown. I'll switch to short wave just to check. You see? Lab-grown diamond's fluorescence is stronger under short waves, which is not the case here. Yes, this is a good first result. Sometimes, the labs try to fool people by irradiating their diamonds, but this does not glow in the dark." The light snapped back on. Both men stood gazing at the red diamond. "Perfect," Hans said, "Of course, we will know for sure it's an actual diamond when I put it in this machine here. It is called a Diamond Tester." He sent the leader a wry smile. "Not a very creative name, I suppose. But it tells you what job it accomplishes."

The man pressed his back to the wall and stood motionless and silent as Hans moved methodically through his review, taking notes on his notepad.

Finally, Hans looked up. "Yes, you see," he tapped on one of his reference books, "my calculations replicate the documentation. On all metrics I can employ, this artifact complies with the description, and I can certify its authenticity with a very high level of certainty."

"Not a hundred percent certainty?" The leader scowled.

"There is never a hundred percent. A 'very high level' is all anyone could offer," Hans said as he polished the ring and placed it gingerly back in its box, handing it off before he made his way back to take his place behind the desk to compose a report from his notes.

His head bent, Hans felt the leader silently communicate the good results to the team members in his office. The room was suddenly bright with excitement.

No one spoke; no one moved until Hans stood to hand his certification to the leader. After reading it over, the man placed his stack of euros on the desk. Then, after checking a final time that the ring was properly in its box, he tucked the paperwork and his treasure away, shutting the briefcase lid and clicking first the lock and then the handcuff back into place around his wrist.

Wordlessly, the men turned on their heels and filed out of the room, the last one closing the door behind him.

Hans dropped his head into his hands as he reviewed the last hour of his life. So many emotions along a broad spectrum. He would take tomorrow off and rest from this experience, he concluded.

But for now, Hans wanted to share this extraordinary event with someone who would understand. With a grin, Hans lifted the receiver on his phone and swirled his finger into the rotary dial, reaching out to Wajeeb, a man who had been a steadfast friend and counterpart throughout Hans's professional life. Wajeeb had done the secretive work to stop Syrian conflict relics from reaching the black market, and the two had conferred on such things since the Syrian civil war began. Wajeeb would value a good mystery such as this one.

Answering on the third ring, Wajeeb barely said hello before Hans's story spilled from his lips. "I was astonished that this ring fit the description perfectly. Wajeeb, I held in my own two hands The Fire—" Mid-sentence, Hans stopped abruptly, "Did you hear that?" He stretched the cord long so he could stand at the window and look for the source of the banging reverberation, unlike the expected car doors slamming shut.

There was another and another in quick succession.

Gripping the phone in a tight fist, Hans cupped his other hand around his eyes as he peered through the dim pane, focusing down on the sidewalk just in time to see the last of the five men fall to the ground.

Hans ducked his head to the side so he would not become a target.

Six bangs. Six shots. Now, silence.

Hans dropped the receiver as he yelled, "Gunshots! There have been gunshots!"

Unthinking, Hans ran toward the door, his body moving in a way he couldn't have imagined was still possible. Unquestionably, someone had come to rob the team of The Fire of the Desert. His clients were in mortal danger.

Had the gunmen waited for this moment and the papers of authenticity?

Had Hans's own actions somehow led to this catastrophe?

Clinging to the handrail with both hands, Hans raced to the ground floor, hoping to somehow help the men. He threw open the street door, then froze mid-stride on the stoop as he stared down at the bodies.

The men's heads were missing chunks of skull.

The handcuff still encircled the leader's wrist, but the briefcase was gone.

As Hans grabbed at the handrail to steady himself, he looked down the street. There, he saw a woman in a black dress and heels lifting the briefcase and placing it into her car before sliding behind the wheel and driving nonchalantly down the road.

Hans lifted his gaze to the building across the road where three men with rifles in their hands stared down at him. One lifted his gun and was taking aim, the barrel lining up to bring Hans down, too.

The pressure of this scene sat like a boulder on Hans's chest. It was too heavy, too much. Hans couldn't find space in his lungs for a breath. Radiant pain shot fire down his left arm, and a greasy sweat stung his eyes.

The colors around him dimmed to gray, then black, as his knees buckled beneath him.

His wife was right, after all, Hans thought as his body collapsed into a heap at the bottom of the stairs. The isolation of his office meant no one would come to help him.

1

———

Red

AN OLD-FASHIONED INCANDESCENT BULB SWUNG NAKED overhead. Its dim light drew fuzzy shadows on the blue-tiled walls. Johnna Red leaned over the sink to scrutinize her appearance past the spider web cracks edging the bathroom mirror.

She looked as shitty as she felt.

Her olive skin had a greasy cast that was oddly gray as if she'd mixed ashes into fat and polished her face. Turning her head this way and then that, Red concluded that blush or lip stain would make her ghastly pallor that much more obvious. Mascara would call attention to her glassy, feverish eyes.

Would her appearance frighten her asset?

Probably.

She wished she could delay their meeting, giving herself a day—or two … maybe three—in bed, recovering. But this was the day Moussa was driving from the capital to his next meeting. Passing through Tal Afaya, he could stop for lunch without raising suspicions about his doings.

He'd said it had to be today, whispering into his phone,

"This needs your government's immediate attention, I would think. Yes, I think this very much."

Skittish, anxious Moussa was a pencil-pushing yes-man who made no decisions and was of no consequence in the grand scheme.

Not to his organization, anyway.

He worked for a major import-export company. Their international dealings came with a veneer of respectability, but credible sources indicated that they dabbled in disruptive activities. Possibly, they were getting bolder and had turned to funding terrorism.

That was what Red aimed to discover.

In Moussa's role at the company, sitting in the same office suite as the owner, jumping to his boss's every demand, he was a shadow that garnered little thought or attention beyond his scrambling efforts to appease.

Keeping the coffee and tea hot and flowing as politicians and government officials stepped through the carved wooden doors—to sit, visit, and accept their side money—meant essential conversations could be overheard.

Yes, to the CIA, a shadow like Moussa could be gold.

Red had been developing him for months, and luckily, she'd found two points where she could leverage him—he wanted money to ease his daily life, and he wanted his son to go to an American university to become a doctor—that meant at least a decade of school so at least a decade of intelligence gathering *if* Moussa proved helpful.

Since Moussa had just agreed to become Red's asset, they hadn't gotten to the point in their relationship where she could train him in the dos and don'ts of his role—how to know what kind of information was useful, how to gather it without tipping his hand, and how to pass it along to her without pulling attention their way.

Regardless, Moussa had reached out, saying he had something, and it was significant. Something that she would want to pay him a great deal of money to know.

What would make Moussa act out of character like this?

Should she have her guard up?

Red turned on the faucet, letting the tepid water run until it was no longer rusty. Cupping her fingers, Red leaned down to splash her face.

Gliding damp hands over her head, she pressed the frizz of black hair that had escaped her ponytail back into place. Then, she reached for a towel to pat herself dry.

This towel had been white at some point in its life cycle. But the hotel paid the rural women to do the laundry in the river, and now the fibers had taken on a faint terracotta cast.

The roughness of the line-dried fabric felt nice in this instance. It seemed to scrub a bit of color into her cheeks. Red buried her face in the towel and drew in a deep breath, filling her nostrils with the scent of sunshine and goat shit. That combination was inescapable even here in the town center.

Did Moussa actually know what kind of information was worth paying for?

Maybe.

He was an educated man. Just … kind of spineless. Or so she'd thought before his phone call.

Yes, his voice on the phone quivered, but it wasn't nerves. It had been excitement.

She glanced at her watch and then ripped open a packet of electrolytes, pouring them into a bottle of room-temperature water. With the top in place, she shook it until the crystals dissolved. That effort exhausted her. She tipped another round of antibiotics into her palm and clapped her hand to her mouth, tossing the white, chalky pill toward the back of her throat, then washed it down with the salty concoction that was supposed to make her feel like a human again.

She popped another anti-diarrheal from its bubble wrap and tucked it into her hip pocket, just in case. So far, the last round of meds was holding, and Red tried to convince herself that she was turning a corner.

After long years in the field, Red had learned a lot of tricks to stave off the travelers' intestinal shit-shows. By reflex, she popped GI-tract-coating pills before every meal. But sometimes she hit bad luck. Her job with the CIA's Color Code, after all, was to befriend anyone who could further her understanding of threats to America. And friends accepted invitations to camps, eating the offered meals, even those that were iffy.

So iffy that her prep pills weren't up to the job.

Her friends were fine.

But Red, even after years in the area, hadn't built resistance to all the local microbes.

Tenacious buggers.

Red reached for her backpack, reassured herself that the banknotes were in place, and pulled the strings tight. *If* Moussa brought valuable intel, she'd exchange this with a matching black bag that Red had given Moussa the last time they had spoken.

If he remembered to bring it along.

Wrapping a scarf over her hair, draping it in such a way that it would obscure the contours of her face, Red left her room, locked the door, then tested it twice before pocketing the key. She was staying on the second floor, at the rear of the hotel, and could go out a back door at the bottom of the stairs where no one would clock her movements.

Red trudged down the worn stairs. No, this wasn't the nicest of hotels.

She was paying for two beautiful rooms in the modern-styled hotel just up the street that housed diplomats, passing military brass, world journalists, and contractors as they moved through this border town near the Syrian crossing. And that was where Red had scheduled her asset meeting. But for safety's sake, Red elected to stay down the road. Here, with the cracked walls, the rusty water, and the lumpy bed. The toilet worked. That was appreciated. Greatly appreciated.

Red recalled how one time she and her informant needed to escape through the countryside on foot. They were both very ill but still needed to follow protocol. So they urinated off the trail and packed out all their solid waste. There had been a single trash bag, and she was the one who carried it. That had been a challenge in ways imaginable and unimaginable. Yeah, that had been bad.

Red wanted to push that story out of her mind.

Memories were like earworms, a melody that played over and over no matter how much she wished it would stop.

The best thing to do was focus on her immediate mission.

Stepping outside, moving around the building and onto the front walkway, the midday sun was a cudgel as she walked the three blocks towards the relief of air conditioning that she'd find in the international hotel.

What was Moussa about to deliver to her?

Hopefully, it was as good as he thought it was.

Something was ramping up. Red could smell it past that ubiquitous sunshine and goat shit. This was a sizzle of expectation like a fatty steak on the grill, making people salivate. There was a greediness for some outcome. After so many years in the field, Red could taste when an attack was in the planning stages. It was bitter on the sides of her tongue.

Who was making the plans? Where was the money coming from?

As a member of the CIA Color Code, it was her job to find the wallet that would spread wide to pay for the impact.

Stop the money, freeze the attack.

Without funding, it was all just fantasy.

With funding, it was an atrocity.

Would this Moussa meeting be consequential to saving innocent lives, or would this turn out to be a nothing burger?

2

———

Red

Red forced her lips into a smile of gratitude when the guy in his construction boots held the heavily carved front door of the Surain Zunai Hotel wide for her. Dipping her head as a silent thank you, she passed into the relief of chilly air and the vibrant clatter of ambient noise bouncing off the tile surfaces.

This venue was a normal CIA dangle, chosen for a specific purpose. The Surain Zunai hotel—with its relative opulence—would give Moussa a taste of what life could be like for him and his family if he gathered the right kind of intelligence.

Under today's operational circumstances, it was bad luck that there were so many people milling around the same space. That wasn't always the case. It depended on the mission goals and what situation worked best. A busy subway staircase with much jostling and bumping was perfect for a brush pass where she handed off a physical item to her confederate. In a public meeting like today, Red preferred a good balance—enough people that she would be one of a crowd, yet sparse enough that she wasn't pressed shoulder to shoulder with strangers. Today, a little more room for a quiet—and more importantly—private exchange would have been nice.

The men opened a path for her as she wended toward the tearoom, where a handful of their team members took advantage of the WIFI, busily pecking at their keyboards.

Everyone sitting in the tearoom chairs looked like they were in their own headspaces, getting their work done, and no one lifted their gaze to observe her.

The others, dressed in desert tactical gear, milled around the lobby, looking like they were gathering up, ready to head out somewhere en force. Their faces were ruddy tan from the intense desert sun. The flesh that peeked from under their shirts showed the milky line between exposed and protected skin.

Did this team know what they were getting themselves into?

The Syrian war had cooled to some degree, but there was no place in the country that didn't experience violence. Terrorists and armed groups still posed a significant threat of kidnapping, serious injury, and, yes, death.

The borderlands area had struck a precarious balance that everyone tried to respect lest that tenuous stalemate shift.

From her local contacts, Red had learned that this group of contractors from an Azerbaijani company had arrived five days ago and would be moving across the border once their equipment caught up with them. Their presence was a burr in the sandals of the tribal leaders on the other side of the border.

No, burr was much too benign—the leaders spoke of this initiative as a significant threat.

If the company got its way, this crew would usurp the elders' power by enticing the youth with jobs that came with plenty of cash flow and a shift in the power structure to a personally enriching, capitalist model.

The tribal elders didn't see this as a threat only to their authority but also a threat to their traditions and way of life.

Red predicted that the talks would prove increasingly contentious—possibly violent—if the contractors didn't carefully respect the norms of the area they wanted to exploit. It was poor timing that she was crossing paths with them. Surely, tribal members were posted about, observing, and reporting back. And Red didn't want her face caught in their surveillance.

She'd keep her head down, literally and figuratively.

Rounding behind a table in the shadow of the back corner, Red could watch the road through the plate glass window as well as the front door. Here, she had a bit more space to keep her conversation private, and she had a quick exit through the kitchen if necessary. By habit, Red always planned three points of egress. But who the hell was she kidding? She'd parked herself here because she was close to the bathroom.

Please let me keep it together just long enough to make the exchange.

Taking her seat and placing the money bag between her feet, Red relished the wafting air-conditioned air that soothed her fevered system.

Maybe she'd buck her standard protocol and let herself have a night or two here until she felt well enough to travel back home to Beirut. Would that be so bad?

Honestly, who would be taking aim at her?

Maybe it wasn't terrible that the contractors were here; perhaps they sucked up all the local vigilance.

With sunlight streaming through the window, the air shimmered with particulates. The staffer outside was using a watering can, sprinkling the sidewalk to keep the dust down.

And stepping past that worker came Moussa's slender form.

Right on time.

Even from here, Red could tell from his quick step and the glow of anticipation on his face that he was bringing her a prize.

A tingle of excitement ran through her system. She couldn't wait to discover what he'd found.

A tearoom server moved into place, blocking Red's view. His pencil poised on a palm-sized pad, he bent at the waist in a quasi-bow and raised eyebrows. This posture was meant to elicit an order from her without the need for opening pleasantries, especially if she didn't speak his language.

Red wondered what might show up in front of her if she mimed drinking from a cup. Instead of following through with that thought, she leaned to the side and pointed toward Moussa, who had pressed through the doors and was elbowing his way through the huddle of contractors. In Arabic, Red said, "My colleague just arrived. Would you let him know where I'm sitting? And also, mint tea for both of us, please."

As the server proceeded to do her bidding, Red removed the scarf from her hair and let it drop over the bag.

Moussa held his arms stiffly to his sides as he wended through the tables toward her. Dressed impeccably in an urban business-man's blue suit, his white shirt looked crisp, and he contrasted with the contractors enough that they turned their heads to watch him.

Red stood. Extending her arm, she shook Moussa's hand, making direct eye contact and maintaining the body language and feel of a business meeting. *Nothing clandestine going on over here.*

His hand was moist and shaky. To be fair, hers probably felt the same to him. Though for very different reasons. "Won't you sit down?" Red gestured toward the seat, which would put his back to the room and block others from seeing her while leaving her view as wide as possible. "I've ordered some tea. Are you hungry for lunch?"

"No. Yes. Well, tea. Good." He sat, undid the button on his jacket, looked left then right, and, gripping his seat, he shuffled the chair a little closer to the table, scraping the back legs enough to make a bright screech.

Red winced as she ducked her head to look at her lap.

When she thought he was done making noise, she raised her gaze to find him sitting very still, blinking at her.

Red sent him a flat-lipped smile, then turned to watch the server gather their tea items on a tray from the workstation while letting Moussa settle his nerves.

This whole exchange was awkward as hell. Red had a lot of work to do to get Moussa up to speed on how to flow through an event like he was water.

Gentle, unobserved water.

As the server glided into place, Red pushed the items on the table to the side to make room for their drinks. And with a flourish, the server poured from high above, letting the syrupy tea stream into the glasses. After placing a vase-shaped tea glass in front of each of them, he set the pot near Red so she could refill their glasses as desired.

"I think we'll be having lunch. Could you bring menus, please?" she asked.

When the server left, Red lifted the top off the pot and moved it closer to her so that she could smell the freshness of the mint. It soothed her system as she closed her eyes and inhaled.

After a moment, she opened them again to find Moussa frowning at her, his head tilted. "What's wrong with you?" he whispered in French.

"I ate something." She batted a hand through the air. "Tell me, how is the family? Your wife? Your son?"

"I left them very well, thank you," he replied stiffly. He patted his breast pocket before quickly glancing around. And now, Red knew precisely where he'd placed the information he wanted to share. He wouldn't be this twitchy about his surroundings if he passed her garbage.

She was itching to get her fingers on whatever was in that pocket.

"Such an excellent scholar, your son. He will make a fine doctor one day. Is he playing sports this year?" Typically, Red would chat this guy up. She'd use this opportunity to continue to grow their friendship. Her work required honest relationships and genuine feelings of amity. It was a maternal kind of friendship that she would develop between them. She would encourage and teach, and if necessary, she'd correct his behaviors. Moussa was her asset, which meant she was responsible for him—for his education on how to do his job for the CIA, meeting his needs, and keeping him safe.

But Red wasn't sure her body would cooperate much longer, so this would be little more than a brush pass. And her initial bantering questions were about as far as she was going to take the chit-chat today.

Red lifted the hot glass, holding the tea just in front of her lips. Looking through the plate glass window, a man across the street had caught her eye. Something about the way he was staring at the hotel without moving sent off her warning bells. Was there some kind of calculation going through his mind? Perhaps this was one of the tribesmen sent to observe and report. Perhaps this was a face she knew from a past mission. As Red pulled her phone from her pocket and opened her camera, her gut knotted painfully, and she had to clench her glutes hard to brace as she curved forward.

The man, dressed in tribal robes, had squared his shoulders and now strode across the street, moving toward the hotel entrance, stopping in the middle for a donkey cart to pass.

Red shifted her gaze toward the ladies' room just a few steps away.

Situational warning bells were clanging, vying for attention with the intensity of her cramps.

Her body had picked one hell of an inconvenient time to scream at her.

With her antennae pinging, she worked to form a practical plan of action. She couldn't handle this basic meeting, let alone a complication, when she was doubled over. Maybe she could run to the bathroom, get the purge over, hustle back, and assess the situation.

Surely, whatever her nervous system had picked up on was of local consequence and had nothing to do with Moussa. Right? He could sit quietly here at the corner table out of the way.

That man and his assessing gaze belonged to someone else's circus and wasn't one of the monkeys she was meant to manage.

As the cart moved on and he was fully visible again, Red tapped the button on her camera. Then she pinned her location with a CIA app that would place her at the center of a ring radiating out thirty-six inches. It still blew her mind that they had that level of precision. When she was back at her sleeping hotel, Red would send that image through the software to see if it couldn't identify him.

Or maybe she'd do it tomorrow.

Or just pass it on to an analyst.

As she slipped the phone into her thigh pocket, Red accepted the menu from their server's outstretched hand.

Once the server left, she dropped her hand to her bag and pulled it onto her lap. Untying the top, Red opened it wide, tipping a view of the contents toward Moussa. She'd offered him a mere glance, but it was enough for him to see what was inside. When his eyes grew round with surprise, Red tied the cords back together and pulled one of the straps over her shoulder.

"Read the menu and hide your face. When you're ready to order, choose something for me. Anything will do. I'll be back as quickly as I can. I need the ladies' room." She waved a hand through the air and said, "My stomach. This might take a while. Apologies."

Moussa's face stretched taut in horror. Whether he was frightened and feeling like he was being abandoned, or he was simply disgusted that women had bodily functions that sometimes went awry, Red couldn't tell. And she couldn't care less. She was up, and as she sidestepped past the table, her hand slid into the breast pocket that Moussa had been tapping.

She pulled out a piece of folded printer paper and moved towards relief.

$$3$$

____

Red

BYPASSING THE PUBLIC RESTROOM, RED REACHED THE SERVICE elevator near the kitchen, positioned for quick room service deliveries.

She climbed on and waited as the car took her upward. She had a strange sense of disorientation that frightened her as she stepped out of the car. Where was she? Did any of this look recognizable? Why was she even here?

Standing in the middle of the hall with its patterned red carpeting, Red blinked at the elevator as the doors slid shut. She looked down the hall and had no idea where or why she was there.

She looked at the piece of white paper in her hand and the room key.

She noticed the number on the key was the room in front of her.

She shifted the bag off her shoulder and looked at the contents, cash.

This feeling was familiar to her. Red had experienced this in her training at The Farm when sleep was a game of finding odd moments to prop herself in a corner and shut her eyes, resting in small sips.

It seemed to work, but in reality, her brain glitched. At The Farm, she'd learned that if she just stood there and gave her mind a moment, it would all come back to her. The trick was not to panic.

A moment later, that technique proved true; Red's mind cleared.

These were the back corner rooms she had rented when she first arrived in town, one beside the other. On both doors, she'd hung a *Do Not Disturb* sign and had monitored the rooms with a remote camera and alarm system to ensure those signs were respected.

Having the second room as a buffer meant no one could press a listening device to the wall and hear what she was about to say.

See? She was fine. She could do this.

Blowing a long breath through pursed lips, Red unlocked the door, went in, then quickly threw the latch back into place.

She stumbled into the pristine white bathroom, tugging her phone from her pocket to reach out to her colleagues, John Black and John Grey, so they could help her think and, if necessary, act.

Dialing over an encrypted channel, Red needed to lean her whole body against the wall for support as she entered her codes and biometrics for identification. Perspiration made her clothes humid as she unfolded the white paper she'd slipped from Moussa's pocket and spread it on the counter with trembling hands.

While Grey's and Black's video feeds showed on her screen,

Red chose to keep her camera off. "I'm sending you a picture of what my asset handed me just now," she said with her phone on speaker. This page—typed in a small font with single spaces and no paragraph indentations—was way too long for Red to read coherently.

Clearly, she was not on her A-game.

After Red snapped the picture and forwarded it, she tapped her phone to mute, then stumbled toward the toilet. Dropping her pants, she flung herself onto the clean white porcelain seat. Her body, given an opportunity to purge, did nothing but spasmodically cramp.

Holding the paper up, Red tried very hard to focus.

Army Sgt. Danny Poole got fifty thousand United States dollars for sensitive information that he downloaded using his top-secret clearance and brought with him to give to my boss. (I calculated the Lebanese pounds three times. It is far more than I am paid in a year. It's an astonishing amount of money.) This money was passed to a bank account in Belize. The money is there now. He didn't get any cash to spend here. My boss was very excited with what was brought to him, and he said that it was worth every cent. Scent? No, it must be cent. Like a small coin. How do I know this? The door was closed, but I had hidden a cell phone in a plant in his office, and I listened to everything all day long. They speak in English so I write this in English so the words don't change with translation. I do my best. While Poole (Spelling is right. I saw it written in the private ledger. 'Army Sgt. Danny' was written. 'Danny,' though I think that name might formally be Daniel, yes?) transferred the information to my boss. Poole said he was on something called "a wall." Poole laughed a lot. I think maybe he was nervous and excited. My boss says to Poole that Poole's girlfriend wishes for him to go back to the Army with a tale of being sick or robbed. In this way, he can get more information. Poole said first he wants to see some of Syria. A colleague—a friend of my boss's—has family there, so this was arranged. I know where his family is, so I found the GPS coordinates, and I put them below. They said he would be in the friend's house from the 26th until the 28th, and then he will go into the city which is Damascus. He wishes to surprise his girlfriend. I believe she is Hellannah. This is why I must see you today. Once Poole is in the city, you will have trouble finding him again. I'm sure you wish to find him. Poole said he would decide while in Syria whether or not to return. Being "a wall" (I don't understand this, and my translator does not help me. It sounds like a single side of a room where there might be perhaps a door or window. Maybe this refers to something he was observing for my boss? Perhaps it means he was silent and listening; there is the phrase, 'a fly on the wall,' correct?) Poole said being a wall was a big deal, and he'd have to make up a very good story. My boss is offering him a lot of money if he goes back. My boss asks Poole how he got into our country without passing through customs, and Poole laughs. He did not answer the question. Poole asked if their tangos (like the dance?) are on the southern border in the United States. My boss tells Poole that friends from Tajikistan were flying to Central America. This group has selected eight members—who had already proven themselves as effective when they attacked in Kabul years ago—this is why they were the ones chosen to go to the United States. They would cross over the southern border and move into place any day now. For their safety, they would not be in touch until the time was closer. Then my boss and Poole speak of other things. But these things had to do with which foods to try and tourist travels.

· · ·

Time passed while everyone read and digested the contents.

One thing for sure, Moussa was right; the United States needed this information. Today was the 27th.

Finally, Grey said, "Move into place? Can you talk to your asset about that?"

Red reached down to tap the unmute and spoke toward the phone lying between her feet. "He's not involved other than transcribing. He won't have any insights that he didn't write down. And yes, I know this page is poor tradecraft. I wasn't expecting this. I thought I had some time to work on his training."

"This is your new shipping asset?" Black asked from stateside.

Black worked out of Langley while Grey did fieldwork like she did. Although, Grey's job had a decidedly more tactical bent than hers. Red's bread and butter was in developing assets and gathering intelligence to act on. Lunch and chit-chat, it was a whole lot of boring with occasional flashes of adrenaline.

She wasn't free of danger—she had to keep herself fit and her tradecraft sharp—but being a CIA officer was much less Bond and a lot more mother hen than most would suspect.

"Import-export asset, yes, sir. I've been building our relationship slowly because he's well-placed but has an anxious personality. He called me out of the blue with this. Speaking of blue, he showed up dressed in his blue business suit in a sea of desert tactical and traditional robes. He stood out, which means I stood out. I'll work with him."

"Craft aside, if this is accurate, it's a hell of a first scoop," Grey said. "It could also be a setup trying to capture CIA or maybe even special forces over the Syrian border. Could he be playing us? What's your read?"

Yeah, that was a danger.

Given her present state of disrepair, Red wasn't sure she

could accurately read the tea leaves here. This she could say with conviction, "He's got that shiny look of victory on his face. He's not ballsy enough to try to pull one over on me, not with a first offering." Yes, that felt correct. She'd go down that path. "I trust the intel is good. But listen, that GPS coordinate listed means if our wayward soldier *is* there, he's moving on tomorrow. We don't have much time for a plan." Was it weird to be talking to her colleagues with her panties around her ankles and her chest resting on her lap?

Yes.

Could she do anything about it?

Absolutely not. "Do we have a friendly in the area that could grab Sgt. Poole and find out what the hell information he downloaded and passed on and why that would trigger eight tangos to head into the United States?" She closed her eyes and took a breath before adding, "Using the word tango is weird, right? It sounds like Poole wants the team to go. But Tango is the target."

"Or terrorist. And he might be working with a group of terrorists and enjoy using the term. I don't know," Grey said. "And I won't know until he and I are face to face having a little chat."

"You'll connect with the FBI to make sure they know to keep a lookout for the team crossing over the southern border?" she asked, then quickly pressed mute to give herself some necessary privacy.

"I'll reach out to Frost on the Joint Task Force as soon as we get off this call," Black said.

There was a muffled discussion on Black's end while Grey asked, "How are you feeling, Red? On the upswing? You sound like shit."

She reluctantly pressed the unmute. "We do *not* say that word right now, please and thank you. I'm still messed up. But duty first, right? Listen, I'm going to head back to my table before my asset's nerves get too raw. Let me know what you find out." She tapped the mute button.

"Stay on the line, Red." Black stopped her. "My analyst is speaking with our Pentagon contact now. Before you hand this guy a bag full of cash, let's see if this Sgt. Danny Poole even exists, what kind of clearance he holds, and if he's on base where he belongs. Those facts are easy enough to corroborate."

"Since the asset information says they have people actively trying to come across the border into the United States, we don't want to take a swing and a miss," Grey said. "As we're waiting to see if the asset uncovered an unfolding act of espionage, let's act as if this is accurate and develop next steps. Tonight, we know where Poole is. Tomorrow, according to the dates on this paper, he'll reach Damascus, where we won't have an address. And even if we did, urban extraction can get messy. We have this window. We need to pull him out."

"It has to be a covert mission," Black said. "And that means we can't reach out to our military even though they're only about four hours away. Our bases are under constant surveillance. Even though Poole's an American citizen, his presence is illegal. While he's breaking American laws, he isn't on American soil, and we would need to defer to the Syrian legal system. With people staging to cross over into the United States with an unknown agenda, we don't have time for Poole's case to work its way through the courts. This is black ops. One minute, Poole is a guest sleeping in a bed; the next minute, he vanishes into thin air."

Red released the mute button. "It would be ideal if we had friends in the area that could keep the American government at arm's length. What about Iniquus? I think Panther Force is somewhere in eastern Africa. If not, my second choice would be to call in a Special Activities Unit. Are any of them close enough to move into place in time?" The Special Activities Unit

—SAC—was the tactical branch of the CIA. In their younger days, both Grey and Black had been members. It was the CIA's special operations forces–who performed covert paramilitary operations–that Uncle Sam wanted the ability to disavow. The U.S. government would deny all knowledge of the team members and their mission, and nobody was going in to save them.

"Neither Panther Force nor a SAC unit is close enough to act as fast as we need them to," Grey said. "But I just finished meeting with a group from the House of Delegates in Türkiye. Delta Force Echo is providing their close protection. Echo could reach our Turkish base in the southeast in short order. I trust they can get the job done if JSOC is willing to sign off."

"Echo won't abandon their principals," Black said. "We need to find another team that are close enough to get in there in our short window of time."

"Echo is the group that pulled me out of my own impossible situation," Grey said. "I like to lean on teams I know. We're talking about special forces being in the country without crossing a border, capturing an American soldier who is also over their border without seeming to have come through proper customs channels? That's a red line. Diplomatically, if anything were to go wrong, they'd have Uncle Sam's nuts in a vice. I'm advocating for Echo if possible."

"Which sounds nice," Red paused. "Let's get real here. Things are heating up in the area. If Echo gets caught, using our regional allies as a jumping-off place isn't going to come with a get-out-of-jail-free card."

"We need to make sure we're not caught."

Red could almost hear the shrug in Grey's words. *Let's make sure we're not caught.* "Yeah, let's work that plan." Red rolled her eyes.

"It's not ideal," Grey said. "I agree. But looking at the map, it's the best of the not-good options. We have to have come in from somewhere. Proximity-wise, it has to be from the southwest.

Red cupped her forehead, hoping the gesture would help her to focus her thoughts. This intel was about to put American military lives on the line. She didn't have the same special operations tactical skill sets that her colleagues had in their timelines. Sure, she'd sat next to decision-makers as they spun up missions. She'd provided her details and her assessment. But in those instances, the U.S. was mandated to be in country. This was operating on foreign soil without that government's agreement or even knowledge, in an area peppered with violent factions.

"And as to the close protection duty. Without going into details," Grey continued, "the timing is good to put the representatives on their plane safely and pivot for a night maneuver. That base in eastern Türkiye is for cargo. We'd have to bring in an appropriate plane and pilot. I've been entering data into the system. The calculations show, obviously, that window is tight. But I think it's doable if we act as if—while waiting for the various stakeholder lights to flash green."

"They'd need to drop in," Black said.

"Looking at this map," Grey said, "I don't see any other way. A HAHO could put them down in a desert area close to a road. It's a new moon, so that runs in our favor. Echo has K9 Rory with them, also a bonus."

Personally, Red preferred a half-moon, enough light to see the hole before she stepped in it, but she also wouldn't stand out against the horizon the way it can happen when it was full.

"Grey, do you have anyone that could deliver a vehicle?" Black asked.

"I have people in the city," Grey said. "I can work that out."

"No one who could just grab Poole and hold him for us?" Red asked.

"No. That would take more time to develop than we have. Positioning a vehicle is something I can swing."

"And from there?" Black asked.

"If they land in the desert area to the south of the lake— depending on how close they come to their X—they might have a hike," Grey said. "Low winds, at least for the next twenty-four hours, so they should be able to get on target. From the desert area to the compound at the GPS coordinate, that's an hour on the road. The residence is rural, but, looking at this satellite map, it's just on the outskirts of the city. If the family called for help, help wouldn't be far."

"That's the grab. What does the extraction look like?" Red asked.

"Well," Grey paused. "Okay, we have a sub off the coast of Cyprus that we can move closer," Grey continued. "If the team can head to the coast—"

"Split the team," Black said. "One goes after our boy, and the other sits over the horizon with an inflatable boat. When they make contact, the boat picks them up and heads to sea. The sub pops up and loads them on. The timing is tight. A boat extraction would have to happen in the dark. The Navy won't surface that sub when it can be seen over a satellite."

"But once Echo has their hands on Poole, they have a lot more flexibility with timing," Grey pointed out. "They could lay low until the next night. Once on the sub, the Navy throws Poole in the brig until we can get him in front of the right people."

"Sounds like a cakewalk," Red said dryly. There was so much that could go wrong with that scenario. And she was ulti- mately responsible. She vouched for the information on the white paper, risking Delta Force lives and American diplomacy.

"Is it possible to do that before the population is awake and paying attention?"

"If everything goes textbook? Yes," Grey said.

"Here we go, I have a report from the Pentagon," Black said, followed by a long pause. "Army Sgt. Daniel Owen Poole does, in fact, exist. He took ten days of leave and has failed to check in. He's a day overdue. Poole holds top-secret clearance. And as part of his duties, he has access to a broad array of information. He could have passed on intel ranging from our advanced weapons systems to operational plans. Red."

Red released the mute button. "Yes?" she gasped.

"Your asset has earned his pay," Black said. "I'll work the phones and get the authorizations from all the stakeholders, looping DIA into the mix. Grey, you and I will coordinate on the mission. It might be a long shot that we can grab him, but this looks like our best chance at getting the information in time to act. Well done, Red."

She offered a weak, "Thank you, sir. Listen, from this point, I'm going to be useless. Less than useless. I'm going to give my asset a pat on the head. Then I'm going to go to bed until I can purge whatever the hell this is from my system."

"Do you need support?" Grey asked.

"I'm popping all the meds. I should be fine in a day or two. Tell Delta Force not to drink the water," she said, her phone balanced on her bare thigh as she tore Moussa's intelligence into tiny pieces. Pulling a plastic container from the money bag, she added the pieces to the solution and watched the paper disintegrate into a mucous blob.

After hanging up with her teammates, Red toppled forward and was now on her knees on the floor. She thought she might be wrong about having some virus or bacterial infection. Maybe this was appendicitis. Maybe her appendix was about to burst, and she'd die here with her bare ass in the air.

There was a local hospital, such as it was. Although she wasn't sure she trusted they could keep her alive. She pressed her abdomen to see if she was being paranoid. She couldn't tell the difference. Everything hurt before she pressed, and it hurt after she pressed.

Was the pain mildly worse, and did it last a little longer under pressure? Maybe.

Red formulated a new plan: Hand the money to Moussa, flag one of the local cars outside the hotel that offered rides for hire, and head to the hospital.

Struggling to her feet, Red pulled herself together enough for this last push. Hell, she'd been through much worse, she encouraged herself. When she was going through her assessment, she walked for days on end until she had no skin on the bottoms of her feet, and her shoes were damp with her blood. She'd been through SERE training where they threw every phobic thing in the book at her, and when that didn't work, they threw punches instead.

Ten minutes at most, and she could collapse in a car on the way to help.

She had this.

This was fine. Right?

4

———

Red

WITH HER HAND PRESSED AGAINST THE ELECTRICAL PANEL AND her head resting on her upper arm, Red realized she was on an elevator when suddenly, the downward momentum stopped with a thump as the car settled.

She blinked as she lifted her gaze, watching the door slide open.

The elevator rumble must have been just enough to coax her brain into Neverland. Hadn't this been her same reaction on the way up?

Time had jumped forward, and Red had no recollection of exiting from her hotel room, shutting the door, or locking it. She tried to believe that muscle memory meant that she'd done everything as it should have been.

As the doors slid wide, Red's hand jerked to her shoulder as a sudden jolt of adrenaline shot shock waves through her system. She grabbed the backpack to assure herself that the strap from the black bag full of asset funds came with her for the ride. She lifted it just enough to assess the weight, checking that all seemed as it should be.

It was fine.

She was fine.

Red stepped into the hallway, spreading her arms wide as the walls whirled in her vision like some kind of funhouse illusion.

These sensations were recognizable. She'd learned during her time at The Farm that if her body ran on autopilot, her consistent application of tradecraft over the years would manifest in steering her zombie-like self through whatever maze presented.

Conversely, it was also essential to change everything up all the time so that her movements weren't predictable to anyone who might be watching.

Which strategy was best?

One never knew until one knew.

She touched the wall to reorient.

To her left, the door stood open to the back alley. The kitchen waste, decomposing in the hot sun, struck her nostrils, and it just seemed mean, like a kick when she was already down. Waves of nausea and cramps hit her again.

The action plan: Get to the table, drop the bag in Moussa's lap, turn toward where the ten-o'clock hand would point, find the front door, find a car—probably any car would help her under these circumstances—ask for the hospital.

Yes, that had to come out of her mouth first in Arabic, then French. *Hôpital. Hôpital. Hôpital.* She practiced as she took a step forward, only to stumble sideways with a cramp.

Appendicitis?

She'd rather not die of something that stupidly banal. She'd much rather go out in some legacy-making shitstorm.

Not shitstorm! She shouldn't have thought that.

Pressing off the wall, she changed her plan.

Women's toilet.

She needed to sit again and rest in private.

Yes, sitting and panting were very high on her needs pyramid.

Red realized she was on the very lowest rung of Maslow's Hierarchy of Needs.

Then, she'd splash cold water on her face before she made for the front door.

No! Moussa came before the door, drop the bag in his lap, *then* the front door. Say *hôpital,* then probably the good people from this area would take care of the rest.

"I'd rather be back in SERE training," she muttered. "I could tap out. And there would be relief." Gripping her stomach, Red rolled a shoulder against the women's room door, slammed her way into the stall, reaching for her belt and then her zipper. She pushed her pants down and sat, closing her eyes and tipping her head back, not knowing how to handle her predicament.

Red once again went through the last few days. And once again she remembered being in that Beirut restaurant with the Russian businessmen.

Was it possible they'd figured out that she was a CIA officer?

Was she brushing too close to one of their operations?

They could have dropped something into her food. She could be poisoned.

Novichok? Polonium?

Yeah, not only did she not have those kinds of symptoms, but they wouldn't risk using something like that on her.

If the Russians wanted to take her out of the game, they could stage a mugging gone wrong and call it a day.

Novichok, for Heaven's sake. "Get yourself together."

She'd been gone from the table way too long.

Anxiety-filled, Moussa would be panicking. He'd think she took the information and disappeared without paying him. He'd think he'd risked his safety and his family for nothing. She could imagine him twiddling his fork in his fingers, rubbing sweaty palms down his thighs, looking around furtively. He'd remember this distress and weigh it against his desire to feed her more intelligence.

For better or for worse, the pills were doing the job, and she sat there without relief. "Move forward," she muttered under her breath. "Moussa, then the hospital. Up we go." Red forced herself to stand. She tugged her panties back into place and was reaching for her pants when the ground beneath her shook her off her feet. She tumbled into the door and was flung back against the toilet bowl.

She would have thought this was her own balance issue if it weren't for the roar of a blast.

Red had been near enough explosions that her body knew how best to survive, and she dropped down until her cheek was on the colorful floor tiles.

The outer door to the bathroom slammed open with a blast concussion that toppled the metal partition of her toilet stall into a triangle over her head, then crumpled downward as a portion of ceiling plaster collapsed on top.

With her hands packaging her head, Red wrapped herself around the toilet so the ceramic structure would take the brunt of any further building collapse, perhaps guarding her chest from being compressed under the weight. She'd survived by hugging a toilet before. There were far worse places to be. This was fine, she told herself. She was fine.

After a moment, the building materials seemed to settle, and there was stillness.

She heard nothing past the ringing in her ears and muffled chaos.

Red blinked, feeling the heaviness of the dust weighing on her lashes and caking her skin.

Stay calm. Act fast. The mantra wiggled her lips with the repetitions.

She had labeled the situation—*explosion.* Possible suicide vest? Possible gas from the kitchen?

She'd figure that out later.

What was her priority?

Safe distance.

No! It was *Moussa!*

Red crawled forward then pushed herself upright, dragging her pants into place, buttoning the top button, leaving them unzipped and unbelted. Red tapped her shoulder to make sure her pack was still in place. Then she tapped her thigh to assure herself that her phone was still with her.

She forced herself to carefully place her feet amongst the sharp edges.

Agony forgotten, masked by adrenaline surging from a system that clearly read this situation as life-or-death, Red made her way painstakingly toward the tearoom, climbing over the ceiling tiles, dodging the electrical wires that sparked and snapped, Red's brain was hard focused and astonishingly clear.

The kitchen walls had buckled and warped with the pressure but still held the ceiling up. Anything that had been hanging on the walls was now on the floor. In her mind's eye, she saw a scene with knives flinging through the air. The workers lay stunned on the floor, dust-covered and in shock. She didn't see blood. Nobody looked like they needed CPR. But she did that triage with a glance, the mere turn of her head.

Stumbling up the corridor, Red fought her way over the debris, trying to get to the front. The damage was worse moving forward. The epicenter had to have been the front of the hotel.

She tapped her leg again, assuring herself the phone was

there. Help was a phone call away. Did she need to set Color Code into action? Just knowing she had options buoyed her.

"Eyes on the prize" became the phrase for her left foot while she kept up, "Stay calm. Act fast," with her right steps. Lifting her knee, kicking out her leg, searching for a solid footing, setting her boot tentatively down, shifting her weight forward, and pulling up her back foot was a process, and the words helped.

Moussa was her goal.

If Moussa survived, she'd get him whatever help he needed. It wasn't probable; it was merely possible. She'd been pulled from such a situation before and had the scars to prove it.

The other thing that needed protecting here was the integrity of her mission. Dead or alive, there could be nothing with Moussa that might identify *why* he was in this hotel today beyond stopping for lunch as part of his business trip.

And certainly nothing that could identify her.

Arms wide to increase her balance, Red's gaze swept across the space where she had been watching out the front window just minutes ago. There was no support wall to do its job. This was a six-story structure, and the beams around her screamed with the sudden weight shift.

Would it hold?

No one was outside. She imagined they'd all dived for cover, waiting to see if more blasts would follow.

Soon, a ring of people would gather outside, hands over their mouths, looking toward each other, looking up at the structure, clearly stupefied by the unexpected event. That was the way this would unfold. It always did. Moments after that, someone—despite the obvious dangers of approaching—would take those first tentative steps forward. In the cell structure of a good portion of humans was the nuclear impetus toward the survival of a species. It would make them braver than they could have imagined acting as they drank their tea and ate breakfast that morning.

Others would follow like ants sniffing the pheromone scent trail.

And others would wait in safety to receive the stunned, the wounded, and the broken.

There was a reason that everyone was born with a role to play.

Hers was to get to Moussa.

And there was movement—a shift in the debris. Gravity, most likely.

The wind was sweeping the particulates down the road, clearing the view.

Look at this place! She pulled her hand away from a sparking electrical cord. Moments ago, the laptops were rata-tat-tatting with ideas and information. Now, there were random hands, strewn body parts, and fires.

But never say never. Red had been in situations where, if assumptions had been made, life would have been overlooked and help left unrendered.

Coughing up the dust as she stumbled forward, Red remembered the solidity of the thick tabletop and the heavy construction of the metal central leg.

Excitement bubbled through Red's system. Hope.

Springing forward, she clawed through the debris to find Moussa's legs. His shoes were gone. His socks didn't match; one was blue, and one was black. But now, they were both powdered with grit. He must have sensed something and ducked; he was indeed under the protection of the table, though the table seemed to have separated from its central post and lay on top of him. Her hands patted up his legs, following along to third-degree burns of his charred hand that held the melted remains of his phone. Red pocketed it.

The area smelled like pork barbeque.

This is why Red declined those Fourth of July picnic invitations back home with the smells that lit her memory with images of atrocities.

She shuffled her feet to get a flat surface under her toes. The color of a *thwab*—the traditional robes worn in this region—caught her eye. It stood out as different from the tactical garb. Red stopped, giving her brain a moment to take in the man woven into the debris. He didn't look hurt, merely dusty and very much dead. She looked at his sandals and thought that when he'd bent that morning to pull the strap over his heel, he had assumed he'd be placing them outside the door that evening.

But no.

This was the man she had photographed crossing behind the donkey cart.

When he'd stood outside the hotel, she'd focused her attention on him for some reason.

If she thought he might be a suicide bomber, she was wrong. This man wasn't the epicenter of the blast that had come from over by the front door.

She pulled her phone from her pocket, and under the cloud of dust, she surreptitiously captured his fingerprints in her app then took pictures of what there was to photograph. She'd look at them later and probably hand them off to one of the Langley teams, which spent their time building understandings of connections. Maybe he was a known entity. She'd send the pictures of Moussa as well. Though, Red didn't like sending people pictures like this or asking them to focus on the details. There was no framing the target images without capturing severed and charred body parts.

Red couldn't imagine what studying them did to someone's mental health.

With her back to the street, Red touched the man's arm that snaked under his body. Without rolling him, she followed his sleeve under the weight of his unsupported chest. He gripped a phone. She dragged it out from under him, swiped it open, and held the phone to his face, angling it down so the software could register his biometrics, his eyelids half open in death. Once she had access, Red changed the security code and added her own facial recognition information to maintain access, then tucked it into one of her tactical pockets.

People began to move into view, forming the ring she had predicted.

With the dust settling, they'd remember someone taking pictures and patting pockets instead of trying to help.

Crouch walking closer to Moussa, Red thrust her weight into her heels and heaved the table top up with enough of an angle that she could roll it to the side. The thick wood tabletop was heavier than expected—or she was weaker than she was used to.

For Moussa's sake, Red didn't know what to hope for as she pressed the table away—not that her hopes had any power here. If he had survived, his life would be forever changed.

Look at this place. Look where he is. Look how he's lying.

Blinking down, Red saw that Moussa's face was recognizable. His torso, where his ribs protected vital organs, seemed fine, and his white shirt was still very white.

But he was very clearly dead.

Dead.

Of course, he was.

And she had only survived because she had the shits.

Wasn't that a strange twist of fate?

5

———————

Nomad

OVER THE LAST THREE NIGHTS IN ANKARA'S CITY CENTER, Nomad's job, along with his Delta Force team, was to ensure his principals slept safe and sound behind the heavy doors of their hotel rooms.

The modern card-locking systems seemed anachronistic amongst the art and statuary stringing the length of the hall.

The place was pristinely clean, but there was that musty smell endemic to centuries-old buildings.

Nomad had paced up and down this hall enough times that he had a mind map of the squeaky floorboards hidden under the golden design on the red carpet.

For this close protection mission, Delta Force Team Echo was traveling with a bi-partisan delegation of representatives from the House.

It wasn't typical for a Delta Force team to be involved when members of the legislature went overseas to a non-combat zone.

A number of variables were weighed when deciding how to keep government officials safe. The reason Nomad was in this hall (keeping himself amused and focused by avoiding the squeaking floor planks) boiled down to three issues—the proximity to the Russian war against Ukraine, the current concerns over the Black Sea just to the north, and the fact that Representative Johnstone tweeted a meme that struck a match then held that flame uncomfortably close to the fuel of regional unrest.

His tweet went viral.

Johnstone followed up the tweeted meme by spending his Sunday morning on talk shows "shooting off his mouth," riling tensions through insults and threats.

In America, Johnstone got what he'd wanted, the pundits opined, suggesting that this tactic made sense from a politically strategic point of view. After all, Johnstone was behind in the polls. Viral outrage was free publicity and nudged his grassroots supporters to take action. With the furor, funds flowed to his coffers.

Nomad didn't have an opinion on any of that.

Nomad's concern focused squarely on ramifications and how the present situation might impact the group's safety.

How it played in America was not necessarily how other countries reacted. Türkiye felt the sting of Johnstone's words and expressed their anger loudly on social media—much more quietly in the halls of government. As a result, the incoming messages were full of vitriol and highly detailed, credible threats.

Usually, the DSS— the State Department's Diplomatic Security Service—would handle the protection of official representatives of the United States government while abroad. But with the ensuing backlash, the FBI got involved. After more hoopla, the protection had upgraded to a CIRG team—the tactical operators in the FBI.

The other representatives scheduled for the Ankara outreach —the ones who had to walk by Johnstone's side and climb into a car with him—were fearful but unwilling to back out of the trip lest they seem cowardly.

And so, one of the delegates called his brother, a top brass with JSOC, and requested Delta Force protection. Though the FBI's CIRG was full of retired Delta Force operators, and both groups had similar skill sets, Echo was handed the assignment.

Dressed, albeit atypically and uncomfortably, in suit and tie, Echo took on the mission of guarding the politicians.

The job of tamping down the political backlash belonged to the State Department.

Politics wasn't Nomad's sphere of present expertise. In the military, as with his parents, who ostensibly worked for the State Department, Nomad had served under both parties' admin-istrations. His loyalty was to the American people. His job was to use his skills to protect American interests. And right now, that meant focusing on the three feet around him. Or, in this case, the fifteen meters of hallway.

Back and forth. Back and forth, he paced the hall.

Nomad was vigilant.

Protection was boring, but it was never light duty.

A great deal of pre-planning and groundwork was included in any protection plan. Every moment of every day. Every stop —and that didn't mean hotel to meeting space, that meant every light, every roundabout, every tunnel, every*thing*—was researched and assessed. And while Türkiye was a NATO member, the team understood there was a war raging just a hop, skip, and a jump away.

Echo team weighed each threat made against the American contingent and mitigated it.

The meme war aside, from the point of embarking on their commercial flight out of D.C. until now, nothing had stood out as particularly dangerous. But that was the thing with mental health and violence; sometimes, there was nothing to see until it was playing out. Nomad knew that you don't focus on the dog that barks; you focus on the one that will stalk and bite.

Back and forth. Back and forth, Nomad strode.

The four days had come and gone with him pacing this hall.

Nomad was the newest member of Delta Force Team Echo. And this happened to be his first Echo mission. A proud member of the United States military since he was old enough to sign on the dotted line—Army boot to Ranger School to Green Beret, and recently a move to The Unit—he'd served both in combat and in peace.

But a military record didn't matter much when you joined a new team.

They tested you.

And rightly so.

Nomad had no expectations that he'd walk through the door with his battle rattle and Echo would embrace him as a brother.

When their lives were on the line, the team needed to know Nomad's character as well as the skill sets listed in his file.

Did it amuse him to be a burr in somebody's backside?

Would he snatch at the cream assignments and try to snake his way out of doing crap jobs?

Would his ego jeopardize a good outcome?

Would he go along to get along? Sometimes, that was a good thing; sometimes, it was deadly. You had to know when to speak up and when to shut it. *Every* choice had ramifications.

Nomad absolutely understood why Delta Force Team Echo needed to test him and see how he performed under stress. And there were few things as good as sleep deprivation coupled with boredom to assess someone's capacity to stay even-keeled and focused.

When assignments were handed out, and Nomad's schedule looked like he was basically on duty twenty-four/seven for the duration, Nomad had planned to hit exhaustion by the time they wrapped up this four-day handshake mission.

Nothing new in that.

Taking night shifts, walking the halls in a five-star hotel *wasn't* a crap job. It was low bandwidth.

Yeah, there were far worse things he could be doing right now. One that came readily to mind was the day Nomad had slithered through a minefield on his belly, wearing a wounded Ranger buddy on his back like a turtle shell. Or the day his Green Beret unit was in Hatari, East Africa, and they raced into the fray as guerilla fighters, hopped up on khat leaves, attacked a village of women and children. That was one of the most horrific days of his life. He still had nightmares about it. He still felt guilty that only one person from that village, his friend Hailey, had survived.

Comparatively, this assignment was cake.

But Nomad didn't have much of a sweet tooth.

He preferred the adrenaline rush and the power of physically and mentally pushing himself.

He wouldn't be pacing the hall that much longer.

The delegates were in their rooms, gathering their bags. Soon, they'd be loading up and heading back to the airport to fly to D.C. The group would spend their weekend overcoming jetlag before they were back in session.

Maybe he could grab some shuteye on the flight back.

The elevator dinged, and two of the DSS officers from the embassy stepped off, followed by Nomad's teammate Havoc, who signaled him over.

The DSS walked to either end of the hall, somehow hitting all the squeaky floorboards along the way.

Nomad stopped in front of the elevator with a lift of his brow.

"Changing of the guard. Echo is heading to the embassy,"

Havoc said in a tone that wouldn't travel the halls and slip under the hotel door cracks.

Nomad followed Havoc onto the elevator. "This is about the delegates?"

"Someone sent up a bat signal." Havoc pushed the starred button. "We're jumping off in a new direction."

They'd be turning on a dime.

Sudden pivots fit Nomad's personality. He enjoyed the challenge. A little like the waltz that he grew up dancing at embassy events with his parents, "slow, slow, quick" was a good metaphor for his job. The change of balance, the constant redirection, never standing with the feet planted. And when one did it well, it seemed effortless and graceful.

The metaphor came readily because of the embassy setting he'd been working in and the memories of his youth that it pulled up for him, but he liked it.

Nomad was sure that wasn't an easy call out of JSOC to redirect Echo. This must be a high-stakes event. If it ever came out that Echo was rerouted from their protective duties and something came at this legislative group, there would be hell to pay.

Yes, it had to be big. They'd know soon enough.

Hopefully, somebody had some gear they'd be handing out because Echo came to Türkiye with wool suits, not battle rattle.

When Nomad walked into the embassy's SCIF—Sensitive Compartmented Information Facility, where classified information could safely pass from one set of hands to another—T-Rex sent him an assessing look. "You good to go? We pushed you these last four days when it comes to sleep cycles."

"I'm squared away." Nomad moved into the room. "I don't need much on a normal day."

Master Chief T-Rex Landry was Echo's number one—then there was Havoc, Nitro, and Jeopardy. Their second in command, a guy named Ty Newcomb, handled Rory—the team's Tactical K9 who was both a nose and a bite on the job and a goofball when hanging with the team. He wasn't just an amazing athlete and a force multiplier but a respected team member and good stress relief.

Nomad? He was, "Hey, new guy."

And if the past defined the present, he would be for quite a while.

The men sat around a long table with a large screen connecting them to their support team back at Fort Liberty. Nomad found a place where he could easily see and pulled his notepad and pen from his bag.

"Gentlemen, we're changing gears," Colonel Watts said by way of greeting. "Keeping our principals out of the public eye served its purpose. The news cycle has moved on to the next topic. Our intelligence community believes that the Diplomatic Security Service can take over our duties regarding the legislators. Right now, JSOC needs you in the field."

There was a shift in the room as the focus sharpened. The only sound was Rory panting under the table.

"We have an AWOL servicemember. Army. A Sergeant Daniel Poole. We believe that Poole is a traitor who committed espionage and has connections with terrorist activity imminently planned for American soil. We need to scoop him up for interrogation." He turned his head to focus on T-Rex. "Master Chief, I've forwarded the intelligence package. It includes what we know of our target and our window." Colonel Watts shifted his gaze to the whole team. "Intelligence has developed initial suggestions for how this might go down, but we're leaving it up to you how you get the job done. We have two asks—that you don't swing and miss and that there is zero footprint."

"Yes, sir," the men responded in unison.

"Where is this?" T-Rex asked.

"Syria."

Arms crossed over chests, chins tucked in. That area was dry tinder. The tiniest of sparks could set off a conflagration that would be time and resource-heavy to put out.

"We need to pick him up in the next few hours and get him someplace with American jurisdiction. Poole can't reach EU territory," Watts said. "He'd fall under our friends' laws, and we simply don't have time to wrangle red tape. We need Poole's information. And honestly, it would have been better to have had our hands on it yesterday."

"Why didn't we?" T-Rex asked. "Was there a hold-up getting this signed off?"

"The field officer got the information during an early lunch meeting today in the Middle Eastern time zone, is my understanding. That means we received this information five hundred hours East Coast time—we pulled people out of bed. We've now had the information in hand for just over an hour. We're pushing this along as quickly as possible."

"To clarify, sir, you've sent us an intelligence package," T-Rex asked, "not orders?"

"Not all the stakeholders have signed off. They're in discussion in the Situation Room. We're waiting to hear back. We think we know where Poole is right now. We lose him at dawn. Until we hear back, you need to act as if—" Watts looked over his shoulder as someone handed him a piece of paper. He paused to read it over, then handed it back. "That can wait." He turned his attention to Echo. "Gentlemen, we're staging as if we have the green light. You'll agree, it's easier to pull down a mission that's ready to go. No sense in wasting time twiddling your thumbs. You have commercial tickets on a flight from Ankara to Adana Şakirpaşa at your sixteen twenty hours. That's the closest airport to the base."

The team scribbled notes on the pads in front of them.

"The flight takes an hour and twenty minutes. We'll have someone there to pick you up. It's thirty minutes by vehicle to the base. They're bringing in a jump plane as we speak. Your intelligence package suggests a HAHO." Watts used the term for a High Altitude High Open parachute jump. "Everyone is packed up already, and you have your bags with you?"

"Yes, sir," Echo said in unison.

"Then I'll leave you to it. T-Rex, once you've come up with a cover story and a list of items you'll need, send them to the base contact. They'll do their best with it. Gentlemen, we trust your training and your professionalism. You're the right team in the right place and time. I'll let you know as soon as we get the nod. Good luck."

Here was one hell of a twist. He was moving from the robotic tedium of hall pacing to a HAHO into a hotspot, chasing an American traitor.

Nomad was ready for it.

6

———

Nomad

Echo moved from the SCIF down to the embassy's gym.

If Rory was going to be on a commercial plane, he'd have to burn through some of his excitement first. Rory could smell a mission rolling up, and his coat twitched with anticipation.

With a Marine guard standing outside the gym's door, keeping others at bay, giving the team the freedom to talk things through, Ty had Rory on a treadmill sprinting a five-mile run. Usually, ten miles was about what it took to wear off Rory's go-go-go energy and keep him comfortable on a plane. But this was his second run of the day. Five should top him off just fine.

The rest of the team dragged chairs to the snack table nearby and found a spot to plunk down.

"Who developed this package?" Spinning his chair around, Havoc sat, crossing his arms across the backrest.

"John Grey." The way T-Rex said it, Nomad interpreted the source as known and trusted. T-Rex's attention turned to the ping on his phone. He swiped the call open as he moved from the table to a back corner.

Jeopardy scowled. "Color Code is involved with an AWOL traitor?"

"Color Code?" Nomad asked under his breath.

"Their focus is on thwarting terrorists from getting their hands on funding," Havoc said. "They work around the ex-USSR block countries up to—I'm guessing—Ukraine, maybe? Down to the Mediterranean, then east into Lebanon and Syria. We've worked with their intel from Eastern Africa, too. I guess they go where the money trail leads."

"All that's speculation," Ty said. "We don't actually know much about Color Code."

"From what Echo's seen," Jeopardy grinned. "Syria is definitely their stomping grounds. My guess is that, in this case, they were in the field and came across an American soldier in a place they weren't supposed to be, doing something they weren't supposed to be doing."

"AWOL in *Syria* of all places." Nitro scratched his fingers along his beard-covered chin. Long enough to touch his clavicle, Nitro had tamed his unruly facial hair into something that might be construed as fashionable for their time with the legislators—more likely, his wife did that.

Since Echo's typical assignments required them to blend with local populations as they moved through their missions, the entire team masked their profiles behind beards. Their hair reached their shoulders. While wearing suits in Ankara, the team pulled their hair back into neat ponytails.

It was rare that Delta Force wore anything approaching a uniform, instead choosing to put on what everyone else was wearing in that locale. Blending allowed for success. And survival.

This was all new to Nomad.

He'd been clean-shaven in the Green Berets with a tight military haircut, wearing a camo combat uniform.

Since he'd joined Echo, his beard was filling out, and he'd categorize the length of his hair as unruly. It would be a few more months before he could gather it in an elastic band like his teammates had. For now, it was just in his way. "This guy who developed the intel package, Grey, he works out of the Syrian region?" Nomad asked Nitro.

"Who the hell knows? Does that make his information less reliable? Absolutely not. Grey's no cake eater. He was boots-on-the-ground and knows what we're capable of accomplishing. More importantly, he knows what's made-for-tv bullshit—bending time and eating bullets like potato chips."

"Potato chips. Man," Havoc rubbed a hand over his lips, "I could go for some salt and crunch. Anyone see a vending machine on the way in here?"

"I've got a bag of BBQ, but it's gonna be chip crumbs by now." Nomad dragged his backpack from between his feet and unclasped the top.

"I'll take it. Thanks," Havoc said. "You're going to hear Color Code a lot working with Echo. You'll know you're working with one of them because the males are Johns. The females are Johnnas. Then, each has a color as their last name. Ty over there met his girl when Johnna White decided to play matchmaker."

"Careful, brother. We don't talk about my girl on duty or in the field."

Nomad snagged the chips from the top of his kit and handed them out. "Color Code is CIA?"

"Affirmative." Havoc accepted the bag. "I bet Grey specifically picked Echo to go in there and grab Poole. Since he owes us big time, that intel will be as squeaky clean as possible. That guy was part of the craziest mission I've ever been on. Sometimes, I think it was a fever dream that stuck with me because it was so damned vivid."

"It was real, brother," Ty said as he pressed the buttons to slowly increase Rory's pace. "That, or the whole team was having the same hallucination."

Laughter went up, punctuated with celebratory high-fives.

T-Rex returned to the group and stood at the top of the table. "Gentlemen, focus in."

"I'll tell you later," Nitro said. "You'll want to hear this."

T-Rex opened his laptop, then turned the screen to show the men a topographical map that included Syria, Lebanon, and the Mediterranean out as far as Cyprus. There were four red Xs: three on land and one over the sea. "Here we go with the broad strokes of the mission, suggested by Grey in the intelligence packet. Elements are moving into place to support this scenario. If we fundamentally disagree, we need to get that to JSOC stat. But I think it's a solid plan."

T-Rex stood even taller than Nomad's six-foot-six frame. Like Nomad, T-Rex's mere presence was intimidating and was often all that was needed to control a situation. Their stature could also make them uncomfortably easy to spot as they moved through a population where the average male came up to chest level. Like T-Rex, Nomad had learned to hug the walls, so his height wasn't as apparent.

"We're going to divide into two groups, Alpha and Bravo," T. Rex said. "Alpha is going to head out on the jump plane, parachuting to this LZ." He tapped the first X that signified their landing zone. "It'll be a HAHO." His gaze moved to his men then back to the map. "The U.S. has an asset in the area moving an SUV to the X. It should be gassed and ready." T-Rex drew his finger along a roadway toward the second X. "Driving lights out, using night vision, it's about an hour to this farmhouse. The neighbors are far enough away that they won't be looking out the windows at us. If the intelligence is correct, that's where Poole will be sleeping tonight. If he's not there," T-Rex continued, "we head to our exfil site. There's nothing more for us to do. If he's there, we package him up and drive to the coast."

"Team Bravo?" Ty asked.

"They'll helicopter out and drop into the sea with an inflatable. Bravo holds over the horizon for a signal. They motor in and do a pickup. The whole team, along with Poole, move out to this last X in international waters for a Navy pickup. Easy day." His gaze swept the team. "Let's talk this through."

"How many boots on the ground?" Ty asked.

"Four Alpha. Two Bravo. You and Rory will be Alpha. We'll need Rory to surveil the house," T-Rex said.

"This guy, Poole, he slunk over the border?" Nomad asked. "Or did he move through customs? I want to know if the authorities know he exists. Could they be keeping eyes on him?"

"They found Poole's papers on base," T-Rex said. "The field officer believes that he either went over a porous section of the border or paid to get waved through and headed right into the arms of his host family."

"I hear a lot of speculative language," Ty said. "They handed us a GPS coordinate. Did anyone get eyes on this guy? I'm not loving the idea of getting lured into Syria. We've dealt with worm-on-a-hook intelligence before, and we're going in without support."

T-Rex posted his hands on his hips. "You know the drill. Intelligence does its best. If they ran this to the Situation Room, there's a reason. That's not for us to decide. We get an order, we make a plan, and execute."

"Impressive," Nomad was reading the report on his tablet. "Not only do they have a GPS coordinate, but it was fast. Poole's still within twenty-four hours of his R&R window shutting."

"Somebody's on the ball," Havoc reached for a chip. "I appreciate the hell out of them."

"Amen to that, brother," Jeopardy said without lifting his eyes from the intelligence report.

"All right. Alpha, we're going to HAHO into the desert just south of the lake. Because of time constraints, you will pretty please, with sugar and cream on it, not take the scenic route that requires a sand jog to what should have been the LZ." T-Rex tapped the X. "Here, we pull off our jump gear and pile up everything that doesn't match the cover story, pull camo netting over the top, fling some sand around the edges to keep it down, and head to the second X. We'll mark the spot on GPS. If there's no activity around the area and nobody's nose goes up to sniff the air, they may be able to send a team of our soldiers from the south to go pick up the equipment and make sure we haven't left any tracks for some curious shepherd to follow. We don't know how the spook got hold of this, and I don't want to put anyone's cover in danger." T-Rex slid his finger along the screen. "This is also where we'll find our transportation. *Should* be an SUV—a gift from an intelligence contract. If there's no SUV, we may have to get creative," T-Rex looked up. "I don't care what that means."

"Because there'll be a lot of options lying around on the edge of the desert," Jeopardy said dryly.

"Goat wrangling." Nitro grinned. "It's a thing. Just lift your feet up so they don't drag."

"Hell or high water," T-Rex continued, "we get to the second GPS coordinates on your map before dawn. That's where Sgt. Poole is going to lay his weary head. This being his last night in a known location, it's our only opportunity to grab him. Like Watts said, this is not a swing and a miss. This is a pile-on. But—and please pay attention to the but—if he dies or his brain gets rattled to the point where he'll be eating pudding and drooling on himself for the rest of his life, we won't find out what information he passed on, and what plans are in the making. We need him to tell the nice interrogators the who, what, where, why, and how of an attack. Sgt Poole is treated with kid gloves."

"Whole and healthy and ready to chat," Ty said.

T-Rex pointed again to the map. "Jump here. Vehicle here. Poole here. Exfil here. Now, we're on an inflatable in the Mediterranean, and the sun is inching over the horizon if everything goes beautifully."

"Once we have Poole in hand," Ty said. "We have a bit more flexibility with our schedule. The goal is to get out of the country without anyone being the wiser. No need to push to get out before the fishermen are on their boats."

Nomad was scanning the map on his tablet. "The topography looks good. We can find a quiet hole to dig into and lay low until nightfall the second night."

"Agreed," T-Rex said. "So Bravo, get yourself geared for that eventuality – food, water, warmth, shelter, and fishing gear just in case someone motors up with questions. And assume that Alpha will need rations when we reach you. Think about a cover story. Let's pick our teams."

"International waters, I'm not answering anyone's questions," Nitro said. "And I call raft duty. I hate HAHO."

"So we load onto the inflatable, and we're out in the Mediterranean, then what?" Havoc asked. "And I'll take the ground team." Deep, dark waters weren't his thing, Havoc had told Nomad, and that was the reason he didn't go the Navy SEAL route for special ops.

"I'll take Bravo," Jeopardy said.

Nomad hadn't weighed in on his preference because he was "new guy," and he'd take whatever role needed filling.

T-Rex gave him a nod. "Okay, once we're loaded onto the raft, Nitro will navigate to a given GPS coordinate. Our sub will pop up, we'll board, collapse the raft, and shove it down the hole. Poole will go straight to the brig, and the sub will descend until someone from the American base rows out and picks us up to take us back to Türkiye. We need to get our documents stamped. For now, we'll leave our papers here with the embassy. We're going in naked. No papers. No weapons. Our cover is hungry, lost hikers."

"Copy," they said in unison.

T-Rex turned his computer screen back toward him. "Now, let's fill in the missing pieces. We need to get our story straight and get it into the right hands so, if needed, they can rally to our side in whatever capacity they can."

"You don't think they'll be told to disavow?" Nomad asked.

T-Rex pressed his lips together and dipped his head. "Always a possibility. But it might work in our favor if we're lost hikers and concerned friends had let area embassies know we'd lost touch. Right?" His gaze slid around the table. "You're using your alias names if it comes to a confrontation. As usual, gentlemen, we won't use our call signs when others are within earshot."

"Our jobs?" Havoc asked.

"We'll make it easy," T-Rex said. "We're all digital nomads. We settle into a place for a month or so, working remotely, using the freedom of being untethered from a desk to see the world. So, there are no permanent addresses in the U.S. Our paychecks come from individual contractors, and the projects are always changing. In our individual capacities, we accept contracts that need marketing and data analysis. We fulfill that contract, wash, and repeat. Same gig we used when we were in Kenya. Right now, everyone in the group is between contracts since we wanted to see the desert and do some hiking and there's no connectivity."

"Copy," the group said.

"That was easy enough," Havoc's fingers busily typed the information into his report.

"Looking at the map," Nomad fixed his attention on his tablet, "if we're lost hikers who are found near our landing zone, that's a six-day hike from somewhere with a government that might support our story. Let's say we were last at Mount of the Beatitudes. How'd we survive lost in the desert for six days? How'd we get hold of a vehicle?"

Nitro pushed his chair back, swinging his heels up onto the table. "Too bad we don't have a dead body."

"What?" Havoc laughed.

"If we had a body, we could say, 'Hey, we found this guy near the car, and we thought we should deliver the body to the authorities, so we drove him in.'"

Jeopardy balled up a piece of paper and tossed it at Nitro's head. "Nomad's the only one who's supposed to be suffering from sleep deprivation. That's the stupidest damned suggestion I've ever heard. 'Hey, we're digital nomads with no addresses, no working phone, no money, no paperwork, we're driving a car that doesn't belong to us with the lights off and night vision strapped to our heads, and oh, here's a dead body. You're welcome.'"

"Wouldn't have to be dead. They could just be sick," Nitro shrugged. "We find someone, roofie them."

"Simple is best," Ty said from over near Rory. "We came upon the car and looked around for the owner. Didn't find him. Keys were in the ignition. The car wasn't working. Nomad went under the hood, found a loose spark plug, tightened it down, and we thought we'd drive into civilization, hand it over to the police, and contact a U.S. embassy. But we're not sure where we are. We're not even sure of what country we're in. Is this Jordan?"

"That'll only work until we get to the first city and an opportunity to turn it in. Then what?" Nomad asked. "With that background story, we wouldn't have Syrian currency to buy or rent a vehicle. And I'm assuming we have no money and no papers because we were robbed along the way, right?"

"Right," T-Rex said.

"We didn't check the license plates to tell us where we were?" Nomad asked.

Jeopardy shook his head. "We're Americans. Could we understand a Syrian license plate?"

"We don't get stopped," Havoc said. "We're driving at night with night vision. We'll see them before they see us. And we're not driving through any cities, right?"

"Spark plugs," T-Rex said. "Not bad. I like that. And yes, we're heading to the coast, taking the scenic route along rural roads. Like Nomad pointed out, there are hills to disappear into."

"That's if they give us a car with the right off-roading capabilities," Ty said.

"Anything better than motorcycles will make me happy," Havoc said. "Though, if they give us a piece of shit with bald tires like they did in Niger—remember that crap?—we'll have to get creative."

Nomad leaned forward. "Why don't we take a pile of cash in there and just bribe them? This is a conflict zone. People are hungry."

"We need to take in some moola as a backup plan anyway, for sure," Havoc said. "I'm adding it to the list. We can hide it in Rory's vest, and if we don't want them to look too close, Ty just signals Rory to tell the guy to back off." Havoc grinned.

"Sorry, my dog's pretty hungry," Ty said, "and he gets cranky when he's low-sugar. Got any bread? Piece of goat?"

T-Rex planted his knuckles on the table and leaned forward. "All right. Scenario A – we're lost and pitiful. Scenario B –

things are going sideways. Maybe they act like they want to call in backup, 'How about we take care of you?' Scenario C – still not going well, we let them go night-night, take their comms and vehicle to give us a bit of time to get clear of the area."

"With you and me pushing the seats as far back as we can," Nomad said, "and Rory in the mix, Poole better be small enough to shove in the hatch."

"That, or we can tie him to the roof like a Christmas tree." Ty laughed.

T-Rex swung his gaze around the table, taking in his team. "Since Nitro brought up dead bodies—bodies, that is, absolutely *not* dead ones, or the mission is a fail—we need to package Poole and get him out. He's not going to like that. And," he rapped his knuckle on the folder in front of him, "zero footprint means we shouldn't wake up the household or put anyone in motion."

"Sedation." Ty was slowly reducing the speed on Rory's treadmill. Soon, it would be time to head to the airport to fly east.

Jeopardy drew his hand down his beard. "Sock in his mouth and a head wrapped in duct tape."

"Sedation only. We can't risk asphyxia." T-Rex rapped the table again for emphasis. "Zero footprints. We need to explain the situation away."

"If we're stopped, and we say he's having a medical emergency, they could very well separate him from us." Nomad said, "He wakes up and talks to the authorities in a stupor. He'd get shipped off to their own little black hole for question-and-answer time."

"How do we explain his situation so he stays in our custody?" Ty asked. "We're lost hikers with a found car. Granted, driving the car at night in the country means we might not see anywhere to stop, so we just kept going. It's a stretch. But so is every other word out of our mouths."

"I did a mission once when we had enough time to develop pocket litter." Nomad referenced the items chosen by operators working a clandestine mission to support a cover story. "We brought in two pharmacy bottles with his name printed on the label. The sleeping pills said, 'Take one.' The other was pain medication, 'take two every four hours.' No one stopped us. But had that happened, we were prepared to say that our guy got the bottles confused and tipped back two pills for a headache, which was double his dose of sleeping pills, and he zonked out on us. We've been checking his breathing. He seems to be okay. Just out like a light. It'll wear off."

T-Rex turned to Havoc. "Get that information to the soldier in charge of putting together our mission kits. Make sure it lists how many pills and that a good number are missing. Make sure the date on the bottles is at least a month old. We need a back-pack with dirty clothes that fit Sgt. Poole that matches what we're taking in, used hygiene items, and sand. Throw every-thing in the dirt and stomp on it. Front pocket of the ruck sack for the meds."

"Wilco." Havoc focused on his screen as he typed out the encrypted message.

"We'll take Poole's stuff out with him, but we'll need to go through it and dump anything that isn't intel or doesn't support our cover. Speaking of meds, we need to get Poole from his host house to the boat. It could be hours," T-Rex said. "He needs to be knocked completely out."

"How big?" Nomad asked.

"He's five-foot-six, a buck sixty," T-Rex read.

"Haloperidol should do it." Havoc didn't look up from the keyboard. "Ketamine, maybe."

"When Poole sees us, he'll know he's going to a black hole

to answer some CIA interrogator's questions," Nomad said, "probably followed by a supermax. His adrenaline's going to be through the roof."

Nitro stretched his arms long and then rested his laced fingers on his head. "We need to B52 his ass."

"B52 gives us options." T-Rex nodded. "Okay the diphenhydramine goes in someone's first aid kit for allergies to bee stings."

"Desert bees?" Nomad lifted a single brow.

"I don't care that there aren't any bees." T-Rex turned to Havoc. "I'm leery of labeling the allergy. Leave specifics off."

"Remember when Foxtrot said their guy was allergic to shellfish," Jeopardy asked, "and the investigators forced him to eat oysters?"

"Well, it made him swell up," Nitro grinned. "But that was him enjoying the smiles of the woman serving him and less about anaphylaxis."

"Wrong head was getting fat." Havoc picked up the chip bag and tipped the last crumbs into his mouth.

"Allergies." T-Rex pointed toward Nomad. "That's you. Sometimes you have a reaction, sometimes you don't. You carry the kit just in case things turn bad."

"Got it."

Havoc dragged his fingertips down his sleeve to clear the oil, then typed that out for the logistics team to gather the items for the mission. In situations like this, Echo had learned that, when time was of the essence, it worked best when they sent the name of items as soon as an element hit their list.

"The Haloperidol and Lorazepam can tuck into the Glucagon kit," T-Rex turned to Havoc. "Let them know our normal procedure for that." He sent his gaze around the table. "Remember that as we relabel the meds, look for the series of numbers. The last number is the number of milligrams to use.

H5—five milligrams of Haloperidol and L2 is the two milli of lorazepam." T-Rex leaned onto the table. "Let's not get sloppy. We need this guy to eventually answer the intelligence community's questions. Again, with emphasis, we can't allow any mistakes to jeopardize this guy's safety and well-being. Take your time. You know the drill. One inch apart. Thigh or deltoid, whichever is thrashing less."

"We have that in the glucagon kit – for the label, which one of you has trouble with hypoglycemia?" Havoc asked.

"You," Jeopardy said. "That'll explain why you're constantly thinking about food."

"Not constantly, just since I met the guy living raisin to raisin. I've come to the conclusion that every meal could be the last for a while. Eat while there's food in front of you, right?"

"Slow learner," Nitro said. "I picked up that lesson when I was in boot."

"In boot, you knew another meal was coming." Havoc rubbed his stomach. "This guy lived raisin to raisin for weeks, thinking he'd never eat again."

"Got a little vicarious PTSD going?" Nomad wanted to hear what that was about; he'd wait until after this mission. One problem with joining a team that had already coalesced with shared mission stories was that a rhythm was in place. The more stories Nomad heard, the more he could get a feel for how the team worked.

"Raisin. To. Raisin." Havoc bunched up the chip bag and tossed it in the trash.

T-Rex spun toward the door at the sound of a knock.

The Marine popped his head in. "Excuse me, Master Chief, the cars are here to take you to the airport."

"Here we go," T-Rex said, closing his computer top. "Let's make Uncle Sam proud."

7

Black

Idling at the security booth at the front of the Iniquus campus, John Black accepted his identification back from the guard. He raised his car window and waited for the massive gates blocking the entrance to edge open.

He'd left a message with his assistant that he'd been called into an emergency meeting this morning, and he'd get to Langley when he could. "If Grey reaches out to you," he'd noted, "no matter what, I need to know immediately."

That mission was at the forefront today. And he didn't need whatever it was that Iniquus was about to throw into the pot. He just didn't.

Impatiently drumming his fingers on the steering wheel, Black hoped against hope that the asset's information about Poole was accurate.

If it was, then Red made a hell of a security save with her new mole.

They'd know one way or another very soon.

Knowing what happened when there were too many cooks in a kitchen, Black didn't want to be an obstacle that confused the forward momentum in the capture of Daniel Poole. He took a step back and had Grey work with JSOC and the White House on this since Grey was boots on the ground in that area.

Still, this was Color Code intel, so it was Black's name and reputation on the top of the Poole report. While that meant he was first in line for congratulations, he was also first in line to deal with negative ramifications.

When Iniquus's gate attendant waved him through, Black slowly pulled forward, tracing his way down the tree-lined drive. A drive that Black typically enjoyed. He found it soothing.

Today?

Every tree irritated him.

That Iniquus Panther Force called this morning, pulling him away from his focus on Poole and Syria, *irritated* him.

The tight window in Syria was what had his nerves frying.

That and it all fell in line a little too neatly. It seemed a little *too* good to be true.

A little more time and a better chance to vet the information would be a "best of all worlds" scenario. But Black didn't live in that world. He lived in a world that could catch fire at any moment, and his team had better have extinguishers in hand.

There was at least *some* information that the Pentagon verified.

Of course, that could be staged. Someone could have snagged Poole and been holding him somewhere, an innocent man.

Black just didn't know. And wouldn't know.

Yeah, the regime in power or any of those elbowing and jostling to gather regional supremacy might have set this up.

What if Color Code sent a team of Delta Force operators to a GPS coordinate in the middle of nowhere, told them to go naked with a lost hikers' tale, and someone threw a net over them?

They'd grab up six elite warriors and a highly trained combat K9.

Four. Two of them would be on a raft off the coast.

Four would still make horrific snuff films. Would be incredibly powerful terrorist recruiting tools. And what those men would suffer … Black's lips pulled into a deep frown.

The intelligence game was not for those with a weak stomach.

And on this one? Yeah, Black could feel his coffee churning around, giving him heartburn.

He pulled into a parking place designated for guests, turned off his engine, and flipped his phone over to see if, somehow, he'd missed a call.

Popping his door open, Black reminded himself he wasn't steering this ship. It wasn't his choice what happened next. All the information had been handed over, and people with higher ranks than his were debating what should happen next.

Echo would be sitting on a tarmac in Türkiye, waiting for the sun to set. They were seven hours ahead of Eastern Standard Time.

Black got out without bothering to lock his door. Iniquus was one of the most secure locations in the world. Black planned to tap all his contacts here at Iniquus to let him in the gate if it looked like a nuclear war was starting. He was sure they had the best fallout plan around. Maybe second to POTUS, but Black wouldn't be on that survival list.

Tucking his phone into his pocket, Black straightened his tie, using his side window as a mirror, then started for the atrium door.

If this went down, Red would have to stay in close touch with her asset to make sure that there wasn't any blowback on the guy, Black thought. Though, if this went down *perfectly*, it should look like Poole disappeared into the night. No one would think that there was a mole telling tales from the office where the asset had listened in.

Never assume. Not everything goes into a report.

As soon as he knew anything, Black would apprise Red. He made the mental note as he walked through the soupy morning air.

Red had sounded like shit when they were on the phone. He and Grey had been on video feed; she had been a black square. Her phone, when she wasn't speaking, had been switched to mute, and her voice was weak and raspy with the hitch-breath delivery of someone who was bracing against pain.

It was the personality of a field officer to bite down on the bullet and get the job done.

That was probably what was happening. Black trusted she could handle whatever was going on.

Red, like all field officers, carried all the standard pharmaceuticals and knew how to treat herself to keep her name, face, and—most importantly—DNA samples away from anything that had governmental control or connection.

Red was definitely on his mind. Not only her health and the Poole situation but also, while Black had no idea why he was here at Iniquus, he did know it was Red-related.

Could it be something to do with her illness?

Since the Iniquus call came in about an hour after Black got off the phone with her, and since Red didn't respond when he reached out, Black would admit that the heat and pressure behind his sternum had become painful.

He reached into his pocket and took out his roll of antacids. He popped one in his mouth, pocketed the roll, then yanked open the atrium door, moving from the ninety-five percent humidity into the crisp air conditioning that made his sweat evaporate and chilled his system.

The waiting escort gave Black a slight bow. Visitors weren't free to move around the building on their own. The CIA had tested some of their best officers, asking them to breach Iniquus and take a picture in the executive suite to prove they had gotten in. No one had been successful. This organization ran with the fine-tuned precision of a hand-crafted watch.

"Sir, if you'll follow me, I'll show you up." No introduction. No further chit-chat, just a crisp turn, and his guide took him to the elevator, up to the corridor that held the Iniquus forces' office spaces, down the hall that Black had traversed many times before, stopping with a quick rap on the door that read "Panther Force War Room."

Panther Force's tactical operations coordinator, Nutsbe, opened the door. The guide gave a slight bow and disappeared toward the elevators. Nutsbe held out his hand for a shake.

When Nutsbe had called this morning, referencing Red with a "this seems time-sensitive" dangle, Black headed straight over.

He'd considered Red's health, but could this possibly be about Poole?

Black's gaze swept past Nutsbe to take in the room where a woman sat at the highly polished conference table. She looked small in the black captain's chair. Her ebony hair and navy blue dress made her sink away until all that was truly visible was a determined face.

"Miss Abadi," he said. This was one of Red's most important assets with essential contacts in both Lebanon and Syria.

"It's Mrs. Ackerman now, but you can call me Sophia," she said without standing. Instead, she opened her hand toward the chair next to her by way of invitation. "I'm sorry if I'm disrupting your day. I tried to reach Red but was unsuccessful. I just received news from a friend of mine." She stopped and slid her hands down her skirt, smoothing the non-existent wrinkles on her lap. "I understand that you and Red are on the same team and that all information is shared between you? I remember you from before."

Okay, she wasn't bringing him bad news about Red. That, at least, was a relief.

"Yes, exactly. That's how I was able to intervene on your behalf when the FBI mistakenly took you into custody."

Sophia bit her lower lip and looked over her shoulder at Nutsbe, who sat just behind her and to her left with an enormous bullmastiff dripping drool onto the carpet. When Nutsbe didn't warn her off, Sophia turned back to Black. "Okay. Red isn't answering, and I don't think holding on to this story is wise. I'm just going to tell you."

Black reached into his breast pocket and pulled out a digital recorder. "May I?"

"I prefer that you don't, actually." She gave a tight shake to her head. "AI can trace voices now, and I'm not interested in getting on anyone's list. I'm meeting you here because it's safe for us to talk at Iniquus. No one would know I was passing on information. I have every reason to be at my husband's office, even if he's out of town."

"Notepad is okay?" Black tucked the device away and extracted a pad and pen. He sat back and waited for her to start in her own time.

"Yes. Okay, so I typically offer Red information about conflict relics sold to fund terror. This time, it's more of a treasure hunt that I want to bring to your attention." Sophia cleared her throat. "There is a man named Zayd Ali Kamal. Do you know of him?"

"Yes." Kamal was one of the wealthiest men in the Middle East.

"He has offered a forty-million-euro prize for anyone who finds his fiancée's great grandmother's wedding gift. It's a ring with a rare red diamond."

"Fire of the Desert." Black nodded. "Last seen at the end of World War II when she was imprisoned in Marrakesh, Morocco."

"Exactly." Sophia licked her lips, then lifted the water bottle resting in her lap for a sip. "Since you know that, did you know it was found?"

"What?" Black edged forward in his seat. "No. By whom?" Forty million euros in the hands of an entity like ISIS could be cataclysmic. And if this had nothing to do with funding terror, why would Sophia Abadi Ackerman be involved?

Sophia drew a hand across her forehead and exhaled hard. "I received a call from my friend, Dr. Wajeeb."

Black nodded. "Syrian antiquities professor."

"Retired. Yes."

That he knew the name and could label him seemed to lower Sophia's distress. That disquiet was understandable since she was out of her chain of command, and the information she dealt with usually put lives on the line.

"Okay. Dr. Wajeeb received a phone call yesterday from a friend, Dr. Klein of Munich." She looked over to his pad when he hesitated and spelled. "K-l-e-i-n. Dr. Klein and Dr. Wajeeb have been friends for decades. They are in similar fields, and they often discuss rarities. Dr. Klein called Dr. Wajeeb and told him that five men had just come to his office—"

"In Munich, Germany?" Black asked.

"Exactly. They had the Fire of the Desert ring with them and asked that Dr. Klein authenticate their find."

"But it's been missing since World War II … How?"

"I know nothing about that." She twisted the cap off the water, then twisted it back on. "I know that Dr. Klein agreed that the ring was authentic, signed the papers verifying his opinion, and the men left his office. Dr. Klein then called Dr. Wajeeb to share this story. Dr. Wajeeb was on the phone when Dr. Klein yelled that there had been gunshots. Dr. Wajeeb said he then heard the sound of the phone thudding, presumably onto the floor, and the sound of running feet leaving the office and going down the stairs."

Black pressed the tip of his ballpoint into the pad.

"Dr. Wajeeb, of course, was horrified. He waited for his friend to get back in touch with him to give an explanation. When day turned to night, Dr. Wajeeb searched the Internet for information about gunshots fired in Munich to see if he could figure out what he had heard over the phone. Dr. Wajeeb discovered that there were five men shot in the head by what was described as more than one sniper on the rooftop across the street from Dr. Klein's office address. Dr. Klein was also dead. Pending autopsy, they believe it was a heart attack. The police, of course, have no idea why someone targeted these men. None of them had identification, though things of value—watches, for example, and phones—weren't taken. At first glance, it didn't look like a robbery. The only thing taken was a briefcase. I can show you this." She pulled out the phone that she had tucked under her thigh. "This video was recorded by the street cameras and shown on the news."

Sophia scrolled, then held the phone out to him.

Black watched a video clip of a woman bending low over a downed man, not to check on him but to take a briefcase. Then, she calmly walked down the road away from the carnage. The cane and the foot of an elderly man slid into view, but from the camera angle, nothing more was visible except the edge of a car door when it opened and the legs of the woman when she slid into the driver's seat.

The car moved sedately into the street and drove away.

"That was on the news," Sophia repeated. "They asked for anyone with information to please come forward."

"When was this?"

"Dr. Wajeeb spoke to Dr. Klein yesterday around eighteen hours, Munich time. This video was on the late-night news in Munich. Dr. Wajeeb waited until he knew I would be back from taking my boys to daycare before he called me. So he waited four hours."

Forty million euros. *Forty million euros.* What were the chances that these were thieves and not terrorists? Murderers who thought all was fair for a pirate on a treasure hunt?

With the names that Sophia was mentioning now? Those odds weren't good. Black made quick notes about the time as he asked, "The woman took the Fire of the Desert. Correct?"

"That's what Wajeeb understands."

"Do any other authorities know this?" Black handed her phone back.

"Dr. Wajeeb is leaving this to our intelligence community to consider. He's afraid if he says anything to anyone else, then well … I guess the closest American phrase would be 'too many cooks in a kitchen.'"

Wasn't it interesting that she'd used the phrase that Black had just been using to describe the Poole situation? Wajeeb was right about this. It was better to hand it to a single trusted resource.

"Dr. Wajeeb told me and me alone. And, of course, I am handing it off immediately. I mentioned a delay between the late-night news in Europe and my taking the call this morning."

Black leaned forward. "You spoke over an encrypted channel?"

"Always. There's a little more. During those hours, Dr. Wajeeb did what he knows to do when something of that value is in the hands of a criminal. He tried to figure out who had possession of the ring and what they might be funding with the sale. His concern was and remains that forty million euros could wreak enormous destruction."

Black felt the blood draining from his face. This was what he was fearful of. He wouldn't be here unless both Dr. Wajeeb and Sophia concluded that this was about terrorism. Otherwise, why involve the United States government? "Who has it?" Black asked as evenly as possible, cutting to the chase.

"A woman. Dostoevskia Elena Yakovna She is Syrian born with a Russian father and a Syrian mother." In Russian paperwork, a name is written with the surname, followed by the person's first name, followed by the patronymic. "A" is often added to the surname, and the female patronymics end in either -ovna or -evna.

Yakov—as an American would write it—was a name familiar to Black. Yakov had been with the military for most of his career and was now retired. And yes, he had worked for the Russian government in Syria from around nineteen eighty on the Treaty of Friendship and Cooperation signed by Russia and Syria. Working between the two countries, Yakov mostly lived in Syria through the outbreak of the civil war, but that was twenty-eleven. Also, the Yakov Dostoevski that Black knew was married to a Russian woman, an oligarch's cousin. They had four children together, all of them grown, some with their own children.

So, Black was thinking of the wrong man. He'd figure out who Elena's father was when he got back to Langley. He needed to work with his targeters to see if this had come within their research. "Keep going."

"Elena is known within the circles who sell conflict relics.

She speaks Arabic, Russian, and English fluently and enough Turkish to get by. She frequently flies to Western Europe to meet with people who would like special items, gathering wish lists from her clients and trying to match that up with available pieces found at archaeological sites."

"As its own crime or to fund terror?" Black asked.

"ISIS maintains control of all the digs in Syria. In order for her to function, it is with the blessing of ISIS."

"Red is familiar with Elena's work?"

"Yes, as am I. Of her name, at least. But we didn't know what she looked like. Now, we do. Dr. Wajeeb figured out that Elena used the last name Savas when she was in Europe. That was the piece missing. We know her as Elena Savas, not her Russian name. Once he connected those dots, he could make progress finding her image."

Black was making quick notes in a shorthand that only he could read. "Savas is a Turkish name?"

"Yes, and somehow she has Turkish papers and a Turkish home near the Syrian border where things are porous, so it's easy for her to cross back and forth."

"How did they decide that was Elena of the video?"

"No one is sure that it is her in the video. It might not be. It could be someone who works with her." Sophia filled her lungs and released a sigh, obviously trying to shed some stress. "Look, Dr. Wajeeb blames Elena for his friend's death. He feels certain that had Dr. Klein not seen the murders, he wouldn't have had the heart attack. Ever since Dr. Wajeeb heard the news, he has been working his considerable web of information. That's how he discovered that Elena Savas had contacted Zayd Ali Kamal's people and told them she had the sought-after ring and authentication papers. And he also discovered that Savas is an alias for Dostoevskia Elena Yakovna of Damascus."

"I see." Black paused, imagining the timeline. "And just so

I'm clear about who possesses the ring, has Elena handed it over to Zayd Ali Kamal? Was Elena paid the money?"

"Not yet." Sophia said, "Kamal is an interesting man. He doesn't follow straight lines and seems to enjoy intrigue. Those are my observations. Kamal's right-hand man—uhm, his name is Joel Brighton—said he—he being Joel—would be at a charity ball in Vienna this week. Saturday. Kamal said he'd provide Elena Savas with a ticket—which, by the way, were sold out at least a year in advance. It's a centuries-old social event. It's called—"

"Secret Order of the Raven's Gate Gala?" Black asked.

"That. Yes. Joel will be there, and he asked Elena to come with the ring and the paperwork to prove this is on the up and up. And if that looks good, he'll give her instructions for how the exchange will go down."

"Interesting." Black would agree that Kamal found life a bore. Money made everything come too easily for him. If there was any drama to be had, Kamal would try to make a meal of it. "Security?"

"Yes, Dr. Wajeeb said he wondered the same thing. He discovered that Security is provided by the Order. No one is allowed—not royalty or heads of state—to bring in their own teams. That's my understanding, but I'm sure you have the resources to figure that out. It should be a safe environment for her to show him."

"Just to be clear, the him is Joel Brighton?"

"Yes, an American. Joel and Kamal went to university together in the U.S. I have his picture." She flipped through the phone again and showed it to Black.

Black knew Sophia wouldn't want to send this to his phone, and he didn't want that traceable connection either. He turned to Nutsbe. "Can you get that to me?"

"I will."

"And pictures, Dr. Wajeeb tried to get pictures of Elena." She scrolled forward. "This is old, but here is a Syrian school picture of her." Sophia showed Black the picture. It didn't pull up any connections for him.

Nutsbe leaned forward to look at the image. "I can put it through our AI to age that photo. How old would she be now?"

"Mid-thirties," Sophia said.

"We have a crime. We have the possibility of the criminal getting a forty-million-euro payout. We have a date for the meet and greet that you're sure of?"

"A hundred percent." Sophia nodded. "While waiting for Red to call me, I reached out to a friend who is part of that charitable society. She was able to check the ball's invitation list. Elena Sava's name was added this morning as Joel Brighton's guest. Before, it was listed as 'Joel Brighton plus one.' And I thought I might be able to use my connection to score a couple of tickets so someone from our government could get in and observe or intervene. But there's no wiggle room. There are no more tickets. I'm sorry."

"What do you think is happening here?" Black asked. He had heard the ramping tension in her voice throughout the interview. He watched as she used both hands, petting the dog's neck and back. Sophia had been doing this kind of work for many years. She should be used to this level of danger. And yet, it was obviously impacting her hard.

"Elena Savas funds terror." Sophia sat with her back ramrod straight. "She develops terror cells outside of Syria. She has had money before—money in what would be, say, a million dollars in a year's time. She has never had forty million. The ring is going to be an international story. Once it is out there, the media will look for the lucky treasure hunter. They'll find Elena. The world is too small for her to hide her identification. And Zayd Ali Kamal and his people have no reason to protect her. That means Elena is about to be exposed, and she doesn't care. Dr. Wajeeb has concluded—and for what it's worth, I concur—that Elena doesn't mind the exposure because she will want to be the victorious face of what comes next. Dr. Wajeeb further believes that what is coming was already planned and is underway. They were simply trying to find a funding source to send it over the finish line."

8

____

Nomad

With everything going on with the Middle Eastern countries along the Mediterranean Sea right now, the United States government had a vested interest in calming the temperatures.

Whatever information this guy Poole had in his back pocket, it couldn't be small.

It had to be a serious threat.

This was one of those missions where any point of failure was a spark to a det cord. It could very well snake itself along to a massive explosion.

Nomad had lived a razor's edge kind of life for nearly two decades.

It was the space he liked to inhabit. It brightened his focus, calmed his nerves, and felt good in his bones. It was what he was made to do.

While that made missions feel natural, it didn't make them easy.

Nomad didn't take anything about his work lightly.

He and Echo Team Alpha spent time trying on the dirty clothes, going through the packs, and familiarizing themselves with all the elements that had been gathered. Whoever was supporting this mission had done an excellent job. How they found worn hiking clothes that fit both him and T-Rex—yeah, they stepped up to the challenge of "Go big or go home."

Their jump gear was squared away. The night was deepening, and now there was nothing to do but be pointed toward their plane and given a thumbs up.

"Focus in." T-Rex pulled the team's attention to him as he looked at his phone. "I'm getting a message from the Diplomatic Security Service."

Ty turned his way. "Out of Ankara?"

"Affirmative."

Nomad scowled. "Is this about our legislators?"

"Reading. Okay, a bomb went off in front of an American-owned hotel in Tal Afaya."

"Lebanese border town, I moved through there on assignment a few years back," Havoc said. "Which hotel? Does it say?"

T- Rex put his finger on the screen. "Surain Zunai."

"That's right in the middle of town where Westerners stay when heading over the border to Syria. It was a good jumping-off place for those traveling to Damascus before the Civil War. It's nice." Havoc paused. "Was nice."

"Does it give any information about the structural damage? Body count? And, I guess, more importantly, if it's bringing scrutiny to that area?" Ty asked. "Our target isn't there, but he's not that far either. We might run into issues if they're suddenly on high alert."

"That's all it says other than it might have been targeted on the government building next door to the hotel."

"And someone set off a bomb in the wrong location by mistake?" Nitro asked.

Jeopardy tipped his head. "Hand got twitchy on a vest, and they didn't reach their destination?"

"There was a significant loss of life. There were almost exclusively foreigners and staff in the hotel. To that end, embassies in Beirut were informed. They don't know yet if any Americans were involved." T-Rex swiped his phone closed. "It might make the border guards jumpy. Lebanon and Syria might put more boots on the ground."

"Good thing we're floating into the desert then," Ty said.

"Note that. *Desert* is where our boots touch down. We are coming mighty close to the lake, and we don't have the time, the equipment, or the manpower to drag your drowning asses out of the drink. Ty is dropping down first with Rory. Follow his beacon in."

"Which is fine until he goes into the water," Havoc said.

"That's why you have a GPS, princess," Ty sent him a grin.

A guy in Air Force coveralls stepped through the door. "Echo," he called out, "your plane is fueled and waiting. If you'd follow me?"

They scraped back their chairs, snagged up their gear, and headed out.

Nomad looked down at Rory, trotting beside him on a short leash. "You ready to play? Does Rory like to be a birdie?"

Rory's tale wagged furiously while he pranced by Ty's side.

Ty scowled. "Don't rile him with promises we don't know we can keep. Look at him grinning like that. Now, if he doesn't get to jump, he's not going to be happy."

"I think that's all of us," Nitro said. "Jeopardy and I will see you on the beach. Go catch us a traitor."

Rory, Echo's Malinois, had trained for a SEAL team. Rory came to work for Delta Force when his handler became ill and had to leave the service. By the time Ty became his handler, Rory was a seasoned and polished force multiplier. His enthusiasm for working in the fray was admirable. And his energy was contagious.

Right now was one of those times. With his helmet strapped under his chin and the ear protectors in place, Rory knew he was going to work—his favorite thing in the world.

Smart as a whip, he paid attention to what kinds of packs the team had hanging from their shoulders and knew they were about to jump.

Possibly, that was true.

The brass in the situation room hadn't greenlighted this mission beyond flying to a specific coordinate where they'd circle until a decision was made. That decision could come from D.C., or the pilot would call it if they got fuel critical.

This was part of their training: Take a knee, ready for the breach, and get called off. It wasn't as easy as that might sound. Hormones being what they were, when all systems were primed for violence, it was hard to sneak away in silence.

If it was hard on them, it was straight-up bad for Rory. If they did get turned around, Ty would have to devise something, possibly even having them jump onto the training field so Rory wouldn't be disappointed. It was the same when Rory went out on a search. If the subject wasn't found, at the end of the day, they'd find some volunteer to lay under a blanket or something so Rory could find them and get his reward. Otherwise, like most working dogs, he could become depressed.

Rory stretched his neck past Ty's knees to capture his jump bag in his teeth and pulled it onto Ty's lap. His butt hit the floor, and he looked expectantly at Ty.

Ty scratched under his chin.

Rory must have a bit of psychic intuition. The pilot came over the comms. "That's the call. We are climbing to altitude and leaving international waters. We have the wind pushing us along, that's going to cut our flight time. We estimate you'll be on target in thirty-five minutes."

The men moved through their preparation slowly. The goal was to—even if nerves were amped for the dangers of a HAHO jump—prevent any sweat. Being damp and experiencing the negative forty-nine-degree temperatures at thirty-five thousand feet could be life-threatening. They donned their thermal HAHO suits that wouldn't keep them toasty but would help prevent frostbite.

Ty loaded Rory into his jump bag, which would keep him warm in the frigid temperatures of high altitude and protect his legs during landing. He wore an oxygen mask like the rest of the team to keep from going hypoxic and passing out.

Nomad was looking forward to the jump every bit as much as Rory was. Nomad's place of peace was floating through the night sky. His favorite kind of jump was the HAHO. It gave him the longest drift of all the jumps.

It was only under extreme circumstances that he got the opportunity to enjoy his time in the sky. Such is life.

The HAHO was chosen when they needed covert insertions. And if a mission needed minimal detection from those on the ground, this qualified.

The pilot called out the two-minute mark.

The back of the plane yawned open.

The brothers lined up.

After the team checked each other's equipment and gave a thumbs up, the jump master signaled them forward.

Ty was out the door with Rory dangling from his front harness.

This was it. The mission was in motion.

Nomad stepped up and jumped out.

Now, to meet the objective without starting World War III.

9

———

Black

Black had asked Nutsbe for a SCIF and was following behind an escort taking him to a room with a secure line. They walked down the hall past men and women in charcoal grey uniforms, looking efficient and well-regulated. That was trained into them on Uncle Sam's dime. Iniquus was a veteran-owned and veteran-staffed business model.

Black's mind raced with the information that Sophia handed him.

Red's assets were stepping up, once again proving to Black that he'd made an excellent choice when he took Red onto his team even though his colleagues had scoffed at having a woman working in the field, especially in that part of the world. He'd taken the blowback. Fine with him. She had proven herself time and again. Just look, her net trapped two dangerous terrorist events unfolding in real-time.

Forty million euros—about the same in U.S. dollars—in the hands of a terrorist organizer could buy a hell of a lot of people's loyalties and the means to create destruction, be it cyberwar or something kinetic. Terrorism was a game of whack-a-mole. It had been from the beginning of history, and it would be until the extinction of humanity.

Right now, he had two pressing questions. Did Elena go after the ring for the money to retire, or did she do it to fund her work in terrorism? If this money wasn't going to a house on the beach with a server bringing her cocktails as she lay on the sand and was indeed about funding terror, would she tuck the money away and begin her plan? Or was Elena planning to use this windfall to fund something she already had underway?

Black tested each of those possibilities, seeing how they settled into his system. If he were a betting man, he'd say the teeth had already taken a bite of the fruit.

The first thing he needed to do was bring Color Code into play.

Sitting in the SCIF, Black watched Grey's image open over the video feed.

Grey lifted his chin by way of hello and jumped right in. "Hey, good, I was about to call you about Red."

"I tried to get her on the feed. She's not answering," Black said.

"Did you hear about the explosion?" Grey was dressed in a suit, which was highly unusual. It looked like he was sitting in a basement somewhere.

"This is about the Poole capture?" Black asked. "Did we lose him?"

"No, it's about Red herself. I got word that a car bomb deto-nated in front of a government building that housed both the court and official records offices. Most of the damage was to the hotel next door where Red met with her asset."

"Government building? Are they sure the hotel wasn't the target?" Black leaned back in the captain's chair, laced his fingers, and rested them on his chest.

"My understanding was that someone called in with a threat. The reporting suggests it was an assassination attempt on the judges."

Black scowled. "What's Red saying about this?"

"That's the thing. I've been reaching out. She's not answering."

"Shit." Black drew a hand over his face as icicles formed along his nervous system.

Silently, Grey nodded and then, after a prolonged pause, added, "Exactly."

"All right, let's talk this out."

"I'm going to share my screen with you. Here's what I have. These are pictures of the exterior of the hotel." Grey slowly moved through the four photographs.

Black took in the six-story building. While it remained standing, the whole front looked like the structure was carved out, blackened from fire. It was a rat's nest of construction material and furniture. There were random detached body parts. A lot of bodies … a *lot* of bodies. And they, like Red, were wearing sand-colored tactical wear. Black leaned forward and found himself searching the debris for some sign that one of those bodies was Red.

Grey moved to a photo of a map. "Red sent me this pin. I'm not sure why. But from what I can tell, it corresponds with the time of the explosion."

"She has the rooms at that hotel as a cover. She has rooms at the hotel down the road, right? When we talked to her, she was going to hand the bag over and walk out, *right*?" Black was having trouble getting air in. Red was *his*. He discovered her at The Farm, trained and mentored her, and brought her on his team. They had been together for over a decade. Setting his work with her aside, he had an avuncular attachment. "Did you try calling the front office of that second hotel?"

"No one answered the phone. She missed her check-in call. I'm thinking someone needs to go in and get eyes on Red. If she's in the hospital and muttering State secrets under her breath, things can go very badly—methods and procedures, and over a decade of service with an extensive list of assets and contacts."

Black rubbed a hand over his chin. "And if she's in the morgue, we need to get her body for repatriation."

There was a long pause.

"Yeah," Grey finally said. "That too. We can't have her buried there when no one claims her. And claiming her would lead to all kinds of uncomfortable questions. One way or another, we've got to get to her and get her out of there. And it's got to be someone that can finesse any situation."

"You?"

"I already looked into that. I'm in Istanbul," Grey explained. "We need someone closer. It'll take me too long. The first flight out is nine-twenty hours here. We can't send anyone from the embassy, not even their security. She's not an American citizen on paper, so that would bring up red flags, no play on words intended. They're good at what they do, but I'm not willing to risk Red's cover if she's caught up in events. She could be delayed getting in touch, or phone lines and cell towers might be impacted by the explosion or the rescue efforts. We need someone with more than just training at The Farm on field methods in their rearview. It has to be someone with experience getting tough jobs done."

"Agreed. It might work in our favor that Delta Force Team Echo went into Syria to gather up Poole. By now, they should be boots on the ground. If I'm guessing at timing."

"They're following the broad strokes mission I outlined," Grey said. "They'll jump when the sky goes dark. If all goes well, they'll have Poole on the beach by astronomical twilight before local fishermen launch their boats, and they still have the cover of dark. If we turn, say, two or three members of Echo around, they could possibly make it to the village by the time the village gets moving."

"Right. I'm looking at the map. Boots on the ground in Syria, to Poole, to the sea, to Red's town—the whole thing is only six hours and twenty minutes of drive time. Not operational time, that's just road time. But we don't want the team driving into the town during pre-dawn hours, anyway. That would call security's attention. They need to blend with the local activity."

"I'll work the phone and see if JSOC will lend a hand." Grey paused. "Thinking this through—Echo is working without identification. No passports, so getting out again would become complicated. Once we know if they can go and which operators they're sending, I can wake up the good people at the embassy and get them involved in creating the proper documentation. Echo can sneak in where the border is porous. I know where. I need to ensure they have money to grease some palms if required." Grey looked away from the camera while he scribbled notes. Without looking up, he asked, "You were calling me about Red, and it wasn't about the explosion. What did you want?"

"You said you're in Istanbul? Do you have a full roster?"

Grey squared himself to the camera and put his pen down.

"We've had something come up."

Grey pulled his brows together. "About Red?"

"One of her assets couldn't get in touch with Red either. She had intelligence that needed our attention at an event this Saturday, and that event will require plenty of prep time, so she brought the problem to me."

"Listening."

"Does the name Elena Savas mean something to you?" Black asked.

"Unfortunately, yes."

"You've met her?" Black asked.

"Name on the bad guy list." Grey leaned forward. "What's going on?"

Black moved through the information that Sophia had shared with him. "I need you to go over the border to Vienna. As a matter of fact, if we can find Red alive—"

Grey's nostrils flared. "That's grim as hell."

"It's Red," Black said through gritted teeth, "so until I hear otherwise, I'm going to believe she's fine but might need help. We'll get that covered. So, if she can safely get to you in Vienna and work with you on this, that would be best. I need to make that happen. Either way, I need someone at a ball this weekend. I'll send you a file with the details."

"Okay. Until then, I'll be working on finding Red. Poole is JSOC's priority, but if they can hand Poole off and move on to check on Red, you're right. That would be ideal. If JSOC says that's a no-go or the team is going to be in the field on the Poole mission past sunrise, we're going to have to go another route." Grey paused. "We have people in the area that can do it. Like you, my concern is that, if possible, I don't want to blow her cover. Having the CIA actively functioning in the area of an explosion right there on the border—with so much else going down and everyone extra sensitive—would be diplomatic chaos. I agree, we need this to be shadow work, which takes a special forces skill set, especially if she somehow got scooped up in someone's net."

"Kidnapping?" Black asked.

"I was thinking hospital. But that kidnapping is a possibility. Suddenly, we have a new asset who shows up with information. Information that we haven't heard verified for accuracy. We don't know what's happening with Echo right now. One of the scenarios was that we were getting played, sending in a SOF for an ambush."

Black glared into the camera. "And at the same time, a bomb goes off, and Red's missing? Game that one out."

"If they grabbed her and then blew the building, and the explosion was devastating enough, it could cover her disappearance. It would take some time for the metaphoric dust to settle. There would be time and space for a thorough and enhanced interrogation."

"Yeah. Agreed,' Black said. "That has to be part of this calculation. I need Red, her body, or if that's not possible at the scene, then a significant DNA sample, or we need to go hard on finding what happened between our phone call and now."

Grey leaned into the camera. "Agreed."

"Okay, get a yay or nay on Echo taking this on, and if it's a no-go on their end, then we need to juice up a different team."

"Got it. I'll let you know what I find out." Grey dragged a hand down his face. "Yeah, this isn't like Red at all. Something is going very wrong."

10

Nomad

Nomad sailed the air, and it was glorious!

The arc of the Milky Way, unimpeded by light pollution or much of a moon's glow, was a river of stars.

The landing, though …

The success of a HAHO depended on precision. Nomad toggled this way and that, using the current to help him get to the exact X to meet up with his team.

This X was in the desert, where a layer of dust and sand covered a surface baked into a hard crust. It was hell on the ankles. Sand landings were abrasive as hell when you hit a dune. But sand landings on baked earth were the worst.

As soon as he got his boots under him, Nomad yanked off his protective clothing and oxygen. Gathering the chute and equipment, Nomad checked the GPS, then jogged the distance to the rendezvous.

He'd come close to the X, but a new pin had dropped, signifying an updated rallying point.

When he joined the team, Nomad saw why. There was a

slight indentation where they dumped everything that wouldn't serve this mission and its cover. The dirt was too hard here to do much with it. They had a shovel with them, but any digging would be obvious, hence the utility of the indent.

"There he is," Havoc said. "We thought we'd lost you, sunshine."

"Had my head in the clouds." Nomad piled his things with the others'.

T-Rex sent that pin to headquarters so the brass could make a decision. American soldiers at a base to the southeast might be able to retrieve the equipment.

They stretched the camo cloth over their pile and moved heavy rocks along the edges so a high wind wouldn't send one of their parachutes sailing off to some sheep farm and rouse curiosity.

Meanwhile, Ty and Rory had gone in search of the vehicle intelligence had promised them. Aside from the multitool that each of them had clipped to their belts, Rory was the team's only weapon.

And if this turned out to be some kind of ambush, Rory could sniff out any bombs or bad guys that might be in the area.

The ping of a pin dropping onto their map told the team that the vehicle had been located; they were good to go.

With Havoc at the wheel, the team drove through the dark of night.

It was an hour's drive, and there was literally no one and nothing out this way. Not even the goats mentioned in jest.

There was no way they would have made it if Grey hadn't come through with an SUV for them.

A day late, a lost opportunity, a traitorous terrorist in the wind, four US operators, and a K9 in a volatile country without food or water.

Yeah, things could have gone to hell.

But they'd arrived at the second X. With the engine off and the car in neutral, Havoc let gravity roll the vehicle into a low-lying area, where he threw the gear into park.

The house was a silhouette against a black nightscape.

Making their way forward, there wasn't much in the way of cover. The men lizard-crawled to keep even the sliver of a moon from spotlighting them.

While the team left every extraneous piece of operational equipment back at the fill site, they had to keep a headset with night vision to drive with the lights off and also the equipment to trick Rory out with his high-dollar electronics.

It was possible—though not probable—that someone declaring authority would believe that the group of friends, lost wandering the Syrian desert, were indeed content developer hobbyists who used their doggo to make side money. There actually was a Tik-Tok with Rory fans, though, on social media, they used his official name, "Glory."

Nomad was told the team call him Rory because that's how Rory pronounced his name himself. They'd laugh like it was the funniest thing ever while Nomad shook his head. Had to be an inside joke.

Glory's fame, though, was developed to cover just such a case when equipment might need an explanation. Rory's doggy helmet had a place to attach a camera that fed to Ty's tablet. There was a two-way mic attached to his collar. He wore a protective vest rated for small-arms fire and stab wounds to his vitals.

And when Rory dressed out, he knew he was badass.

He embraced it, strutting around, tongue hanging long as he panted with anticipation.

Send me in, coach!

Ty dispatched Rory to circle the farmhouse, managing Rory's movements through commands softly spoken over the comms collar. This skill was trained and drilled until Rory could work independently. From past experience, Nomad knew that the images that would come back were, unfortunately, only as high as Rory's head, about hip height to most. Even though Ty had taught Rory to lift his chin and scan, the angle still wouldn't be ideal. But it would still be invaluable information.

Besides showing the team the exterior, Rory's current task was to draw any dog barks so there wouldn't be surprises later.

While their dog was a force multiplier, the other guy's dogs were an impediment.

"Rory, sit." Ty pointed at the tablet's screen with the eerie green images. "See the open window there? I can get Rory up onto that wall. There, he gets up some speed for momentum as he moves over this lower roof and jumps through the window."

The team's eyes had adjusted to the dim light. And they could see enough to have a sense of the environment, losing only details and color.

"There's enough clearance for his equipment?" Havoc asked.

"Rory will figure it out." Ty was confident.

"That looks like a good place to infiltrate from a ground game," T-Rex said. "Depending on what's on the other side of that window. Yup. We can try that. I didn't see another access point that's workable. And I'd rather not kick a door down and go hand to hand tonight."

"Agreed." Ty recalled Rory.

When Rory came back to Ty to sit and wait for commands, Nomad noticed that he caught Ty's eye in the meaningful way that dogs do. From working alongside dogs and their handlers for nearly two decades, Nomad knew they passed pictures back and forth, silently communicating. After a moment, Ty handed off the tablet to T-Rex and came up to a crouch. When Rory turned to focus on the window, Nomad knew that Rory agreed with the game plan. "Rory, sit and wait."

Rory's body quivered with the effort to follow the command as Ty lined himself up with the window and jogged to the wall. Rory's ears twitched toward Ty, waiting for the command so soft that only Rory could pick it up.

Once Ty reached the wall, he used his body to make a ramp.

Rory was a bolt of lightning. He flashed across the ground, ran up Ty's body, and up the wall until his front paws looped over the top of the second-story roof and scrambled over.

Ty moved back so the team could assess the images and get a feel for the interior.

Nomad watched as Rory stopped and assessed the window, then took a run at it. Leaping through, he dropped to a crouch, completely silent and still to avoid notice.

No other heat signatures were showing up in the warm end of the spectrum. "Rory, hold," Ty commanded through the mic.

"Door's shut," Nomad whispered.

Ty enlarged the screen. "If it's not locked, Rory can open that kind of lever." He toggled the mic and made his command. Slowly, silently, Rory cased the entire house following Ty's instructions.

The team evaluated the heat signatures and relied on the AI readout to tell them the approximate heights of the people asleep in their beds. From this, the team had a good idea of where Poole was and how to get to him.

They were risking their lives on the intelligence packet.

Some terrorist cell might well have set a trap for the Deltas to step into.

It could also be that there was no Poole in this house, and they were about to break in on an innocent family.

Life was rarely clear-cut and well-defined.

In this line of work, that was especially true.

Nomad prepped three syringes and taped them to his chest, ready.

Ty recalled Rory, who continued out in stealth mode. He made his way over to the edge of the roof, and Ty held out his arms as Rory leaped down. "Good job, buddy." The reward would come later. Rory could be patient. He knew Ty wouldn't forget.

T-Rex handed off the night vision to Nomad since it would be his job to administer the meds to Poole.

Ty moved back out of view with Rory, his job done.

Now, T-Rex, Ty, and Havoc were up.

Over at the compound, Havoc put his hands on the wall as Nomad and T-Rex bent and grabbed his lower legs. Havoc stepped into their palms and, walking his hands up the wall for stability, T-Rex and Nomad stood, then extended their arms to their full length, lifting Havoc cheerleader style.

Havoc reached up, gripping the edge, then did a Russian pull-up, swinging a leg over. There, he secured a rope. And moments later, walking up the wall, Nomad then T-Rex climbed the rope hand over hand to join him.

Through the window, down the hall, Nomad, with night vision in place, led the way to the bedroom where they had identified a figure that was their best guess on Poole.

Comparing a guy with his face pressed into a pillow, mouth wide to accommodate heavy snores, to a memorized photo could be tricky with night vision. Sometimes, they needed an AI assist, but not this time. This guy was obviously blond. He sported a fresh military-tight hairstyle. And then, there was also the big old bald eagle with the American flag tattoo on his bicep, right where it was supposed to be.

When Nomad gave his teammates a thumbs up, T-Rex turned his hip to sit violently on the sleeping man's back, pressing all the air from Poole's chest. Simultaneously, he wrapped Poole's mouth to suppress any noise. T-Rex's pinky and ring finger curved under Poole's chin, trapping his jaw together so Poole couldn't bite or spit.

"Hey there," T-Rex curved to whisper into Poole's ear, "your buddies were missing you back at the base. Looks like you got a little lost. We're gonna take you home."

Guttural sounds resonated from Poole's throat, and Nomad thought he might be trying to barf.

Nomad stepped forward, pulling the first syringe from his t-shirt, and plunged it into Poole's deltoid.

Poole flailed his feet, pounding them into the bed to make noise.

Havoc simply laid across them as Nomad took the top off the second syringe and administered that dose, carefully putting each top into his pocket. *Leave no trace.*

"This is what we call a B52," T-Rex explained, lifting his weight off Poole so he could breathe again. "You know why? 'Cause it's the bomb, man."

As Poole sucked in a giant gulp of air, Nomad plunged the third shot into his thigh.

Havoc stayed on Poole's legs. T-Rex kept Poole's mouth tightly shut.

Soon enough, he was out.

As they pulled back his sheet, they found Poole was naked.

Of course, he was.

They wrapped him up in his covers, and Nomad threw him over his shoulder.

Havoc grabbed Poole's belongings and shoved them into his duffle. The men stole their way down the hall, back through the storage room, and out the window. They handed Poole down to the rooftop. Then they tied the rope under his arms and lowered him to Ty.

"Naked? Serious?" Ty was dressing him as the three climbed back down the rope.

"He's ready?" T-Rex asked. They put Poole in the middle of the blanket. T-Rex and Nomad took hold of the front corners since they were the same height. Havoc took both back corners with the weight of Poole's legs and feet.

With Rory leading the way, on the command, "Rory, find the car." They headed to their vehicle, dumped Poole in the back with Nomad, and made a beeline for the coast.

So far, so good.

11

Nomad

THE INFRARED LIGHT THAT NOMAD LASSOED ACROSS THE NIGHT sky signaled Echo Team Bravo that Alpha had arrived on the beach, and it pinpointed their location.

Within minutes, they saw one in return—message received.

"That was surprisingly easy." Rory was positioned between Ty's knees, getting a well-deserved scritch.

Havoc looked over his shoulder. "Too easy?

"I'll take too easy," Ty responded.

"Hear that?" Havoc whispered.

They sat silently, listening to the motor approach. T-Rex tipped down the night vision apparatus, checking that it was their teammates in the boat roaring forward. He stood. "Here they come."

Jeopardy and Nitro cut the engine, and their forward momentum pushed the inflatable up on the beach. "Hey, change of plans," Jeopardy called, jumping out of the boat and reaching for a bag.

"How's that?" T-Rex headed forward.

Jeopardy pulled a tablet from the backpack and squatted as he initiated an encrypted satellite link.

T-Rex squatted next to him, reaching for the screen when the connection came through. "Colonel Watts."

"You have Poole?"

T-Rex looked over to where Jeopardy and Nitro moved over to their prisoner. "Yes, sir."

"Anything I need to know about?"

"Clean mission, sir." He walked the screen over to the sleeping Poole to show Colonel Watts.

"You have no bruising, no blood," Watts said. "You must have had an okay time of it."

"It all went to plan, sir."

"Outstanding. I'm rerouting three of your team. Ty and Rory, Nitro, and Jeopardy are heading to the sub to complete the last leg of the Poole mission. I want Nomad and Havoc to gather 'round."

T-Rex lifted his chin. "Havoc. Nomad. We're not done here. Nitro. Jeopardy. Ty, get Poole and Rory onto the boat and get ready to launch."

Once the three had gathered around the screen, Watts said. "CIA has an MIA. Johnna Red was doing fieldwork on the Lebanese side of the Syrian and Lebanese border, southeast of your position. There was a hotel explosion."

"Yes, sir," T-Rex answered. "We were briefed on the event prior to our mission. It's in the same vicinity as our operation took place. The CIA thinks Red was caught up in that?"

"The bomb went off at the time and place where she was last in contact with her team. Langley needs to make sure she's healthy and functioning."

"Is her role important to this conversation at all? Is anyone trying to get to her or hurt her?" T-Rex asked.

"That we don't know. What I can tell you is that we got a call there's an American secret squirrel in possible danger. She's high-dollar, and they need her back in whatever condition. You need to find her or her remains and get her moved. If she's in a hospital, you need to come up with a silent exit strategy. She can't be mumbling under her breath no matter what."

The screen changed to a map. "I've sent these to your phone."

"I have your phones," Nitro called and moved back to his bag. He dug out a plastic container and handed it to Nomad. It held their three cell phones.

Nomad handed them out, then swiped to open his encrypted channel to find the map.

"So here's how this is supposed to go down. You get to this area with Pin A. You ditch the Syrian car. The owner will retrieve his vehicle at that point, so hit your mark precisely. We're indebted to the person. Next, you're going to walk to this wall. You'll know you're in the right place when you see this symbol." Watts held up a photograph of graffiti. "You're going to cough three times."

"Cough?" T-Rex asked.

"Three times." Colonel Watts repeated. "Someone will be there to help you."

"With a lozenge," Havoc said.

"They'll provide you with a car, money, and embassy-produced documents. You keep driving to the town. You'll find basic intelligence in that file I uploaded for you." He moved the cursor to a red pin. "This is the hotel that exploded." He moved the cursor slightly down the road. "This is where she was staying."

"Not in the hotel?"

"Red had two rooms that were decoys in the hotel that blew. They were rigged to see if anyone was interested in her. Don't go after the equipment. It'll call too much attention, and we don't know how stable the structure is. I'm not getting one of you hurt over a motion-activated camera. She used an alias there, so it's clean. Down the street," he circled the third pin again, "this was the place she was sleeping. No one has heard from her since the explosion."

"Johnna Red, do you have her photo?" T-Rex asked.

Colonel Watts said. "Your team will use their normal aliases. This is your cousin, T-Rex. They put a photo in your album. Her cover name and other basic information are in the intel file. You should memorize it. It's not as important for the others. You were in Lebanon to visit her. She didn't show up at her apartment. You heard about a bomb and came to check on her because she was visiting friends in this area. You don't know the friends. You know nothing more."

"Yes, sir." T-Rex swiped it open. "Sir, how are we supposed to identify this woman?" The team leaned in. It was T-Rex's picture with a photoshopped woman wearing a ball cap and turning her head to the side.

"Her fingerprints are in the app," Colonel Watts replied. "We gave you what Langley was willing to have out there."

"Serious?" Havoc asked. "We just walk down the road and ask people to stick out their hands?"

"You've got more than that," Watts replied. "Long dark brown hair. Mid-thirties. Athletic build. Those are the descriptors."

"In Lebanon," Havoc said under his breath as he looked at it. "Great."

"All right. All right. Havoc," the colonel said, "I'm giving you some leeway. I understand you're functioning on no sleep. But watch it."

"Sir."

"Now listen, her room at the hotel needs to be stripped and polished. We can't be seen as having a footprint in the area. If there's a body, we need it back. That might get challenging because you won't be going through normal channels. She's ours. You take her and get her back home."

"If she's wounded?" Nomad asked. "Is there a hospital in the area?"

"There is." Colonel Watts said. "And they're full and over-whelmed. My understanding is they're shipping people to nearby cities. She could be in pieces. She could be in hospital. Any hospital." His eyes were hard and unblinking. "If she's alive, we need her in an American hospital and under guard. What's in her head would make her extremely vulnerable – and America at the same time. If she was able, she would have reported in. Move on silent feet."

"Yes, sir," T-Rex said. "The clothes on our backs are the clothes we have with us. They were specifically developed to support the last op. We look in rough shape."

"State understands the situation. They have your sizes and are working to find something that will function for you in short order. Shops aren't open yet. Both T-Rex and Nomad will pose a challenge, but I think our people are up to it. You'll be dressed to blend. Luckily, there are a lot of contractors in the area. More importantly, State will produce your diplomatic papers and State credentials. There are no stamps. So these are replacements after yours were stolen. You picked them up at the embassy last night when you let them know your cousin hadn't come in as scheduled."

"Last night, yes, sir," T-Rex said.

"Once you're over the wall, you'll find a rental car parked directly in front of you. That's where you'll find what they were able to gather. We're putting the car in T-Rex's name."

"With added drivers? Properly insured?" Havoc raised his brows. "I don't want to do anything contrary to the laws. It's the little things that can trip us up."

"I-s will be dotted, T-s will be crossed," their commander said. "Look, I get it's been a while since the team has slept, and we'll need a little more time to get the elements together. I suggest you pull around behind a hill, take a short nap, get fed and hydrated. We're balancing a lot of variables. We want to get this woman out as soon as possible, or minimally, to assess her situation and find a solution. But going in before the village is awake is going to call attention to you. They'll have guards posted. Questions."

"Are people after her?" Nomad asked. "Could she have been taken?"

"A distinct possibility."

"Could the explosion have been focused on her?" T-Rex asked.

"I damned well hope that's not the case. Possible? Yes. Probable? I can't take anything off the table. I don't have the intel. To that end, we received a pin that indicated the exact spot where she was meeting with a man in a blue suit. If you get into the area, see what's there. *Start* there. Her last interaction with her team was sending that pin."

"Wilco," T-Rex said.

Watts drew his lips into a hard line. "Listen up. She's highly skilled and will be using tradecraft. She doesn't know you're coming in. She doesn't know you, so be aware. Her code this week is, 'Did you buy Johnny new crayons for school?' The answer is, 'Can you believe he's in first grade?' and lastly, 'He loves to color.'"

The three repeated the phrases.

"At this point," Colonel Watts said, "with two check-ins

missed, we have to assume that she's incapable of initiating comms. She has backup routes if she loses the means to use an encrypted channel. None of them were acted on, which tells me we need to be prepared for repatriation or a medical emergency. If the latter, time will be of the essence."

12

───────

Nomad

"Hey, Ty, hand me all the money under Rory's vest. We'll take it with us in case we need to bribe our way out of a situation." T-Rex reached out his hand and waited for Ty to pass the stacks of Syrian pounds. He shoved them into his thigh pocket. "All right. You three need to get Poole out of here. I don't know if they'll pop the sub up without the cover of darkness, and his meds aren't going to last much longer."

They waited to ensure their team got safely over the horizon, then returned to the car. "Havoc, you're driving."

Havoc slid into the driver's seat, pulled the night vision apparatus into place, and adjusted the straps on his head. T-Rex sat shotgun, and Nomad put the back seats down and climbed into the hatch where he could find more room for his legs without sitting like a frog on a lily pad.

T-Rex pointed. "Head back down the road and follow it around to the east. As they got underway, T-Rex opened his phone and dimmed the light. "Listen up – this is information on where we're going in. We're headed to the town of Tal Afaya in eastern Lebanon. It sits at the bottom foothills of the eastern mountains. That'll be good if we have to tuck ourselves away. The town is a jumping-off point for the Lebanese and Syrian borders. If we had taken the western road last night instead of our trek to Poole, we would have been to the town in less than an hour."

"Wow, close. Isn't that interesting?" Nomad asked.

"Put that thought on the back burner. Let me get through this data. All right, we're looking at around twenty thousand people. So that's not an insignificant number. The town is populated with U.S., Canadian, and French immigrants. But they're rooted here now. Looks-wise, we shouldn't have trouble fitting in. We'll see what the embassy does about our clothes. Lastly, it's not an industrial or tourist town. This is agricultural."

"Johnna Red. This is a member of Color Code, right? Grey's team? And this is the same Grey that sent us after Poole?" Nomad asked T-Rex.

"Same."

"And now we're looking for her only an hour away?" Nomad asked.

"Don't jump to conclusions."

"Okay, how about this," Havoc said. "We don't know what Red was doing on the Syrian border. But it's possible she wasn't in the bombing, and she was taken hostage. She might have tipped her hand as a field officer, or it's also possible that someone realized she was American and wanted a payday."

"Kidnapped." T-Rex's voice was flat.

Yeah, that was a scenario that no one wanted to have played out.

"You know what happens in the moments after an attack," Havoc said. "All hell lets loose. Someone grabs a woman, and she starts screaming. She looks like every other screaming woman. If she's not hurt, then the guy is dragging her away because he doesn't want her diving for a dead relative. No one is paying attention to that."

"In that case, they wouldn't have to suspect she was American. They could just see an opportunity for a slave. If she doesn't want to expose her skills, she might have to go along with the scenario to get to a place where she could free herself without blowing her cover."

"It would be nice to know what her cover is." Nomad leaned over the front seat,

"We have her fingerprints; what more do we need?" T-Rex laughed.

"So I take it you haven't worked an op with her before." Nomad settled back in the space, trying to figure out where to put his legs.

"I haven't crossed paths with her, no." T-Rex opened his phone's album. "But we have a photo of a hat."

"She has a chin," Havoc said. "Neck. Shoulders. Everything where it belongs."

"Lips," Nomad said.

Havoc turned his head, then focused back on the road. "Ah, but are they uniquely recognizable lips?"

"When I was in Afghanistan," Nomad ventured, "we trained some locals who were working for one of the CIA's Numbers Group, called Double Zero. Is this the same kind of thing as Color Code? Colors and Numbers…"

"Different character to those two groups," T-Rex said. "Color Code is more like you."

"How so?" Nomad asked.

"Color Code is polished," Havoc said. "A lot of their work involves conflict relics and the like. So we're talking about brushing up against a population of people with money to burn. Working in that world, Color Code has to fit in. High society, fine wine, five different forks at their table setting, seven different glasses. I'd stick out like a sore thumb. With your background growing up in the embassies, you'd call it Wednesday dinner."

"Interesting." Nomad flipped onto his back and scooted down to pillow his head on his laced fingers, bending his knees and planting his feet. "And yet there she was in a rat hole hotel room on the Syrian border, dodging terrorist car bombers."

"Yeah, I can't tell you what all they do," Havoc said. "But I can tell you that Grey is part of Echo legend."

Nomad lifted his chin to get Havoc in his view. "I was promised this story."

"Yup. Ready for some shit?" Havoc's grin was wide.

"I'm ready for some shit."

"We take off from an Iraqi FOB—" Havoc used the acronym for forward operating base. "And we're dividing into two groups to jump onto helicopters – Blackhawk and a Little Bird. Ty, T-Rex, and I are on the Little Bird. Our pilot flies us over the border into Syria. Broad daylight. Why risk it? We got word that Grey was captured and, like Red, what's between his ears cannot be pried loose under any circumstances. We save him or bless him with a triple tap, but the enemy would not get a chance to beat names and means out of him."

"Where was he being held?"

"Prison." T-Rex grinned.

"Prison ..." Nomad let the word drift off.

"Yup. fifth floor," T-Rex said, "eleventh window from the south corner."

"Keep going."

"The pilot on the Blackhawk hangs back," Havoc said. "The

Little Bird—D-Day Rochambeau, a Night Stalker and—what was the co-pilot's name?"

"Nick of Time," T-Rex said.

"Yeah, Nick of Time. So D-Day flies her bird straight down the middle of Main Street.

"Broad daylight," T-Rex said. "She has balls of steel."

"Nick is trying to direct her," Havoc said. "It's hard to see with all the dust from the wash."

"I can imagine." Nomad actually *couldn't* imagine. That image was nuts.

"Someone came out of their shop," T-Rex said, "and was under us shooting."

"Where was D-Day trying to drop you?" Nomad asked.

"She wasn't." T-Rex skated a hand out to approximate the movement of the helicopter. "She flew us to his window."

"The prison window?"

"Yup, fifth-floor eleventh window. She flew us right up like we were ordering a hamburger at the drive-through," Havoc said. "We looked in the window and saw a guy. Nick holds up the photo for comparison and yells, 'We've got him!' It was Grey. We pushed a ladder out to make a bridge from the heli to the sill."

"What?" Nomad barked a laugh.

"Swear on my grandfather's grave," Havoc held up a hand. "We stuck a ladder out the door and rested it on the window ledge. I was the lightest guy, so I went out. There's backwash everywhere, filling my lungs, sandblasting my goggles. There's a guy with a gun underneath me who fired his rounds, then loaded up and fired some more. Ty and T-Rex held down my legs because the windowsill was only a couple of inches wide. The ladder is rubbing and screeching against the rock. D-Day held us steady while I used the plasma cutter to slice through the bars. And I mean, one little twitch of her finger and we would have crashed and burned. There were buildings just feet away from her blades.”

“Shit.”

“So I’m through the bars, I broke the glass. Grey is standing there with the wildest look on his face. He had to think this was the acid trip to end all acid trips. I mean, who would believe that shit? I grabbed Grey, then Ty and T-Rex dragged both of us back onto the helicopter.”

“Easy day,” Nomad was still grinning. The adrenaline rush had to have been crazy.

“Not so easy. The shithead beneath us shot a hole into the fuel tank, so things got a little hairy from there. We set down. And we weren’t alone.”

“Grey was on the phone, so I guess you turned the fighters around?”

“In the end,” T-Rex said. “Grey is alive and well, working to keep America safe by finding and stopping terror funding.”

That whole thing of getting dragged out of the prison from a helicopter flying down the street? That was some wicked badassery performed by all. Man, Nomad would have loved to have been part of that mission. That would have been a story to tell his grandchildren when he was sitting in his wheelchair, eating mush with a bib tied under his chin. “So, honestly, you don’t think it’s a great big coincidence that we went into Syria after Poole, and she’s working on the border?”

“I seriously doubt it,” T-Rex said. “Hand me that water, will yah?”

Nomad uncapped the bottle and handed it forward.

After a swig, T-Rex added. “From what I know of Red—and these are things I picked up working with John Grey and John Green, Red’s focus is on finding the western millionaires that buy conflict relics, thereby funding ISIS at the height of the

Syrian war. Some of that money went into Afghanistan. But the relics that were being sold came mostly out of Iraq and Syria."

"Okay, that's how she rubs elbows with social circles."

"Rumint—" Havoc used the term for rumor-intelligence "—says that her father was from a royal family, and he worked for the American State Department."

"No royal blood in my family. But if she's about my age, then maybe I know her. Does the rumint place her in any particular location? Are we talking European royalty?"

"No. Jordan? Syrian, maybe?" Havoc shrugged.

"Grain of salt," T-Rex said slowly. "And don't spread rumint about Middle Eastern royalty around Ty."

"There's a story there?" Nomad asked.

"Not mine to tell, brother," T-Rex said. "But yeah, from what I heard Grey and Green saying, with Red's background, she could be your sister."

"I don't think so," Nomad said, "at least not from the shape of her lips and chin."

"We need a better photograph." Havoc reached up to adjust the lenses on his night vision.

T-Rex swiped to bring up the GPS map. "We're getting close to the turn, Havoc. I'll let you know. Okay, let's talk this through. You're Red; what would you do?"

"If I was in the field, hurt and disoriented," Nomad said, trying to imagine a polished socialite moving through this kind of situation. And he couldn't. "I'd go to ground until I could figure out how to reach out to my team."

"Unless you had a gaping wound," Havoc said. "Is this where I turn?"

"Almost there." T-Rex was focused on the phone. The men were silent until T-Rex said. "Okay, here."

"Depends on how gaping," Nomad said. "I carry a tube of bonding glue. Wash it out, stick it back together.

"The intel file says that Red's been sick and not containing the illness with the normal meds they carry." T- Rex pointed out his window. "And turn again here." He waited for Havoc to get on the new road. "It's straight on. So in about thirty minutes, you can start looking for a nice little space to tuck us into so we can get some shut-eye."

"Wilco."

"No more information about the illness?" Nomad asked. "This is *before* the bombing."

"About the same time," T-Rex said. "Grey noted that when they were on a video call, Red didn't turn on her camera to show her face."

"Did she think that if they saw that she was in rough shape, they'd make her stand down, and whatever she was up to wouldn't get covered?"

"If that's true," Havoc said, "she must have been latched onto something important.

She might know of a local doctor who would let her slip in after hours. That might be where she's holed up."

"Great, how do you suggest we find this local doctor?" Nomad asked.

"Wouldn't all the doctors be at the hospital dealing with the mass casualty event?" Havoc asked.

"Havoc, pull behind that hill. I see headlights coming up. If we get stopped," T-Rex said, "we have the bribe money. But let's try to talk our way out of this."

"If they ask about the night vision, I'll offer it to them as a gift." Havoc grinned. "And say that we wanted to go fishing, but our lights would scare away the fish."

"Yeah, fishing. That might work better if we had some poles or tackle and weren't heading in the wrong direction for finding water." Nomad had his binoculars trained on the truck. "AKs,"

Nomad whispered so they could focus on any exterior noises. "I'm counting seven in the back.

The men held their breath as an open-bed truck rumbled by.

Once the taillight moved over the next berm, T-Rex lassoed a finger in the air. "Let's move. The sky is brightening up. I want to be within shouting distance of that wall and hunkered down until our rally time."

13

———

Nomad

Hɪs ʙᴀᴄᴋ ᴛᴏ ᴛʜᴇ ᴡᴀʟʟ, ʜɪᴅᴅᴇɴ ʙʏ ᴛʜᴇ ᴇᴀʀʟʏ-ᴍᴏʀɴɪɴɢ shadows, Nomad trained his binoculars on the horizon, scanning for any movement. T-Rex and Havoc ranged further out to keep from bunching into an easy target should things go south.

When Nomad signaled an all-clear, T-Rex raised his fist to his mouth and coughed three times.

A moment later, a rope ladder flew over the twenty-foot wall, placed exactly over the graffiti. T-Rex grabbed it before it smacked him in the face. He climbed in silence and once over the top, he signaled Nomad and Havoc to follow.

What limited gear they had chosen to bring with them was in a single backpack.

They left the Syrian cash in the car they abandoned at the designated GPS coordinate. Hopefully, it would land in the hands of the guy risking his safety and vehicle to accomplish the Poole mission.

It was best that they weren't carrying Syrian pounds in Lebanon.

Throwing a leg over the wall, Nomad took a moment, using the height to scan. He'd imagined that there would be a house and garden, a bit of an olive grove, and a dairy goat or two. But no, there was nothing and no one. Just dirt and a vehicle. "Who threw the rope over?" he asked.

"Cloud of dust from spinning tires was all I could see by the time I got over the top." T-Rex looked toward the van, which was unremarkable in every way imaginable. "Rory would come in handy right about now."

"If there are papers on the front seat like we were told," Havoc was making his way over to the passenger side, "I say we're golden." He put a gloved hand to his brow and looked in. "Good to go," he called.

The keys sat in the drink holder. There was a file with papers. On the second-row bench, shopping bags stamped with golden clothing store logos lined up in a neat row.

"I'm about starved," Havoc said, pulling out a bag and handing it off to T-Rex.

"Nothing new there." T-Rex dragged a pair of desert tactical pants out, held them to his waist, and then handed them to Havoc. "I hope like hell these are for you. What do you want to do about eats?"

Havoc dragged another bag over and handed it to Nomad. "Remi's been working with you on your accent, right T-Rex? Just go in and act like a local and grab us something."

"If he walks in and just glowers at anyone who wants to talk to him, I think they'll shut up," Nomad said, opening another bag. "Here we go. Extra longs, these are for us." Nomad looked over to Havoc. "Some bread and cheese would be easy."

"And a bottle of wine, we can have a romantic picnic in the mountains." Havoc opened a third bag. "Hey, hey, hey! Look what I found. Someone's taking good care of us!"

"What's there?" T- Rex asked, standing on the toes of his boots as he stripped down to his boxers.

"Let's see. The bread and cheese Nomad wanted. Olives … dolma, a bag of tomatoes. Another of dates. What is this? Anyone know what this is?" Havoc pulled the lid off a plastic container.

"Cherries with herbs." Nomad dragged his new pants up his leg.

Havoc used a plastic spork to shovel up a bite. He closed his eyes as he chewed. "Oh, man, wow. Hey, that's good."

Nomad looked up from clasping his belt. "Are you getting a little teary-eyed, Havoc?"

"I always do around food ever since that mission in Kyrgyzstan."

"That or you miss your mom's pot roast," T-Rex said. "*I* miss your mom's pot roast."

"Yup. Always." Havoc tucked the food back in the bag and worked on changing his own clothes. They kept their boots. There were new ones, but new hurt. And new stood out as unauthentic.

With the water bottles and hygiene kits provided, the men did what they could to clean up. Beards made the process easier. Once dressed, they threw their old clothes back over the wall, then took a minute to eat. Parked on a hill overlooking the town, they hoped to time their appearance to coincide with other traffic. But Nomad felt the pressure of the wait. His gut said to get to Red and get to her now. It took a sizeable amount of constraint not to rush forward.

T-Rex threw his paper napkin and spork into the empty paper bag, then lifted the binoculars. "Still not a lot of activity."

"You know how it is with the heat," Nomad said. "Folks are up and doing at night and sleeping in come morning. Still, I'd appreciate a coffee vendor." Nomad dragged a napkin across his face, tossed it in the bag, then turned to look through the gear pack sitting on the floor behind the driver's seat. "No weapons. An advanced first aid kit. Of course, the documents and the fresh clothes might be the most important. The embassy folks did well for a middle-of-the-night call with a short window. Everything fits with the character profile of a concerned family member coming in with friends to find his cousin. Nothing here stands out as tactical beyond work gloves and a folding shovel."

T-Rex stood on the running board, scanning. "Both hotels are on the main road. That means more eyes. It looks like there's a street running parallel behind Red's sleeping hotel." T-Rex pointed. "And an alley here running perpendicular. If we come into town and turn to follow that parallel street with the van, we'll call less attention to our presence."

"They have barriers up," Nomad said. "We can't drive down that main road, anyway." He lowered his binoculars. "They wanted us to check the flag Red dropped first." Nomad pulled out his phone to get his bearings. Moving up to stand beside T-Rex, he suggested, "Park here. There's only a two-minute walk from one pin to the other. We can use this alleyway just south of the bombed hotel."

With his binoculars up, T-Rex pointed. "Do you see the heavy equipment parked at the north end of the road? They probably got in last night. My guess is that they'll spend the morning shoring up the building to keep it from toppling. If they got the living out last night, I bet they didn't take risks for the dead. That and they need to assess this forensically. The report said no one's claimed credit for the bomb."

"We need to beat them in," Nomad said. "If the crew is pulling up, they'll bar access."

T-Rex dropped the binoculars, letting them hang from the strap around his neck. "Yeah, from the setup, it looks like the locals are letting the national government handle the site. And as we all know, there's a certain pace to government intervention."

"Molasses?" Havoc asked.

"Can be." Nomad opened the driver's side door. "I say let's move." He climbed in, and as the others found their places, he started the engine, anxious to get going.

They drove sedately into town and followed the plan for staging the vehicle on the parallel street for a quick exit.

Dressed in desert tan tactical gear from t-shirts to boots, they blended into the colors of the environment.

No matter how hard the townspeople worked to conquer dirt and dust, the debris rode the winds in from the desert. This morning, the shop workers hadn't yet swept and watered the sidewalks to tame the powder, and the team's boots left ridged tracks as they made their way to the hotel.

Once in front of the bombsite, Nomad took video of the area on his phone. There were bodies and parts of bodies laced into the construction materials. If Red was in the restaurant with her asset, there was zero chance she'd survived.

A guard walked over to him. "Peace be with you, brother."

"And with you." T-Rex placed his hand on his heart. "I am missing my cousin. I am afraid that perhaps she was here having lunch."

"I hope this was not the case." The guard had probably stood at this scene for hours. It was taking a visible toll on him.

"When they took survivors out, the wounded, were any found in this front area?" Nomad asked.

"Here?" The guard swept his arm to take in the front of the hotel. "No. There are no survivors here. Above, upstairs, some, yes, and the kitchen workers, yes."

Grey had said she'd been sick. "Bathroom?" Nomad asked.

"The public bathrooms, no – the bathrooms were empty."

Red had her CIA rooms on the sixth floor. Nomad leaned back and looked up to the top of the hotel. "How high up were the injured? All the way up?"

"One story up, there is serious destruction. Third floor and above, there are cuts from the windows and bruises from the shaking and falling, popped eardrums, we got them out the back of the building."

Nomad adjusted the strap of the bag on his shoulder. "Thank you." Nomad pointed toward the debris, raising his brows, and the guard walked away.

That was enough permission for Nomad. He pulled a plastic drink straw from the first aid kit, which he always kept in his left thigh pocket. He'd filled that straw with camphor rub and sealed it with a hot iron. Nomad used the masking smell of menthol on days like this. Slicing off the top of the straw with his multi-tool, Nomad rubbed a glob under his nose, offering the rest to T-Rex and Havoc. There were a lot of bodies. And the smell could be overwhelming. Vomiting on a crime scene was a no-go. "I'll take the blue suit," Nomad offered, still aware that as "new guy," he should be reaching for the shittiest of the shit jobs.

This fitted that bill.

"Fine." T-Rex tapped Nomad's chest with the back of his hand. "Document everything you find interesting. Havoc, you take the bathrooms and kitchen. I'm going to take a look in the back. But be aware, someone has eyes on us twelve o'clock, third floor." They adjusted their baseball caps lower on their foreheads and dragged shemaghs from their pack pockets, wrapping them around their lower faces.

Coming in from the southeast corner, nearest the pin, it took patience to climb over the debris field in a way that avoided desecrating the deceased. But it took little effort for Nomad to find the guy in his blue suit. Nomad hoped against hope that he wouldn't find Red in that tangle.

In his bones, he felt her alive and desperate. Still, any clue might point the team in her direction.

Right away, Nomad spotted a black drawstring pack. It was dust-covered but not buried like the things around it. Nomad guessed it was placed there after the explosion but before the debris cloud settled. He took a picture and imprinted the image with the GPS location.

Then Nomad picked it up and looked inside.

The banded stacks of Lebanese pounds had to be worth thousands of dollars.

Nomad slid that strap over his arm along with his other pack.

The other thing that had caught his eye was the table leaning on top of the debris turned to the side, exposing the man with the blue suit. Though the top and sides of the heavy wooden table were destroyed, the underside had withstood and was in pretty good shape. It seemed to have shielded the suited man's head and chest, but that didn't make him any less dead.

He was definitely in decomp.

Some flies were in the area, but with the cold desert night temperatures and the steady breeze, this scene was in better shape than he'd expected.

T-Rex moved over to Nomad's side.

Nomad pointed down at the man in the robes. "I know this guy. That's Imraan el-Jafri." Nomad used the man's sleeve to lift his hand and look at his fingers. "Might be able to get a print."

"On it," T-Rex said, moving forward. "Get photos. What was he known for?"

"Contraband funded terror activity. I thought he'd met his maker. I guess I was wrong."

"You're sure of his identification?" Using a gloved hand, T-

Rex pressed el-Jafri's fingers one at a time onto the phone screen to be read by the Intelligence app.

"See the Big Dipper?" Nomad pointed to the man's brow. "How many guys have eyebrows like his *and* a big dipper of moles perfectly positioned to frame his eye?" Nomad crouched to get a picture of the left side of the man's face. "He worked with ISIS to move their goods along trade routes to the Mediterranean for the European market."

"A true believer?" T-Rex asked.

"My take was that it was financial, plus they offered him a consistently refreshed choice of slave women. Girls. He preferred girls. May he rot in hell." Nomad snapped pictures of the right side of el-Jafri's face.

"I have what I need." T-Rex swiped his phone down his pants leg. "What have you got in that bag?"

"Looks like an asset payout." Nomad pointed to the man in the blue suit. "He's not going to be spending it now."

"Hopeful sign. If he was paid, maybe Red was already gone." From his squatted position, T-Rex looked over to where Havoc clambered over debris toward the front of the building.

"Nothing back here. The bathroom and kitchen were destroyed but survivable. The back door goes out to an enclosed yard with an open gate door. It's where they dump their trash. Unless she was upstairs—and upstairs doesn't look affected. No sign of her here?" He glanced around.

"If she's in here, it's going to take heavy equipment to find her." Nomad's gut clenched.

"After we check the hotel up the street," Havoc moved toward the sidewalk, "we can start down the list of hospitals where they've sent the wounded. When the crew starts putting the victims in body bags, we can check them."

"The guard's signing for us to clear out." T-Rex raised a hand, then brought it to his chest to signal gratitude, and the team moved clear of the bombsite. "Let's get back to the vehicle and make our way over to her hotel. Look for a back exit we can avail ourselves of."

Havoc took the black bag from Nomad and looked in, letting out a whistle under his breath. "Whatever information she was given must have been significant." He opened the van door and threw the money bag in before sliding the door shut with the tiniest click.

They continued up the street, running parallel to the main drag.

"I mean, that's a ton of money," Havoc said, "Maybe not life-changing, but it certainly would be life-enhancing. What do you think he was handing her? Could that be part of the reason she disappeared?"

"My guess is she didn't know what she was getting and had a bag to mete out the appropriate payment." As a Green Beret, Nomad had been involved in similar scenarios.

T-Rex turned his head, keeping an eye on the surroundings as they moved. "Fact is, we don't know that it had any connection to Red."

"Are you kidding me?" Nomad pulled his brow together. "I found it at the pinned location. It was hers. And from here, Damascus is only an hour away," Nomad reminded them. "Poole's farm host is even closer."

"But was it a payment for Poole?" T- Rex asked, lengthening his stride. "That time frame's too short. When this happened, we were getting a phone call to head out. She would have been involved with this event at the same time we were getting rerouted."

"The farmhouse is waking up now and checking on him," Havoc said, turning into the alley.

"He's an American; they probably think he's tired, so let him sleep in." T-Rex stopped and looked at the building in front of them. "Here it is, room six, second floor. Let's go knock on the door."

The men walked right in the side door.

Nomad noted that Red could have come and gone from the back staircase without having to smile and be pleasant to the front desk.

The tradecraft was good. This hotel was clean but run down. The kind of setup where they'd have a sink and a toilet. Visitors would go to a hammam—a public bathhouse—to get cleaned up. There would be none of the modern amenities that the hotel up the street would have. No one would look for a Westerner here.

A huge step down in quality of stay. It would be tough to be sick in a place like this.

Not seeking relief from air conditioning and a shower would take fortitude.

Nomad knocked and then put his ear to the door lest someone mutter or moan in response. But the only thing he heard was the drip, drip of a leaky faucet.

The lock used an old-fashioned brass key. Their pickpocket tools weren't going to work here. After examining the situation, the men decided that they weren't getting into that room by kicking down the door, especially if Red had put her locking systems in place. They'd need a C4 blast, which was a no-go.

"Ideas?" T-Rex asked.

"Sob story to the front desk?" Havoc suggested. "We could always use some of the cash from the money bag. It's just sitting there in the van."

"They were adamant about preserving her cover. We need to keep our faces separate from her."

"Look in the window?" Havoc asked. "Maybe there's a ladder?"

"That might be wishful thinking," Nomad said, "but why not come down from above?"

"I'll go see if I can't rent the room above hers." T-Rex went down the outside stairs so he could enter through the front door.

Havoc and Nomad waited in the hallway.

Standing there, Nomad knew Red was inside. *Knew it.* And he knew it was for him to get to her and save her.

Hang in there, Red. I'm coming.

14

———

Nomad

T-Rex was back with an old-fashioned brass key.

"What's the plan?" Havoc asked.

"You stay here, Havoc. I'm taking New Guy upstairs with me. There's someone in the room above, but I was able to get the one above that."

"No rope," Nomad said. "On the way in, I checked. There's not enough ledge for me to hang from the window and get my toes on the sill."

"We make do." There was a twinkle in T-Rex's eyes. "We tie the sheets together. I hold them on one end, and you dangle from the other. You should be able to see and report the situation."

Sheets. Fair enough. While he trusted T-Rex's strength, Nomad weighed in at two sixty-five. Those sheets had better have a damned high thread count, or he'd be plummeting from the fourth floor.

Once they were upstairs and dragging the comforter off the bed, it was evident that pulling those sheets off was a no-go.

They were threadbare and patched already. Instead, the men yanked down the drapes, cut them into strips, lashed them together, then braided them into a rope.

The shutter-style window opened inward; Nomad straddled the ledge. Looking over his shoulder, it was a long-damned way down, and there was nothing, not even a heap of garbage, to break his fall.

Those thoughts came and went as Nomad adjusted into position, moving with the precision of a man who had done this a thousand times before.

Nomad felt the pressure of time and knew he had to get to Red *now*.

He dropped the roping down the wall, checking that there was sufficient length.

"Good?"

"Good enough." Nomad planted his foot on the wall, then walked his way down, moving hand over hand for the second time in less than twelve hours.

"That's the one," T-Rex signaled him.

Nomad locked the rope between his feet. A bit more and Nomad dangled from one hand as he used the other to block the light to see in.

A woman sprawled half on the bed, half draping off, one foot on the floor. Fully dressed, boots on her feet, she was white with plaster dust. Reaching up to grab the rope above a knot, Nomad called up, "I've got her. He pressed his toes onto the sill, adjusted his grip into a less awkward position, then pulled one foot back, slamming it into the line that held the two sides of windows together with a locking latch.

The windows flew apart, hitting against either side of the wall, shattering the glass.

Swinging through, Nomad landed on the blue tile floor in a crouch.

Glass shards crunched under his soles as Nomad quickly cleared the room, then moved to the woman's side, not at all sure she was still alive.

He licked the back of his hand and held it under her nose.

Her exhale felt cool on his skin as the moisture evaporated.

Over his years in combat zones, Nomad had learned to go slow and not touch unless and until it became absolutely necessary. Extremists sometimes hid grenades or other incendiaries under the sick and the dead. That tactic took out the helpers and dropped morale among the survivors. It made it less likely that anyone would run in to render aid in future attacks.

Covered in dust so thick that Nomad couldn't see her skin color, her hair was powdered to seem gray. A pool of dried blood stained her ear and neck.

Alive but unresponsive.

If this was merely sleep, his entrance would have brought her around.

Nomad moved to her door, where he checked for any booby traps she might have laid or other complications. An unused door wedge with a triggering alarm was set off to the side. She must have come in, locked the door, and dropped onto the bed, he thought as he turned the old-fashioned key and swung the door open for his team.

"Is it her?" T-Rex asked.

"Right lips." Nomad stepped to the side. His heart was pounding. What about this situation was triggering him?

He didn't know her, but his system was reacting in a way completely foreign to him. Nomad wished he had a moment to regroup.

Staying frosty meant surviving the day.

As T-Rex pulled out his phone and opened the fingerprint app, he called, "Ma'am? Ma'am, can you hear me?"

Her lids fluttered.

"Ma'am, don't open your eyes yet." Nomad calibrated his voice to a tone that would slide behind the veil of semi-consciousness. "Let me wash your face first so you don't scratch your corneas." He moved into the bathroom. It looked exactly how he had expected it to, clean but primitive and aged. Reaching for the small cloth hanging on a hook, he held it under the warm water, wringing it out. He filled the pitcher and grabbed up the trash can. Looking in, he didn't see anything that might give them information. Nomad brought it into the room just as T-Rex announced, "She's a match."

T-Rex shuffled from a squat to take a knee. "Johnna Red, American support is here to rescue you. I'm going to reach under you to make sure there are no surprises left by combatants."

Nomad stepped past T-Rex while his teammate swept under her legs and torso. "Clean."

"Red," T-Rex said slowly and clearly. "Did you buy Johnny new crayons for school?"

T-Rex leaned his ear right over her lips.

Nomad could read that she tried for "First grade."

"He loves to color," T-Rex finished. Since T-Rex had identi-fied Red through the fingerprints, Nomad knew he'd moved through that series to let Red know this team was on her side. She could trust them.

Dropping to the floor, Nomad leaned in. "Ma'am, I'm flushing your eyes with warm water. Just keep them closed." He wasn't sure how much she could hear or understand him. That coagulated blood by her ear might indicate a perforated ear drum.

As he poured the warm water over her eyes, letting it slowly stream down the side of her face into the bucket, Nomad went through a mental list of things that might have happened to her.

Obviously, she'd been on-site during the explosion; bomb dust coated every inch of her.

Surviving the initial detonation was only half the battle. Then came the after-concussion. She didn't need to be that close to the bomb detonation to suffer the wave of energy that followed. If that were the case, she could have stumbled to her room and succumbed.

The effects of blast injuries weren't always immediate.

Primary blast injuries, beyond blast ear, could mean the barotrauma affected her brain, eyes, lungs, or gastrointestinal tract.

Perforations, hemorrhage, and even a rupture of the globe of the eyes were possible.

As he cleaned her face, Nomad discovered that, thankfully, the blood wasn't coming from her ear canal but was a superficial cut. Luckily, that ear hadn't pressed into the pillowcase, so the scab was unaffected when Nomad turned her onto her back.

Red had sweated and thrashed enough that the plaster dust had formed a paste, and that paste had dried. He was afraid to pick it off lest he scratch her skin. He had no idea what kinds of microbes were involved here, and she obviously didn't need anything more in her system to fight off. Oddly, her belt was unbuckled, her zipper unzipped, but she was buttoned at the top of her pants. In Nomad's experience, women unbutton before unzipping when getting undressed.

Did this scene make sense?

Havoc was gathering her belongings and shoving them into a suitcase.

T-Rex was on the phone getting in touch with Command and apprising them of the situation.

"Ma'am," Nomad rested his hand on her shoulder. "May I have permission to cut you out of your clothes to ensure you have no hidden bleeds?"

She gave him the slightest of nods. But he appreciated the go-ahead. Even if this was a medical emergency, Nomad didn't ever want to touch a woman in a way that didn't have her knowledge and permission.

Using his trauma sheers, Nomad got her outer clothes removed and performed the usual assessments.

"I have Colonel Watts on the line. What have you got, Nomad?" T-Rex asked. "I'm putting you on speaker."

Nomad lifted his voice. "Sir, there are no open wounds. She has heavy bruising on either side of her body. No signs of serious crush injuries. No palpable broken bones. She's feverish, only semi-conscious. She's murmuring unintelligibly."

"She can't go to the hospital then," Colonel Watts's voice came over T-Rex's speaker. "I need Grey in on this. Hold."

T-Rex caught Havoc's eye, "Make sure you get everything in the bathroom. They'll want any meds or supplements in a separate bag to hand off to the doctors so they can assess. Nomad, get her as comfortable as possible while the colonel loops the Color Code into the call."

Havoc went into the bathroom to get soap and refill the pitcher with warm water and brought it to Nomad T-Rex found a loose pair of harem-styled pants and an oversized t-shirt in her suitcase and handed it off. Nomad thought they'd be comfortable for her to wear and easy for him to get her into.

As Nomad cleaned Red up, he tried to understand the scene she'd survived.

From the placement of Red's bruises, Nomad could imagine her being thrown to the ground and something crushing in on her. The high fever was worrisome, and as Nomad washed her, she shivered violently.

"T-Rex," Nomad said softly, "if she has sepsis, any extra time might crash her system. I say, grab her up and get her out of here ASAP. Let the closest hospital take over." Nomad tried to advocate. "Time is of the essence."

"The local hospitals are full," T-Rex reminded him. "She won't get immediate attention."

"Beirut?" Nomad asked.

"Not if she's out of it and talking, no," Colonel Watts was back on the speaker. "Grey? Thoughts?"

"If we send her to the airport for a private flight, her illness would be probed by customs officials. Even if the team somehow got her awake and upright, getting her out would be delayed. The questions they'd ask would be problematic, especially if they had a doctor inspect her, and she's suffering from blast trauma."

Nomad thought of the sub that picked up Poole. It might be able to pop back up. But it had been over near Cyprus. That, too, would be a long route. They couldn't get her loaded until dark and the sea clear. No guarantees there. He'd put it out there anyway. "A water exfil?"

"Boats, Grey?" Watts asked.

"I can get hold of a boat." Grey's voice sounded as purposeful and stressed as Nomad felt. "If Echo can navigate the vessel northwest into International waters. We can send a helicopter from the eastern Turkish base to pluck Red—who is your medic?"

"Nomad," T-Rex said.

"Red and Nomad come out and fly to the same base Echo started from yesterday evening," Colonel Watts said, "Hell of a twenty-four hours, gentlemen."

Nomad thought his last twenty-four hours were a cakewalk compared to what this woman had been through.

"Looking at the complicating factors, the sea looks like the fastest route to get her to medical help," the colonel said. "So the team knows, the instructions to keep Red out of a non-

American hospital under the circumstances that you've described came from the Situation Room. Those orders are not from JSOC nor Color Code."

Interesting. Red going missing went up to the Situation Room? Not only had someone signed off on Delta Force pulling Grey out of the prison, but now they'd prioritized the secrets Red knew over her wellbeing. That meant the work she did was high stakes.

"I think a sea extraction is our fastest route," Watts said.

"Grey, this is Nomad. We were told she was ill prior to the bombing." The heat radiating off her body was alarming. Nomad's medical training had to do with battle wounds and basic humanitarian interventions. This was way past his knowledge and the equipment he had available to keep her safe. He felt like Red could very easily slip away. He worked to keep the urgency out of his voice. "Do you know what was wrong? Did she tell you any symptoms?"

"Negative." Grey paused. "She's not coming around?" Yeah, his voice sounded like Nomad felt—vexed and frightened by an inability to fix this.

"I have nothing beyond she's dangerously hot." Odd that Nomad wanted a clear definition of Red's relationship with Grey. Was this a worried teammate, or were they more to each other? Why would Nomad care? "She's dehydrated, sir. We don't have saline bags with us."

"We're moving," T-Rex ended the discussion. "We'll do what we can."

"I'll get that boat lined up. You get Red into your vehicle and aim for the coast." Grey's voice was thick with emotion when he added. "And thank you."

15

———————

Red

DREAD WAS THE WEIGHT MOORED TO HER CHEST, ANCHORING IN her stomach. Red's eyelids squeezed tightly shut to keep reality at bay. When she opened them, she'd have to deal with the cause of her anguish.

She could physically feel that her lids were shut. And yet, there she was, looking out across the park. Twitching her head this way and that, Red tried to get her bearings, yet the view didn't change.

That was when Red realized she was asleep; this was a dream.

It was such an unusual occurrence.

Typically, when she put her head down, Red—physically or emotionally exhausted from her day—grabbed at sleep. Clung to it.

Sleep had always been an ally, healing and restoring her.

And when it was time to wake up, Red never used her alarm. She'd never had to. Red simply said to her brain what time worked with her schedule. "Tomorrow morning, I need to be up by six thirty. I want to lie in bed for ten minutes to organize my day." And it worked. Red would become aware around six fifteen, blinking her eyes open by six twenty.

Sleep was reliable and dreamless.

She didn't like this experience. Red was aware that she was lying in a bed, her body heavy, and a movie playing—not a movie unless she was an actor, right? That was what it felt like —like being on a movie scene and acting in some kind of improv. It was fiction, but the set, the other actors, and everything about this made her believe it was real.

I want to wake up now!

No, she didn't like these sensations at all, and this wasn't a particularly useful dream. Red didn't really understand it.

The corners of her lips twitched with irritation.

Wake up! Open your eyes.

For some reason, Red had decided not to park her car where she always parked when she came here to this place.

What place?

It seemed familiar. It reminded her of school.

Was this one of those dreams she'd heard about where people forgot to study for an exam? Or the one where they forgot to show up to a class until the last day of the semester? Or maybe her clothes would disappear, and she'd walk into the lecture hall naked?

If this place wasn't college, maybe it related to what she'd learned at The Farm?

Red processed with the part of the brain that stood to the side, watching events unfold. Why not just go with the dream and see what happened? Though it seemed like a whole lot of nothing, maybe her brain had something to tell her.

Red got out of the car and locked the doors. A woman, bending over to pick up a pair of eyeglasses from the ground, distracted her.

Another woman said, "Hey, those are mine. I guess they dropped when I fell. Give them back." There was an accusation in the tone of her words that Red didn't like.

With keys in hand, Red turned to her car, but now she was somewhere with all grass and no streets for parking.

She had to find the car, and she needed to get going.

When people dreamed, was it always this much work? How did they wake up in the morning feeling refreshed?

"You could take the train," Helper-woman finder-of-glasses said.

"Thanks," Red answered.

Queasy and floaty, Red saw a children's train—the kind that takes kiddos back to the parking lot at amusement parks. When she climbed in, she was the only person on the train; there wasn't even a conductor at the front running things.

The train chugged upward in a steep climb. The ride was rollercoaster-like. As she looked to her left and the right, there was no bottom. She would just freefall into nothingness if the train were to skip the track. Clinging to the sides, Red looked for a safety strap, a harness, something that could hold her in the car as it plunged down the rails. The car swooped down and rattled her back and forth as it straightened out.

"I don't dream. This *must* be important," she stuttered out through clacking teeth. Biting her tongue, her mouth filled with the metallic taste of blood. "I need to pay attention." And with that thought, the train came to a sudden, lurching stop that threw her body forward, then back again.

As she winged around another loop, plastered to the side of the car by centrifugal force, she screamed into an empty sky that she really, really hated the sensation of being between the conscious world and this bizarro make-believe space.

She found herself in the car she'd parked earlier, her fingers wrapped around the steering wheel, the airbag deflating in front of her. She couldn't feel her legs. "Are you okay?" she managed to ask the person beside her. When he didn't answer, she reached a hand toward him. "Are you okay?" she mustered.

The dream stopped.

She was awake now, lying there with heavy lids, not knowing what to do. Not knowing how to feel normal in her body. What was wrong with her?

Think! What's happening here?

Her brain didn't feel like her own. Red remembered the meeting that Color Code had about Havana Syndrome and the pressure that CIA victims felt in the atmosphere, and then something happened in their brains.

Red hadn't paid close attention the day of that lecture. The attacks came at embassies. John Green should be worried. He worked out of the embassy in Bratislava. But she was a field officer, and nobody focused a secret brain-destroying weapon attack on her.

No one knew who she was.

And as meanspirited as her assessment felt, it was better that Green get hit with the danger waves and not her. The CIA didn't treat women well when they showed up with a job-related disability. Yeah, things went really badly for them. And some even died from that inattention.

Now that Red had moved her thoughts to illness, she remembered she was in recovery. She'd been in an explosion on top of being sick.

This stupid dream about losing her car and getting stuck on the kiddie train from hell must be a fever dream.

Red hoped that once she was well again, she'd go back to her dreamless sleep.

And with that thought, Red blinked her eyes open to green tiles and fresh white sheets with not the slightest pink tinge from the Lebanese river water.

Did she slide into a new dream?

What was all this?

She skated her hand over the surface of her sheets. They weren't soft, but they weren't thin and rough like at the hotel.

An I.V. was stuck in her arm. That was it as far as medical equipment went—no heart monitors, no automatic cuff that would check her blood pressure every so many minutes.

She'd woken up to that before. This setup told her she wasn't in a life-or-death fight for survival. Whatever her situation, she was stable.

Then she remembered that in her dream, she was in some kind of event that left her without sensations.

Was that real?

With a sudden jerk, eyelids held rigidly open, Red threw back the covers and looked down her body. The visual of legs and toes wasn't enough. She curled up and touched her body parts, pinching until the sensation registered. Ten toes, two legs. Fingers, hands, arms. She touched her ears and felt her face and neck for bandaging.

Her eyes felt wild in her head as she looked around. She was so disoriented. So fuzzy.

Where the hell was she?

How did she get here?

A nurse in blue scrubs watched Red's odd behaviors as she drew up a syringe then pressed the liquid into Red's IV line. "Well, hello there. That was a surprising way to wake up." She chuckled. "I'm Tomi. I'm your nurse today."

Red shifted her leg as she twisted to see better. "What's wrong with me?" It seemed like the most reasonable place to start. Much higher on the need-to-know list than "Where the heck am I?"

"Salmonella Typhoid, I bet you got that typhoid vaccination, not the oral dose." Tomi wrinkled her nose.

"Yeah, that's right. I …" This woman was American. That meant Red hadn't gotten herself to the hospital down the road. That was the last plan she remembered. Drop the bag of money into Moussa's lap, walk out the door to a car, and ask for a ride to the hospital.

They didn't have American nurses at that Lebanese hospital.

Where the hell was she? How did she get here?

Red's mind scurried around, trying to find a way out from under the blanket of panic.

"Well, it's good you were taking your antibiotic pills." Tomi's voice was too bright for the darkness that covered Red. Something terrible had happened.

The explosion.

Moussa was dead.

She hadn't given him the money. He couldn't use it anymore.

Where was it? Where did she put the bag?

"You're probably feeling odd. You've been sedated to get some deep rest." Tomi smiled.

Red followed the tubing from her arm up to the IV.

"You should be coming around now. I just added your last dose of antibiotics. Your blood work is looking good. Counting backward, you were on the last days of this beast. You got severely dehydrated. How are you feeling?"

"I'm not cramping. Tired. A little woozy and disoriented. Other than that, okay." In Red's mind, she was back at the scene of the explosion. She was stepping over bodies and crushed walls. She's stumbled down the road out of the cloud of dust, coughing.

And now, she remembered deciding that no matter how sick she was, she shouldn't go to the hospital. It was going to fill with victims from the blast. They'd need all their medical staff to cover the bombing. She'd lie in some hallway, ignored because she was low on the triage scale. No one would be assessing her to see if her appendix burst.

She'd just be in the way.

For everyone's sake, Red decided she might as well go back to bed and try to survive.

But this scene didn't make any sense at all. "How'd I get here?"

"Some concerned friends went to find you and brought you in."

"Where's 'in' exactly?"

"You're at a US Army base in eastern Türkiye." Tomi smiled. "Not many people know we exist, but here we are. And here you are."

Türkiye?

"I'm told your hotel was bombed. I'm sorry that happened to you. You came out of that relatively unscathed. You had crap in your lungs, but no ear issues, no brain trauma, no bruising or internal bleeding."

"I was in the women's room, sitting on the toilet, cramping from salmonella."

"That's your story?" Tomi laughed hard, the medical version of gallows humor, Red guessed.

"Yeah. Very glam, right?"

Tomi picked up her tablet and tucked it under her arm. "Well, if you feel up to it, you have a visitor."

Who in the world? "Yes. Thanks."

As Tomi went out, she held the door wide. "She's awake. You can see her now."

16

Red

"Look at you, all pale and thin." Her teammate Grey walked into her room—handsome guy, smart, talented at his job. But there was no chemistry between them. It was all deep friendship and work ethic.

"Surprisingly, I'm alive. Who woulda thunk it?"

"What the hell was wrong with you?" Grey wandered over to her I.V. bag and read the prescription. It didn't seem to interest him. Probably just saline.

"Meh, just a little salmonella typhoid."

"I told you to get the oral vaccine." He pulled a chair over and sat.

"Yeah, except I'm not a virologist and didn't know how to whip one up. The shot was the only thing available. But also, they debunked the difference in efficacy. It's fifty-fifty on a good day.

"Antibiotics, hydration, and time?" He inched down in his chair, then raised an ankle onto his knee, looking like they were kicking back and having a beer together.

"Luckily enough."

"So good to go?"

"Go?" Red quirked a brow.

"We're told you're over whatever and are resting. Are you rested?"

She pulled her brows together. "That depends. Rested for what" *Not really. What the heck?*

"Dancing?" he asked.

"With whom?"

"Me." He hitched a thumb toward his chest. Grey was a good dancer, smooth and confident on the dance floor.

"No. But thanks for the invite. Why are you asking? Maybe I can think of someone willing to have her toes trod upon all night."

Grey gave her a slow smile, letting her know he found her teasing amusing instead of an offense. After a moment, he licked his lips and said, "Sophia Abadi Ackerman passed a message from your buddy, Wajeeb, to Black." He shifted his weight and reached behind him to pull a folded English-language newspaper from his back pocket. As he handed it out to her. He pointed at the article he wanted her to see. "Speaking of Wajeeb, there was an earthquake yesterday in Zaghreen. If you'd been conscious, you would have felt it in Lebanon. It hit as your extraction team was loading you onto the boat. Good thing they didn't drop you in."

"Yeah, good thing." Frowning, Red scanned through the article. *More horror. Those poor people.* After a moment, she looked up and pressed the paper back at Grey. "How is it Sophia was passing on a message to Black? I mean, she met him when the FBI arrested her, but it's not like she can ring Langley and say, 'Hey, can you put me through to John Black?'"

Grey reached between his knees to grab the chair, pulled it

closer to the top of the bed, and lowered his voice. "She asked Iniquus to develop a meeting."

"Smart. Yeah, she's married to that guy with Panther Force."

"Exactly. Their TOC called Black and asked him to swing by so she could pass some information."

"Wow. It must have been big."

"That's what he thought. Knowing Black, he thought a more colorful word." Grey offered up a lopsided smile. "I have to say, your assets are batting a thousand for Team USA right now."

"Poole?" She pressed the button to raise her bed so she was sitting upright. "Tell me what's going on."

"He's with the interrogators."

"So the intel was good. That's huge. But also, Sophia and Wajeeb would have nothing to do with him."

"There's a woman named Elena Savas. She works in our sphere."

"Savas, yes, I know her name. It's an alias. I recently discovered she has a Russian name that I can't recall right now. An asset was telling me about her recently and filled in some of my questions." Red licked her lips.

Grey reached over to the side table, poured her a plastic cup of water, and then handed it over. "We have an old school picture that's getting AI age corrected. I'm going to forward that to you."

"That's good because I've never seen her or her picture. So what's up with Elena?"

Red listened intently as Grey recounted Black's meeting at Iniquus.

It was a lot to process, given the sedated condition of her brain. It made Red think about a bottle of medicine. The useful stuff at the bottom was tightly packed by a wad of cotton that held it still. Did that batting have its place? Sure. Was it helpful? For a time.

That time was over, and Red needed to be alert.

She pinched her thigh to find something sharp to clear her thoughts. It was an idea that didn't help. She smoothed a hand over the leg, offering up. "That woman is amazing."

"Agreed," Grey said, then his smile fell off. "We're talking about Sophia here, right?"

"Yes. But Elena is pretty amazing, too. Smart. It turns out that she has a degree in antiquities. Minored in business. Skilled. And angry. So she's very focused."

"Tell me about the angry part," Grey said.

"Her dad is Russian. He worked between Russia and Syria. Elena and her mother were in Damascus. They lived a very comfortable, even luxurious life. Good schools, European vacations. The Civil War broke out just after Elena graduated from university. At the same time, Elena's mother got an ALS diagnosis. That was when her dad disappeared from the scene. He wasn't answering her phone calls. Money stopped coming into their bank account. So Elena decided to jump on a plane and fly to Russia. She's a dual citizen. When she got to Moscow, Elena discovered that her dad had a whole other family—a wife and four children around Elena's age. Some a little older than she. There are nieces and nephews. As it turned out, her dad had been living a double life while it was convenient for him. When Elena confronted him, he told her he'd have her arrested and sent to Siberia if he ever heard from her again."

"That explains the angry part, all right. You got this story from your asset?" Grey asked.

"Yes, I was trying to understand why a woman as polished and educated as Elena was reputed to be would get mixed up with conflict relics. And I wanted to know where the money was going."

"Not to an offshore bank account, I take it."

"Yes, to that. But also, she can only get to the relics and

fulfill her client orders because part of her proceeds goes to supporting ISIS. I thought it was transactional—to trade in the Syrian relics black markets, you also have to be involved with ISIS bureaucracy. I have nothing definitive or actionable, or I would have handed it off to the right agencies. This story of a ring that Sophia told Black … Does that make sense?" She pulled her brow together and tipped her head. "It's not Elena's usual M.O. That kind of treasure hunting is a different stomping ground."

Red paused. "Okay, thanks for sharing the story about Elena. But what has she got to do with dancing?" Had Grey asked about dancing? Or had that been part of her dream? "You started by asking me if I felt like dancing, right?" *Right?*

"There's a charity ball on Saturday in Vienna, the annual—"

"Saturday? The Secret Order of the Raven's Gate Gala? That's huge. We're talking about royalty, stars, and the world's bajillionaires."

"That's the one."

"Nope." Red shook her head. "We can't get in. We'd need tickets, and they go up for sale a year in advance. There's no stealth mode into the ball."

Grey popped his brows mischievously. "I have two tickets in hand."

Red's eyes stretched wide with surprise. "How?"

"The ambassador and his wife."

Red grimaced. "Making enemies?"

"True, they're none too pleased. Or so I understand. I didn't make the ask. A call from the White House was persuasive."

"The President?" she whispered.

"Secretary of State, but since she serves at the pleasure of the president, close enough."

"Close enough, yeah. So they're pissed, the ambassador and

wife? Because if things turn to shit—as well they might—the ambassador is our first line of defense."

Grey shrugged. "Right now, that's not my worry. We need to get into the ball and see what's up."

"You're planning to steal the ring?"

"Steal … well, no ring, no reward money. We wouldn't keep the ring, of course. We'd make sure it got into the hands of the heir, right? In effect, Elena doesn't own the ring. She simply has *possession* of it. She got it via the assassination of five men. And Dr. Klein as collateral damage. So six down, that we know of."

"Dr. Klein is a loss. He was a grumpy old man, set in his ways. But he knew his stuff. And he always helped when he could." Red tipped her head. "You're sure the woman who took the briefcase is this woman making contact? One and the same?"

"With Dr. Wajeeb providing us with a name, we were able to get more examples of Savas on security cameras, airports mostly. AI compared those samples to the woman at Dr. Klein's address. It has a high probability of the right body composition, height, and walking patterns. We had no face for comparison. We have some now. But it's CCTV crap. The clarity isn't there. Better to wait on what Iniquus hands us from the aging process."

"Okay. And you think Elena will have the ring on her at the ball? What if she doesn't?"

"She's meeting the guy, Joel Brighton who has the passwords and the bank account number. Joel asked to meet Elena at the ball to make the exchange happen. So one assumes she'll have the ring on her somewhere."

"Forty million." Red drummed her fingers on her thigh.

Grey nodded. "It's a lot."

"They aren't going to do that at the ball." Red pursed her lips as she paused. "They'll just be setting up the handover."

"That's what Black and I decided as well."

"So it could be anyone who shows up," Red said. "It might not even be her. I mean, she would be exposing herself."

"True."

"And this guy, Joel, he'd have to have had his ticket well in advance?"

"He did. Two tickets, one for himself and a plus one."

Suddenly, Red's eyelids grew heavy. Her head clanged. She so wanted to go back to sleep even though that damned dream was an oily sheen on her thoughts, and she didn't want to sleep if it meant revisiting those sensations. "Grey, you figured this all out. I'm not enjoying this game. Let's cut to the chase. What's the plan?"

"We're told Elena was offered a ticket. Until then, she'll be a mole in the ground, right?"

"Yes," Red acknowledged. "So we go to the ball, you and I? To what end? I mean, taking the ring would be the simplest task. But when do we ever do simple?"

A grin spread across Grey's face. "Simple is boring. What would you like to get out of seeing Elena talking with Joel?"

"What I want to know is the end goal of this transaction. Is Elena heading into a cushy retirement? Or is she planning something? I want to know if this reward will fund something big and bad. Saturday? I can dance on Saturday, but I don't have a ball gown."

"That's being handled."

"Thanks, fairy godmother. And if you could turn my pumpkin into a coach?"

"I'll do my best," Grey said, then added, "The assignment needs to answer the following questions: What is the money paying for? What's plan?"

The truth about terrorist plans was that they were hard to extinguish once conceived. If you kill the planner, the plan survives. If you kill the financing, there are other ways, other times, and other avenues. In order to kill the plan, you needed to know the plan, and you needed to destroy the plan and all of its pieces and parts.

How?

Typically, sunlight did the job. Tell everyone about the plan. Tell the public the day, the time, and the perpetrators.

Getting Elena Savas might possibly—but improbably stop the plan.

Getting the ring *wouldn't* stop the plan.

Red needed to follow the money.

That meant that Red needed to protect Elena's ability to get to her payday so they could watch the money move, find out who the players were, and where the money was spent.

Find the plan. Kill the plan.

What did that look like? Above her pay grade. Those decisions had absolutely nothing to do with her.

She was a field officer who discovered the dangers. That was *her* kind of treasure.

And now, she was on the hunt.

17

Nomad

NOMAD LAY ON HIS BED IN THE AMERICAN BARRACKS. AT THE end, he'd positioned a chair with a stack of pillows to give himself the extra inches he needed so his feet weren't dangling off the mattress.

T-Rex stood at the open door and caught Nomad's gaze. "Up and at 'em. Looks like rest time has come to an end."

Nomad swung his legs around, sliding his feet into the boots he always kept prepped for a quick transition. He pulled the laces into efficient bows and followed along behind T-Rex.

"Where's Echo heading next?"

"Not Echo." T-Rex pointed. "You."

Me? Interesting. Nomad silently followed T-Rex out the door into the hallway to the elevator and pressed the button. "Did the CIA update you on how she's doing?" Nomad wouldn't speak Red's name outside of the mission. But T-Rex would know exactly whom he was asking about.

With his hands on his hips, his lips pressed tight, T-Rex shook his head, and Nomad felt a vice tighten around his heart.

During the extraction, Nomad had taken charge of Red. In the back of their vehicle, Nomad had cradled Red in his arms from the hotel to the docks with her head resting on his chest. He'd carried her to the boat and held her, draped across his lap, as he protected her from the swells while T-Rex motored them farther out to sea where the rescue helicopter could reach them.

Red had been oblivious to all of it.

Nomad had been scared; he'd admit it. He'd felt her clinging to life. They had arrived when she held to the last thread, and it was probable that their last push was too little, too late.

Throughout the race to get her to an American hospital on an American base, Nomad had this crazy thought that if he held her tight, he could hold her in her body. That if he sang her name and just plain asked, "Can you reach down deep? Can you find the thing that can get you through and anchor yourself to it? Can you listen to my voice and stay with me?" she would try harder to stay alive. Like when his buddies were hurt on the battlefield, and he'd yelled at them to keep their eyes open, "Stay with me." He just kept asking, terrified that he was watching her take her last breath. Angry that this rescue was taking too long.

Yeah, it had been bad.

When T-Rex walked through his door to get him, Nomad had been lying there staring at the ceiling, flinging those questions out into the universe. "Red, are you trying? Are you holding on?" In his imagination, Nomad had been reliving the relief he'd felt as the helicopter crew sent the basket down. Arranging her as comfortably as he could, Nomad had pulled the straps securely into place to keep her safe.

As the rope lifted her, Nomad steadied the swing of the basket. It was an honor to do it. He'd felt that acutely. And it was his privilege to fly back to the base with her, to be the one who got an I.V. into her arm, to run beside the gurney as the rescue EMTs took over her care.

But as the ambulance receded from view, a sensation flooded Nomad's system, rocking him like a rogue wave.

It was a lot.

Big.

Hard as hell.

He didn't know her name.

He'd never get to talk to her.

He'd never see her smile.

This mission was the embodiment of those damned lines from Longfellow:

Ships that pass in the night, and speak each other in passing,
Only a signal shown and a distant voice in the darkness;
So on the ocean of life we pass and speak one another,
Only a look and a voice, then darkness again and a silence.

Nomad had never read that poem as bleak. He lived that life and loved it. Everchanging missions and postings, people came, people went. His family was a distant, calm harbor he could return to at any time, which was enough for him.

The passings in the night was a life choice.

He was a novelty-seeker. An adventurer. He had the DNA of his Viking ancestors racing through his blood. Tired of the rocks and snow and needing to see other things, they climbed into a boat and headed to sea, driven by something deep inside, hungry for the next adventure.

And yet, this mission. *This mission.* He didn't want to let it go. Didn't want to see the ambulance fade into the distance.

He wanted her back in his arms.

Crazy, right? he asked himself. Nomad held his breath, waiting for the update, terrified that T-Rex would say, "We did our best, but it wasn't enough."

As the elevator doors drew open, he said, "I have nothing on her status." T-Rex tipped his ear toward the door. "I do have Colonel Watts holding. Let's move."

They exited the elevator, and Nomad followed T-Rex into an empty room. Colonel Watts was on the screen, looking down at a report that held his focus.

"Sir," T-Rex and Nomad stood at attention in front of the camera.

"At ease. Take a seat, both of you. Nomad, I wanted to review a few things from your file with you."

"Yes, sir."

"Let me catch you up to speed." He turned toward T-Rex. "You, too. I just got some interesting information from the Mediterranean. I'm going to put you on split screen." Another man's face came up in the frame on the right. "This is Javeed Hasan, DIA." DIA was military intelligence similar to the CIA.

Nomad had assumed intelligence would be taking the reins when dealing with Poole. Maybe Javeed Hasan was the one interrogating the guy.

"Call me Hasan. I'm going to cut to the chase. Our AI system spat out your name, Nomad, as the right guy, in the right place, at the right time, with the right skills—technical and otherwise."

"Sir."

"Thank you for your assistance in bringing Sgt. Poole back into the fold."

"Yes, sir."

"We want to keep the circle tight with this information for many reasons," Hasan said.

Nomad thought they didn't want to affect morale, encourage copycats, or look like idiots for giving this guy clearance. No good could come from broadcasting the issue or spreading the knowledge.

"So we needed to pick wisely for this next step," Hasan continued. "My understanding is that you have an association with the Viennese embassy. Tell me about that."

Nomad crossed his arms over his chest. DIA and the Viennese embassy in the same breath with mentioning Poole?

What was *his* association? Nomad's parents had been CIA field officers who worked under the guise of jobs with the diplomatic corps. One of the places they worked was out of the Viennese Embassy.

Was that what this DIA officer wanted, for Nomad to out his parents?

When he hit high school, his family moved to Vienna. Nomad had slowly been figuring out his parents' true professions. It was at that time that his family had gone to a dinner party where Nomad met a Green Beret, some relative of the Viennese ambassador, and his wife.

Was that what Hasan wanted to chat about?

That night had been pivotal for him. At eighteen, he'd been an idealist and a patriot. When this Green Beret had talked about his work as a diplomatic special forces operator, the kind of special forces nobody made movies about, Nomad was honed in. He did his research and signed the contracts. He'd go to boot right after graduation and then on to Ranger school.

His parents had taken the news with gray faces, their muscles held tight under their skin. Usually, they were better about masking. Well, if anything happened to him, they'd have his twin, who was heading toward medical school to become a brain surgeon. The contrast was stark. His parents treated

Nomad's career decisions like personal affronts to their life's sacrifices.

Since no one knew what they had done for a living, Nomad was pretty sure that his grandparents on both sides would have met their choices with the same strain around the eyes and tightened lips.

To this day, the extended family didn't know about his parents' CIA service, and even for Nomad, it had been a guess, a source of curiosity.

After spending a decade with the Green Berets, Nomad had been asked to consider joining Delta Force because of his unique background as a kid growing up with parents in the State Department, moving every year or two, picking up not just the languages but also the mannerisms, the etiquette nuances, and high cultural intelligence.

He could blend.

He was a nomad.

Of course, his parents had also taught their sons spy skills. They'd treated it like a series of games to learn new cities as they moved about. When the CIA was providing the new Delta Force members training in spy craft, Nomad already knew how to do handoffs, how to change appearance and disappear into a crowd, how to work with dead drops, to follow a rabbit—the name for a person you were tracking—to set up a safe house, the hows and whys, and wheres of caches. All of it. None of it was new.

In training, Nomad was so good at it that they looked into his background.

And Nomad knew precisely when that happened because his parents had shown up.

Their visit was an in-person plea that Nomad keep the family secret quiet. They just went for a sail and made sure that he wasn't wondering and therefore digging and asking questions.

It was all good. He had been eighteen when he'd made peace with all that. The affirmation was appreciated, though.

Was *that* what Hasan wanted him to reveal?

"You know Vienna?" Hasan asked. "You speak German?" Hasan already knew that if he'd read Nomad's folder.

"I speak German. My father worked at the Viennese Embassy for a time. If you gave me an address, I'd need a GPS to get there. It's been almost twenty years."

"And you have social skills?"

"What does that mean?" Nomad hadn't been asked these kinds of questions before. It had always been, "Go here. Accomplish this."

"Dancing skills, and by that I specifically mean ballroom dancing skills, the waltz at the very least." Hasan glared through the camera at Nomad. "Delta Force and ballroom don't usually pair together."

"Yes, sir. I'm comfortable with all of that."

"Okay," Hasan spoke to someone off camera. "I think this is our guy. He has the right look if he were in white tie and tails. Do you have his measurements? Good. Get everything ordered. Correct car. Correct hotel. The works. And with the car, you must remember his height, yes?" Hasan turned back to the camera.

"Sir?"

"Solo mission. It's going to take some creativity on your part. There's a woman, her name is Elena Savas. She's supposed to attend a ball in Vienna this Saturday, and we want you there with eyes on her."

There had been the mention of Poole, keeping a tight circle, and now a woman named Elena …

Poole was most likely still in a brig under the Mediterranean Sea.

Not everyone was trained to withstand interrogation.

It wasn't easy.

Nomad learned this the hard way in SERE school. Survival being the goal—escape was the best of all worlds. But when necessary, they knew how to resist, which could be an external resistance or an internal one. And they'd been trained to escape.

There was no escaping a submarine.

Obviously, Poole had given something up.

"Yes, sir."

Hasan drummed his fingers on the table. It had the quality not of impatience but of anxiety to get the job done. The sense that he wanted boots on the ground. And he wanted them to be aggressive. "Poole is a traitor. We have a limited understanding of his actions and their implications. Right now, we recognize that there are people out of the Iraqi attack who are staging to go over our southern border to mole into our communities and to affect some large-scale act of terror. We want to know their end goal and net them before they burrow into some hole where we can't find them anymore."

"Yes, sir. Do you know Poole's motivation for his involvement?"

"It looks like he was a bored soldier with a high-security clearance that an attractive woman developed for intelligence. And a car that he wanted to buy."

"And this has to do with Elena Savas?"

"Exactly. We need you to turn that whole honey pot thing around on her."

Nomad didn't respond.

"Elena presents as Poole's girlfriend. In her messages, she mentioned she'd be in Damascus this week."

Nomad sat stoically. Was Elena the reason why Poole risked going AWOL?

"We believe he'd planned to surprise her. Poole told Elena he'd been paid for the information he'd brought in from his base. She congratulated him. He said he wasn't going back, and she tried to change his mind. She mentioned a group that was heading over the southern border of the U.S. and that the information he'd brought in was crucial for the success of that team—"

"Team?" T-Rex jutted forward.

Hasan's gaze turned to t-Rex. "That was the English term she used, yes. This came from a text exchange. She texted that the information he'd provided the team would make their infiltration and ultimate success possible. The mission would be a go very soon."

Shit.

"From the discussion, we know that Poole agrees with the purpose of the event. He knows that the event will be taking place in the United States and is a terrorist event, but he doesn't know who, what, or where. That's why we need Elena."

"And she'll be at the ball," Nomad said. Yup. This was big. Innocent lives would be on the line.

"A ball in Vienna will be the perfect place to meet her in public and make contact. Perhaps, make a move toward some kind of romantic connection. If not making a move, at least place bugs and trackers on everything she has with her, her phone especially, then we can follow along until we have a better opportunity. That night, we need to know with whom she's interacting. Whatever happens, time is of the essence. We need Elena's information fast to stay three steps ahead of the event."

"Yes, sir. But why the ball, sir? Is there a connection?"

"From the texts, going to the ball sounds like it will result in a big payday. It came up in her texts just a couple of days ago that she'd made contact with the buyer who wants to meet her there to look at the ring."

"Ring. So, a piece of high-dollar jewelry?" Nomad asked.

"We believe so—could be code for something else. The DIA knows that Elena Savas has been dealing with sales of specialized items—cultural artifacts, for example—to European elites since the Civil War began in Syria and that business models in that region include a hefty cut of the profits going to ISIS. Further than a basic file, the DIA hasn't been involved. Up until now, she's outside the scope of our directives."

"Is Interpol prepared to pick her up for questioning?" Nomad asked.

"I have nothing to do with that. I will be sending you a file with your plan of action. It will include some of Elena's pictures that we found on Poole's phone. Enough that you can identify her. We discovered through the FBI that Elena Savas is on the attendance list as the guest of Joel Brighton, an American citizen living mostly in Dubai. We'll have his images available as well."

"You had mentioned making a romantic connection, sir?" Nomad asked.

"We need to ask Elena some pointed questions, and we need to do it in such a way that we are not tipping off the group that she's targeted so they scatter to reorganize later like some damned murmuration of starlings."

Nomad suppressed a smile. "Poetic, sir."

"I liked that image." He held up a finger. "Here's the challenge, we want to ask Elena our questions. To do that, we need to get her into international waters. And she needs to go there willingly. Or maybe, quasi willingly."

"Drugging her would be illegal," T-Rex said.

"Alcohol, freely consumed, is not," Hasan countered. "*Romance* is not."

Nomad leaned back in his chair. "I see." Surreal. This fell under private life skills he'd never considered applying to his soldiering career.

"Be creative. We can provide you with a yacht, for example—maybe she and her friends, if that made her feel safe—would enjoy that. You could, for example, ask, 'Would you all like to go out onto the water to see the stars or the sunrise?' *Be creative*. We could have a helicopter available. Would she like to fly and see the lights? And that helicopter could move to a ship in—"

"International waters." Yeah, he got it.

"Correct. Son, I'm not saying this is going to be easy. I'm also not saying it has to be done the night of the ball. If we can get trackers on her and her things, that would be a step forward."

"Do you think she's in an actual relationship with Poole?" T-Rex asked.

"He does."

Foreign spy or not, this kind of operation didn't align with his ethics. He didn't lie to a woman for manipulation—kidnapping. Nomad taught fighting skills and blew shit up. This op was someone else's bailiwick. "Is there a reason that JSOC is turning to Delta Force instead of CIA or DIA?"

"You know how this works," Hasan must have caught something in Nomad's tone. "The number of people who have to sign off if we shift to a new team. The pebble hits the water, and the rings expand outward." Hasan glowered through the camera. "For myriad reasons that I don't feel compelled to share with you, we'd like to limit the number of pebbles that get tossed. Frankly, we think your unique situation and … attributes will make it more likely that you will be successful. Those officers in the area might have less hair on their heads than you and more jowls. You've already been read in on Poole. The more people who know, the more chance that this might somehow, for example, get into the ears of a reporter and the story finds its way into the papers. That would be a bullhorn blaring out our position when we want to sneak up on the tigers, catch them in our nets, and turn them to our will."

"Yes, sir." So they needed someone young and fit to try to attract her enough to move her to a place where the laws were more plastic.

But did that make sense? The CIA, after all, knew about Poole. They had developed the intelligence packet for Echo to find him that was dead on. Of course, having handed off the package to JSOC, the field officer would have no idea what had come of it.

"Need to know" meant the players often had no idea how a puzzle fit together.

If Echo had missed, JSOC might have asked the officer to work their asset and try to get their next coordinates but that was about it.

"The problem," Hasad said, "is getting you in there. Security is tight. Tickets to the Secret Order of the Raven's Gate Gala are impossible to come by."

"We reach out to the American embassy," Nomad offered. "Surely, the ambassador would have procured tickets when they became available. My parents went to that ball when they worked in Vienna. I remember them talking about it."

"We called the ambassador. State confiscated their tickets for national security reasons. Others needed them."

"But not us?" T-Rex asked. "Some other team that needs to be there for a different reason?"

"The CIA might be on hand, possibly the FBI. But they'd be working a different case."

Ah, here was another reason for tapping him for this mission; Nomad might have some strings he could pull. "Some of my parents' society friends will be going, I'm sure," Nomad said. "Do I have permission to reach out to my mother for contact names and numbers?"

"You do. Other than that, you might end up needing to come down the chimney like Santa Claus."

18

———

Nomad

Growing up, Nomad's unusual childhood exposed him to a plethora of languages that he tucked under his belt—some more fluent and others more at a survival level—he thought that was probably why his commanders tapped him for Delta Force assessment.

Born Algernon Leeland Kesling—yeah, that was a mouthful—Nomad renamed himself when he was in high school.

Moving from country to country, embassy to embassy had been a life he'd liked.

Nomad's father's work meant he often took off at a moment's notice, sometimes for extended periods. His dad was unreliable when it came to a presence in his life but was never undependable with his love and concern.

His parents' devotion to each other, him, and his twin brother was probably why being a nomad was adventurous instead of disorienting.

It had been like having family scattered around the world to have his parents in the diplomatic (or so he'd thought) profession.

Nomad's last assignment - providing close protection to the group of legislators in Türkiye - felt like old home week. It had been 30ish years, but he knew the woman who sat in the front room. She used to sneak him pieces of candy, and she'd bring her pet rabbit for him to play with. Nomad knew that she wouldn't remember him—after all, he'd been five years old at the time—but Nomad looked enough like his dad that he could tell she was trying to place him.

Nomad had noticed that front-room assistants at the various embassies had a remarkable knack for remembering names and faces. Knowing it would continue to bother her, Nomad had decided to reintroduce himself before the team left to fly back to the United States.

As Robert Burns observed, "The best-laid schemes of mice and men often go awry."

Plan B: Nomad's mother kept copious notes about people and connections. He'd call her and get the right name and home address to send the lady a note with his memories of her kindness to a young kid.

Having added that task to his mental to-do list, when Nomad made the DIA-sanctioned call to ask his mom for help getting into the ball, Nomad had decided to lead with Ankara since they weren't on a secure line, and he couldn't just say what he wanted to say.

He talked about missing the embassy life and the fun he'd had going to the balls to dance. She'd know that was bunk. But his mom could read between the lines.

The conversation wended lazily into the "Hey, by the way …"

And by the end of their call, Nomad had concluded that his mom would find some way to get him into that ball, even if it meant he was going in as catering staff. Of this, Nomad had no doubt. But the means to that entree wasn't tip of the tongue; his mom would have to make some calls.

"Love you, Mom. And thanks for this."

"Yes, all right. But I'm extracting a price. I want to see you for your birthday this year."

"If it's in my power, I'll be there," Nomad promised. "But with my job, I never know. You remember this from Dad, right? The apple and the tree thing?"

"I appreciate your trying. Okay, lovebug, let me get going on this. I'm six hours behind you. People in Europe will go to bed soon."

Later that night, a message dropped: **Frau Leitner, high tea at 16h tomorrow (Friday).** And the address.

Landing in Vienna that Friday morning. Nomad set off on his mission development tasks. He had about thirty-six hours before the ball. So far, he'd been to the tailor to have his tails properly fitted and shoes purchased. There were little details, the correct cuff links, and pocket litter he needed to gather. Even if he ended up sneaking into the manor house—now used as a venue for weddings, galas, and receptions—he'd still need to transform himself into a persona that might entice Elena Sava onto a yacht.

Nomad drove a high-dollar sports car past the Viennese American Embassy on his way to Frau Leitner's house. Unfortunately, few luxury car options were left with all the glitterati coming into the city for the ball. Yes, the car fit the profile he'd be trying to sell. But whoever rented this car didn't truly understand the concept of six foot six. Once Nomad had wedged himself in, he realized how little flexibility he had in the driver's seat. Even with a powerful engine, there would be no tactical driving possible in this thing.

Fortunately for him, none would be needed.

As Nomad drove toward the high tea, he was surprised that he knew exactly where he was. He'd been in this city as a seventeen- and an eighteen-year-old, one of their family's longer stays anywhere. For the first time, he and his brother had left their parents when it had typically been the other way around. Returning to the States, Nomad showed up for boot camp and his brother for university orientation.

But now, Nomad was back in the world of diplomacy.

His adult life had been shaped by the lessons he'd been conscientiously taught and those he'd absorbed from the atmosphere. Nomad had spent his formative years listening to and learning about the intricacies of peace and friendship, of maintaining relationships when the outcomes were precarious. He'd learned to listen carefully to the music that was playing and to match his steps to it, like the ballroom classes his mom had insisted her sons not just take but excel at.

Nomad and his brother hated those classes and rebelled against them until they eventually figured out that girls had been put into dance classes to become ballerinas when they were two. It was rude for parents to prepare their daughters for the mating dances that happen worldwide during adolescence but not equip their sons similarly. The girls had been beautiful and graceful and mightily put out when the boys, new to their fast-growing feet and gangly limbs, stepped on toes already pinched by the girls' first high heels.

Awkward just by age and that flush of new hormones – squeaking voices and sweaty palms and now thrust out onto a dance floor to socialize and make their cases for being good boyfriends? It was a lot.

And that was when Nomad and his twin learned that their ease on the dance floor was a commodity. Their skill sought after.

Nomad wasn't sure if he or his brother ever thanked their

mother for their dating success. And sure, he'd admit, he and his twin were both athletic, top of their classes, they had attributes that played in their favor. But so did other guys in their class. The Kesling brothers' ability to dance won them a cloud of butterfly girls.

He should tell his mom he was grateful.

For a lot.

He knew that any time he needed her, she would be there for him. There was never a single doubt in his mind that was also true for his brother and dad. And once again, Nomad wondered what it would be like to have the support of a loving partner like his dad had found. Nomad wanted to experience that, too, but his mom was one in a million.

And while Nomad was open to loving deeply and all that went with it—the joys and the sacrifices—he had never met anyone who had sparked anything like those emotions in him.

His mind shifted to Lebanon. The last time he was in a vehicle, he was cradling Red. He hoped she made it. Hoped she was alive.

That mission was in his rearview, Nomad thought as he struggled to get his feet onto the correct pedals to parallel park with a stick shift grinding into his thigh and the steering wheel between his knees.

Now, here he was, outside of his mom's "dear Viennese friend's" mansion, walking up the marble steps to the elaborate front doors to say hello and share his mother's best wishes.

He knew his mom had already made a deal; this was performative.

A maid led Nomad to the salon, where afternoon tea was laid. An elegant woman with silver hair pulled back in a knot, perched behind the pot that Nomad thought would be too heavy for her to lift.

He sat and sipped tea from a teacup so delicate it was

translucent. They spoke in niceties about the weather and books they had read. After a while, she angled her face and looked at him with a side-eye. Frau Leitner switched to impeccable English. "Young man, I'm sure you didn't mean to spend your day over tea with an old lady. How can I help you?"

Yes, she knew. She simply needed the conversation to take place.

"I'm going to be in town tomorrow when the Secret Order of the Raven's Gate Gala will be held. My parents fondly remember the time they attended. I'm wondering if you might know how I could get a ticket to join. I know it's last minute."

"Lovely that you should ask!" she responded. "And perfect timing. I plan to attend the ball this year and just got word that my escort broke his hip. I'm in need of a gallant arm. Shall you be my escort?"

"I'd be honored."

From her age, Nomad had to wonder if this woman had been a Cold War spy.

She knew something was up. She even went so far as to touch her nose and give him a knowing nod of the head.

19

———————

Red

"WHAT ARE YOU DOING?" RED'S VOICE WAS THICK AS SHE spoke into her cell phone.

"Trying to figure out how to tie this damned bow tie," Grey grunted. "It keeps slanting up on the left. Are you getting dressed for the ball we need to leave soon?"

"I just woke up from a nap."

"You feeling okay?" His voice had the strained sound of exasperation, but she knew that was aimed at the tie, not her.

"I'm off my game. But I can get the job done. I mean, look, I pushed through when I needed to meet Moussa."

"I hate that you did that, and, man, what a miracle you did. What are you thinking about all that?"

What? So much. Too much.

Moussa was an anvil sitting on her chest. Fine one minute, destroyed by the circumstances the next. He had been sitting at the table ordering lunch for himself and her.

He would wonder how much money was in the black bag.

He was probably sitting there planning what he would do with it.

Where would he hide it? Would he tell his wife?

Something made Moussa lunge under the table prior to the bomb.

And there was that guy dodging the donkey cart, the one that she'd somehow recognized and photographed. He had been standing at Moussa's side. Did Moussa know him? Were they talking when the bomb exploded? It had occurred to Red that Moussa lunged under the table because of the donkey cart guy, the one with the strange design of dark moles around his eye that reminded Red of a star constellation.

She had access to his phone. After the ball, she'd look through it and see if there was anything at all that was interesting to the CIA.

When Grey asked what she thought about all that, it churned up those questions and got the thoughts and images roiling again.

Red tapped her phone onto speaker as she crawled out of bed and walked to her open suitcase. Reaching down, she pulled the stranger's phone she'd picked up along with Moussa's melted cell. "Oh, I was thinking I might have some octopus DNA in me somehow."

Grey chuckled.

"I'm serious, Grey. At the time of the bombing, I was out of my mind with a fever. Like, I kept arriving at places and wondering how I got there."

"That had to be frightening. But octopus-like? In my mind, I'm picturing blending into the environment. Is that what you're talking about?"

"I'm holding the phone from a guy I think was talking to Moussa when they died. I had recognized him before he came into the hotel, and, at that time, I took his picture to hand to the targeters."

"Okay, good."

"After the bomb, I found his camera and switched the biometrics on that phone to my own."

"Perfect. But octopus?" Grey asked.

"Each arm of an octopus has its own brain and therefore can function separately from the other arms. And yeah, I know that I was leaning into training and muscle memory throughout that event, but I prefer the idea of being an octopus."

Grey snort-laughed.

"You sound happier. Did you get the bow tie done?" Red opened the man's encryption messaging app and scrolled through his recent text exchanges to determine if she had access. She'd work with it later when she had time and focus. That would come after the ball.

"I'll try the tie again in a second. I'm working on my cuff links."

"Oh." Red scowled. "Wow. Isn't that something?"

"Cuff links?" Grey's voice was muffled. "No, not really."

"Synchronicity, I guess. The world is indeed a small place when it comes to treasure hunters and conflict relics. There are only so many names on a list. The web is spun of fine silk."

"Spiders, now, I see you're following the theme of eight-legged creatures. I'll bite," Grey said. "What are we talking about?"

"Wajeeb sent me on the track of Moussa, who stumbled across Poole. Of course, I was looking for information about conflict relics, and Poole was a surprise. I'm thinking that means Poole has some connection with conflict relics, too, or why would he be working with the import-export guy that Wajeeb identified?"

When she paused, Grey repeated, "Keep going."

"I'm looking at the phone from that guy I recognized heading toward the hotel. As an aside, someone collected Moussa's from my hospital room. Black wanted it at Langley."

"It arrived," Grey verified. "They're working on it. It was melted, but they might be able to get something. One cuff link down, one to go. It would probably help if I didn't have my phone clamped between my ear and shoulder."

"Probably."

"Do you think this guy is someone that might prove useful?" Grey asked.

"Well, he's dead." Red scrolled back and forth through his texts. "So I'd say no. But his phone at least gives me a little explanation of why he was there in the explosion."

"This is the 'Wow. Isn't that something?'" Grey asked.

"Mmm. Loose translations of the exchange go like this: 'I found a phone in my office. I believe it belongs to my secretary, Moussa. I believe he's been spying on me.' The guy answers, 'What shall I do about it?'"

"That's true, correct?" Grey asked. "Your asset, Moussa did you say? Moussa hid a burner in his boss's office."

"That's my understanding. Listen, the boss answers, 'He's going to a meeting. I am tracking his phone. Stop him before he tells anyone about Poole. If you see him with someone, take care of it.'" What was that saying about nine lives? It looked like she'd used three of them that day—the typhoid, the bomb, and an assassin.

How many did she have left?

Ice dumped through her system as she remembered the drug-enhanced hospital dream that kept peeking around her consciousness and peering at her. She shook her head to reset. "I hope they put that phone in a Faraday bag. Otherwise, they'll know the CIA is in the mix."

"Protocol. So yes. Stop here. I'll hold while you get the

spyware on that phone. I want Langley's AI to be culling that for any information useful to this mission."

Red did as asked. "I got the green light. The data should be flowing to our targeters."

"I'll send a message to Black. So this guy in Lebanon was a hitman? And you honed right in," Grey's voice was congratulatory. "Good instincts."

"Ah, but for the shits, I would have faced an assassin and a bomb."

"Huzzah for the runs. Also, huzzah for the second cufflink achieved. I'm going to need to hang up to do the damn tie. But I called to make sure you were up and animated. Are you getting dressed?"

"I'll be ready and downstairs in twenty minutes. If you can't get the tie, I'll help you in the car."

"Good enough. See you downstairs in twenty." Grey ended the call.

Grey. He was good stuff. She'd always liked him. And he'd always had her back. Right from the very start when they met at the CIA training institute called The Farm.

As unlikely as it was for a woman at the CIA, Red had seen herself as a field officer from the get-go. That's where she'd wanted to be, out using her languages, background, and gift of sitting next to people and having them spill their life stories and deep, dark secrets. All Red had to do was sit and nod, and the most remarkable things came out of people's mouths. Since it had been such a natural occurrence in her life, as a teen, she'd been startled to realize that wasn't true for everyone.

Her friends, figuring out this talent, would send her out to find out if "Jimmy likes me" or if "Bill cheated."

And very quickly, Red realized that people didn't want the truth.

They wanted to hear what they wanted to hear.

Friendships burned quickly. Luckily for Red, her father moved frequently from country to country and embassy to embassy for his job, so the losses and malicious rumors stemming from embarrassment or hurt feelings were short-lived pains.

She continued to use her secret powers; she simply didn't talk about it.

In the context of her life, Red hadn't thought it would have applicability.

In the American high school Red attended, juniors took an aptitude test to point them toward a good career fit. Red's report indicated she should either be a dress designer or a language professor. To this day, Red was hard-pressed to explain, on a Venn Diagram, what aspects of her personality might have been shared by such oddly divergent results that the guidance counselor offered her.

But then, after reading an article about Virginia Hall, an American spy who was one of the most accomplished secret agents in the French Resistance in WWII, Red found her calling.

She would join the CIA and become a spy, too.

Virginia and Red had things in common. They were both women born to affluence with various languages under their belts. Both were well-traveled. They had both been born in Maryland, though Red's father was from Jordan, and her mother liked to tell her that she was of royal blood.

Red couldn't care less about her pedigree.

She looked Middle Eastern, and that was gift enough when it came to doing her present job. That and her father taught her to speak flawless Arabic alongside Russian and French.

Her Mom and America gave her English and the most rudimentary Spanish possible. And her work with the CIA had given her a smattering of regional languages.

There was a serious divergence between Red's and

Virginia's backgrounds. Virginia shot herself (literally) in the foot, leading to her leg amputation.

Red shot herself (figuratively) in the foot. But that had to do with self-sabotage. She doubted her intellect, her skills, and her ability. She thought perhaps she was wrong to believe she could make it into the CIA, so she set her sights elsewhere. She changed her studies, thinking she might like to collect for a museum or an art gallery.

But luckily, one of her professors quietly worked for Langley, pointing out students he thought had the secret sauce.

Because this professor spotted her, the CIA knocked on Red's door.

Red would get the opportunity to follow in Virginia's footsteps, after all.

Virginia, too, had been discovered and recruited, though that was a much more exciting story. The person who tapped Virginia was the one and only Vera Atkins, the woman who many thought was Ian Fleming's template for Miss Moneypenny. Atkins got Virginia involved in Churchill's new Special Operations Executive (SOE), and she went after the Nazis in every way she could imagine.

Was Color Code equivalent to the SOE?

No. Their jobs weren't the same.

Virginia was crisscrossing Nazi-filled France, and Red was dealing with the business end of funding terror.

But still, Virginia Hall was her inspiration.

Would Red hobble around war-torn France with a wooden leg she named Cuthbert like Virginia had?

Certainly not.

Red would give her prosthetic limb a *much* better name.

But becoming a spy? That had excited her imagination in a way nothing had before.

Once Langley tapped on her door, Red had done her

research. She didn't go into this career blindly. She knew all about how the women went through the Farm and then were relegated to the basement to do research as "targeters."

At the CIA, the men got the attaboys, fist bumps, promotions, pay raises, and field assignments.

Luckily, Black pulled her onto his team, and she didn't fall into the toxic swill the other women had to swim through.

"Look, Virginia," Red said aloud. "I made it."

She'd done it like Virginia would, with strategic alliances. Red had teamed up with a fellow recruit at the Farm. The man who would eventually become John Grey. And when Color Code wanted Grey on their team, Grey brought her to Black's attention.

She made the team on merit. She *deserved* to be there.

It was just a shame that her success depended on a man seeing past her XX chromosomes to understand she was value-added to the team.

Over the decade she'd worked for them, the CIA remained an old-boy, patriarchal, often misogynistic organization that had barely made cultural strides since the nineteen-fifties despite Director Haspel's ascendance.

Just look at the women who suffered injury and illness in the field and were cast aside in ways that the men weren't. Yes, her team had sent someone to save her. Yes, she got the medical help she needed. But what if her illness made fieldwork impossible? She would have ended up in the same straits as, say, those women who had been exposed to the Havana Syndrome shit. Many of them developed aggressive and unusual cancers.

Did the CIA stand by them? Support them? Care for them? Questionable.

No, Red was under zero illusions. She worked for the CIA, and she loved her job. They would love her and the results of her work just as long as she was still producing. And then they'd kick her to the curb.

Not her team, though. Her team was family, and she believed they had her back.

But do you have time for continued warm friendships when you spend every day trying to save the world?

Color Code would remain busy, and Red was prepared to live out her life alone.

It was a price she'd decided to pay.

But tonight? Tonight, she'd be with Grey, and they'd be waltzing.

Red had to look very different at the ball than she usually did. She needed to ensure that if she showed up on any viral royal watch feed or influencer social media, moving forward, no one would recognize her, including AI software.

Her transformation was easily accomplished with the shading and highlights of her makeup.

She'd had the salon thin her brow and create stylish arches, which changed her look. Typically, Red wore her hair in a low ponytail or simply draped over her shoulders to obscure the sides of her face. Tonight, the stylist had swept her hair into a sleek updo and sprayed it with some titanium-like hairspray, which meant no strand of hair was out of place even after napping.

Standing in front of her bathroom mirror, Red inserted chandelier earrings with man-made diamonds that looked like they were worth a fortune. They were heavy, and she wasn't used to the tug on her earlobes. But as she turned her head from side to side, Red had to admit, they looked amazing. They weren't just decorative. They were digital cameras. Technology was miraculous.

Besides that, Red would have a couple of GPS dots to press

onto Elena if possible. Tiny, she might even be able to hide one on the Fire of the Desert if she could get close enough.

Other than that, she was going in naked, equipment and weapons-wise.

Back in the bedroom, the full skirt of her red taffeta gown spread wide across the bed. The matching high heels with their pointy toes and crystal clustered embellishments lay on the carpet.

Red was sure that Grey had asked someone to "get Red a dress," and they'd heard "get a red dress" because this was very red. Very. It was a lovely red, though, she thought as she rubbed the fabric between her fingers. As far as formal wear went, she liked it. Tactically, it was an impossible gown. There would be no stealth with its rustling sound, no running with its yards of voluminous skirt, and certainly no hand-to-hand in a bodice that wouldn't allow a deep breath or sleeves that constricted her range of motion.

Fortunately, none of that really came up in her job. Dodging bombs aside—observation, contact, and manipulation were the daily skills she applied.

And this get up?

This looked as far from spy as she could get.

This looked a little *prima donna* if Red was being honest.

Good. That would make life a little easier for her tonight.

As tired as she was from her bout with typhoid, easy would be greatly appreciated.

20

———

Red

When Red was in grad school, one of the ways that she took a break from the books was playing poker. Playing for pennies was about stress relief and friendship instead of a payday. But that didn't mean that it wasn't a cut-throat game. The stakes felt real, even if they weren't.

Red, by nature, was competitive, but she liked a slow game.

She was the turtle in the "Rabbit and the Turtle Race." She liked to bide her time and make measured but steady progress. It meant fewer people noticed her success. And that always proved a good thing. She could just inch on by the pack.

While others enjoyed big-ego bluster and talking smack, Red, sitting behind a hand of cards, was quietly observing, learning, and honing her skills.

Poker taught Red to spot a bluff. She'd learned to read a whole body, where some people tried to read just the eyes. The subtle tells of body language weren't lists she'd memorized from a book or heard in a behavioral psychology class at The Farm. Red's capacity was a hard-earned knowledge from hours, days, and years of observation. Trial and error, stakes-driven outcomes, she'd learned a lot from penny-ante.

Her body language reading skills were a hallmark of those who came up through violent childhoods. And Red was forever grateful that she built this skillset purposefully and safely; it hadn't been thrust upon her.

What she read about Elena at this moment was that she was dancing with a stranger while waiting to connect with someone else.

And that stranger was *very* into the nuances of Elena.

They looked lovely together as a couple. They had parallel good looks that seemed to come from the same social upbringing. But Red would swear they were strangers.

A head taller than most in the room, this man was basketball-player-tall if he were in America. Six foot four? Five? Six maybe?

Elena was supposed to be Red's height of five foot seven, and in her heels, she came up to his chin.

His beard was shaped, and his hair was styled with product to keep the length looking romantically Prince Charming-esque. But he was too comfortable in this setting, too relaxed and graceful in his dance steps to be anyone but an elite, someone of noble birth, probably old European money.

Not security. Not a foreign intelligence officer—even Grey, who was fine in these settings when not fumbling with his bowtie, didn't have the effortless hyper-masculine grace this guy exuded.

It put Red oddly in mind of knights in shining armor riding against the dragon in service of his lady.

The really odd thing about this man was that when Red looked at him, something short-circuited in her body.

Yes, really just the strangest thing. She was utterly unprepared for this visceral reaction, having never experienced it before. She'd like to assign it to her professional grief or her recovery from either bomb blast or salmonella typhoid, but she knew that categorization was cowardice on her part. This was something else.

Handsome?

Yes, handsome. Handsome-enough. Not handsome in a way that was over the top.

He was handsome in that his tails were tailored to his body, draping beautifully over his broad shoulders, powerful arms, and long muscular legs.

Something … *Something* about him was making her go haywire, and Red was growing pissed at the distraction.

Crazily enough, she was jealous of Elena right now. Red wanted to be the one in his arms gliding over the polished floor.

Shake it off, she mentally scolded herself.

Focus in.

Red still hadn't found an opportunity to get any spyware in place. She wasn't even sure that Elena had a phone with her tonight. Elena had to get off the dance floor and move somewhere where they could bump into each other. A little sleight of hand, a few bashful apologies, and it would be a done deal.

Letting her gaze take mini sips of the environment, Red looked for where Grey had gotten himself off to. Ah, there he was, waltzing with an older woman very near Elena. Nicely done.

Steady Grey, affable Grey, deadly as hell, and dependable Grey; he was bedrock. And she needed something solid to counter the crazy effects that Elena's dance partner was having on Red's system.

The questions looped like the twirls of the dancers. Why did Red think it was *her* place to be in that man's arms, to have *her* head resting on his chest. In fact, Red felt that she had been in that place before and that this man wasn't a stranger.

There was a component of life or death, an element of gentle care.

But Red was good with faces. Hadn't she recognized the man from Moussa's office as he approached?

So weird.

As a matter of fact, Red had clocked this guy from the moment she had entered the ballroom. She and Grey moved through the doors and handed their invitation to the man in golden livery at the top of the stairs. He accepted their invitation and called out their names to announce their presence.

"The Ambassador to the United States, Mr. and Mrs. Archibald Bland."

No, Color Code hadn't tried to change the names on the invitation. It might have called attention to them from the organizers. There might have been questions that no one wanted to answer.

When Red and Grey descended the red-carpeted stairs, on a couch against the far wall directly in front of them, an elderly lady sat in a lovely emerald-green dress—demurely cut and fitted. Behind her had stood *that* man, looking attentive and companionate. And Red had thought he was probably the woman's grandson.

Their eyes caught as Red took the last step, and she would swear something sizzled between them, recognition but not. Emotion, but not. Actually, she had no definition for the exchange. He'd bent and whispered something into the woman's ear, and the grandmotherly figure looked directly at Red and Grey as she shook her head no.

Maybe Dapper Dan knew that she and Grey were not, in fact, Mr. Ambassador and Mrs. Bland.

And he'd been wiggling there in her awareness, like a brain worm, ever since.

Maybe it wasn't just her.

Red widened her perceptions.

He was attracting attention amongst the women. There was a stir of jealousy that they, too, wished to be swept around the dance floor by someone gallant enough to have this guy's skills and not use them to boost his own ego but to showcase the woman in his arms.

He was the ball's Pied Piper, mesmerizing the women with dance instead of music.

Charming, yes. But *uninteresting* to her mission unless he turned out to be part of the ring deal.

And since Elena's gaze wasn't locked on his, and she was continuously scanning, Red thought Elena was immune to the man's elegance. She was here for the deal.

Understandable. It was about forty million euros sliding into her bank account and averting a possible indictment for the murder of five men and whatever the German equivalent was to manslaughter for Dr. Klein's death.

So no, Elena wasn't distracted by him.

But he, most certainly, was fixated on Elena.

It didn't matter.

He didn't matter.

Elena was the goal.

As the last strains of the dance were played, Red watched as the man bowed and Elena curtsied. Red watched as he seemed to notice something on the floor and crouched to pick it up right near the heel of Elena's shoe.

At that moment, Grey arrived by Red's side, and she repositioned him so she could keep her eyes on Elena.

Elena's gaze was on the door that exited toward the ladies' room. The man rose fluidly, holding out his discovery. Elena touched her ear and shook her head; no, it wasn't her earring. "She's going to head to the ladies' room," Red told Grey. "Keep an eye on her in case I'm wrong. I want to get there first. Time to plant some electronics." And time to get away from this guy and his strange effect.

"Get to it," Grey said. "Good luck."

Red bent over the sink, reapplying her lipstick as Elena entered the ladies' room.

With a quick look around to see the attendant adjusting a woman's dress and smoothing the back for her, Elena pulled out her phone and texted.

Red put her lipstick back in the pocket hidden in the folds of her dress. She caught Elena's gaze in the mirror. "Pockets!" she said victoriously, feigning a French accent.

"I'm jealous," Elena said, pulling her bag forward. It hung on a black beaded chain that blended with her gown. "But in a dress cut as this one, it would not work."

"Your gown is stunning, if impractical. But who wishes to be practical on such a night as this?" Red reached into her pockets and pulled out a handkerchief, her phone, and a tiny bottle of hairspray, placing each on the counter before reaching into the other pocket to retrieve a comb. "The designers this year are not our friends. Have you noticed the waistlines? How do they expect us to breathe?" Red pretended to use the comb and spray her hair and used her hands to smooth any frizzes into place. In fact, with the salon's spray, Red wasn't sure she'd ever need to comb her hair again.

With her banter and primping, Red was trying to accomplish two things simultaneously.

She used her chandelier earrings to take pictures of the rings on Elena's hands.

And, with Red's phone lying inches from Elena's. Red pressed the side button to activate the spiderware that moved through the WIFI. Within moments, it should reach into all the crevices of Elena's world—any app, file, connection, or contact that had been accessed from Elena's phone was now accessible to Langley. That was unless Elena had protections that could thwart CIA software. And it wouldn't be helpful if this was Elena's burner phone. From the tiny scratches on the corner, Red was sure that wasn't the case.

Elena's phone pinged. She sent Red a flat-lipped, this-chat-is-over smile and moved to a stall. Red walked down to the end and entered a booth far enough away that Elena wouldn't feel crowded or, worse, followed.

Red opened her own phone expectantly.

There it was.

Spyware success. On the app's display was the phone number that had called in and the readout of voices being recorded.

Red inserted earbuds to listen, and every time Elena spoke, Red tapped the program, flagging the AI.

From this, their AI software would learn Elena's voice. Red could simply tell the program to open Elena's cell phone mic and record. The recordings were two-fold. One included the ambient sounds. In another, the AI software focused on Elena's voice and the voice she was conversing with, removing that ambient noise for clarity.

In this way, the unimportant should not distract, but the important shouldn't be overlooked—someone sidling up to Elena and passing information by a quick passing phrase, for example.

While Elena was put on hold, Red opened her photo album.

Langley had floated the idea that Color Code might be able to find a way to exchange the Fire of the Desert for a fake that Red now carried in her pocket.

Finding such an opportunity was a stretch of the imagination.

Elena would have to be roofied or something to make that possible.

Someone at Langley—certainly not Black—had cooked up that scenario. If they did switch the ring, Grey and Red were told, then the US government could message Kamal that the ring was a fake and Dr. Klein's signature was a forgery should that be the route the government chose.

The pictures showed that each of Elena's fingers was decorated with a different ring with red stones. In her body-hugging black velvet dress, Elena made this look elegant. Not a single one of those rings, in and of themselves, looked like the Fire of the Desert. One wrapped Elena's right ring finger, embellished with stones from knuckle to knuckle in a Gothic swirl that incorporated a large stone and a starburst of smaller stones. Red was convinced that the Gothic-style ring was the Fire of the Desert hugged by a ring guard.

If you didn't know, you'd never know.

Smart woman.

Clever.

Red would have to remember that about Elena.

21

Red

HAVING WAITED IN THE BATHROOM STALL UNTIL SHE WAS SURE Elena was back in the ballroom. Red followed after her, listening to a conversation between Elena and a man that the AI had labeled as Joel Brighton, Kamal's representative.

Red glanced around and almost immediately spotted Grey. Red sent a piercing glance across the room until he turned her way, and then she telegraphed that Grey should come join her.

And he started purposefully over.

Without a preamble, Red handed him a bud that he popped into his ear that was closest to the wall. He leaned his shoulder into the wall, casually swirling a martini glass. His other hand debonairly thrust into his pocket, looking like the kind of man who should be at a Great Gadsby soirée.

"I am so confused," Elena's frustrated voice was heard clearly. "Why can't we simply perform the transaction this evening? It's simple enough to do. If not here, then your hotel, for example?"

"Kamal wishes to make the circle complete. You see,

Sireen's great-grandmother Haamida and her sister tried to blend in with the local population, hiding from the Gestapo in the Marrakech Medina. Despite their best efforts, the Nazis found them, obviously. That is where the sisters were arrested, and the ring was stolen from Haamida. We know the sisters lived in the Secret Garden, *Le Jardin Secret.* You will meet Kamal there. And in the garden—which is very tranquil and beautiful after its restoration—you will hand him the ring, and he will transfer the money to your account in the currency of your choice."

"I *thought* I was here to affect the transaction."

"No. I am merely verifying that you are not playing a game."

"And if I were?"

"I would not have looked kindly on the act. And discipline would be applied so that a naughty girl would learn to act in a mannerly way." He said it in a cheeky way, as though he were commenting on an absurdity with an absurdity. But Red knew from the slight acidity that gave his last syllables their bite that he had very much meant it. His boss was not to be toyed with. "But here I find that you have refined taste, a beautiful waltz, and you are a woman who acts with integrity."

So weird, Red thought. People with too much money like Kamal were just super weird—everything was a go, and yet, Morocco? Full circle? Red was frustrated for Elena. And herself. How would Red discover where the money was going until she could follow the transactions?

Morocco?

If he wanted things to be full circle, why wouldn't Kamal simply invite his fiancée and present the ring to her in the Secret Garden? Would Sireen even know what had taken place?

What was the game here?

Red caught Grey's gaze, asking him his read on this.

Grey's read was a shrug and a twitch of the head with raised eyebrows.

"You brought the paperwork from Dr. Klein?" Joel asked.

"Of course."

"I will accept that now."

"No," Elena said.

"What, no?" Joel stopped dancing and took a step away from her.

Elena had put him back on his heel. He thought he was in control, and yet there she was exerting her power.

Yeah, Elena was a dangerous, murderous woman, but still, in this situation where everyone would be inconvenienced for the amusement of a bajillionaire, *you go, girl!*

"No," Elena repeated smoothly. "The paperwork is part of the sale. With no money for me, there is nothing tangible for you."

"But I can see it?"

"No, you would simply take it from me." She gestured down the length of her dress. "I came here to waltz, not fight. Besides, I've sent you images of the documentation so that the signature can be verified in advance. Obviously, you know that the paperwork is in order, or you would not be here talking to me now."

For whatever reason, silence had fallen between Elena and Joel.

"I'm not going to be able to switch the rings," Red whispered.

"I figured," Grey said. "I saw her hands. I think it's on the right ring finger."

"I thought the same. It's not coming off," Red said.

"I have a flight for you," Joel took Elena back in his arms and picked up his simple box step, "for tomorrow morning. You will fly from Vienna to Amsterdam, then to Casablanca, and from there to Marrakesh."

"Why such a round about route?" Her voice was suddenly suspicious.

"There were no direct flights available from Vienna to Morocco. But it's all first class. And you'll have comfortable accommodations in the Medina for tomorrow night. I'm sending you the information now."

"That will have to do." She sighed.

They continued their boxed step, though they dropped their hands to pull out their phones.

"If I must. I must."

Red opened the tracking app and waited for a moment, then watched as the airline and hotel information dropped into an encrypted messaging app bypassed by the CIA spyware.

Grey leaned over the top, reading it upside down. "Send that to Langley, have them get you on those planes in any way they need to. You are going to befriend Elena. We need to figure out a cover story to make that happen. Something beyond, 'Oh! What a coincidence. Are you going to Marrakech, too?'"

Red lifted her brows. She had nothing. "Any ideas?"

Both stopped talking as the conversation began again between Elena and Joel. "When you go to the gardens for the exchange, please be dressed beautifully. Kamal wants to receive the ring and be able to tell the story at his wedding party. The story is as important to him as—well, maybe not *as* important as the ring itself— but the story from the 1920s over the century, through love, pain, loss … Yes, Kamal enjoys a good plot arc in his stories. And this is how he wants things to play out. There will be a videographer."

"No," Elena said, quiet but firm.

"What, no?" Joel's brow crisscrossed with lines.

"Hire an actress to reenact the scene. I will not be partici- pating in a video. That would make me a mark for anyone who wants to try to steal my money. I worked hard for it. I need it to pay my team. And I am *not* going to pay for security for the rest of my life."

"No?" Joel dipped her low. From that vulnerable position, he looked down into her face when he asked, "And what do you plan to do with this new wealth?"

Elena waited until she was lifted upright once more, then laughed lightly. "I will luxuriate in beauty."

"You mentioned a team?"

"Do you think I found the object on my own? I had a team of treasure hunters."

"Are they here?" Joel's gaze scanned over the room.

"My team? I don't know how it would make any difference to you one way or another."

As Red heard that in her ear, she thought the group of men she spotted circling Elena all evening made a lot more sense. She had counted four, possibly five.

The Pied Piper guy didn't quite fit with the others. But he was one of a handful that circled Elena. Red had almost convinced herself it was Kamal's security. Kamal would have enough money to pay someone to stay home that night so they could access the much-sought-after tickets.

Did Elena have that kind of cash and connection, too?

Now, Red was assessing the idea of Elena on a deadly team. Elena was probably in her early thirties. Like most thirty-something women she'd met, Elena took her exercise routines seriously.

How seriously? "I want to be strong and healthy" seriously or "prepared to go hand to hand, trained for military missions" seriously?

Was she just there to hire the shooters and saunter onto the scene to take control of the briefcase containing the Fire of the Desert? Or was she the leader of the pack with sharp enough teeth and claws that she was able to take down anyone and everyone who stood in her way?

Red's mind went to the movies she'd seen about Russians who took control of beautiful girls who they trained as special agents with feats of incredible (and off-screen impossible) gravitation-be-damned acrobatics, killing a whole platoon as she raced down the stairs.

Red tried to imagine that of Elena, but she wasn't sure.

Luckily, in a setting like this, with her mission being to "follow the ring," Red's job was to absolutely not get into a fight with the lovely Elena.

Red turned her attention to the grandmotherly woman with her chin drooped to her chest, sitting upright but asleep on the sofa. She hadn't budged.

And there behind her was Pied Piper.

Their eyes locked momentarily.

He'd clocked *her* and not Grey.

She was on his radar.

In Red's experience, if this exchange happened as a romantic overture, the man immediately slid his gaze to her dance partner to see if they had noticed. To see if they made some physical display of dominance or possession, a puffed chest, or physically turning to block the visual path to the woman.

Pied Piper didn't do that. His eyes were on her. She got nothing else—not curiosity, not interest, not a decision to invite her to dance next.

Nope. He was as stoic as a seasoned operator when he locked in on her face. He'd remember who she was later.

Why would that matter?

Why. Would. That. Matter?

It mattered. Red was sure of it.

22

———

Nomad

RED HAUNTED NOMAD'S THOUGHTS.

Ever since he'd looked through the window of that Lebanese hotel, something about that woman had caught hold of him. That sensation stayed with him even as her ambulance roared away amidst flashing lights and blaring sirens. There, left standing in the shadows, Nomad felt raw and strangely directionless.

Command deemed the mission a success because the team met their objective: Find Johnna Red and get her back into American hands.

Nomad didn't know, from her point of view, if Red would consider the mission successful or not.

Had the operation prioritized institutional needs over basic human care by insisting they avoid Lebanese doctors and hospitals?

Had she survived those choices?

Yeah, ever since he'd watched the ambulance pull away

from him, the only word that seemed close to describing his emotions was bereft.

Wasn't that funny?

Not only that but now Nomad found himself looking for her. It was as if she was near, and he should have been able to reach out and touch her and take her back into his arms.

He was seeing Red in the women in his sphere.

Long black hair caught his attention, full lips. Anyone around five foot seven.

Even that woman who had descended the stairs under the name Mrs. Bland brought Red to mind. Nomad was simply associating the code name with the beautiful red gown that drew his attention to Mrs. Bland like a spotlight.

Not-Mrs. Bland.

Frau Leitner said the woman wasn't, in fact, the U.S. ambassador's wife, and the man offering his arm wasn't Ambassador Bland.

"Who do you think they are?" Nomad had asked. Perhaps other socialites had traded something of significance for the tickets.

Frau Leitner sent him a secretive smile.

Yes, she knew who they were. Maybe it was just the number of ears around them that made her keep those names to herself. He'd press her later when he was driving her home.

Frau Leitner was a date that required little of him. She'd been napping on the sofa almost from the beginning. Nomad had felt free to function, though he kept an eye on her.

Nomad had danced with Elena three different times. She danced effortlessly and wordlessly while her mind was clearly elsewhere. She seemed to be using him as a means to keep moving. And he thought she was either looking for someone or actively avoiding someone.

Though he'd made no headway as a honeypot, he'd try not to let that bruise his ego.

Throughout the evening, there was only one man that she might have connected with. They'd pulled out their phones and seemed to be following each other's social media or maybe even getting each other's phone numbers. But they only danced the one dance and ignored each other the rest of the evening. On the other hand, Nomad spotted plenty of eyes following Elena. There were not-Ambassador and Mrs. Bland, though that was really subtle, and again, Nomad might just be extra attracted to the color red right now. There was a group of four men that he thought might be her security by the way they formed a box and kept their rabbit inside of it.

As for rings? She had one on every finger. None of them looked particularly remarkable to him. But rings weren't really Nomad's expertise.

The one thing he'd accomplished was the application of various electronics to Elena's shoes, rings, dress, and tiara. Each dance, more electronics.

He worried he was underperforming because he was so distracted by that low-level hum of worry about Red. It irritated Nomad that he couldn't clear his mind of her. It was his own fault for becoming emotionally invested. He had never held precious cargo against him before. Nomad used the phrase that was supposed to keep the survivors at arm's length, but in this instance, it was too late in the game for that to help. During rescues and extractions, he'd tended to people with vigilance, but there was a difference between caring for them and *caring* for them in all the definitions of that word.

Red was messing with his circuitry.

She was making him see ghosts. He had no idea who that woman in the red gown was. But since she seemed to be circling Elena all evening, Nomad gave himself permission to approach her when it seemed natural to find out if she spoke English with an accent, to cleanse his pallet of the niggling desire to be physically close to her. He thought if he could just verify that this was no one of interest, he could refocus.

Nomad tapped the comms button that he'd placed under his lapel and connected with the encrypted channel patched into the command center. "Glad you're checking in," T-Rex said. "From the photos you've been sending in, we've made an interesting connection for you to be aware of."

"Listening." Standing in a shadow shielded by a column, Nomad's gaze settled on Elena, fixing herself in the mirror and the absolute uniqueness of the woman dressed like a feathery egg.

"The photos of Elena's dance partners are of no consequence except for one. His name is Joel Brighton. He's the right-hand man of Zayd Ali Kamal."

"Middle Eastern multi-billionaire."

"That's the one. Zayd Ali Kamal became engaged last year. At that time, he set up a reward for anyone who could find his fiancée's great-grandmother's ring. It's a two-carat red diamond stolen from the family by the Gestapo in Morocco during WWII."

"That's the ring? Elena found it?"

"Possibly. Or perhaps she's the middleman."

"How big is that prize?" Nomad asked. "It's got to be substantial."

"Forty million euros."

Forty million could fund extremism in a big way. "She has red rings on all her fingers. One of them could be it. Or she might have handed it to this Joel guy already."

T-Rex said. "Asad and his team at the DIA are monitoring the mic you placed before their dance. Outstanding effort."

It didn't feel like an outstanding effort to Nomad. It was

pretty rudimentary stuff. "Should I get the rings? Or is the plan still to entice the woman? Because I'm going to be straight with you. I don't seem to be her type."

"It's being debated by the brass. Right now, the job is to keep eyes on."

"Speaking of which, I'm not the only one interested in this woman. Do you know this couple?"

Nomad pulled his phone from his pocket and held it by his leg as he pulled up a photo of the not-ambassador and the back of the woman in red. He'd tried a few times to get not-Mrs. Bland in a photo, but it seemed she had a sixth sense and kept her face averted.

"I can't tell from the woman's back, but the guy is John Grey from the Color Code," T-Rex said as soon as the photo pinged into his messages. "Interesting that you're in the same sphere."

"And focused on the same woman. I mean, he's subtle, but once you've seen how a magic trick is performed, you know how the CIA handles their rabbits."

So that was the legendary John Grey, pulled from the upper cell of a prison before his secrets could be tortured out of him.

"Grey," Nomad pitched his voice so that it could be picked up by his comms but wouldn't carry to others around him, "He's good people? Trustworthy?"

"All his team were handpicked for skill and ethic," T-Rex explained.

"Should I let him know I'm here?"

"Not the assignment," T-Rex said. "You do you."

"Right now, I've accomplished Plan A. The electronics have been planted. Elena's obviously working tonight and focused. I'm not going to be able to offer to whisk her away on my helicopter into the sunset. I think we need to take that off the table. What's our next move?"

Colonel Watts's voice joined the conversation. "I'll have the DIA reach out to the Color Code leader at Langley and see if they'll tell us why Grey is at the ball. If the CIA, Interpol, or anyone else is interested in Elena, you might need to get more aggressive. We need Elena more. Poole is *our* guy. We need *our* questions answered without dicking around."

"Copy." He was in Vienna, Austria. What did Watts mean by 'get more aggressive?' "Wilco."

"For now," Colonel Watts finished, "keep an eye on Elena. We'll work out a strategy and get back to you."

23

———

Red

After Elena's dance partner bowed to kiss her hand. "*Enchanté,*" the murmured word came over the earbud in Red's ear. The man had been counting steps under his breath the whole time—one, two, three. One, two, three. There had been no chatter. Red had learned nothing new about Elena.

As Elena rose from her curtsy, her dance partner lost himself in the crowd. Dancers shifted, some moving off the floor like Elena, others moving into place as a violinist drew her bow along the string, testing a C note.

And now Elena stopped, facing the wall in front of a woman wearing a dress constructed from an enormous cloud of white feathers that seemed improbably difficult—and hot—to dance in. That woman was both the chicken and the egg.

Elena wasn't speaking to cloud woman. Instead, she focused over the woman's shoulder into the surface of a gilded mirror, using the reflection to adjust her dress strap and then a tendril of hair curling down her cheek to the delicate bones of her clavicle, softening the austerity of her French chignon.

With a tilt of her chin, Elena scanned the entirety of the room.

Suddenly, she visibly braced. Red would swear Elena had stopped breathing. Her brows drew upward, and she held her eyes wide and unblinking. It was a survival reaction.

Elena had transformed into a mouse by the chair leg as a cat slunk through the room.

She was terrified.

Red decided to take the risk of moving her focus off Elena to scan the room and see if she couldn't find the person who had elicited this reaction.

Ah, not one, four.

Here were the men that Red had been aware of all evening —the ones that Red had thought were probably on Elena's team, possibly the ones she had alluded to in her chat with Joel Brighton.

But now that a benign understanding of the situation was off the table, Red had questions.

Tonight's ball was tightly secured. The event security team had blocked the road in front of the venue.

Car keys were handed off to valets and guests had to approach on foot.

The tickets were sold out on the first night they were offered, and availability was a year in advance. It had taken a phone call from the United States Secretary of State to the ambassador to pry the tickets that Red and Grey were using from covetous fingers.

Elena was Joel's plus-one.

Who was chasing after Elena if this wasn't her security team?

And how did they have the wherewithal to get in?

By the time these thoughts passed through Red's mind, she'd captured all four of their images both on her earring cams and in her memory and swung her focus back toward the mirror.

But Elena was gone.

Red took three backward steps up the staircase, out of the press of the crowd, to gain height and possibly a better view.

Elena's tiara bobbed as she quickly wove through the crowd, a viper amongst the weeds.

And there was that Pied Piper guy, tall enough that he was easy to spot, moving in the same direction as Elena, looking nonchalant. But there was purpose to his movement. He was caught by a crowd that formed in front of him, and there was no easy way for him to continue to follow without seeming extremely rude. He backtracked to find a different route.

Elena made it to the staircase, brushing past Red without a second glance. And behind her came the group of men. They had fanned out in the room, but now they drew together like a net capturing prey.

Red watched as Elena turned into the hallway, not to the left toward the ladies' room but to the right, where the caterers staged the trays of hors d'oeuvres and drinks for the waitstaff to circulate. Beyond that was the kitchen.

Elena could probably find a way to escape out into the back alley.

Red was momentarily unsure what to do.

There was hidden security here at the ball. There had to be. These were the elite of the elite. Royalty, for Heaven's sake. But that security blended into the evening so everyone could simply enjoy. It was one of the ball's calling cards. Freedom from their ubiquitous security detail was much coveted.

So, were these men part of the ball-sanctioned security?

No, Elena wouldn't recognize them as a threat.

Possibly Interpol?

After all, Elena wasn't just involved in selling conflict relics, but she'd been on the scene of five men's deaths when they were sniped in Munich. Had someone besides Color Code and their CIA assets figured that out?

It would be unlikely that Interpol would send anyone that Elena might recognize.

If Red were to insert herself into a security scenario, the very least that would happen would be a blown cover.

What if the waitstaff were all members of elite forces? Could happen. Why not?

Red could be wrong about her interpretation of the unfolding scene, but she had over a decade of fieldwork under her belt. And she read people very well.

Reading Elena—she was afraid she would be killed, slowly, painfully, while giving up every piece of information she knew or made up just to make the pain stop. The fear Red saw wasn't worry about a quick bullet to the brainstem. Uh-uh. No. It just wasn't. She'd seen enough people in enough of these scenarios —there was a reactionary difference. When the person knew they lived in a dangerous world and played a dangerous game, death was often met with a sense of inevitability and resignation.

Play stupid games, win stupid prizes.

It was torture that turned someone into a wild animal.

And the men?

Their faces weren't set with determination to meet the moment and finish a mission.

Those were the expressions of men who wanted to exact vengeance.

If Red was forced to define those four men and make a call on what was happening, she'd stake her reputation that they were part of the treasure-hunting group that had successfully found the Fire of the Desert and taken it to Dr. Klien for identification. Five of them should have been sufficient to maintain control of the ring. Any more, and it would have gone negative in terms of attention and pressure on Klein.

Yes, Red believed these were the four that were left behind.

Their teammates dead, their work vanished, they wanted the ring, and they wanted retribution.

If they had the skill to find the ring, they had the skill to find Elena. In doing so, they'd probably come to the same conclusion as Color Code: that the ball was a public opportunity. Otherwise, she'd go to ground and finding her would be all but impossible.

This team was singularly focused.

And so was Red.

They just had very different needs.

Red needed to know the plan for the forty million euros.

Where was their target?

What was their message, and what would have been their gain if the terrorist event had been successful?

Red would get none of that if anyone hurt a hair on Elena's beautifully coiffed head.

Reaching for the front of her dress, lifting it, and moving her hands to the rear of her hips, she tried to free herself of the cumbersome lawn of skirt. The ridiculousness and look-at-me red of this gown impeded Red's ability to function.

What was she going to do?

Red had no idea. Just getting in the same space was the goal at this moment.

Once there, she could see what options presented themselves. Screaming at the top of her lungs, for example, would pull every eye and every resource forward.

But as she screamed, Elena could use that opportunity to slip into the night.

That might not be a bad choice, Elena's escaping since Red

knew what flight she was taking to Marrakech, and Red had full access to Elena's phone.

It made more sense for Elena to refuse to make this silly trip to Morocco that Joel Brighton proposed. Reaching out privately, Elena could explain that she wasn't playing games, that there was money for the ring, or the ring would disappear again. She had leverage.

Scenarios presented, were processed at lightning speed, and set aside as Red made her way through the revelers with a pointy elbow held up like the bow of a ship, forcing the tide of glitterati to shift out of her way.

Damned stupid time for Grey to have had to go to the bathroom.

Red wanted to pull out her phone and tap the button to let him know this was an emergency, zip up his pants, and get here. Now! But the time and distraction of looking down was a price that Red wouldn't pay.

This event wasn't supposed to turn kinetic. Red and Grey hadn't come with comms taped to their sternums lest their voices be picked up on security radios or seen on scanning machines at the front door.

Maybe it was a mistake to come ill-prepared for things turning FUBAR.

And if—*if*—Red couldn't help her, and Elena didn't get away from this team, Color Code could track her via phone and a GPS Grey had placed on Elena's dress.

But surely these men knew enough to toss the phone and force Elena to change clothes.

And then what? And *then* what?

Red's mission was to keep Elena in play. Anything less would be a failure. *I don't do failure,* she growled in her mind as she reached the last man on the team with enough time to grab an empty party tray. Using the swing toward the man's carotid, dragging the long edge of the rim slowly down his artery, depriving his brain of blood flow, he dropped into a heap, unconscious.

Three instead of four, that would be a short-lived reprieve. The man would quickly revive.

Red, of course, carried no weapons, or she wouldn't have made it through the X-ray machine. Here, the kitchen was filled with possibilities, but that worked both ways; a knife in her hand was a cleaver in theirs.

Bursting through the doors, Red found a kidnapping underway.

A man on either side of Elena gripped her arms above her wrists, dragging her toward the back door held wide by the third tango. The man at the door pointed a gun at the kitchen staff, who were cowering together in the back corner in confusion and fright.

He wouldn't aim or fire at Red. First, even with his silencer, it would make noise and pull attention. Second, he'd have to be a damned good shot because his teammates and Elena were grappling between them. A hand clamped around her mouth, muffling her screams.

The gasps from the kitchen workers dragged the gunman's attention their way, allowing Red to grab a cloth and wrap it around the handle of a cast iron skillet. Lifting it high, food flying out, Red brought the pan squarely down on the head of the goon holding Elena's left arm. Red failed to knock the guy out cold. Dazed, he sprawled on the floor, but his grip hadn't loosened.

As he fell, Red set up for her next swing.

To protect Elena from being hit, Red spun, gripping the handle like a tennis racket, the heat from the cast iron now burning her palms.

While the standing man maintained his grip on Elena, he threw up a middle block to protect his own head.

The cracking noise was nauseating. She did some damage to his forearm. Maybe even broke it.

But the men didn't let go of their quarry. The man on the ground dragged Elena toward the floor. The standing man held Elena upright. She was like a tug toy in the jaws of two alpha dogs.

Red tried to spin again to take another swing at the standing man.

But the guy on the ground had been gathering the cloth of Red's gown, and when she spun, she effectively trussed herself in the fabric.

The swing still landed. But it lost its oomph. Red fell, taking Elena and the standing man down with her.

The gunman kept his gun on the kitchen staff. There were too many of them for him to lose control because of a woman with a skillet.

The man that Red had taken out with the tray was back on the scene. He grabbed Elena under the arms, bodily lifted her into the air, and went out the back door.

The man on her left clawed up a fistful of Red's hair as he stood and dragged her out the back door.

There, a catering truck stood with yawning doors. A plastic tarp lined the floor. Above was a pipe. Someone had developed this catering van as a mobile interrogation site.

With the light from the alley shining into the van, Red focused on a pile of four bodies, naked but for their undershorts, heaped at the back. And now Red knew a few things.

She knew how this team had thwarted security—dressing as catering staff, coming in with boxes or bags with their evening wear, and changing surreptitiously.

She knew they were deadly, brutal, and mad as hell.

Red knew Grey had no idea she was no longer in the ballroom, waiting for him by the stairs.

And she knew that if something wildly improbable didn't happen, Red would be subjected to whatever was coming Elena's way.

The man whose arm dangled at an improbable angle—*yup, broken. Shit.* Held a gun on her.

If Red thought they'd take a kill shot, she might opt to go that route.

But no. The gun, with the silencer, was aimed at her leg. They'd just add shooting her until she looked like Swiss cheese to one of their questioning techniques.

Miracles happened. Red tried to reassure herself as the men first attached Elena and then moved on to attach Red to the overhead pipe. The thick riot-style zip ties ratcheted tightly and wouldn't be easy to thwart.

Before losing the ability, Red took every opportunity to snap pictures with her earring, knowing they would flow to Color Code computers. Her team would have pictures of these faces, the van, and the circumstances.

Someone could avenge her.

The man from the door, the only one Red hadn't hit, took Elena's purse from her. They patted her over and found nothing more.

Red was next, her pockets emptied of comb and hairspray, lipstick and phone. She watched the fake Fire of the Desert fall to the ground unheeded.

The doors slammed.

Elena and Red were alone in the back of the windowless van.

Surely, the kitchen staff were raising the alarm. When they did, the police would swarm.

Surely, Grey was done in the damned bathroom. As he came

down the hallway, he'd see the stunned and confused catering staff racing out of the kitchen. He'd check his app and see the phones in the alley where Red imagined the team had tossed them. It wouldn't help Grey to find her, but it would let him know to look. And Langley had systems for that.

Miracles happened.

She just needed to survive and keep Elena alive until they did.

In the darkness, Red heard Elena whisper, "Who are you?"

24

Nomad

N OMAD HAD WATCHED E LENA TAKE FLIGHT THROUGH THE ballroom.

Not-Mrs. Bland had been right on her heels. Though she stayed in character, to his eye, she was definitely racing after Elena. What Nomad couldn't tell was if it not-Mrs. Bland was a menace or a help to Elena.

Getting to them had been a game of bumper cars as he dodged the now very tipsy revelers.

By the time Nomad got to the hall and pressed through the kitchen door, he found the staff huddled in the back corner, sobbing and yelling. Quickly enough, he understood two women had been kidnapped at gunpoint.

There was a blood smear on the floor. Some blood, but not a life-threatening amount.

"Who was bleeding?" Nomad demanded.

"One woman fought and failed. They dragged them away." She pointed to the exit. Nomad grabbed the handle and yanked the door wide. The alley was empty. "How many people were taken?"

"Two women," the chef said, climbing to his feet, cookie sheet shield grasped in his hands.

"How many dragged the women away?"

There was a conference as they worked out the number. "Four," a woman said. Three fighters and another one with a long gun." But she drew her hands out in a way that Nomad understood she didn't mean it was a rifle but a gun that was longer than usual. The gunman had a silencer.

"What were these women wearing?" Nomad asked just to be sure Elena was in the mix.

"Slim black dress. There's her tiara."

Nomad turned in the direction of the woman's pointed finger. Yes, that belonged to Elena.

"And then a big red dress. She was the lady who fought," the woman continued.

"She knew how to fight," a man said. "She knew what she was doing."

"Broke that one man's arm with the skillet."

"Yes, that's right. She broke his arm. The blood on the floor was from the other man." The woman reached up and touched the back of her head, where Nomad assumed the kidnapper had been hit.

"But the man with the gun … She could not stop that," the chef concluded.

Another man was on his feet. "One of our catering vans was out there, but I heard the motor start, and they drove away."

"There's nothing out there now. Can you describe the van to me?" Time was ticking. Nomad needed to be on the move. "Do you have a picture? The license plate number?"

"Yes. Yes. We took a picture of us as we were unloading that one." He held up his phone, and Nomad took a picture of the image, turned, and ran out of the kitchen, down the hall, up the stairs, and out the front door.

A valet pulled up as Nomad leaped down the steps toward the street. Nomad looked over his shoulder to see an elderly couple descending the granite stairs. Nomad raced around the front of the sedan. "Excuse me," he said, pressing the valet out of his way. "I just need to adjust." Nomad toggled the seat's motor, moving the driver's chair toward the rear as far as it would go. He pressed another toggle to lean the seat back as far as it would go.

The man on the stairs raised his cane. "You there. Hey, you there!"

The valet realized that something was amiss and reached for Nomad's arm. "There's and emergency inside," Nomad said as he thrust the valet away. This provided enough space and distraction to accordion-fold into the vehicle.

Nomad would never be one of those badasses that ran up to a car, threw himself behind the wheel, and took off with squealing tires. His frame just wasn't made for such things.

Squeezed into the small space, Nomad pulled up the GPS on his phone, tracking one of the electronics he'd placed on Elena throughout their dances. As he tore down the block, he tried to figure out where the truck might be going so he could get out in front of them. There wasn't much maneuverability in this older area of Vienna with its narrow streets.

Twice, he had thought he could guess their trajectory and tried to position himself to intercept, but then the van's path changed. Nomad hadn't put eyes on the van in this cat-and-mouse chase. The only reason he knew he wasn't chasing a decoy was that there were too many trackers placed on Elena—her shoes, dress, purse, tiara (still in the kitchen)—for all of them to have been found and a plan constructed to send him on a chase.

Nomad called it in to command.

"Get her out of there," came Colonel Watts's command. "I don't care how. Just do it."

Nomad had already decided that was his tack. Elena had answers between her ears. And the Pentagon needed to know what they were.

"There you are," he growled as he wove through the sparse late-evening traffic, moving up fast. He knew the driver had spotted him when the van took a sudden tire-squealing sharp left. The driver pressed the gas to juice the maneuver, making his backend fishtail.

"Tactical techniques perform differently in cars and delivery vans, my man," Nomad said. He'd use that to his advantage. Nomad gunned his car, feeling the latent power of a German-made engine. This was tricky business. The goal here was to stop the vehicle in such a way that he could maintain Elena's safety and extract her from the hands of four kidnappers with at least one gun. And then there was Grey's date, the not-Mrs. Bland. She had to be on the good guy team. Right?

Other possibilities surfaced, such as Grey being the honeypot guy playing some role in her sphere.

Never assume.

As they moved up the road, doubling the speed in a residential neighborhood and dodging around the slower cars, Nomad heard the sirens.

Nomad edged up on the speeding vehicle. He was going to have to tap the bumper and spin the van. When he was weapons-ready, that was a no-brain decision. He was hesitant under these circumstances. Which was the bigger risk, stopping her here or waiting until the van reached its destination?

The van's occupants must have heard the sirens, too. The driver's foot became lead as he dragged the wheel sharply to the left, trying to make a last-second turn onto a ramp.

Take the risk.

Nomad pressed the gas and made a looser turn onto the ramp, hitting the far corner of the van's bumper. It was enough impact to jar him, but he'd carefully positioned that strike so as not to set off his airbags. Immediately, he pulled his foot off the gas, letting the steep incline slow his speed rather than jamming on the brake.

Nomad pulled to the side and forced his body out of the car.

Already in a left-hand, over-juiced turn, Nomad's tap had been enough to send the van into a wild ride around and around until it came to rest against the wall, trapping the passenger side door shut.

Nomad, already in motion, reached into the trunk, grabbed a tire iron, and sprinted across the street. A mighty swing at the driver's side window broke the glass as the driver threw himself to the side to dodge the blow.

Nomad punched the dazed driver in the temple, and he collapsed against the man in the middle.

The middle guy held up a protective hand to block the strike coming his way. *What a useless waste of energy.* Nomad put his lights out.

The third guy was trapped by the door and his companions. He wasn't going to get in Nomad's way.

Stalking to the back of the van, he found the door unlocked. He positioned himself so a bullet wouldn't easily find him.

Inside, someone was screaming in agony.

With a tactical cleansing breath and the tire iron ready to swing into action, Nomad threw the doors wide.

Elena's wrists were bound to a pipe overhead. There were bodies in underwear strewn across the floor surrounding a man, a screaming man.

Not-Mrs. Bland was also zip-tied to the pipe.

Nomad followed her body down her leg to her foot, where

her high heel stabbed into the man's palm with her full weight. A gun with a silencer rested between her feet.

Damn, that was some badassery right there.

Nomad pulled off his formal dress pump and retrieved a razor blade hidden in the cavity of his heel, along with the other pre-positioned survival objects. He quickly stepped into his shoe and climbed into the back, his focus on the woman in red. She was the wild card. "Are you okay?"

"Fine. Just, you know, hanging out." She rattled her hands on the pipe.

Nomad sawed the thick plastic of the military-style zip-ties holding Elena trapped. Elena stared up at him wide-eyed.

"Hi. Do you remember me? We danced together a few times tonight." He used the timbre of his voice to soothe her, hoping that she would trust him and come away quietly.

Elena was white and shaking.

"Just hold still, I'm going to get you down. All right?"

She answered with shivering nods.

After releasing Elena from the pipe, Nomad took her full weight against him as he held her up. Her knees weren't locking. She dangled like the ragdoll that Rory liked to hug when he was sleeping on his doggy bed.

The police were one street over. They'd be within sight soon. Elena was his mission.

Nomad pressed the razor blade into not-Mrs. Bland's fingers. "You're okay?"

Pinching the razor, she stammered, "Yes, I—" She seemed astonished that he wasn't going to rescue her.

Instead, he'd squatted down, draped Elena over his shoulder, and carried her out the back of the truck, around to the passenger seat of the stolen car, and set her inside.

After slamming the door and racing around to the driver's

side, things slowed as he folded himself under the steering wheel again.

Putting the car in motion, he reached an arm across Elena, grabbed the belt, and strapped her in safely.

He tapped his lapel to open comms, knowing T-Rex would listen to the update. "Elena, they kidnapped you. I'm glad to get you back."

Elena turned toward him with a slack-jawed frown. "Who *are* you?"

25

———

Nomad

Here I go, figuring out a creative solution. Nomad sent a quick glance Elena's way.

Clearly in shock, she hugged herself and trembled.

That was okay by Nomad. As soon as she got her wits about her, she'd start asking questions and making demands.

If she asked to get out of the car, and he refused, it would be kidnapping.

He decided to stay on the highway and keep his speed up so they didn't hit a stop where she might try to jump out of the car.

He was still waiting on his orders.

And now, Elena was pulling herself together.

Wing it. "I'm undercover security," Nomad said softly but authoritatively. "I'm sorry those men got as far as they did. That shouldn't have happened. It was our duty to protect you, Elena."

"Me?" She pulled her chin back. "How do you know my name?"

Glancing quickly her way, Nomad realized his two mistakes.

He'd said her name when she hadn't introduced herself that evening. And he'd saved her and left the other woman zip-tied in the van. He'd lean on his training to get out of this mess— obfuscate and then hand her the reins. "It is my duty to create a safe environment this evening. How do I know your name? It's listed on the security roll. We took pictures as the guests came through the checkpoint. We're aware of everyone who attended the ball." He sent her a smile. "My turn; do you know who that other woman was back in the truck with you?"

"No." Elena shook her head vigorously. "I mean, she tried to help me. But no. I have no idea who she is. I think she maybe wanted to rob me of my ring." She folded one hand over the other. On each finger, Elena wore various sizes of red-stoned rings. No one had stolen them from her. Nomad had no idea which one was the ring she'd hoped to sell. But she had absolutely used the singular in that sentence.

"Your ring?" He shot her a glance that he hoped read as confused. "Of all the jewels in the room tonight, why would she want your ring?"

"Oh." She tucked her hands under her thighs. "I don't know. I simply can't imagine another reason for her ... Unless she ..." Elena turned her head to look out the back window. "Wait, you asked me if I knew her. I don't. Why don't you know her name when you know mine?"

"Her name is Mrs. Bland," Nomad said evenly. "I asked if *you* knew her. I never said that I didn't." Nomad thought that played smoothly. "But what was that thought you just had?"

"I was at the ball this evening to speak to a man about an important business transaction. I noticed that this woman was paying attention to him. She seemed to be consistently in his vicinity, shadowing him but looking around him, not at him. I'm thinking," Elena's gaze was on her lap, but she was clearly reimagining the ball, "Yes, I'm quite sure she must be part of his security. And that makes sense, doesn't it?" Elena looked over at Nomad, eyebrows pulling tightly together. "He would want to ensure my safety until we've completed the transaction."

Nomad decided that he should align with this thought process. Let her see that he was in lockstep with her. "There are places that a woman goes that a man cannot. So a female undercover—"

Elena cut him off. "And he would have been right to care for me this way. I was heading to the ladies' room when the men grabbed me. They held a knife to my ribs and forced me down the hallway to the kitchen. I thought that once I was in the kitchen, guards would be at the back door to help me. But they were not."

"And this woman?" Nomad asked.

"Yes, she came behind me, bursting through the doors. She threw a pan at one of the men holding me, and it hit him in the head. Did you see her dress? Her shoes? So impractical." Elena pinched her bottom lip. "And yet there she was fighting them. Fighting to get me free from them. She broke one of the men's arms. I heard it crack. I thought I was going to vomit." Elena pulled her hands up to cover her face. Speaking into her palms, she said, "The kitchen staff crouched on the ground, holding pans over their heads to protect themselves. She was succeeding. I thought she would get me free even if there was a man by the back door with a gun." Elena dropped her hands and faced Nomad. "You're security? You are part of the ball's security?"

"Security," Nomad said.

"But you didn't know her? I mean beyond her name."

"She's not on my team." Yeah, he didn't know how to play this scene. He simply didn't have enough information. Elena might be right about Kamal sending personal protection to cover her. That would make all the sense in the world, except for the impracticality of her red dress and high heels. Okay, he'd try this, "It sounds reasonable that the person who invited you to the ball would—"

As they drove, in his rearview, Nomad spotted a car suddenly speeding up, moving to the right of a truck already in the righthand lane. Now, all three vehicles vied for the same limited space between the walls of the underpass. The other car's driver blared his horn which echoed off the cement.

The truck driver must have startled and tried to pull away from an accident with her but over-corrected, shrieking to a stop just before he hit the wall in front of Nomad.

In his mind, it was slow motion, and that move was both ballsy and genius.

"Brace!" he yelled.

They were flung forward and back again as Nomad slammed on the brakes, bringing them to a sudden and complete stop. Elena screamed and flailed her arms. One of her rings caught on his face. As the truck came to rest directly in their path, Nomad felt the bite of the prongs slashing his forehead.

The person driving the truck applied their brakes, bringing them to a sudden shrieking stop.

The other car that put him in this tactical configuration was now in front of the truck.

The truck rested diagonally across the underpass, blocking any forward movement on this highway.

Nomad's stolen vehicle was a hair's breadth from the wall.

Not a single vehicle was damaged.

Not a single person hurt.

But just like with the van accident earlier, Nomad could not open his door. He couldn't back up for the traffic piling up behind him. And he certainly couldn't find a way out of the passenger's side because of his size. He was trapped.

A tickle of blood dripped down his cheek.

Nomad watched with zero surprise as not-Mrs. Bland approached their car, her voluminous skirt piled over her arm, exposing shapely legs. She was like something out of Hollywood, and Nomad felt compelled to give her a round of applause. Instead, he pulled a handkerchief from his pocket.

Not-Mrs. Bland opened the door, crouching down to be eye-to-eye with Elena. "Thank goodness!" she said, all care and concern. She reached over and unclasped Elena's seatbelt. "I've got you. You're safe now, Elena." She handed Elena a phone.

Elena stared at it with confusion, then looked up to catch not-Mrs. Bland's gaze. "Thank you for getting this back to me."

Now, the woman in red was close enough that Nomad could see heavy bruising up the side of her legs.

Nomad's heart pounded in his chest.

Was it possible?

He stared hard at her in the partial glow of the overhead light, trying to see past any CIA-taught makeup skills.

Then he snapped himself back to reality. He didn't know who this woman was. *Elena* was his mission. How could he keep control?

He didn't grab at Elena or try to stop this. It would have been illegal and also pointless. Men trapped in the traffic jam behind him would climb from their cars and intervene. The best he could do was let Elena go and track her to the next site with the trackers he'd planted.

Nomad pressed his handkerchief to staunch the blood flow before it hit his white shirt. He did have to go back and retrieve Frau Leitner.

Elena was obviously weighing the situation. He had saved her, and the woman in red had fought to save her. In the end, Nomad imagined her reasoning that not-Mrs. Bland was connected to the ring and Kamal, while Nomad was event security. She made the decision that Nomad would have made; she went willingly with the woman in red.

Holding Elena's hand, not-Mrs. Bland leaned in and pointed at his wound. "You're good, right?"

He felt the rebuke like the sting of a whip's lash. He felt like an utter cad.

The truck driver apologized, corrected the truck on the road, and continued with his night. Nomad drove back to the city where he parked the car a few miles from the gala, found a taxi on the cross street, and gave them an address around the corner from the ball.

Hard to hide where he was heading; he was wearing a penguin suit.

After dabbing his forehead to ensure he hadn't started bleeding again, Nomad paid the taxi in cash and walked toward the ball. He was surprised that there weren't police cars everywhere. He had some guesses as to why. The Society had a great deal of pull and would handle things quietly. Their guests should not be upset, and the paparazzi would have no access to pictures or stories.

But they wouldn't know about the dead bodies yet. This event wasn't going to go quietly into the night.

It was actually kind of eerie and strange that he could just pull his valet ticket from his pocket and let the same man that he'd shoved on his butt know that he was ready to leave.

Undoubtedly, the man knew who he was. And yet, nothing.

"Little bit creepy," as his mom liked to say on dark nights in ancient cities.

After showing his ticket at the entrance, Nomad moved through the security steps, then down the grand staircase to the ballroom where Frau Leitner, still asleep, perched like a china doll on the satin couch. He crouched in front of her, capturing her neatly folded hands in his.

When she blinked her eyes open, he smiled at her, "Cinderella, the clock is about to strike midnight. Do you think I should take you home?"

26

———

Red

As Red drove back into the old part of the city, Elena turned to her, "Where are you taking me?"

"Back to your hotel. I'm sure getting cleaned up and lying down to rest will feel good."

"Who *are* you?"

Having jumped from the back of the van, Red prioritized getting Elena's and her phone back. Locking the back door to trap the man with the broken arm, then grabbing up the abandoned tire iron, Red had rounded the van to confront the men who had taken her. The tire iron raised and ready to land, the man, pinned in his seat by his two unconscious teammates, handed over the phones. From there, a flagged car was easily carjacked, and Red was in hot—adrenaline-fueled—pursuit. Of course, too bad Red couldn't just open the mic and listen to the conversation with the Pied Piper.

Pied Piper could be event security.

Did Red believe that?

She a little bit believed that.

He had the social graces. He had the strength. He had the height, so his supervisor would put him on the floor.

But Elena had decided to come with her.

She trusted her more than the Pied Piper. That might be because Red had gotten Elena's phone back and handed it to her. Phone's being a lifeline in most people's psyches, giving Elena the ability to communicate or call for help should have, and seemed to, establish safety between the two women.

Red would lay money on a bet that Elena had concluded that she was on a security team associated with Kamal and Joel Brighten.

Red tested those waters, "I'm private security. My job is to watch over you and protect your free movement until the transaction that you are arranging with Zayd Ali Kamal is accomplished. For example, I am sure Joel Brighton informed you that you will leave tomorrow morning to start the trip to Marrakech." Red sent Elena a wry smile. "I'll be making the same journey with you. It'll be a long day with all the legs we have to take. But you will be far more comfortable than I in that while you have first-class seating, Brighton arranged for my tickets—well, his secretary, Mr. Brighton delegates that kind of work—in coach." These were all details that should settle her nerves and help Elena to believe.

Elena nodded. "I need a drink."

Thankfully, from the information in Elena's phone, Langley had pinged Red and Grey with Elena's hotel, directions, suite number and layout as well as a list of available amenities. Having scanned over the information at the ball, Red was prepared. "There's a bar in your suite. When we go up, I'll make you one. Once you're more comfortable, I'll head to my room. Your suite has extra security through the hotel. Brighton knows I need to sleep at some point." Red grinned, hoping to make a human connection, but failed. "I'll be available when you wake up tomorrow."

They arrived at the hotel, and Red checked the car with the valet, which took a bit of brio since it was a five-star hotel, and she was driving a stolen car that she jacked from some poor guy who stopped to help back at the van accident.

As she'd driven after the Pied Piper to retake Elena, Red had touched base with Grey. He wanted Elena roofied if possible, so they'd have planning time. And they decided Red should take Elena to the hotel if possible. That's where they'd meet.

As Red and Elena made their way to the elevator, Grey did a brush pass with a hotel room key card—presumably so she could access the elevator, and a small vial with meds.

So far, so good.

Up in the suite, Elena kicked off her shoes and draped herself across the couch like a Regency damsel who had collapsed and was calling for her smelling salts.

Red made Elena a drink and roofied her with the pills. Granted, waiting for Elena to get herself undressed and tucked into bed first would have been so much easier.

A quick call to Grey, and he arrived to move Elena from the salon to bed. "I say we pull off her gown, and everything else stays on. Tuck her in, call it a day."

"Fine," Red agreed.

Grey held a noodley Elena up while Red unzipped her, then tugged the tight-fitting black velvet sheath over her head with a lot of hands shifting and teamwork. This was not their first rodeo. Red didn't know how many people she and Grey had undressed and put to bed over the years.

After Red pulled back the covers, Grey laid Elena down and tucked her in.

Then, both started pulling out the pins that held Elena's chignon in place and piled them on the bedside table.

Grey gathered Elena's dress and shoes and threw them out the window.

"The ring?" Red stared down at them. "We could take it now. It's a risk to continue with the mission as we outlined it. But the fake is somewhere in the back of the van. It fell from my pocket, and I didn't take the time to try to find it."

Grey pulled a foil packet from his pocket, shook it, and tipped his ear toward the door. Together, they moved into the salon, Grey shutting the bedroom door behind them. "I might take a *known* bite of pie over a *possible* slice on some occasions." He moved to the sofa. "But not this one ..." he let the thought trail off.

"Oh, this sounds good. Orange juice?" Red moved to the fridge and poured them each a glass.

Grey waited until she was sitting next to him, then said in a low tone. "The phone you picked up at the blast site belonged to Imraan el-Jafri."

Red leaned in. "I don't know that name."

"Interestingly, it was the DIA who identified him. One of your rescue crew recognized him in the blast zone when they were looking for you and took his fingerprints for confirmation. His team sent the information on to the DIA."

"But why would the DIA know about el-Jafri?" Red asked.

"That I can't tell you. What I can say is that el-Jafri is an exporter, mainly of opium. Very much in the ISIS fold. I understand he's part of a new group out of Northern Afghanistan and is very busy making their name known worldwide. That you grabbed up his phone is gold."

Red tucked her feet under her hip. "Good?"

"Excellent. First, el-Jafri is Elena's fiancé."

Red leaned forward, "Are you kidding me right now? It's not Poole?" She leaned back. "I kind of felt like she was just using everyone to get to her own ends, whatever they might be.

I had some begrudging respect for that. Fiancé? Yup," she took a sip of her juice, "now I've lost all regard. Tell me about the intelligence. It must have something to do with the ring and the money, or we'd just take the damned ring."

"The terror cell is planning three separate attacks. One is sending their people to various cities in the United States. Divide and conquer. They want to set off simultaneous events in different cities at a synchronized time."

Red pressed her lips together as she listened.

"Langley is developing the data. They're working with the FBI Joint Task Force on this."

"Who's leading that?" Red asked. "Frost?"

"Frost and Prescott."

"Good. Good. Okay, that's the one on the home front."

"One in Russia," Grey said. "That seems to be pure retribution and has something to do with daddy issues. And one is scheduled for a European concert."

"Okay, which concert? Where?"

"Right now, I only have the broad brush strokes. The U.S. is being treated separately because it is already funded and already in motion now that they have the information from Poole."

"But Russia and the concert?"

"That's vague. Langley needs more information. That's why we're not taking the ring. I am merely attaching a tracker to it." He pointed to the foil packet. "The money is destined for a group of arms dealers in Algeria."

"We're heading in that direction. Elena just found that out tonight. She's not the one pushing Morocco."

"Odd how synchronicity works." Gray adjusted himself on the sofa. "Elena contacted someone via text with her travel plans, and they replied that they would meet her at the border, and she should follow the same route as last time."

"When did she have a chance to send that?" Red asked.

"I read it when I went to the can."

All right, that's what Elena was doing when she was standing by the feathered woman near the mirror.

"Okay. Did Elena say which border?" Red asked. "We can't assume Algeria. And did she indicate which route? She won't have the ring at the border. She's selling it to Kamal."

"Right, we follow the ring to the exchange, and then follow Elena to the border and see what happens next. The arms have already been purchased. Elena simply needs to show up with the money."

"Forty Million?" Red asked, shaking her head. What would that buy? A dirty bomb?

"Could be a lot less. Just because she has the money doesn't mean she'll put it all into explosives. The more we know, the better we can break up this cell. I don't want to just cut the head off and watch another one pop into place. I want their operation stopped." He held up the packet he'd shown Red earlier. "Micro trackers, a gift from DARPA."

"Thank you, DARPA. Okay, we follow the ring."

"I don't. I have a situation on the front burner that needs my attention first thing in the morning. You're doing this. You and someone the DIA is sending your way."

"Seriously?" Red asked. "Who? Someone I know, at least?"

Grey shrugged. "I'm sure they'll introduce themselves to you along the way." He patted his knee. "What I'd like you to do now is go shower, get in bed with Elena, and get some sleep. I'll stay here and guard the situation."

Red just stood and looked toward the bedroom with a frown.

"You almost died in Lebanon," Grey said. "I never intended to tax you further by having the fight or the car chase. You need to sleep."

Red followed his instructions gratefully.

In the morning, he roused her as Elena was coming to, then slunk out the door.

Dressed in a simple skirt and heels, hoping to look professional and match what Elena might wear, Red sat in the chair, watching Elena sit up and reach drowsily for the light switch. "You," Elena said, focusing Red's way.

"Me." Red smiled. "I'm glad you were able to get some sleep. "Mr. Brighton wants to ensure you get on your plane to Morocco without glitches."

"Glitches, is that what you call last night?"

"You're here. You're safe. That was just a little upheaval." There was a tap at the door. "I ordered room service," Red said. "I thought we could both use a cup of coffee."

The rest of the early morning unfolded uneventfully.

Elena had luxuriated in first class, and Red was just so *not* in first class, but they made it to Amsterdam in less than three hours. It was now nine o'clock, and Elena could rest in the lounge until their afternoon flight. She had to be hung over from last night's sedation.

Elena had been first off the plane and had not waited for Red as Red had asked.

But how far away could she get? In order to get on the international flight to Morocco, they needed to go through a passport check, and then they'd leave from the same gate. Red had the trackers. Everything was fine.

In the line, Red was behind Elena, but not by much.

When Elena turned around and stared at her, Red sent her a smile and a finger wave. *Friendly, see?*

This happened again. And Again. And Again. Elena looked agitated. Frightened even, and Red didn't see a reason why. Was Elena trying to signal her?

Elena was up at the window, handing over her passport. She was talking to the man animatedly.

A guard tapped Red's shoulder and pointed to the open window next to Elena's.

"There. Her!" Elena said in a panicked voice as she accepted her passport. "She's the one talking on her phone about bombing the plane. You must stop her and her bags from going wherever she's flying today."

Instantly, sirens sounded. Guards with hands on weapons raced toward Red.

Red sent a shocked, wide-eyed glance toward a smirking Elena, who, passport in hand, winked and moved through the doors to her plane.

The guards slammed Red against the booth. Her arms were wrenched to her back, handcuffs snapped in place as a gun was trained on the little space at the top of her nose between her eyes where a bullet could kill her so thoroughly dead, that a finger on a suicide switch couldn't retract even from a left-over electrical impulse.

Red closed her eyes and held very still.

She really didn't want to die in a line at the airport.

27

———————

Nomad

"You're flying to Marrakech this morning," Colonel Watts's voice was in Nomad's earpiece.

His phone dinged as flight information dropped into Nomad's messages. "Long layover in Amsterdam." When they said this morning, they meant right now. Nomad was in motion, gathering his things.

"It is," T-Rex said. "Best we could do under the circumstances. You'll be functioning in support of CIA's Color Code, Johnna Red."

"Yes, Master Chief." Nomad's heart filled his chest, and he stopped breathing. "She's out of the hospital? She's good?"

"You met her last night," Colonel Watts said. "You two were playing do-si-do with Elena Savas."

It *was* her. He hadn't been imagining things. "Got it."

"And you have a relationship with Elena now. So you don't have to start from scratch," Watts said. "You have a sense of her."

"Elena knows my face. Am I going into this as a known

quantity? Last night, I told her I was ball security, so arriving in Morocco would set off alarms. Are we still trying to do the international waters?"

"Undercover," T-Rex said. "Change your appearance. Get clean-shaven and get a haircut. Not military, but short and neat, think American businessman climbing the corporate ladder."

"Master Chief, I don't want to be the "new guy" here. I don't need any landmines that are being tossed out to see if I blow or not. What's the real reason I'm going in?"

It was Colonel Watts who answered. "Who the hell knows, son. Whatever it is, get the job done."

"Yes, sir. So, I'm not taking point. And I have no mission objectives." This was wild. Delta Force was a new world for him. He wondered if this was what it was like for people in intelligence. Just out there walking around, seeing if they didn't happen to bump into a terrorist along the way. "Am I under her command?"

"You're a partnership. She's representing the CIA, and you're representing the DIA."

"Yes, sir."

By sheer luck, Nomad made it in time for his flight to Amsterdam. He'd come with his toiletries, boxer briefs, and an otherwise empty roller case that needed filling. He'd dumped the rest of his things in an alley trash bin. After deplaning, Nomad grabbed lunch on the go. Barbershop and then clothes shopping. It was guesswork to know how to pack to fit a persona he wasn't sure of. He went for quality travel wear that had a decided urban tactical feel. A couple of dressier silk button-down shirts and a pair of slacks that would blend. If he needed something more along the way, he'd grab it on the go.

Now that he was set, Nomad would spend the layover working through tutorials that explained the difference between Moroccan Arabic and the Egyptian Arabic that Nomad had learned in his travel-with-State childhood.

Sitting in a lounge area, glad the design had bench seats, Nomad's phone buzzed in his thigh pocket.

"Side quest," T-Rex said when Nomad answered his phone.

"Yeah? What's that."

"You ready for some shit?"

"I don't know, should I brace?" Nomad stood and moved to a quiet corridor to talk.

"Red tried to convince Elena that she was private security for Kamal."

"Risky," Nomad said. "That could be blown with a phone call."

"Which is what I think happened. Red was on a plane with Elena this morning from Vienna to Amsterdam. They were standing in line to go through passport control to catch their flight to Casablanca. Are you through passport?"

"Not yet, I wanted to keep my options open. Sounds like I'm going to need to exercise those options. What happened in passport control?"

"Elena told the good security officers that she'd overheard Red talking on her phone about bringing a bomb onto her plane."

"What?" That was some brazen stuff. Elena wasn't playing.

"Red's spent the day in interrogation."

Nomad started toward the ticket gate to check his roller bag. He had a feeling that he'd need to have his hands free. "What's State doing about this?"

"Staying the hell out of it until absolutely necessary. This is ongoing but is being monitored via her phone's mic. The DIA thinks it's winding down. Color Code got her a new ticket for tomorrow's flight and a hotel room for tonight. I'm sending the hotel information to you now. The game plan is for you to introduce yourself to Red as an ally before she shows up in Morocco. Once you're both boots on the ground, everything has to flow like a married couple."

"Got it. So what's the phrase or signal to let her know I am what I say I am?"

28

───────

Red

Red held off calling for an ambassador because it was all just so stupid.

Elena's tactic had been a surprise. And Red was begrudgingly impressed.

It could have backfired on Elena. It could have gone very much against her. It was probably against some law to make a false bomb accusation. Things could have snowballed if Elena had been traveling on a fake passport.

But they hadn't. And Red was tucking this experience into her mental file of desperate escape plans.

Despite rescuing Elena twice last night, apparently Elena didn't buy Red's cover story of working for Kamal's security.

As Red had navigated the new twist with Amsterdam airport security, her team, of course, knew what was happening. Even when handcuffed, she was able to tap the panic button on her phone, which opened her phone's mic to her support. They had listened in from the point that the guards marched Red to their offices.

Color Code didn't send anyone from State, so they must have wanted her to handle the situation on her own.

Red had been detained for hours now.

Hours.

She'd missed her plane, though she was assured that her luggage had made it through.

The guards found her suitcase and brought it into the interrogation room, where Red followed the instructions to open it and remove every article. Tampons be damned. Everything went through machines and scanners. Gloved professionals wiped down the contents with towelettes to find explosives residue. Dogs were sniffing through her stuff, and one of them locked onto her personal toy—which, granted from a dog's point of view, probably looked like a throw toy—but, still, disconcerting as hell. *I mean, what the actual heck?*

They put her in a machine that blew air over her that would detect any explosives. Red considered the possibility. It was hard to get explosive particulates off the skin, even with soap and water. And there was that bombing just days ago.

Yes, saved by the stall. But still, explosive residue hovered in that cloud of dust. And she'd swum through that mess to check on Moussa.

The blowing air machine was the only time Red was mildly concerned since she couldn't use Lebanon as an excuse. There was nothing in her passport that would say that Lebanon was possible. If the blow test came back positive for explosives, she'd have to get the embassy involved.

She had been silent through it all, simply nodding or performing the commanded action.

The first rule when dealing with law enforcement was "zip it and keep it zipped."

At that point, her phone still had some juice. She could open her phone log to show the officials that no calls had come in or out since the day before, and that was from her cat sitter. There were no texts beyond the fake back-and-forth of pet videos, cookie recipes, and occasional haircuts or doctor's appointments. There was a group at Langley who had the job of populating burner phones this way.

Nothing on this phone supported what that woman was saying, and just like that, Red was free to go.

Meanwhile, Elena was flying over the Mediterranean, being served dinner.

Red was starving.

Once she was calm enough to sound professional, Red reached out to the team. "Do you have me on the next flight?"

"The last flight was booked solid. Overbooked," the voice at support said. There was no chance she was going anywhere tonight. They had her on a flight the following day. "Sorry about the seat. We have you booked into a hotel tonight. Sorry about that one, too."

"It's fine. Just message me the info. I'm going to find food."

Red was so damned pissed.

She drove the anger down her legs out her heels as they clacked over the terrazzo flooring across the expanse of airport corridors to the main exit. Overnight with only the things in her purse. She did a mental inventory—a water bottle, an extra pair of panties, a sweater. An extra-large T-shirt had multiple uses— a mini dress or pjs, a safe cover for a dubious pillow, or a pillow in and of itself if she stuffed it with her sweater. Toothbrush and toothpaste, comb. From a make-do point of view, she was set.

She pushed through a door marked "Ground Transportation" out into a pleasant night.

A gale would have fit her mood better.

Her ego bruised, Red's pissed-off meter was still ranging in the orange space.

She stood at the end of the taxi queue and read her messages about essential operational awareness for the city. There was a soccer match and not much else.

That must have been why they were sorry about the hotel; they were probably all full of fans.

Fleabag it is.

Red copied and pasted the address into her map's search engine. It was a two-star and not in the best part of town. Actually in a kind of shitty part of town, but beggars can't be choosers.

Red wasn't on her A-game. The illness, the fights, and this whole "you're being accused of terrorism schtick" had really drained her. Luckily, she was only a twelve-minute walk from the hotel. The taxi line was long. And people looked like they were fed up, which meant they'd probably been standing there for a while.

She'd hoof it.

Once she got there, she'd start with that longed-for shower she'd been promising herself, then find some dinner. She messaged in: **Outside the airport. Walking to hotel.**

The battery was red, so she quickly memorized the route before the screen went black.

Her power pack was devoid of juice.

It was fine.

It should be fine.

29

———

Nomad

IN THE EYES OF THE PUBLIC, MEN LIKE NOMAD WERE EASY TO pigeonhole.

They were hard.

They drank hard, hit hard, worked hard. And well … yeah, women made them hard—a fact they acted on often and with both gusto and at least some finesse—at least in the retelling.

Was that myth true for all special forces operators?

Who the hell knew? Some of it, sure.

It was a perception that Nomad blamed on movies and popular fiction.

That and the visual.

His lifestyle of physical training day in and day out, year after year, made him look the part conjured in fiction.

There were benefits. Ladies aside, there were times when Nomad knew he skated through a situation because of his size.

Unfortunately, tonight didn't look like it would work out that way.

Nomad had simply walked into a pub along the route a taxi would use to transport Red to her hotel.

If she came on foot or by car, he'd see her.

And not knowing her time frame, this was a place that gave Nomad significant cover.

The goals were simple: initiate contact, then escort Red back to the airport where a brush pass would provide Red with her new persona. Then, he'd jump on his final flight to Casablanca. Easy day. All he needed to do was sit in front of a beer and wait.

Once inside the bar, Nomad spotted the perfect vantage point.

But on his way to the stool in front of the plate glass window, he was stopped in his tracks by a guy who locked Nomad in an unblinking stare.

Shorter by five or six inches, he weighed about fifty pounds less than Nomad, but he looked wiry under his faded T. Looked like someone who fought dirty and enjoyed the sensations of dominance. Thrived on it. The kind of guy that ate other's pain and fear for its nutritional value to fuel whatever the crap messed up this man's ego.

This isn't good timing, my dude.

Right now, Faded-T looked like his ego needed a boost. And he thought squaring off with Nomad was the way to get that dopamine hit he craved.

While men got violent when they felt powerless in their personal situations, that was none of Nomad's business.

Faded-T was stepping on his op.

"Hey, big man, you *think* you're a big man?" He spoke in Dutch. It had been a while since Nomad had spoken the language. Decades. It took a hot second for Nomad's brain to adjust to the language and register the words. "You think you can come in here to this place—my place—without my express permission?"

Resting his focus on the man's chest—the best place to focus in a fight—Nomad's peripheral vision took in the movement in the small room.

On the way in, he'd clocked two exits—the front and the other in the back between the kitchen and the bathroom.

He'd noticed the television was playing a soccer match. And he knew from his walk down a road filled with pubs that Germany was up two points. Everyone on this street had been shaking their fists and yelling at the screens.

Nomad had picked this place because it seemed relatively settled.

But he'd been wrong. Not only was this the pub's bully. But the patrons were used to his antics. As soon as this guy's chest puffed up, they were choosing a door.

Those who pressed toward the back looked like they'd lived their violence in earlier days and now enjoyed it as a spectator sport. They chuckled with anticipation.

Okay, if things get bad, they'll try to get out back. That will block that egress. That's a no-go.

The others stood up from their seats and stacked behind Faded-T, effectively blocking the front door.

And that way out is a no-go, too.

Nomad decided that he'd pick up a stool, hold it like a shield, and leap through the plate glass window, making a new way out. Probably less injury in that direction than fighting an entire pub full of brawlers. His job was to stay operational and on mission, whatever that took.

Man, he'd rather not jump through glass.

Nomad pulled some words from his memory. He'd been eleven when his family lived here. "Just a stranger passing through." He smiled and held out open palms. "No disrespect to you, sir." The "sir" felt like it could be taken either way, a sign of respect and appeasement, like a dog rolling onto its back and exposing its belly—which was Nomad's hope—or it could be read as sarcasm.

Faded-T read it as sarcasm.

A wounded ego was fragile that way.

No reason to stare the guy down. This was obviously heading for a fight. But Nomad wouldn't take a preemptive strike. He watched Faded-T's chest for the split-second tells that the fight was a go—a deep inhale, a shift of balance, one of the four limbs retracting backward to gather momentum. It was the physics of the fight.

Faded-T ballooned the cotton fabric of his shirt, loosening the cloth, giving the man's hand practice for his next move. He shrugged his shoulders and adjusted his stance.

Now, Nomad knew this guy had a weapon. He'd lay money on it being a butterfly knife. Whipped out and swirled in the fingers to open. It looked badass. It was terrifying to have that slash through the air. Nomad's guts clenched at the visual.

Rightly so.

It was lethal as hell. And intel or no intel, Nomad planned on walking out of the bar with his intestines still folded into their normal place in his abdominal cavity and not pooled out onto the cement floor.

"Hey, man," Nomad kept his voice soft and friendly. "Can I buy you a drink?" Without shifting his attention, he lifted his voice, "How about I buy drinks for the house? Bartender, this next round is on me, with gratitude for the warm hospitality I've received in your beautiful country."

Nobody cracked a smile. No cheers celebrated a free drink.

Nope. This was going to be a thing. And Nomad knew he had to make it fast and decisive, or the men blocking the front door were going to join in the fun of pummeling the out-of-towner.

He was still going to wait until the man made an aggressive move.

Jail, too, would be a deterrent to Nomad's mission.

His phone pinged with a message.

He needed to find a way to scoop this goat turd out of the mission punch bowl.

And as if a miracle was sent from the Heavens above, the Netherlands got a goal.

All attention swung to the television. Fists went victoriously into the air. As the men jumped and yelled, Nomad squirmed his way out of the bar, moved down the street, and around the corner.

He took a minute to breathe in relief from his reprieve, then opened his messages: **She's on foot. Heading your way. Lost phone signal. No longer tracking her.**

An anguished outcry could be heard up and down the street. Who knew what had happened on the field? Europe's football season was no joke. Rivalries simmered. Drinking was heavy. Fighting was frequent and part of the sport's culture.

And now, Red was walking the gauntlet from the airport to the hotel alone in the dark?

30

Red

Red would admit, as she moved through the night down the street in the skirt and heels, that walking wasn't her best decision.

With the soccer match on the televisions, the pubs were overflowing. Beer steins overfull. And the men's alcohol levels seemed to be maxing out.

She moved off the sidewalk and into the street, hugging close to the parked cars, angry at the fashionable shoe choice she had thought would help her align with Elena. Now, she was clack-clack-clacking along. Not another female in sight.

All she had to do was get up this street and turn left. It wasn't that much farther.

And yet.

A group of men drifted out of a pub door, surrounding her. Rowdy. Angry.

A drunk called out to her in Dutch, but she knew what he said by tone alone. Without Dutch language skills, Red wouldn't be talking her way out of this one.

Red rolled her eyes skyward. "Seriously? I mean, honestly, are you serious right now?"

Scanning for her best exit route, for the possibility of someone who might help her, Red realized that screaming would get her nowhere.

The streets echoed with yelling people. Her voice would just blend right in.

She looked behind her. Could she somehow backtrack?

Suddenly, from behind her came a man. He twisted, dropped into a squat, grabbed her wrist, wrenched her purse from her grasp, and dragged her over his shoulder. While yelling out something in inebriated Dutch that got him a rousing cheer, he started down the street.

It was the universal sound of an attaboy.

What should she do?

Red lifted her head enough to see the crowd of guys' fists pumping and following. She felt like a carrot hanging in front of a donkey, a lure.

They called out, and the guy called back. With his booming voice, Red thought of Jack and the Bean Stalk. "Fe Fi Fo Fum, I smell the blood of an American chick." Well, an American trying to get to Morocco to save the world.

There was menace in this guy's tone. But not completely. There was some chiding bro-speak. Hard to interpret—foreign language, foreign culture, and the testosterone that was ankle-thick from some kind of soccer victory on one side and defeat on the other.

Why was this man carrying her? *Where* was he carrying her?

Red wasn't going to fight—yet. She ran through a list of possible defensive moves and why they wouldn't work. She couldn't kick at him; his arm locked her calves to his chest. And her shoes weren't hard enough at the toe. She'd rethink her footwear another time. She couldn't slide from his shoulder;

another massive arm reached across her hips, and his fingers circled into her pelvic girdle. If she twisted, he could dig in.

She decided her best defense was no defense. Red would dangle and think, saving her energy for whatever happened next.

When he put her down, it had to be in one of two ways.

One, he could throw her down. It would hurt—probably hurt like hell—but she could roll, get her shoes off, get her feet under her, and bolt. These alleys weren't a safe bet, but if she could get a car between her and this guy, even with his height, she could play cat and mouse with him all damned night long. Yes, that's what she'd do if he threw her.

Two, he could yank her legs and force her to slide down his body. Then she'd stay in his grasp. What would she do then?

The blood was rushing to her head. She could feel pins and needles as her arms fell long down his back. She wasn't tall enough, her limbs not long enough to grab between his legs for her signature "squeeze, twist, and pull," which made her male opponents leave their bodies in sudden shock and pain. She considered giving him a wedgie, but he'd probably just laugh. Maybe he'd laugh hard enough that he'd drop her?

As the revelers behind her started singing and brushing up closer to her. One reached out as if to grab her hair.

The giant lengthened his strides. He wasn't running. He was just gliding faster. It was like an adult walking along when it would take a child two steps for every one of his. This gave her a glimmer of hope, and then it made her think that he wanted her for himself—the prize he had snatched up.

He had done this before. The scoop was easy, natural, and fast. Who practices scooping up a woman like that?

Serial rapist?

He had her purse over his shoulder. He wasn't just trying to rob her.

The blood in her upside-down head sounded like a washing

machine churning in her ears. She could go down the path of trying to remember how long it was safe to hang upside down before the pressure of her organs on her lungs caused hypoxia, but she thought that the bend in her waist was holding things in place.

And, too, that's not where her mind should be.

Focused, aware, processing, and coming up with defensive maneuvers.

The stream of men had become a trickle and then had run dry.

It was just the two of them now. And a dark street.

He stopped walking.

Here we go.

31

———

Red

"Red, we're at your hotel. I'm going to set you down
now. I'd appreciate it if I could keep my balls attached to my
body." His voice was warm, and there was a mild chuckle with
maybe a dash of concern in the timbre. "All right, Red?" He
pronounced her name extra clearly. "We're agreed?"

What? Who? "Sure. Agreed."

He slid her slowly down his body, and that was quite the
sensation. Truthfully?

Whew.

Yeah, there was the "he's a whole lot of man with a very fine
body" kind of whew, and there was the "my head is spinning
hard" kind of whew.

She was experiencing both at the same time.

Red staggered and collapsed against the guy.

Not wholly intentional.

Not entirely against her will.

There was a solid storefront that would have supported her
just fine.

"Give it a second," he said. "You've been upside down for a couple of blocks."

"I'm sure you had your reasons." It came out sarcastic as hell. She thought that was fair.

His hands wrapped her upper arms, balancing her as Red pressed her forehead to his chest. She'd be more stable if she kicked off the shoes, but she could feel the crunch of broken glass under the thin soles of her high heels.

"Look, I speak Dutch, and it doesn't seem like you do."

"True."

"You didn't understand what those men were saying to you, what they were planning."

She lifted her chin to look him in the eye, but with the streetlight out, he'd chosen the darkest spot on a very dark night. "Also true." *Nope, I'm not ready for that yet.* Her head went back to his chest. His English was as American as apple pie, and he knew her code name. She would go with this until there was a reason not to. "So you saved me from—well, we both know." She took a step back. "I'd rather not discuss that." She licked her lips. "I am interested in the technique. What was that about?"

"When you're my size—"

"Unimaginable." He'd kept steadying hands on her arms; Red liked the warmth they radiated.

"Or when people learn that you're with special forces."

"Which?" Now that she was steadier on her feet, he handed her bag back to her. He hadn't mentioned his name. In her business, it was rude to ask. Still, he knew hers. So, things felt uneven. Red didn't like that he had the upper hand.

"Right now, I am working on a mission that aligns with yours."

"I see. So, it's not a SEAL. They'll tell you if you sneeze

near them. Not a ranger, there's no—ah. Got you. You're a member of the silent profession, I'd bet."

"Finishing my thought, when someone my size goes out mellow-fellow in the wilds—"

"Men size you up."

He smiled. "Women, too."

"Same reason?"

"What reason are you sizing me up?" A chuckle and maybe a dash of flirtation.

True, most women would wonder what it would be like to take a guy with his obvious attributes for a roll in the hay. And yes, maybe the idea flashed through Red's mind as she stood outside her hotel. But no, she wouldn't admit it. "Let's assume that the person—male or female, or a designation of their choosing—is sizing you up. Does that lead to many fights?"

"I try to avoid it by being proactive and a little creative."

"Like tonight?" Red asked. "What did you tell them?"

"That you were my wife, and sometimes you get out past your bedtime." He shrugged to soften the misogyny. "Luckily, you didn't fight me."

"In that position? Is it possible?"

"No." It was said in a matter-of-fact tone because it was, indeed, a matter of fact.

"So the naughty wife, that's why they were laughing. But then they were following along."

"They were drunk enough and surprised enough that when I showed up and threw you over my back—"

"Like a sack of potatoes," she grumped.

"Really? Nah. Less lumpy, I think." He was laughing at her now. "More pliable and soft."

"Soft?" Her eyebrows went up to her hairline.

"Soft compared to a sack of potatoes, yes." He canted his head. "Is that really offensive?"

"What were they saying that they were following along."

"They started to think I wasn't your husband because neither of us wore a ring. Then they started to get mad because they found you first."

Red thought she might vomit.

Some of it had to do with the close call, some from hanging upside down, and some from not having anything to eat since breakfast. But yeah, she was pretty nauseated. She tried to keep that look off her face.

"Do you want to go in?" The giant pointed toward her hotel.

Red looked at the hotel door, then back to him, and licked her lips, unsure.

"You don't trust me?" He sounded genuinely wounded.

She'd been played once that day, and Red simply wasn't in the mood. "No. I don't."

"Yet, I saved you." He turned to lean a shoulder against the wall, forcing her to pivot toward him.

"You came along and changed the trajectory. Saved me?" She lifted a palm. "We'll never know about that."

"Fair point as far as tonight goes. What's wrong with your phone? They can't get in touch with you."

Well, he knew that much, and her name, and her hotel. And her arrival time. Had she been hacked? And what did he mean by 'as far as tonight goes'? There was something that pulled Red to him. Something very familiar. But here, in the black of night, she couldn't look into his eyes and place him. "I ran out of juice."

Nomad pulled a power bank from his pocket and handed it to her.

"Thank you." She pulled one from her purse for the exchange. "The charger at my seat on the plane wasn't working. Maybe you'll have better luck."

He held up a no-thank-you hand, "I have another one."

She slid her charger back into her purse. "Two is one, and one is none?" She pulled out her phone and connected it to the bank.

"Just life experience."

"Okay."

"Maybe this will help," Nomad paused and waited until she was facing him, "'In a box of crayons, Black is the most opaque color. The color I've been using lately is Grey. And Grey works well with Red. Don't you think?'"

"I'm not really the artistic type." She intoned this week's response dryly.

He finished with his line of the code. "I think you live a colorful life."

When a car moved up the street and the headlights shined on his face, Red squinted her eyes at him.

"If you're trying to place me, we've met a few times now." He grinned. "You don't recognize me?" He ran a hand over his cheek and chin.

She felt they knew each other, that he was a good guy, and she could trust him.

Trust but verify.

Brains could glitch. There could be something about him that reminded her of good people in her past. He was painted in that latent lethality of special forces who had been doing the job for a long enough that their cocky shine was burnished off. Then, it struck her. Yeah. He was the guy who left her zip-tied in the van.

"You?" she asked. "You're the Pied Piper."

"Okay." He laughed.

Yeah, that didn't come out the way she meant it to. Red tried again. "You shaved your beard and got a haircut since the car accident. It suits you."

What she didn't know was for whom he played and what

were his circumstances now? Obviously, Color Code wanted them to work together, or he wouldn't have known this week's code.

"You look different from the first time I saw you, too." Pied Piper's voice hit a different note, warm and caring, maybe a little concerned. "How are you feeling now?"

Red blinked.

He put his hand on his chest. "I was part of the team that got you from your hotel in Lebanon to the Türkiye base. You seem to have made a near-miraculous recovery. You're back on your feet fast."

"Fast-ish, to be honest." It *was* him. Her whole system flooded with the same sensations she'd had when she lay in his lap, and he stroked his hand over her hair and whispered encouragement and kindness whenever she moved or opened her eyes. He'd held her tightly against him as he climbed onto a boat and kept her from getting slammed about as the boat rocketed out to sea. He was the one who clasped the spider straps over her as she was lifting into the sky.

The sudden loss of contact with his skin had unnerved her. It was like she was leaving a piece of herself behind.

And then there he'd been, crouching next to her in the heli, running an I.V., calling out orders, taking complete control of her safety and care. And she had been whole again just by his being there.

She suddenly wanted that back. The sensation of being cared for and, maybe more importantly, cared about.

A stranger, no less.

It had been such a gift.

But it also felt mean that she had experienced those sensations and then had them snatched away from her. She hadn't known that was missing from her life.

It was depressing to make that discovery.

Was she really getting misty-eyed here? She cleared her throat. "Sorry about your head wound. Are you okay?"

"Friendly fire. Actually, it was not so friendly. The cut came from the Fire of the Desert." The guy pressed a button to illuminate his watch face. "Elena's ring did that. You know what happens, especially when there's an intelligence breakdown. I didn't know we were playing for the same team, you and I. It seems we were also playing at cross purposes. I think our handlers have figured out a shared strategy."

"Okay, you had a code word for me. Tell me who you are and why someone sent you."

"Your phone died, so you didn't get the message. They need you to go back to the airport with me. Your old cover is blown. You can't use it anymore. We need to be there together for a brush pass to get you your new credentials. You'll have to do something with your look to change things up. The computers will be looking for you to do something dangerous. You don't want to be caught with fake documents."

"You don't need to go with me," Red said flatly.

"My message said they'll identify us by standing together. Besides, I have to get on the plane to Casablanca. Then, I'll head to Marrakesh to set up surveillance."

"You're doing that."

"Yes. We're presenting as a husband and wife on vacation. I thought I was following behind you and would catch up with you there. But you got outfoxed."

"I was indeed." Husband and wife cover?

He lifted a hand and flagged a cab. "Safer not to walk." The cab pulled over. "Okay, let's find out who you're going to be next."

32

Red

"Today was a string of unexpected events," Pied Piper said as he shut the cab door, and they started toward the front entrance of the airport. "I'm sorry you went through all that."

Red was off balance right now. She'd like a few minutes to adjust to the shit show that had been her day.

She still hadn't eaten and was hangry.

Knowing that, Red should watch her mouth, but despite the guy's tone being gentlemanly and concerned, Red bristled at the idea that he didn't think she could do her job. "Did you think I was looking for sympathy from you?"

"Empathy, maybe? I mean, you're a human being. Or," he smiled, "human-like. Perhaps cyborg. In a snap, you went from death's doorstep to La Femme Nikita."

"Nikita. Funny." She looked around to ensure they were out of earshot. "Am I putting off the image that I'm a cutthroat?"

Pied Piper held his eyes wide. "Literally, are you?"

"Cut throats are very messy." She was tired, and this felt like banter. Like they were teasing each other. Like this was flirty. But flirty took energy.

"Stop," she said, coming up on her toes and holding his face in hers. She pressed against him, lifting her lips as if she was going to kiss him on the cheek. "Do you want me to keep calling you Pied Piper in my head, or do you want to give me a name?" Rude? She was fine with that.

"Nomad," he said, pulling his brows together. "Why Pied Piper?"

Red lowered her heels to the ground and took his hand as they walked toward their X again.

Nomad …

She liked it.

"You asked me if I was a cutthroat. I can't imagine asking you the same question. It's part of the job, right? You're handed a mission. You fulfill the mission. Does that violence define you?"

"To some extent, yes," he said.

"Can a man do his job and go home to his spouse and kiddos to have a barbeque with the neighbors all Mr. Suburbia?"

"Not very effectively, honestly. Just look at the divorce rate in our respective fields."

She wore his button-down shirt over her outfit, the sleeves rolled to the elbow, and her hair in her face. She should look different enough, though she'd been cleared by security, and she shouldn't be sucking up anyone's attention.

And the T-shirt he'd worn under the shirt he'd handed her fit him very well.

"Some marriages survive. How do you think they can do that?" He squeezed her hand, released it to reach for the door, and held it wide for her.

Once through, Red adjusted her bag onto her shoulder,

accepting the arm he offered her. Why had she jumped right into talking about marriage and divorces? Who does that?

She leaned heavily on it like an old woman with arthritic feet.

Red would admit to exhaustion. And for once, she understood the allure of a man sweeping her up in his arms and carrying her to the bedroom—but to sleep. She wasn't used to thoughts like these and wondered if her brain had shrunk in the dehydration of her bout of typhoid fever.

After a few steps, Nomad reached around her waist and held her tightly to him, supportively.

Their strides lined up beautifully, and they walked together easily.

"How can someone with our general job description manage a marriage?" he asked as if everyone knew the answer was that it was impossible.

Was it impossible? She took a few more steps. "Good question." Her arm came up to wrap his waist as well, and she let her ear rest against his bicep. "Both partners would have to understand that their relationship isn't the stuff of romance novels. Our jobs demand that we manipulate. And that becomes a skillset so natural that perhaps we don't see how it works in our off-the-clock relationships as well."

"Unfortunately, I agree." Nomad stopped in the designated spot and pulled her into his arms.

Red knew it was so he could look over her head and scan. But she also thought he wanted her to rest and that he was being kind. They were going to be a good team. This was all coming naturally. Anyone looking at them would believe they were in a relationship.

With her ear against Nomad's heart, Red could see a couple approaching, arguing as one pulled their luggage and the other pushed a baby carriage with a screaming toddler.

As they passed, a bag riding on top of a carry-on fell at their feet, spreading the items across the floor.

The man looked up at Nomad and said preemptively, "I've got it."

"Sorry about that," the woman said.

After they gathered their things, a white envelope lay on the white floor between Red's feet.

The woman handed the baby a pacifier, and calm was restored as they continued down the corridor.

Nomad had used the time to step on his lace and untie his shoe. Red pointed, "Shoe."

"Thanks." He bent to tie it, palmed the envelope, and stood, sliding it into her purse.

Red pulled it back out, opened it, and flipped through her new credit cards, driver's license, and passport. "Cassandra Kromos." She blinked at her passport. "Cassandra is kind of rude." Red frowned.

"You don't like the name? They called you Kromos because My papers are for Nicholi Kromos. You're playing the role of my wife. In Morocco, it's against the law for a man and woman who are not married to meet in a hotel room. That would make developing the case much more difficult. It's easier for us to be married."

"Who would ask?" This meant that they would be sleeping in the same room. Most likely in the same bed. While Red's body sent out signals that it was delighted by this particular turn of events, her mind tried to shut that shit down.

"They take your identification when you sign in. They're required to watch and call it in if there is a breach. Speaking of calling we need to exchange numbers." He opened his phone and opened his contacts and typed in: **CASSIE: wife** then added her as his ICE contact.

"Kromos is Greek?" Red asked as she did the same:
Nicholi: hubby

He put his hand on his heart. "I speak Greek."

"Spanish would have made more sense, wouldn't it? I mean, as a second language, a lot of Moroccans speak Spanish."

"Our support team is probably trying to give us a language barrier if needed."

"But I don't speak Greek," Red smiled. "How's your pig Latin?"

"I can get by. I need to get through the security check now, Cassie. My plane will be boarding in the next hour."

She put her paperwork in her purse, reached for his hand, and they set off.

"Cassie's better. Thank you. So if I have to be Cassandra, why couldn't you be Sisyphus?" She looked up at him with a half-smile so he'd know she was teasing him. "You out there pushing that rock up the mountainside, and it tumbling back down … Doesn't it sometimes feel that way when we go on missions? We just do the work and then return to the starting point." She lifted her purse strap and ducked under the loop so it settled across her body instead of sliding down her arm.

Nomad was moving along next to her with an easy stride, not breathing harder, not misting with sweat, and probably his heart wasn't pounding in his chest. Red would like to blame her body's reaction on her recent illness and exertion, but she knew that was a lie. She wanted to get this man on her own and see if the old saying was true about knowing how well a man performed in bed by his skill at dancing. If the Viennese ball was any indication, it would be luxurious.

"Here we are." Nomad turned once they'd reached the back of the line. "When you get into Marrakesh tomorrow, call me, okay?"

They were belly to belly. "I can do that." She smiled up at him.

"Good." He brushed her hair from her face. "Be safe, sweetheart. I love you."

Love? He was just in character.

Red could be in character, too.

She raised on her toes, and, with his face between her hands, she kissed him.

It was not the kiss she wanted to give him but a see-you-soon wifey kiss.

But still, it made her lips buzz awake.

And it was harder than anticipated to turn and walk away.

33

Nomad

Nomad was one of the very last ones on the plane. Good thing he didn't have a carry-on. There would be no space for it. He had learned a long time ago that he needed every inch of space around him, and he couldn't share it with a bag shoved under the seat in front of him. Not if he wanted someplace to put his size fifteen feet.

When he saw the seat row and number, he knew it would be a tight fit for him.

But he had no idea he would be jealous of a sardine packed in its tin.

Nomad ducked his head and sidestepped his way to the back.

The very back.

The two people already in his row had to stand up and squish themselves to the side to let him in. He could see they were calculating and didn't know how this would work.

Nomad didn't either.

But the plane was packed. There were no other options.

He'd hoped perhaps the person on the aisle would take pity and switch seats with him or even let him pay. But the woman's right leg was broken. She had to stick it out in the aisle.

This was fine. He'd been in worse circumstances.

When Nomad had wedged himself into the seat and had his belt in place, the other two gave him a minute to figure out his legs. This seat had his shoulder to the side of the plane. Where a window should be was an indentation in the plastic. Honestly, that seemed like a taunt rather than a design choice. With the lavatory wall directly behind him, his seat didn't lean back.

He'd be upright for the duration.

With his toes on the floor to allow a tighter bend in his knees. He got his shins up along the back of the seat in front of him. There was no way he'd be able to lower his tray.

Once Nomad had settled, his row mates found their seats again, and they all pressed together. Being this intimate with a stranger was socially awkward, and Nomad understood why the women coped by flirting with him. Nomad wanted to be polite but also to shut it down.

It went on through the flight instructions and the takeoff.

It went on through the "You're free to move about the cabin" announcement.

Nomad wanted to think about Red. Wanted to relive their parting kiss. Wanted to get some sleep if possible. But, most certainly, he didn't want to flirt with these women all the way from Amsterdam to Casablanca. So he pulled out his old standby. "Ladies, I'm sorry. I'm narcoleptic and need to close my eyes. Please don't take offense."

The funny thing was that neither seemed to know the word.

Nomad lolled his head against the wall and pretended to sleep.

"What was that?" One whisper asked the other. "Did he say narcoleptic?"

"He did."

"Isn't that when you want to have sex with dead bodies?" Middle seat whispered

"Now that you say that, I think it is."

From under his lashes, Nomad could see both of them peering at him.

"How do you think he comes across the bodies to do that with?"

"He's strong. Maybe he digs them up?"

"Wouldn't that be too tiring?"

"Do you think that's why he fell asleep so quick just now?"

Nomad felt them lean and peer again.

"Hard to tell. But look, he has manicured fingernails. There's no dirt under them."

"Isn't that what the bad guy would do after hitting someone with their car? They go to the car wash to clean off all the evidence?"

"I don't know. Maybe."

"Do you think he hits them with a car? The dead bodies he sleeps with? You know, like makes his own?"

Nomad was having trouble keeping his face slack. He'd remember this conversation to share with his Echo brothers. This was nuts.

"Then he'd be a serial killer, wouldn't he?"

"He would, and he didn't say that. He said he had narcolepsy."

After watching him fold into his spot, the woman in front had been kind enough to leave her chair upright. But she leaned it back and looked at his row mates through the crack. "That word you're using is necrophilia. Necrophilia has to do with dead bodies. The word he said was *narcolepsy.* Narcolepsy is a sleeping disorder that makes someone sleepy during the day. And they can go to sleep at any time. He was probably kidding. He was trying to tell you he was tired and going to sleep."

"Oh, he was tired," the middle seat said. "He was just tired. That's different than what I was thinking."

The woman in front pulled her head out of the crack and turned around, putting the chair back upright.

Nomad worked to keep his chuckle internal.

"Yeah." The aisle seat said, "I wonder if there's a step down from—what did she say? Necrophilia?—like not wanting to get with someone who's dead, but maybe just sleeping."

"I honestly wouldn't mind with a guy that looks like him."

"He *is* pretty while he sleeps."

"Ladies," the flight attendant held out napkins, "what can I get you to drink?"

34

Nomad

Nomad took the rental car to the Marrakech airport. He wasn't missing anything. With the mic on Elena's phone open, he could hear her snoring lightly in her sleep. As long as her phone held some battery life and there was a bit of WIFI, Langley would record her continuously, and the AI would pull out the conversation pockets.

Besides, it fit their cover better that Nicholi went to collect his wife, Cassie.

After Red made it through exit security, Nomad took the handle of her suitcase and wheeled it out. "Hey Cassie, how was your flight?" He laced her fingers with his.

"Good. And yours, Nicholi?"

"I survived," he laughed. "Elena is taking a siesta. And I thought it would be nicer for you if you didn't have to navigate to our place on your own."

He was mission-focused.

So, the fact that he missed her and looked forward to being with her was pressed to the recesses of his awareness.

"Much appreciated." Red climbed into the left-hand passenger seat while he put the luggage in the back. As soon as Nomad slid under the wheel on the right-hand side, she asked. "What have you found out?"

"We're in a riad around the corner from Elena's hotel."

"Her hotel is in the Medina? That's a surprise." Red twisted in her seat to better face him. "At the ball, Joel said it was a five-star. Mmm, maybe he didn't say five-star, but it was implied."

"It is." Nomad reached onto his dashboard to grab the parking ticket and headed toward the booth to pay. "Once you get inside, the hotel is luxurious. I had breakfast there this morning to check it out. I considered signing up for a spa day." He sent her a grin.

"So now you know why I became a spy." She adjusted his button-down shirt and flicked her hair out of the way.

Something about her wearing his shirt made him feel possessive of her. Like he'd planted a flag for other men to see. *She chose me.* Which wasn't true at all. But the flash told Nomad where he was with his thoughts about Red, and he needed to watch that he kept those ideas internal.

Lives were on the line. His heart and libido be damned.

"All the spa treatments I get when following people around," Red lifted her hand to cover a fake yawn. "It's almost to the point of losing my appetite for pampering. So, the hotel— you were saying something about getting back there?"

"It's buried in the labyrinth of alleys in the Medina. I can see how someone might like to experience the Medina's color and bustle and then be able to wend back away from the crowds to luxury."

"Hmm," Red wrinkled her nose. "The way you say that tells me ours—"

"Is not quite as luxurious, no." He offered a wry smile. "It's a riad, so the typical set up of rooms surrounding an open courtyard. Our riad has an orange tree in the middle with ripened fruit. Orange and green against cobalt blue tiles."

"Picturesque"

"Also loud. We're going to have to be extraordinarily careful in maintaining our cover. Those tile floors and walls are great for dealing with the heat and cleaning up the dirt and sand, but the hard surfaces coupled with the old doors that don't quite sit into their jambs correctly—"

"The sounds travel. Yes, I remember that from my previous stays in Morocco. Okay, so does that mean we should stage some tiff to sell our cover? Maybe I can be angry at you that you left your socks on while you were seducing me."

Nomad's eyes glittered. "An infraction I couldn't imagine." Scooters roared up and dodged around their car to speed off into the distance. "Elena is meeting with Joel and Kamal at the garden tomorrow."

"You have the time?" Red asked.

"Fifteen hundred."

"Right after nap."

"Ha." Nomad adjusted his rearview mirror. "Now, as to what I've found out. There's a married couple that Elena met up with for breakfast this morning."

"That's right, breakfast. Did they spot you?"

"I was drinking my Turkish coffee behind a column with a large palm."

"Nice. And the couple—"

"Is pretending to be Parisian tourists. But their French is Lebanese."

Red closed her eyes as an elderly woman stepped off the curb and walked out into the six lanes of traffic that were going forty miles an hour. It was a Moroccan skill crossing the street, and every time it felt death-defying. "You recorded their conversation?" she asked, blinking her eyes open again.

"I did. The two women will visit the Mouassine Hammam before Elena meets Kamal."

"Interesting." Red looked at her lap as she focused on that information. "Her hair's going to be wet."

"Why is that interesting?"

"Kamal wanted to make a video of the exchange. Joel told Elena about that at the ball. And she put her foot down, no video."

"That's a shame because I spent quite a bit of time today in the Secret Garden making sure every square inch is covered with audio-video equipment so no one and nothing would be lost. What has that got to do with wet hair?"

"Joel wanted her to be beautiful. If she put on a headscarf and he forced her to remove it, she'd have dripping wet hair. It wouldn't look nice for the video. That particular hammam is right outside the garden entrance, which may be a minute's walk away."

Nomad thought that listening to a spy go through their thought process would be a valuable opportunity for him to learn. "There's a hammam at the spa in her hotel. Why would staging at the Mouassine make sense?"

"Elena could completely transform her look. And it might be a way to arrive at the garden early so she's not being tracked. The Mouassine Hammam has been women-only since the fifteen hundreds. A man wouldn't be allowed to enter." A smile slid across Red's face, "And then there's the wonderful experience of a hammam that isn't about spa treatments but the opportunity to be in a comfortable women's space. Hammams are part of a cool economic eco-structure."

"How's that?" Nomad asked.

"Morocco can be insanely hot, a hundred degrees, with no

air conditioning available. Nobody wants to cook in their houses in the heat and make it unbearable, right? So, it all works symbiotically. It starts with the men who work a wood-burning oven."

Nomad nodded.

"The oven heats the floors and walls of the hammam so people who are naked and wet while getting clean are warm and comfy."

"I'm following."

"A woman makes her bread dough for the day and prepares a *tangia*—a tangia is an earthen vase-shaped cooking vessel—which she packs with beef, garlic, oil, and preserved lemons, and she takes the tangia and her dough to the oven guy. The man with the wood-burning oven bakes the bread. Then he rakes the ashes out and piles them around the tangia, where the beef slowly cooks all day. Fresh and clean from the hammam, the woman gets her bread and meat and goes home. Her house is cool, and the guy with the oven earns his pay in three ways."

"And they're getting cleaned at the bathhouse because their houses have limited running water like in your hotel in Lebanon?"

"Some have no water at all. In the Medina, they can get their water from the public fountain by filling jugs."

"We have water at our place," Nomad reassured her.

"Good to hear." She leaned back to look into the side mirror, then turned back to Nomad.

"What's it like to go to the hammam?" he asked.

"Men go, too."

Nomad sent her a one-sided smile. "Yeah, I've heard my mom talking about it. I'm not letting someone scrub me like I'm a child."

Red pulled her brows together. "Ego can't handle it?"

"Nope, gotta draw the line somewhere." He entered the

crazy driving of a six-lane roundabout with bumper-to-bumper traffic trying to get to the street they wanted.

"Well, it's one of my favorite experiences because it normalizes the human body."

Nomad kept his eyes on the traffic flow. Morocco had a reputation for traffic accidents, and he thought they'd had enough of that the night of the ball. "Go on."

"You remove your clothes and put them in the locker."

"What will Elena do with her ring?"

"Good question. Probably keep it on. The married women wear their wedding rings. So you walk into the cleaning area naked, and an attendant takes you to her section of the floor where you lie down. These attendants are usually grandmotherly types with big bellies with their breasts draped over the top. They're usually dressed in briefs, and that's all. And just so *beautiful*. When I'm there, and I look at these women with their lives etched into their faces with creases and wrinkles, I think someone should be painting them, capturing the glory of these women."

"You lay on the ground?" Nomad was trying to picture this, and he was thinking about a car wash with vehicles parked in a row for the owners to vacuum them out. That couldn't be right.

"Marble," Red qualified. "Heated by the fire guy. It's comfortable. The attendant rubs you with black soap. This sets for five minutes and loosens all the dead skin cells. Not to gross you out, but it's pretty wild. They take a special mitt and scrub, and as they scrub, the skin comes off in rolls of white. And when you think that's done, there's more and more. I feel very snake-shedding-my-skin-like when I do this. They scrub until you are pink from the friction. The women are working hard, their breasts swinging like pendulums, as they rub up and down the woman's limbs. A fabulously different cultural experience. Absolutely magnificent. One of my favorite things in this world is the public hammams. The care one receives is almost spiritual, you know? No, you don't know. Well, I could take it or leave it in the spa hammams. I get clean. It's just not the same experience. But that's not the end of it."

Nomad chuckled, charmed by her enthusiasm.

"Then they coat you with clay infused with herbs, and you sit in another room. The clay draws out impurities. After that, they rinse you off by throwing bowls of warm water on you. And the funniest part is when the women stand with their heels together and do a *plié* so the attendant can swing the bowl, sending the water up to clean a lady's nether regions."

"Huh."

"A surprising sensation, I grant you that. Yes, a hammam is one of life's great good things."

"Sounds like you want to go and hang out with Elena tomorrow," Nomad said.

"You know, I just might. So that's the end of it? These two women are going to the hammam in advance of the Secret Garden exchange?" Red reached up and scratched the nape of her neck. "Where's the Parisian's husband going to be? What else did they say?"

"I have nothing on the husband's plans," Nomad said. "And as to the other, nothing read as important. But you know how passing information goes. You hide it in the stories." He exited the traffic circle. "Another ten minutes 'til we get to the wall."

They drove in silence down the road, and just because he felt like it, maybe to test the waters, Nomad reached for Red's hand. They weren't in character here, so he would know her genuine reaction.

When Red turned her hand to lace their fingers, something eased in his body. "You look like you're plotting," Nomad said as they continued down the palm-tree-lined street.

"I was thinking about which techniques for following these

women would be applicable in the Medina. You've been there. You know what we're facing."

"It's disorienting. There are a thousand ways to slip out of sight. If I was being tracked, it's where I'd want to be. Doing the tracking, it's going to test my skills."

"Is this your first time in Marrakech?" she asked.

"I was here as a little kid. I thought it was a storybook come to life—the colors and all the people. I remember a big square with men playing music. They had monkeys, but my mom wouldn't let my brother or me near them. She was afraid they'd bite us. Then, there were the snake charmers with their fake cobras set out for tourist pictures and their little garden snakes to put on the tourists' heads. We'd go up on the rooftops and look down at the activity at night, the fire dancers, and those men playing the *gimbri*."

"The string instrument where the man wears the hat tassel and spins it round and round? Okay, that's one thing I don't like. They make me seasick." And when she said that, Red lifted the back of his hand to her lips and pressed a kiss there that felt like gratitude. Nomad wondered if she remembered that he'd been holding her as they went out to sea during her rescue.

He didn't ask.

He let her have the moment, and then she settled their linked hands on her lap. "I like to sit up on the rooftop and have a drink, watching the sun go down. All that hustle and bustle going on below. I like feeling like I'm floating above the fray. But it sounds like you enjoyed the fray."

"Sometimes. So you're the spook, and I am not. What conclusions did you reach about the best ways to follow our rabbits?"

"With just the two of us. We have the advantage of having control of her phone and the DARPA micro-tracker on the ring.

We still need to figure out why the friends are here getting involved. Are they staying at Elena's hotel?"

"Yes."

"It'll be harder to do handoffs without blowing our cover, especially with your height. The clothing, in my case, will help. I can keep changing the colors of my scarves. No makeup. Present as a generic Moroccan woman in the market. What's in our favor is that Elena thinks she ditched me. She'll be focused on the task at hand, figuring out how the billionaire wants to make the exchange."

"I think that Kamal's eccentricities are a challenge for Elena. She wanted a clean pass."

"Right, and that's also to our advantage. Don't sleep on the idea of the modern distaste for inconvenience."

"I think I'm going to need more there." He slid across three lanes of tightly packed traffic to make his next turn.

"Have you tried to tell anyone a story lately?" Red asked.

"In general, I'm not a storytelling guy."

"Fair. Well, this is observational, anyway. Many people get their information in sips, from starter plates instead of whole meals. Memes and social media posts are all synthesized down for the biggest dopamine hit in the shortest amount of time. If you don't like it, scroll on by. If you really don't like it, block and move on. It's too much work to try to understand a divergent opinion. People are overstimulated and overworked, and they just want to get through their day feeling somewhat okay in their skin. Again, observational."

"Observational."

"I've been doing my work for a while now. I was recruited in college and graduated from my university to The Farm. And in that time, I have to tell you, it's getting harder for me to find people willing to build a relationship and deepen—" Red's mouth pulled down, and Nomad was surprised to find her chin wobbling.

He waited for her to decide what came next.

"I'm thinking of an asset who just died. He had been an exception. He wanted our connection for friendship, and I had wanted the connection for exploitation." She took a minute to steady her emotions. "I very much enjoyed our conversations. My feelings for him were genuine." She exhaled. "He was only in harm's way because I created that connection. He's dead because I had an agenda." She turned to the window and said so softly that Nomad almost didn't catch it, "It's getting harder and harder to be okay with all that. Though, I get that my work has a bigger meaning."

Nomad understood. He squeezed her hand a little tighter.

Red swallowed loudly, sighed, and looked out the window, probably trying to find some privacy. After a moment, she took up the narrative again. "So if something is inconvenient to them, doesn't fit their narrowed worldview, or interrupts their life flow, it's ignored. Connection-making is harder. That's the downside. I've found that sometimes, this makes my job easier. Inconvenience is a powerful tool. And I've only seen it become that much stronger with time as algorithms are honed and people are popping their dopamine like popcorn at the theater."

"You were talking about people's stories ..." Nomad squeezed Red's hand and then released. This swarm of motorbikes required two hands on the wheel, and it had been a while since he'd driven on the left-hand side.

"I can't tell a whole story with nuance and descriptors without eyes sliding toward the activity they want to do. Usually, a phone. Sometimes, it's a weight shifted to the foot closest to the door."

"It could be that you're a shit storyteller." He stole a glance her way so she could see his smile was teasing.

"Again, fair. I think my mother's Irish lineage is pronounced in my DNA because I enjoy the oral tradition of storytelling. I'm an epic-sagas gal more than a short story enthusiast."

He reached for her again, and her hand was right there, open and waiting. "Side characters, red herrings, descriptions, and backstory?"

"It starts out that way, then there's the shifting and sliding narrative, but I wrap it up in a neat little bow as fast as I can even if I find the abruptness dissatisfying."

"Can you listen like that?"

"It's my job to listen like that, right? I need to know everything. The longer the story, the more I understand what motivates the storyteller and what characteristics they express with the most emphasis for good or for bad. What makes a hero to them? What makes an evil-doer? What do they perceive to be a reward? For some, it's money and fame. For others, it's the safety of their family and a hug from a beloved friend. Listening to the story *is* my job."

"I like that."

"It's funny how things work. Stories in the real world can have a plot twist. And it's only a plot twist if the characters think that life will continue on like a normal day, but no. Something happens."

Like you're about to fly home with a delegation, get rerouted, get rerouted again, and meet someone astonishing.

"I see just how random fate is. Two people standing side by side. One is blown into mist, and the other is coated with the mist of his friend but otherwise unscathed. Or me—"

"Yes, you. You survived the bombing at the hotel. You had to have, or you wouldn't have been coated with plaster the way you were when we found you."

"I was supposed to be sitting at the table with an asset. But leading up to the bombing, I ate a random campsite meal that gave me a random bacterial overload that sent me to the random toilet clutching my stomach. My asset is killed, and I am protected by the collapse of the metal stalls taking the blow and the aftershock."

"Saved by the shits."

"That's what I said. Absolutely random."

"But someone has your back. We had you out of there within twenty-four hours, and the only heads-up anyone had was that you didn't check in."

"And had you not been in the area, no one would have found me, and I could well have died. Dehydration leading to sepsis or what have you." She lifted her chin. "Why were you in the area? How did you get to me so quickly?"

"I was fishing in the Mediterranean."

"As one does."

Nomad pulled into a dusty plot used as a parking area. "This is as far as we can go with a car." He shifted into park. "We'll act like tourists and hire a pushcart to take your bag to the riad. You ready, Cassie?"

35

———————

Red

Nomad caught Red's gaze. "Elena's on the move."

Red looked down at her phone screen. "She has her map search open. It looks like they're heading to the Djemaa El Fna, the main square with the monkeys you wanted to pet."

"Given the time, they must be going out to see the sunset."

Red stood and stretched. "That would be an affirmative. They're heading to a rooftop restaurant. They just put the name into their map app."

"What do you think?"

Red moved closer to him so she could whisper their conversation. "I'd like to get eyes on them. I have the pictures you took. Some people do well making the leap from photo to in-person recognition, but I've found that when I'm trying to find someone in public, it's rare that they look like they did in a photo or that I get a good look at their face. As a matter of fact, if I get a good look at their face, it means they're getting a good look at mine."

"Can you tell me about that?" Nomad wrapped his hands

around her hips and pulled her into his lap so she didn't have to bend over to speak in his ear. He gave her a slight lift of the brow, asking if this was all right.

It was very all right. Natural even. Flashes of her rescue came back to Red. She decided to go ahead and say it out loud. "I've been in your arms before. I want to tell you how much I appreciate your care during my rescue. For a while there, I assumed I was going to die. And when you had me up against you," tears welled, but Red thought that was a little too damsel-in-distress-like, so she pushed those feelings down, "I knew I wouldn't."

Those words seemed to affect Nomad, too. He drew her tighter in his arms, and she rested her head on his shoulder.

"I'm going to wade away from those emotions and go back to your question," Red continued without lifting from his embrace. "What I like to do is minimally get film of the person. It's better if I can observe over time. Everyone has a style. I focus on how they like to sit. How fast they like to walk, how they swing their arms. How observant are they? Do they walk with their phone in their hand? All of that. Picking out someone's movement patterns is so much easier in a crowd."

"I get that. And you're right. When I get home from deployment, and we're all dressed exactly alike, with the same haircut and the same hat shielding half our faces, the families don't hesitate. They see their soldier, and they race into their arms. That has to be body mechanics. And yet, I never put that together. I've always looked for the face." He patted her hip. "Are you ready to head out? Do you need to change or anything?" Nomad asked. "I need to use the bathroom, and then I'm ready to go."

"I'll change into traditional clothes and head scarf. I love to wear them when I'm near the desert. They keep the sand and dust out of my hair. And they give me a certain level of anonymity."

"Okay, I'll put on slacks and a shirt. I think that will fit your look better than if I keep wearing these tactical pants."

A few minutes later, they were out the door. Nomad locked up with the heavy brass key and slipped it into his pants pocket. "Where are we going?"

Red pulled out her app. "They're heading here." She pointed. "And there's another roof-top restaurant here with a shared wall. I think that we'll be close enough to see them. But they will probably only scan their own restaurant if they're paying attention at all."

The walk from their riad to the square was a crush of humans. Since cars and trucks were only allowed in the early morning hours for deliveries, the paths were shared with motor-cycles that laced through the crowds.

All along their path, vendors in their tiny shops—only about eight feet wide—called out, trying to grab the attention of passing tourists and make a sale.

On some days, Red found the atmosphere to be carnival-like and fun. That night, still recovering, Red found the walk exhausting.

Nomad seemed to realize that and put his arm around her, using his body to carve a path and keep her from the crush.

Still, it was a relief when they found a table that gave them a good view of Elena and her friends through the veil of palm fronds.

The server placed menus in front of them and left them to decide.

Red pulled out her phone. She popped an earbud in one ear, then Red opened the mic on Elena's phone. Ambient sounds around Elena's table were picked up, but their group wasn't talking. They were all on their phones, scrolling.

"Those two are calling themselves Gustav and Simone Delacroix," Nomad said.

"Gustav. Interesting." Red popped her brow. "I'll flag my team and let them know to focus on the contents of those phones for their primary research." Red could see that the spider software she'd placed on Elena's phone did its job crawling into the other woman's phone, giving Langley full access.

With the mic open, Red could monitor their conversation, but so far, all they'd done was order banana juices.

Red wrinkled her nose. "Mmm, not my favorite. When the server comes, I'll do mango, please."

Nomad raised a finger, and the server came over. "A mango and a mixed fruit, please. We'll order dinner in a bit. Oh, and a bottle of still water." The man bowed and backed away from their table.

"They're all three on social media," Red said with her eye on her screen, "doom scrolling."

"Anything telling?"

Red leaned closer to share her screen. "Cat videos." His warmth as the night grew chilly was pleasant.

A tuxedo cat came over to their table and meowed insistently. "Sorry, baby," Red cooed. "We haven't been served yet."

The cat meowed angrily. Where was her food? Red knew that would keep up all night.

"The cats are everywhere," Nomad said. "I've never seen so many cats in my life."

"They're holy beings. No vet care, probably rabid, eaten up with fleas and diseases." She held out a hand. "Please don't pet. But also never shoo a cat away."

"Walking around the Medina, I've seen water bowls at nearly every stand. They're clean and filled."

"They never go hungry, either. The cats know they can sit in front of anyone and meow with the expectation that a bit of food will come out of the person's tote bag. None of them are hungry. One thing I find charming about Marrakech is that the animals don't cower and scurry. There are no angry kicks or fists. There's humanity in that." Red looked around as the server came with a tray. Setting their drinks down and leaving.

Red twirled her glass in her fingers. "I think the cats of Marrakech are prophets here to teach." She looked up to catch Nomad's gaze. "I do." She smiled nostalgically. "One of the biggest life lessons I received was at a chicken restaurant in Rabat one night. I was eating outside, and the cats arrived and meowed, wanting the patrons to throw a bit of food their way. Waiting for my dinner, I watched people tossing morsels out. The cats were generally fat and happy. But there was this one cat. He was obviously very sick and in terrible condition. I watched as people happily tossed food to the pretty and healthy cats and ignored the cat that most needed attention."

Red liked how Nomad listened and that her words elicited emotion in his eyes.

"By the time my dinner arrived, the sick cat was gone. I put some food in my napkin, and as I left to head back to my hotel, I looked for the sick cat but couldn't find him."

"That had to have been disappointing."

"I opened the napkin, placed it on the stoop, and said, 'This is for you. I wanted to help. I'm so sorry for everything you're going through, and I broke down crying."

Nomad took her hand in his.

"Yup. Right there in the street. I felt so bad because as I observed others' behavior, I saw my own. The cute, the pretty, the healthy, why are those the ones who get the attention in a crisis? While those that need it the most are ignored, even eschewed." She looked down at the black and white cat curled around Nomad's foot. "That story and those images pain me to this day. Yeah. I knew that cat was there as a guru to teach me—

as self-absorbed as that might sound. I've tried to watch my behavior, to turn my attention to those that might be overlooked because their circumstances are visually tough to handle." To change the mood, Red sent Nomad a teasing smile. "You, for example. I've taken pity on you. Your life with that face must have been lonely and difficult."

"Yes, thank you. You're right. Being hideous has been a life-long struggle," Nomad said resignedly. "But it's so much worse for my identical twin brother. He's a doctor, and his brain swelled from each textbook he memorized. He walks around with my face, but, you know, an enormous head."

"My sympathy to you both."

And as Nomad absentmindedly reached toward his foot, Red smacked his hand. "Nicholi, they are fed and given water but not treated for disease. Are you up on your rabies shots? Don't. Touch. The. Cats."

Now that it was dark, Elena and the Delacroixes were heading back to their hotel. Simone talked about what time they'd leave for the hammam the next day. Gustav made plans for how he'd case the gardens and get a feel for what Kamal was setting up for the exchange, the security in place, and to reassure Elena that all was safe for the sale.

"After we're sure that's cleared," Gustav said. "I found a tour going over the Atlas Mountains to a spot right along the Algerian border."

"Did you make reservations for that tour?" Simone asked.

"Not yet. I sent word to our supplier to see if they could arrange to pick us up there. We can't have any official contact with Algeria. I'm not getting a stamp on my passport."

"No, of course not," Elena said. "I have three months on the

Moroccan tourist stamp in my passport. So I can work with our suppliers, see the mission through, and have them bring me back to the Moroccan border."

"Three months' time frame," Red whispered to Nomad as they leaned against the closed security gate on a vendors shop around the corner of their riad.

"Do you think the tour will report us missing to the authorities?" Simone asked.

"After they've been paid? Probably not," Gustav said. "They're laissez-faire in Morocco."

"Once we've accomplished the sale tomorrow and hear back from our suppliers—if that's all a go—we set off on this tour," Elena said. "What kind of tour?"

"Glamping," Gustav said. "It's an eleven-hour drive from here to there. But you'll get to ride a camel."

"Joy," Elena said sarcastically.

The Delacroixes told Elena good night. There was a click of the door, and now there were just the sounds of water running and items rustling.

Nomad and Red moved into their tiny room on the first floor.

Red was dead tired and must have looked it because Nomad turned to her and said, "I'd anticipated sleeping on the floor, but there's not enough floor for me to stretch out on in here."

When he said that, Red felt a mild stab of disappointment.

Of course, he would say that. She'd seen him at the ball. He was raised a gentleman. "I had planned on sharing the bed with you." Why not be honest? She sat down on the corner to take off her shoes. "For what it's worth, neither of us will be comfortable on this mattress."

He gave her a nod and a smile. Cogs were whirring. Yeah, he was a soldier boy and not an intelligence officer. He didn't seem like he was used to this kind of assignment. They wouldn't send him to work with her unless he had training, but things were different when you learned about them in theory. "When on assignment, there will be times when you will be playing the role …"

He was navigating new waters.

Interesting though—Red thought as she gathered her toiletries and an oversized T-shirt that she slept in—his smile wasn't lascivious. It wasn't a "he-he-he, I'm gonna get me some." smile. It was a smile that warmed his eyes. She couldn't quite read it. She'd never seen someone smile at her like that before.

Shutting the door to keep the steam out of the bedroom, Red didn't throw the lock. It would be okay if he wandered in.

I like him. He likes me, too.

She'd taken a lot of comfort from him over the last few days.

Yes, he'd left her hanging in the van. And maybe she should be miffed about that. But she would have done the same thing. Red stood in front of the mirror, unwound the scarf from her hair, and pulled her long dress over her head. The night of the ball, he didn't know who she was or what position she played. And he didn't have a lot of time before the authorities arrived. If he'd stayed, he probably would have blown his mission. With all those dead bodies in the van, no one would have let him go free for days. Elena would have seemed to be the victim, cared for, and out there in the wilds.

He had no other choice.

At least he made sure she could get free. He didn't need to.

Stepping into the shower, with warm water and soap, her hands moving over her skin, Red's mind went to the bed. She knew Nomad wouldn't make a move on her.

It was fine. Sex, for her, was stress relief. She didn't have the luxury of a relationship that would make the experience anything more than moving body parts.

She'd had her orgasms.

She'd faked a few because—yeah, sometimes she just wasn't going to get there no matter how long that SEAL could snorkel.

There was always a conscious emotional distancing, the understanding she and her lover were ships in the night.

Nomad was, too. Red reminded herself. *I don't know his name. I'll never know his name. And I won't see him again once this mission is complete.*

She steeped in the flow of hot water, feeling her heart squeeze with grief at that thought.

It had been a lot in a week. And her asset had died. She shouldn't feel an emotion right now and assign it a definition. Yes, she liked Nomad. She liked him in a way that was surprising and intense. But it wasn't love.

It wasn't.

It was … something else.

She remembered the airport when Nicholi said goodbye to Cassie, "Love you." If only that wasn't make-believe, that might actually be really wonderful.

36

———

Red

RED BEGAN DREAMING THE DREAM AGAIN. NO HELPER-WOMAN was pointing Red toward the rollercoaster train. This time, the dream jumped right to the car crash, the holding of hands, and the blood.

In her semi-awake state, she wondered if this was all just a metaphor for what had happened to Moussa.

Trying to rouse herself, Red found her face tucked into the curve of Nomad's neck. She must have woken him because he wrapped her in his arms and pulled her against the length of his body.

Tears ran thick and hot and silent down her cheeks.

He didn't ask her for anything—not an explanation, not that she move back to her own side of the bed. He stroked her hair and held her tightly against him with enough force that she knew that not only did he want her there, but it felt like he needed her there.

She remembered this feeling. He did this when she moved from the hotel to the shore, from the shore to the sea.

The strength of his arms meant she could relax and allow. That she didn't have to be strong all the time. He not only could care for her, but he chose to.

And she remembered the devastation of losing the feeling of comfort when he placed her in the rescue basket and let go. Relief flooded through her when his voice was in her ear, and she knew he was back beside her on the helicopter.

Relief, that's what Nomad's arms brought her.

In the dark, her lips sought his. Her hands painted over his skin. Her fingers worked his clothes free, then hers.

Nomad's kisses traced her tears from lid to cheek down her neck to her breasts.

The ease of him, the utter rightness of this moment, was what struck Red.

For the first time, she felt like she was the focus of someone who intuited her desire. Red hoped Nomad felt the same because everything that felt natural to her seemed to bring him pleasure.

Was intimacy really this easy?

That was the thought she took with her when, wholly sated, she fell back asleep.

A dreamless and restorative sleep.

Red and Nomad, still holding each other, woke to the call to prayer intoned from the minaret with a rich baritone.

Sliding off the end of the bed, Red wanted to avoid any discussion of last night. She didn't have a neat place to file all of this and didn't want words to get in the way of her feelings. She pointed to the bathroom.

"Yeah, you go first," Nomad said huskily.

Gathering her clothes, Red went in to get ready for the day. After showering, Red covered herself respectfully from collar-bone to ankle, the long sleeves covering her to the wrists. Marrakesh could go either way. There were tourists in shorts and spaghetti string tops, and women dressed conservatively to follow Muslim traditions. Red often chose the traditional route, especially when moving through airports and places where she might be confronted with authority figures. Culturally mindful and respectful were important.

When she came out, ready for the day, Nomad was still in bed. The sheet covered him from the hips down. He had his hands laced behind his head and looked like he'd been deep in thought.

He caught her gaze and waited for Red to set the tone.

"If you'll monitor Elena's phone, I'll get us breakfast."

Nomad agreed.

And now she was out in the paths of the Medina. Where there had been a crush of humanity the night before, there was little movement in the first signs of light. Here, Red would have privacy to call Black and file her report on having sex with Nomad.

It was all part of her security protocols, and it was one of the reasons Red's sex life was in the shape it was. This report sucked any romance from a physical encounter. Even the thought of "calling it in" and having the event cataloged in her file meant that Red would often just take any desire to bed with her and her plastic, packable boyfriend.

"Where do you think that's going?" Black asked.

"Nowhere," Red's response sounded deflated.

CIA preferred that their employees have sexual relationships within the agency. Their second preference was that their employees have sex with others of equal security status. Nomad, of course, would have top-secret clearance, or he wouldn't know her name.

"I approve your continued sexual contact."

"Thank you, sir." It was like getting approved for a car rental.

That wasn't at all what Red was feeling.

She had a lot of feelings, and one of them was oddly grief. She was in anticipatory mourning.

When had that ever happened with a lover before?

A Turkish coffee shop was opening its front shutters, and Red walked over. Sitting at a little café table, she held up two fingers and, in French, asked for coffees to go. She'd grab some pastries as well.

As the man went through the ritual of mixing warming seasonings into the coffee—cardamom, cinnamon, cloves and nutmeg, fennel, a bit of anise—and swirling his pot in the heated sand, Red mused over the way Black responded over the phone this morning. There might be clues there as to Nomad's affiliation. Red had speculated that Nomad was a Delta Force operator.

He could be FBI CIRG. Definitely not CIA or Black would have told her.

Nomad did have tradecraft, though, very good tradecraft.

Having worked with Delta Force before, Red knew the operators all had FBI and CIA training—some were better at fieldwork than others. Nomad was as smooth in the field as on the dance floor.

And she spent the rest of the time enjoying memories of the night before, startled when the man placed the cups on his counter and called to her.

Red paid with colorful Moroccan dirham and went back to make a plan for the day.

A day of work.

A day of saving people from terrorist threats.

Honestly, Red, focus!

37

Nomad

Standing under a tree outside the ticket kiosk in the Secret Garden, Nomad awaited Red's signal.

Besides watching passing faces for someone on their watch list, he had time to think.

And what he thought about was Red.

Nomad knew that their love-making wouldn't stay between the two of them. Red had called this in. It was CIA protocol. His taking her into his arms last night was now part of a CIA report.

That felt all kinds of wrong to him. It hadn't just been sex. It had been … sacred was the word that came to mind.

Nomad thought that over his years of experience, he'd become pretty good at reading women in bed. He needed to keep up the reputation of special forces as being especially good. And in that, he made sure to put in the effort. And while sex sometimes became formulaic, it was still fun, if not somewhat ego-driven.

Those elements were missing from last night with Red in his arms: effort, ego, and formula.

He'd been thoughtless throughout.

It wasn't that he didn't care about Red's experience. It was just that it seemed so natural.

There was an ease there that he'd never had before.

After they'd orgasmed and Red had draped her sweaty body over him, he could feel her heart galloping. She'd lifted herself momentarily, then flopped back across him. It wasn't graceful; she was a rag doll, and he had been proud.

No, wrong word. Fulfilled.

Her satiety *fulfilled* something in him. When this mission wrapped up, and he finally had to say goodbye to her, that would be a hard day.

Something in his chest growled, *Mine!*

But she wasn't.

And wouldn't be.

Their lives didn't line up like that. She'd move back into her shadow life, and he'd head out on his next mission.

That thought was a hard kick in the gut.

Red's voice in his ear bud refocused him. He had his ticket in his pocket and could maneuver as needed.

"She's out of the hammam. As anticipated, Elena's changed into traditional clothes. She's in black, head to foot. Simone is walking a few steps behind in grey robes and a rose head scarf."

"Copy."

"Something—" The sounds of the Medina filled Nomad's earbud. He knew to wait. He didn't want to step on her information or concentration. "Something's wrong."

She was steps away, in the shop across the pathway. Nomad rounded to a place where he could see the entrance to the hammam and—with a brief window where the tourists shifted—Nomad caught a glance of Red's back, heading into the Medina's labyrinth rather than toward the garden.

"Okay. This is bad." And he could hear the squeeze of her

ribs that prevented breath. This was a combat call. This was how soldiers sounded when a tango was in play.

Ice dumped through his system.

"She's running," Red called out. "Okay. Okay. I didn't plan for this." She was heavy breathing into the phone. "I recognize this man. Elena is turning. Okay. Moving."

"What guy, Cassie?"

Red switched to Turkish. "There was a robbery in Germany. Do you know that?"

"Negative." That word in Turkish was enough to let Red know he was conversant in that language. He knew she'd switched so those around her would have less of a shot of understanding.

"Five men killed?"

"Negative."

"Treasure hunters found Kamal's ring, and Elena stole it from them?"

Why wasn't he brought up to speed? "Negative. I know that Elena has the ring."

"I'll give you details later. I believe the men at the ball who took Elena from the kitchen were part of a team. Five members of that team were sniped in Munich. At that scene, Elena stole the ring. That's how she came to be in possession of it. The men in the van—you saved us from them—are probably treasure hunters trying to get the ring back before Elena can collect the prize. And we can't let them do that. My orders are to make sure Elena succeeds at getting the money."

Okay, retribution and robbery were on the table. "You see one of them?"

"Affirma—two. One with a broken arm, right arm, in a cast. One with—Sharing my screen." Red was breathing hard.

Nomad whipped his phone from his pocket, swiped open the app, and watched the movement of the flag representing the ring dance across the map, sliding up and down and around the pathways.

If Elena could hide, she'd hide. That was the easiest survival move. If the men were on her heels, she wouldn't have the time or space to make the feint.

She certainly wouldn't head for the gardens.

As he watched, Nomad thought something about Elena's movements was off.

And that was when he realized, "Cassie. There are more than two. They're herding her."

"To where? Can you get ahead of them?"

"Moving."

If it were him running from his captors, Nomad would conclude that his best shot of escape would be to dive into the back of a random taxi. While taxis were everywhere on the street outside the Medina's ancient walls, flagging one down would make Elena slow and conspicuous. The closest taxi stand was in front of the Palais Royale, where a line of military men —a representative of each branch—stood guard.

If Elena could get anywhere near the Palais, she'd be safe.

Two kilometers.

If the men were good enough to find Elena here in Marrakech, they were good enough to think that through. They would want Elena to devise the plan and work herself in that direction. They would push her toward that decision strategically because there were undercover police interspersed with the crowds, ensuring the tourists' safety.

One scared influencer posting about their survival story could aim those tourist budgets to safer places.

Tourists were the lifeblood of the Medina economy.

Two kilometers. "Heading toward the Grand Palais."

"I thought so, too," Red panted. She had been hospitalized

days before; Red was probably wringing the last ounces of energy from her system.

Scaffolding hugged the buildings all along the route from the Secret Garden to the Grand Palais. Placed there after the earthquakes to keep the ancient facades from tumbling, building materials were stacked above and below as the restoration took place.

The tourists had to decide how to move down the road, either under the scaffolding or in the center of the pathway.

Nomad chose to be under and close to the wall, wanting to avoid notice as he strode forward, using the length of his legs to his advantage.

On the app, Nomad saw the pin representing Elena advancing toward his position. He'd been right.

Red was a heavy breath in his ear.

Turning at the corner, Nomad told her, "I'm at the taxis. I can see the length of the path. I'll see her coming." As he leaned his shoulder into the wall, the drivers called out, offering rides. Nomad waved them off. He switched his screen to locate Red, and she moved up fast. Soon, she'd catch up to Elena.

He wondered what the plan was.

"Nomad!" Red yelled. It was a call to action. She'd forgotten to use his code name, Nicholi. "Nomad! Your three o'clock!"

Nomad whipped his head toward the line of soldiers near the door. People were milling about. He didn't see any concerning movement. He spun back to look down the path. From his height, Nomad saw Elena, followed by Simone and Red. Behind Red was a man with a broken arm.

Elena looked over her shoulder and sprinted forward.

As she did, at Nomad's three o'clock, a man tapped his phone and ducked behind the soldiers' station at the Palais.

The scaffolding above Elena shifted and collapsed. The area

filled with screams. A dense cloud of dust rose, blocking the view of the scene.

"Cassie? Shit!" Nomad yelled into his phone.

He heard coughing, then the miracle of Red's voice. "Down, not hurt."

Elena was the only one of the three women under the section of collapsed scaffolding. But many others happened to be in the wrong place at the wrong time.

The man who had caused the collapse was pulling bags of cement off the victims. The three other men from the kidnapping joined in. Nomad knew they were trying to get to the ring.

From here, he didn't know how this should play out. The idea was the ring would lead to a payday for the terrorists *not* the treasure hunters, and that payday would lead them to lifesaving information.

But what if Elena was dead?

Then what?

Nomad decided his play was to observe and then act.

Nomad watched as Red got herself to her feet and moved purposefully forward. As the bystanders and soldiers scrambled to help, they quickly formed a chain, lifting the building materials and passing them hand to hand. Out of the way, Nomad watched as Red used her body to block helpers, facilitating Simone's grapple to get to Elena first. Nomad knew Simone had succeeded when she straightened and stumbled toward the taxis because the ring pin on his phone moved with her.

Brushing her dress to clean herself, Simone climbed into a cab.

As Red followed, she avoided Nomad's gaze. But once in the cab, she asked, "Can you still hear me?"

"Copy." He had to work to keep his communications simple and professional. Everything about this scene was counterintuitive.

"It's not likely Elena's alive."

"I'll stay with that," Nomad said.

"I'm following Simone. She got hold of both Elena's phone and *the* ring."

"I can verify both," Nomad was watching his screen. "Both pins are moving."

"I'll follow at a distance to see what she's up to. I don't think Simone was involved with the collapse. She didn't flinch before it came down, and she was cut. Her face is bleeding. Can you figure out how that scaffolding came down? And find out if Elena survived?"

"Wilco. Out."

With all the hands at work clearing the scene, it quickly became apparent that the people under the scaffold had died. The task went from frenzied ant-like effort to solemnity as the bodies were moved to the sidewalk and laid side by side.

As the man with the broken arm blocked people, three men from the Austrian van—two with ugly jaw bruises the size of Nomad's fist—lifted Elena's body and carried her to the side-walk where the other victims lay. Their acted-out grief allowed them to remove the rings from each of Elena's fingers and pat her over for her phone.

Kamal's treasure hunt had now killed six people that Nomad had heard about. He had to assume there were more bodies along the way. Kamal did like his deadly games.

The three men stepped back as the ambulances arrived and then walked away.

After taking a look at how the treasure hunters had collapsed the scaffolding, Nomad circled toward a different entrance to the Medina, feeling the weight of the tragedy.

So many had died right there, not twenty feet away, as he watched.

Red had survived the bombing of the courthouse by needing a bathroom break.

She survived the scaffolding collapse because she and Simone were four steps behind.

Four steps from death.

Four steps.

His heart slammed against his chest.

38

─────

Nomad

When Nomad's phone rang, he snatched it up and swiped the call open.

Without preamble, Red said, "Simone called Kamal and spoke to him as if she were Elena. Simone accused him of trying to kill her to take the ring and not have to pay the prize."

"Could Simone actually believe that?"

"She might. I mean," Red was speaking in Turkish again, making herself heard over the sound of traffic. "It's possible. Simone may have no idea about the treasure hunters that came after Elena at the ball, and honestly, we don't know what happened. That's speculation, right?"

"I don't think they had anything to do with Joel if that's what you're asking me. Too many easier ways to handle that. And those men had vengeance in their eyes. That wasn't a mission tasked to hired help," Nomad said. "That was personal."

"I agree. So Simone told Kamal she was not going to the garden. And Kamal was pissed. Simone blew the whole 'perfect circle through time' scenario that Kamal wanted to draw. It was apparent that he wasn't used to someone saying no to him. And honestly, Simone is in the catbird's seat. Forty million euros would be nice. But if that doesn't work, there are other buyers. She could get at least four million on the merits of the diamond. Disappointing, sure. But not chump change."

"What did Kamal end up telling her? Are you walking?" Nomad asked.

"Sitting." Her words drowned in the blare of horns. "Simone told Kamal to meet her outside of police headquarters, and they could make the exchange there. She wasn't playing games, and she wasn't taking chances."

"Yeah, I saw that her pin has been there for about ten minutes now. What's she doing?"

"She's perched on the wall."

"You think he's going to buy it that Simone is Elena?"

"I think that entirely depends. If Kamal has only seen Elena's photograph, it could work. It's hard to tell a real-life, moving, breathing person from a person in a photo. Especially if it's a still photo that the person posed for. That's why front-facing grinning photos are terrible to take. They remove the humanity. Now, if Joel is with him, there would be a problem. Elena danced in Joel's arms. He'd know right away."

"So what are you doing?"

"Having a pistachio ice cream across the street, picking construction materials off my clothes. And you?"

"I have some things I'm following up on. I'll update you later. How's the ice cream?"

"Oddly, it's tasteless. But I think that my senses are still in fight-or-flight. That's twice in one week where I lost someone who was mission-critical just feet away."

"I thought about that. You're going to have to take some time to process it."

"Once I've saved the world."

"Agreed, world-saving takes priority," Nomad said lightly, but these weren't nameless tangos squirting out the back of a terror nest. These were humans. They had voices, emotions, and faces that Red had interacted with over time. Nomad knew enough people who pushed that shit down and pressed on, and they paid a heavy price for it. He didn't want that for Red.

"Out of curiosity, do you have any idea how the team got the scaffold to fall? I didn't hear an explosion. There was no fire flare."

Nomad was aware that she'd gracefully but purposefully changed the subject. "Yeah, I have a pretty good picture of what happened. There was a steel cable around the base of the scaffold. It was attached to a motor that was attached to the building."

"Battery-powered winch?"

"Exactly, no noise. I'd imagine the team's job was to get Elena under the scaffold. My guess is that the guy at my three o'clock had the motor running silently, waiting for her. Then, as she stepped under, he pressed the app button that would make the cable drag the leg out. It was a temporary structure. Workable but not all that stable."

"You saw all this?"

"I saw the guy at my three o'clock tap his screen a second before the structure came down. I saw a cable attached to the leg," Nomad said. "Not wanting anyone to mark my face as the one who figured out the cable, I didn't trace it to the wall. But the cable was thick, the kind you might use to pull someone out of a ditch if you're in an off-road vehicle."

"That's some sinister stuff. And creative."

"The three men took all the rings off Elena's hands while the guy with the broken arm blocked people's view."

"Simone has the correct one, of course," Red said. "I saw her pull off the right-hand, ring-finger ring, pop the Fire of the

Desert out of the ring guard, and put the guard back on Elena's finger. The tracker says the Fire of the Desert is right there across the street. I'm just waiting to see if Kamal shows."

"Simone and Elena, what do you think their relationship is? Was?" Nomad corrected himself.

"Simone has to be a cover name. I don't recognize her. But Color Code has a team of targeters who are very good at what they do. The spider software on Elena's phone will give them access to everything available. Since both Gustav and Simone contacted Elena on that phone, their phones have also been corrupted. The targeters will be putting together the pieces of the puzzle to get a clearer picture. Though I'm never allowed to see the whole picture, I just act on orders."

"Need to know."

"Yeah. Do you know what I n*eed* to know right now?" Red deadpanned. "If and when is Kamal going to show? I need the ladies' room."

"Ah, the joys of a stake out."

"Exactly. Someone's moving to the table near mine," she said in a low tone. "Hanging up."

When Red unlocked the door at the Riad and walked in, she put her phone on the shelf with her key. "I just got off the phone with Grey."

"Yeah?" Nomad lifted his brows. "What did he have to say?"

She shut the door before answering, moving over to Nomad and lowering her voice. "I quote, 'You two are hitting it out of the ballpark. Great work. This is exactly the information we needed.' Since I was in the middle of the Medina, I just said, 'Good news.' And we hung up. I assumed you'd know what he was talking about or that I could call him back at some point." She looked at him pointedly. "But I can tell you're pleased." She toed her shoes off. "Fill me in."

"I figured I'd go to Elena's room before the police arrived, so I could document her things. Taking pictures of her passport gives us some important information."

"Agreed. Did you have trouble getting in?" She unwound her head scarf and tossed it into the corner.

"It was a straightforward security system. What I found was that Elena had two computers and she had a burner phone."

Red reached for the hem of her robe and pulled it over her head, muffling her words as she said, "If data flowed between the devices, we'd have all that, right?"

"I called our support team to ask for instructions. One of the laptops was files only and wasn't connected to WIFI."

"To protect the data from the very thing we tried to do." She pitched the robe into the corner, leaving her dressed in a bra and panties. "I'm begrudgingly impressed with Elena."

"There was no cross-contamination with the second phone either. It's all fresh data."

"You took the computer?" Red asked.

"Didn't need to. I put in the flash drive, and it bypassed her security. The team made copies of the hard drive and phone. That information was sent to the AI software to develop preliminary reports on imminent attacks. They can remotely wipe it if they see it moving somewhere that Uncle Sam doesn't like."

"Congratulations, that was a coup." Red moved into the bathroom and ran the water. From the reflection in the mirror, he saw her wash her face and hands. "That's not all." She came to the door, toweling off as she caught his eyes. "You've got more."

"I have our next task."

"So we're not done." She leaned into the door jamb.

"Sadly, no."

They stilled and looked into each other's eyes. Yeah, it would be good to have this wrapped up, to have the terrorists cornered, their plan thwarted. But when it was done, so were they. That would be it.

"Sadly no," Nomad modified, "in terms of protecting innocent lives."

"That's how I took it."

"I found out that the Algeria connection is still a go," Nomad said. "Simone and Gustav will take a tourist trip over the Atlas Mountains."

"Is that what you were working on when I came in?"

"Yes. Gustav went to a tourist guide in the Medina and set up the glamping trip. I got us places on that trip, too. The bus will pick us up in the morning."

"What's the goal? Wait." She paused and looked at the floor. "Okay, that clarifies their last phone conversation. So Simone will break off from Gustav and go with someone else to Algeria."

"Exactly. And I think I've figured out how they're going to pull it off without alerting anyone on the Moroccan side. Command wants us to take pictures of the people that connect with Simone."

"That's it? Pictures in Algeria of Simone making contact?"

"Sarcasm?"

"I'm waiting to hear how you think this going to go down. How are we going to accomplish the goal of photographing people meeting Simone in Algeria?"

Nomad pointed at the boxes on the nightstand— a honking big smartphone zoom lens. "Photography is my hobby. I can't wait to capture sunrise on the Sahara dunes."

"You do love it so much." She hung up the towel. "What's

the range? I'm guessing we can probably hang out—What?—like a kilometer away with a lens like that?"

"It depends on the atmosphere. But on a good day, that might be true. Of course, it's going to depend on topography, too. If we're still in the dunes, and they're down in the trough, things could get sketchy. The rallying point isn't that far distant from our ATV tour. Look at this map. Nomad scooted to the end of the bed and held up his tablet. "This is the glamping site." He pointed at a picture of two rows of cloth tents with a cement sidewalk and footlights.

"That's romantic."

Nomad popped his brows. "They have bathrooms."

"Bonus. Where does the water come from?"

"My question, too. I discovered that there are deep wells dug out in the desert, and they have pipes that lie across the top of the sand that bring the water in. The itinerary. Eleven-hour bus ride. Take camels to our tents. In the morning, we take ATVs to watch the sun rise over the dunes, and then we return to the bus for a ride home."

"I don't think I'd have chosen a twenty-two-hour bus ride for camels, tents, and ATVs."

"You get to see the breadth of Morocco. And Simone gets to go to Algeria."

"You said rallying point?" Red reached for an oversized T-shirt that covered her to her knees, and Nomad was disappointed when she pulled it on.

"Gustav got a GPS meeting point ping in his messages." Nomad moved back to the map. "Here. This other pin is the well. This one is our tent. And this one is the nearest town."

"Close."

"If you get to the well and head east—"

"Which would be apparent if you're going to watch the sunrise."

"Exactly. This is the red line that would move us from the Morocco to Algeria. It's a hard kilometer of walking the dunes." Nomad moved the tablet to the side table, then scooted back in the bed with his head resting on a stack of pillows. "Come here, please." Nomad held out his hand. "I'd like you to come lay down for a few minutes."

"Why, what did you have in mind?" She crawled on top of him and lay down with her head to his heart.

"I had in mind that we have a lot of planning to do, but it can wait for a bit. I've had a chance to turn off the engines and rest. You haven't."

"When did you have this time? I'm calculating all the things you were up to, and I was eating ice cream." She didn't sound like she minded this. But maybe she wasn't used to someone helping her to stop and take a breath.

He was part of a team; they looked out for each other. From what Nomad could tell, Red's team was all over the place, and she worked solo on missions.

Since Red seemed to be resting but not sleeping, after a while, Nomad ventured, "Have you ever found love?" He'd said it from out of the blue, without thinking through how Red would hear that question. But honestly, he knew nothing about her. She could be married, have someone at home…

Love had been on his mind a lot these last few days. He'd listened to plenty of "How I Met Your Mother" stories. But he couldn't recall anyone ever telling him how they knew they were in love. He wondered if it was a gradual awakening or if it were a flash of lightning.

"I have loved in my lifetime, yes." She kissed his chest. "Loved deeply. Loved hard. Loved many. But one by one, they've slipped out of my arms until my arms were left empty."

He was sure by her tone that she wasn't talking about couple relationships that had come and gone but love in general. And it expanded his heart to know that she had the capacity to love and to keep on loving. That took courage. "And then what do you do?" he whispered, pressing the clasp of her claw open and setting it on the side table so he could comb his fingers through her hair.

"I have all that love and nowhere to put it. It piles up around me, and I stumble over it all the time. I try to shift it to the side to make room and space to move freely. But it's liquid – a thick sticky ooze, and it slides right back in my path, gets on my shoes, and I track it wherever I go. I find that it's easier to wash off if I have a hard outer shell. But it's still there, nonetheless."

"And you're aware of it."

"All the time. It still catches at my feet and sometimes tumbles me end over end." She pressed up to look him in the eyes. "But I don't think that's what you're asking me. I think you want to know if I've ever *fallen* in love before. And the answer is no. I don't know what that feels like. I don't know what this is between us, but it's something. Don't you think? It's like we were offered an opportunity. It could be there, we could have that, but it wouldn't be free. The price would probably be very high."

She curled back into his arms, and Nomad pressed a kiss into her hair. That was exactly right. It was there for the taking. But there would be a cost extracted.

Nomad knew that he had to treat every moment with her as precious.

He would have this mission, and then she'd be gone.

39

Red

THE MORNING HAD COME, AND THE DAY HAD GONE. ELEVEN long hours in a bus traveling east over the mountains into the rocky and monochrome distance.

They had arrived at a buffet dinner in the community tent and drummers who did their earnest best to entertain the travelers. But everyone was exhausted from the ride, and their attention was polite but not engaged.

After making love that night, she and Nomad curled into the Berber blankets, which kept them cozy against the sudden drop in desert temperatures.

She'd had her hospital dream again. Each time, it started further along the story. Last night, she'd started on the rollercoaster train but woke before things got too wild because Nomad wrapped an arm around her waist and tugged her to him until her bottom rested against the inside curve of his hips. Curled around her like a nautilus shell, he'd whispered, "Shh-shh-shh, I've got you." He kissed her hair, and she fell into a restorative rest.

Now, Red stood outside the open doorway, taking in the last scattering of stars and embracing the cold desert air. Today, it would heat up to a hundred, making the sand glisten with mirages.

It was the time between dawn and sunrise. She listened to the sonorous call to prayer that hummed meditatively through her body. It rested her soul. When silence fell again, Red stepped into the tent and shut the door behind her.

Nomad lay on the bed with his booted feet extending a good six inches over the edge. A squeaky fan sang overhead as it twirled shadows across the tent ceiling. The air was hazy with dust in the dim light, and there was nothing to do but wait. And listen to the open mic on Simone's phone. "Do you ever get a comfortable night's sleep?"

"At my house, I have a bed made for someone my size."

"I didn't know such a thing existed. So, anything?" She lifted her chin toward the notepad that rested on his chest.

"Nothing beyond this." Nomad unbent an arm he had used to pillow his head and waved his hand in a circle, indicating the static that hissed and crackled from his phone. "They're not up and chatting with their handlers, that's for sure. Good that we have WIFI here in the camp. We'll lose connectivity once we're out on the ATVs."

"Now that we're here and you've met the people on our tour, seen the people who run the place, have a feel for things, give me your best guess." She moved over to snuggle into his body and lowered her voice to a mere whisper. "What percentage that we're right and this will go to plan."

"Eighty-two percent."

"Oddly specific. And oddly tip of the tongue."

"That's the number that flashed into my mind." He grinned.

Red's phone pinged, and she locked eyes with Nomad. "A hundred percent chance that's the eighteen percent you were missing." She flipped her phone over. "I need to call." They moved up in the bed until they sat shoulder to shoulder, balancing the phone between their ears to keep the information to themselves. The only privacy was the thick tent cloth and a few feet of grass.

"Yes," she said.

"Brava." It was Grey.

"Thank you?"

"No, thank *you*. I have a lot to catch you up on. We have a lot of answers. For the moment, what you need to know is there was a change of mission objectives."

Red turned to Nomad and popped her brows up, mouthing, "Eighteen percent."

"We still need you to get pictures of the people who show up to meet with Simone. We're depending on the fact that this is a big-money sale, and they will send competent, high-level people into the desert to pick her up. Stepping back about the ring sale. We now know there is a three-day delay on the funds moving from Kamal to Elena's accounts. International laws and the amount of money come into play. Elena's account will be out of reach of U.S. influence. We'd hoped to trace the money. We now know that's not going to be possible."

"Okay."

"The new game plan is to move the money ourselves or to make sure that no one can access those funds."

"I'm not following."

"Work in progress. Our intelligence suggests that Elena's bank needs Elena to present herself in person to access that account or that she needs to perform the commands from the phone that has been previously identified as hers."

"So we can't spoof that through our access?" Red asked.

"No."

Red frowned in thought. "But you saw it drop? The money is there?"

"We see that it's pending," Grey assured her.

"What you're telling me is that you need that phone."

"Exactly."

"But I can't go get it now where that task is easy here in this camp because you also want pictures of the person who wants to pick her up."

"Yes."

"We don't know how many people will meet her," Nomad pointed out.

"Correct," Grey said.

"We don't have weapons," Red reminded him.

"Also correct."

Red pursed her lips. "And yet, our mission is to get the phone."

"After you take the pictures."

Red tried to stuff her frustration. "Okay, let me ask it a different way. Which is your priority?"

"The photos," Grey said. "So if you get out there, it's a guy on a camel, take his picture, take the phone. If you get out there and it's a tactical team arriving on a helicopter brandishing AKs, take their pictures and let the phone go. If you can get the phone and not get shot, do that. I'd tell you to get the phone and plant GPS tracker to get the photos, but—"

"But there's Gustav involved and possibly others on this tour that we haven't identified, and we don't want them to wave the Algerians off," Red concluded. "Why would you risk letting the phone get away? For a few possible photos? The phone represents forty million dollars."

"From here, we can reset the phone to factory specs like you would if you were selling the phone to someone new, "Grey said. "The money would be in the bank. And we're not sure if anyone else has access. From the profile the targeters are developing, Elena didn't trust anyone except her fiancé and—"

"He was in the Lebanon explosion."

"Exactly. That plays in our favor, and the loop might be closed."

"Okay," Red said. "Orders received."

"Be safe. Out."

Red caught Nomad's gaze. "Fabulous."

Red and Nomad each perched on an ATV. It seemed like the night of research that they'd spent in their Marrakech riad developing plans and contingency plans, and contingency for the contingency plans was paying off.

The tour operator guys were young. This was their job, and they did it efficiently, but they were used to tourists who had never seen sand before. They weren't looking for spies. And they would never think that someone was using their services to escape over the border into Algeria.

One of the greatest dangers is the failure of the imagination.

At the first dune, Red and Nomad were at the back of the pack. As soon as the last kid gunned his ATV up the side, Nomad put the plastic tube in the gas tank, sucked up enough gas to get the siphon flowing, and filled the bottle they'd brought for this specific purpose. Luckily, the gauge said that he only had a quarter tank.

Having done the calculations the night before, the full water bottle should be enough to prime the engine and get them to the closest town, which was within easy sight but a challenging walk. Nomad let the rest of the gas pour into the sand, leaving just enough in the tank, he hoped, to get them to the well. He could always drain the last while they were regrouping and counting heads.

Nomad and Red knew Simone and Gustav had paid for a single ATV they would share. They speculated that the kids running the show would count ATVs and not heads to ensure everyone kept up. Therefore, Simone could just get off the ATV, hide behind a dune, and never be missed.

Since Red and Nomad needed to stay together. Their ATV shuffle was a bit more complex. They wanted to leave an ATV in the dunes for escape or comfort as they returned from following Simone to the rally point. If they ran out of gas, that would take one ATV out of the equation for the headcount.

Now, they needed to hand off an ATV to someone else to drive in for them.

At the next dune, the tourists lined up and waited for their turn to gun it up the slope with enough speed to try to get some lift as they flew over the top.

Nomad approached the father of a British family. "I wonder if I could ask you a favor." He pointed over to Red. "My wife thought this would be great fun but has realized this is too much. She wants to ride on my ATV with me, and I was wondering if one of your boys would be willing to drive hers the rest of the trip?"

That morning, Red noticed the man's tweenaged sons fighting about having to share an ATV. This made the dad a hero, the boys happy, and it would make the head count accurate when Red and Nomad left the tour.

Away from Simone and Gustav's view, the switch was made. And with everyone dressed in similar clothes and wearing helmets, it worked.

Red tapped Nomad's arm as they got the water well into view. Gustav had positioned himself as last in line, and Red watched as Simone slipped behind the well enclosure and out of sight.

At the next dune, Red got off and slipped over the top.

Nomad got to the front of the pack. He revved his bike, trying to use up the last drops of gas. He waved Gustav around them, and Gustav raced his ATV up the dune. The first in their group to fly into the sky and disappear from view.

Nomad was next in line.

After a couple more revs, Nomad's ATV started sputtering.

A few minutes later, the helper was beside him. "Out of gas." Nomad tapped the gauge. "Don't worry about it. I'll get on with my wife."

The boy gave him a thumbs up, and Nomad walked to the back of the group as if he were finding his wife but slipped over the dune.

Nomad knew that they only had limited time until the group returned their ATVs and got on the bus. And that's when the three missing tourists might be noticed. The boys would bring a gas can out to the dune to retrieve their quad, fill it up, and return it to their garage. Still, it would be nice if, somehow, Red and he beat them to it and could exfil on the ATV. Dunes took enormous energy to cross on foot.

Once the sound of ATVs had receded, Nomad caught up with Red, and they gave each other silent high-fives. "Look at her." Red pointed. She's walking down each dune.

"If we keep to this line, and we're sledding, we'll get out in front of her."

"Lots of ifs in the next stage."

"We're creative. We'll figure it out. Nomad winked at her. "You know, wing it."

Red scowled back at him. "Sounds like a solid plan."

40

———

Nomad

NOMAD LOOKED THROUGH HIS SAFARI-QUALITY ZOOM LENS. "Camels."

"Of course, there are."

"Three men are riding. They have two camels with what looks like camping gear. And a sixth camel is set up for riding. That's probably for Simone."

"Can you see their faces?" Red asked. "If you can get their photos, we could just go bully the phone away from Simone, and it could be an easy day."

"The only easy day was yesterday."

"That's for SEALs. That's not me," Red said dryly. "My days are spent chatting over tea. They're all easy."

Nomad turned to catch her eye and gave her a shake of the head. "We both know that's not true. Also, with this wind blowing sand around, they've wrapped shemaghs around their faces. I'm going to have to pull them off to get the images."

"Yeah, the wind is picking up, and I'm getting sandblasted. So what do we do?"

"Here's one way this could play out: one guy will dismount. He's going to get the camel to lay down so Simone can climb on. We've already figured out that the phones are in her backpack. You're going to get the backpack from her."

"I'm going to get the backpack worth forty million euros from that woman. Sure. Piece of cake."

"You are. You're going to sit on the garbage bag and slide onto the scene. We have surprise on our side. They won't know what's going on. They're not ready for this."

"Weapons?" Red asked. "If so, we're just going to have to track them on foot until they set up their camp for the night."

Nomad spent some time assessing that possibility. "No weapons are out. My experience is they carry knives and AKs, but this area is empty of anyone and anything. There's nothing they need to defend against. They're not ready for combat."

"Are you sure?" Red asked.

"They look bored."

"All right. So I slide down to Simone."

"After the camel starts to go down, and everyone has their attention on the process, I'll go in from the east side. All I have to do is get their photos, and then we're out of there."

Red blinked at him. "You know that makes no sense."

"Doesn't matter. We have a mission to complete. Use your trash bag as a weapon. I know you know this, but I feel compelled to say it out loud. If someone gets control of the bag and puts it over your head, don't try to move their hands and fight your way free. Preserve what air you have while you puncture a hole so you can breathe."

She held her eyes wide.

"I'm calling them by their shirt colors. Brown, Blue, Green. If you hear me call out a color, you know whom I'm looking at."

"But not Red."

He kissed her nose. "There are no Reds out here, just a Cassie."

She breathed in and held it.

Nomad waited for her to exhale. "Good?" he asked.

"We're about to find out."

He patted her thigh and made his way to the position he'd chosen for himself, where the men would have to look straight into the glare of the sun to see him.

The eastern dune was shorter than the others, which worked for his plan. Nomad was on his plastic bag, ready to go, when Simone started her sidestep over the dune.

That Simone was walking up and down each hill in sand that came up to her ankles meant that he and Red had the opportunity to get out in front of her by using their thick black garbage bags as sleds at a distance that kept them out of her line of sight. It not only cut their time, it saved their energy. Simone had to be exhausted. She was moving from west to east, with her head hanging, watching her steps.

Red was lying on the northern dune.

The six camels and three men were in the basin below.

Nomad was counting on Simone being worn out because, no matter the front Red put up, Red hadn't fully recovered from her bout of typhoid.

Laying at the top of his dune, camouflaged in his Sahara-sand-colored tactical wear, he watched the scene unfold.

As Simone approached, Blue called out the commands to get his camel to lie down. As soon as the camel's front knees touched the sand, Nomad slid down the slope, aiming straight for the man wearing a green T-shirt who had twisted away from the glare of the sun. Nomad grasped Green's ankle and jerked him from his camel. Green yelled out as he slid over the top, stopping his call abruptly when he saw the size of Nomad hovering over him. Grabbing at the man's robes, Nomad pulled Green far enough off the ground that his strike would do the most damage. Nomad chambered his fist and then let the punch fly to the full extent of his arm so the physics of the strike to the man's jaw would whip his head fast enough to put him out.

Though Nomad's knuckles slid along the man's beard, diminishing the impact slightly, the man was unconscious when Nomad released Green's robes. Doubling into a crouch, Nomad moved under the belly of Green's anxious camel.

"Mohammed, what did you do? What are you doing?" Brown demanded.

Blue had his camel halfway through the front back, front back shifts of getting to the ground where he could dismount. Neither up nor down, Blue was twisting his head, looking at his comrades and then at Simone, ankle-deep in the sand, as she moved slowly down the slope.

Green's camel didn't like Nomad underneath her and pressed sideways into her herd mate, trapping Brown's leg.

Brown leaned over to press the camel away. And when Nomad saw Brown's leg shift downward, signaling that he was off balance, Nomad wrapped his hand around the guy's ankle and jerked hard.

The guy landed between the two camels, clinging with one hand to the saddle cloth, jaw slack with astonishment.

The call of warning from Blue signaled that Red was sledding down the dune toward Simone.

Brown reached up and pawed at the blankets, and Nomad knew he was looking for his weapon. Nomad didn't have the angle for a jaw strike. He wrenched the guy around as he squatted to tuck Brown into the crook of his arm. With his free hand, he clasped his wrist and tightened the pressure on the man's artery. At the same time, he pushed into his heels and stood. The man dangled a foot off the ground, kicking and flailing. But that didn't last long.

Nomad dropped the unconscious man to the ground.

With a hand wrapped into the belly strap of each of the camels to keep them as cover, Nomad walked forward.

Two down, one to go.

But that one had a knife to Red's throat, looking around wildly, trying to figure out what was happening.

Simone had decided she was out of there and had turned around. Using hands and feet, she was scrambling up the dune.

Blue focused on Simone, beseeching her in Arabic to come back.

He was clearly the youngest. And he was lowest in rank, or he would not have been tasked with getting the woman saddled up.

Red called in Arabic, "Friend, may God's blessing be upon you. Why are you treating me with violence?"

"Are you … Who are you? You are not the woman we are to meet."

"Two women. You were told two women, were you not? Do you think I would let my niece travel alone in the desert with men who are not her kin?"

"You are her auntie?"

"Of course. You know this. Take your blade from my neck. This is inhospitable."

She was pitch-perfect. Nomad would have believed her. A mix of incredulity, kindness, and offense. But he also saw that she was twisting the black plastic garbage bag into a rope, getting ready.

The knife hadn't moved.

"Then why is she running?" The man's voice was pitched an octave higher, and he seemed wild-eyed and desperate that he was suddenly here in a situation he didn't understand, and his comrades had disappeared.

"Would you not run if a stranger took out their knife and held it to your aunt's throat? What else is she to do—a woman?"

Green was moaning. And that made Blue shift toward the sound.

That was all Red needed.

Wrapping the man's wrist in her bag rope, she was able to get control of it while giving herself space from the blade. She used the hard edge of her sole to scrape the length of the man's shin, hitting all the pain points. Lifting her knee to chest, she stomped his toes, unprotected in his leather sandals. That would have been a better move on a hard surface, but it still had to hurt.

Nomad was at her side, relieving Blue of the knife.

Once Red saw the weapon had been cleared, she reached between the man's legs, grabbed what Nomad had to assume was the man's scrotal sack, and twisted her hand as she pulled her elbow back like she was starting a lawn mower.

In sympathy with the man who must be seeing his life flash in front of his eyes, Nomad winced, drawing one knee over the other as he bent protectively. "Shit, Cassie."

"He had a knife to my throat, *Nicholi*."

"Fair."

The man was on all fours, vomiting into the sand.

Catching Nomad's eye, Red asked, "Did you get their pictures?"

"Not yet. Doing it now." Nomad moved from one man to the next, snapping photos—front, left and right. And took their fingerprints for good measure. "I think I'm done walking up and down these dunes," he said. "Let's ride the camels. And, so these guys can't catch up once they've recovered, we'll take all of them with us."

"Catch up to Simone, get her pack, get back to the ATV, fill up with gas—"

"And let the camels go," Nomad finished. "Someone will find them."

"Now that sounds like a winning strategy." Red looked over at Green as he started to rouse. Brown was still out cold. "Is he still alive?"

Red

"WHERE ARE YOU TWO RIGHT NOW?" BLACK ASKED OVER THE speakerphone.

"We rented a car to drive to Rabat," Nomad said as he slowed for a turn. "So we can catch our flight."

"I have updates."

Red leaned forward against her seatbelt. "You sound like you sunk your teeth into something juicy."

"I can tell you broad strokes of your successes this week," Black said. "First, about Moussa's death. I am sorry for your loss."

Red swallowed and audibly sniffed air into her lungs before she could say, "Thank you."

"But his death is heroic. He saved thousands of lives. Possibly tens of thousands of lives."

Tension formed around Red's eye sockets as she held her lids open and unblinking. "What have you found?"

"From the various sources of information, we got a list of the terrorists that are on American soil. We have their safe houses and their targets. The FBI is staging a simultaneous raid of each location. No other information offered."

"Good." Red and Nomad said together.

"I can confirm that the men who took you and Elena at the ball were indeed members of the treasure-hunting team. The hit in Munich was well-planned and executed, but Elena et al didn't wipe out the entire team for whatever reason. Only those present would be killed. The hole in that plan? Dangerous, capable team members who would seek the ring, the money from the bounty, and vengeance. Those four are in the wind. The CIA has no interest in pursuing them. They are not associated with terror or crimes against America. If the Moroccan government wants to figure out the murders outside of the Palais Royale, they will have received an anonymous intelligence report with the details that we have that are unassociated with the ring."

"Okay." Red sat back in her chair and popped her seat belt over her chest. "There were two other terrorist targets. Did you figure them out?"

"One was planned for a concert this fall. The organizer, the host city, and the head of state received that information. They were planning to use explosives that they obtained in Algeria and bring them across the Mediterranean. No money, so that one might peter out anyway. But plenty of eyes on the situation. The last one was nick of time and is planned for outside of Moscow."

Red said, "Elena had daddy issues."

"Yes, aggressively angry daddy issues," Black agreed. "And daddy owns a sports park where there is to be a soccer match."

"When?" Nomad asked.

"Today."

"Wait." Red's brows flew up to her brow. "Today?"

"Elena's mom's birthday. They planned a Trojan horse attack and have had tangoes on site for months."

"But the government knows," Red pressed. "We have a duty to warn."

"They were warned with plenty of time. We were able to give them not only the detailed plans but also the names, addresses, and even the phone numbers of the men who planned to execute the directives."

"So safe?"

"Safe," Grey confirmed. "I'm heading into a meeting. Let me know when you land."

"Will do. Thanks, Black."

"Out."

"And they all lived happily ever after." Red turned to Nomad. "Ties up with a nice neat little bow."

They drove in silence, holding hands. Red felt the weight of the next few hours.

She roused from her thoughts when Nomad squeezed her hand. "Talk to me, I'm falling asleep."

"Do you want me to drive?"

"In a bit. I'm good for another hour except in the silence. The radio is doing nothing for me." They had the French news as background noise to hear if anyone said anything about missing tourists in the east. "What are you thinking about?" Nomad asked.

"Have you ever considered what you'll do after you leave the military?"

"I have some friends who work for a group named Iniquus. That might be something I'd consider. I might like to go to university. Working for the State Department interests me."

"Who are your friends at Iniquus? I know some of the operators working there."

"My team's K9 used to be handled by a guy named Tripwire. He left the SEALs because he contracted an illness that affected his lung capacity. He's on Cerberus Team Alpha.

We're in regular contact with him to share updates and K9 antics. And then, back when I was a Green Beret, I worked with a guy named Ares in East Africa. He's now head of Cerberus Team Bravo. I haven't talked to him in a good while. I should catch up with him and see what he's up to. He left to take care of his K9 after his dog was seriously injured during an op."

"That's unusual, isn't it?" Red asked.

"His dog, Judge, dove off the vehicle Ares was driving because it wasn't going fast enough to get to Ares's fiancée, who was about to have her throat slit by a guy hopped up on khat and wielding a machete."

"Woah!"

"The machete sliced down Judge's side when Judge was destroying the man."

"Did Ares fiancée survive?"

"She's alive. As far as I know, the psychological damage was too much. She shut down, and their relationship is in the rearview. Still, Ares loved—loves Hailey and felt like he owed Judge. Last I heard, after rehab, Judge and Ares had that new gig, and they like it there."

"You're not a Green Beret, now," Red said.

"I am not. I'm what you think I am."

She nodded. "Iniquus is headquartered in Washington, D.C. Do you think you'd like to do that then? Private security?"

"I don't think so. I know Iniquus is putting together Cerberus Team Charlie. Cerberus Teams are all tactical working K9s and their handlers. For the most part, their work is about getting people out of hot zones or pulling clients from mass disaster areas."

"Wholesome." Red smiled.

"Exactly. But I think I'd like to go to university. I have a lot of real-world experience under my belt. And a unique childhood that I think could be put to better use. I think working for the State Department makes sense."

"With all your languages? I'd say they'd be lucky to have you."

"What about you?" Nomad asked. "Is this where you'll stay until you retire, or have you thought about other things you might like to pursue?"

"This whole assignment is not what I do. I'm a field officer. I'm trained for the tactical side, of course. I don't enjoy the kind of work I've been called to do on this assignment. I'm a coffee and schmooze person. I manage my people. Yeah, I feel beat to hell by this last week."

Nomad rubbed her arm. "Did you tell your team?"

"They know."

"And what are they saying?"

Red turned toward the side window. "That I need to come in from the field for a bit. Take a rest."

"What's a bit?"

"A month?" She shrugged, looking back at him. "Six weeks?"

"But that's R&R, right? Or are you working out of Langley?"

"I'm lying in a hammock with a ginger beer in my hand, a book resting open in my lap, while I enjoy the tall trees of a very old forest, preferably on a mountain with a babbling brook. Perhaps I can go to town—where I don't speak the language, so I don't have to talk to anyone—and have some lovely woman with magic fingers massage my feet."

"I didn't know that was your kink." Nomad paused, then said speculatively, "I have some time accrued. I could go to the mountains with you and do the foot rubbing if you'd like. Ginger beer's not my thing, but I bet I could find something else to drink."

She lifted her hips and twisted in the seat so she could better look at him.

"I'd like to get to know you better," Nomad said. "I'm totally into you when you're high adrenaline. But you can't always be functioning in that mode. I'd like to know who you are half-awake in a hammock."

"Are you the same in the field and in your private life?" Red asked. "I'd like to know things about you, too."

"Like?"

"Having known my share of operators, I guess I'd like to know if you're the kind of man that squirms in his seat looking for the next rush."

"Fair. What do you think the answer is?"

"If you're a pipe hitter that never lets down, you're masking it well." She canted her head speculatively. "Yeah, it would be nice if you could join me."

"Here's a question for you along those same lines: What name will you check in under at the guest house? Will I be getting to know the real you or another pseudonym and the personality that goes with it?"

"Me." Red put her hand to her chest. "I'm Anaïs Rousseau. Johnna Red isn't me. It's merely a lotion that I wear like sunscreen."

A smile spread across Nomad's face as if he was charmed by the visual. "How's that?"

"I'm protecting my skin. I don't want to get burned." She smiled back at him. "Are you able to share your name, or will you remain Nomad?"

"I prefer you call me Nomad. It's been decades since I went by my given name."

"Rumpelstiltskin?"

"Close. Algernon Kesling."

"And your family likes you?" Red laughed.

"Yeah, actually, they really do." He squeezed her hand. "What was that look?"

"What?" Red blinked innocently.

"You wrinkled your nose. You don't like the name Algernon?"

"I read a book once, *Flowers for Algernon*. And I was remembering that. I liked the name a lot, but I didn't like what happened in the book. It made me sad and—I don't know—uneasy."

"Ah, I see. But you like me." There was no question in his tone.

"I extra like you. Absolutely." They smiled at each other like teenagers, and it felt strange but exciting. "What did they call you as a kid?"

"Leeland. My middle name.

"I bet when you were a kid, your schoolmates called you Greenland."

"Iceland. But it's the same genre of funny."

"I love Iceland. It's rugged and beautiful." Red replayed those words in her head. He would hear her inserting his name into that phrase. Good. It was what she was inferring. She watched his reaction, which was amusement and warmth. "I think they had you pegged—Nomad seems—"

Red stopped. Adrenaline was shooting through her system. She grabbed at the dial and cranked the volume.

In French, the newscaster droned through information about an ongoing terrorist attack taking place at a sporting complex just outside of Moscow.

"Nomad!"

"I heard."

"They didn't stop it. Black said that Russia had the information. Could it have been wrong? Did we not get it to them fast enough?"

"More likely, it was America handing it over, and the Russian government didn't want to believe we knew something they did not. Or maybe they'd rather take the attack and not be beholden."

Red dropped her head into her hands. "I knew it," she whispered.

"Yes, we knew," Nomad's voice was patient. "We warned them."

"That's not what I mean. I knew that nothing would come from our intelligence."

Nomad's body tightened as he drove down the road.

"I'm getting a little superstitious, I think," Red whispered. "Premonitions." She waved a hand by her ear.

"What are we talking about here?" Nomad asked.

"I've started to see a pattern. I guess pattern is a better way to say this than premonition in this case. There's a pattern in the names they give me when I am handed a temporary identity."

"Beyond Red? This is Cassandra? I remember it upset you when you saw it in the papers at the Amsterdam airport."

"Cassandra, the Greek goddess who knows the truth but is cursed that no one ever believes her. She told Troy about the Trojan Horse."

"And Black mentioned a Trojan horse. That's a little too spot on. It actually sent a chill down my spine."

"I am so angry right now," Red clutched her chest. "I am so angr—"

A sudden shriek of rubber against asphalt filled her ears. Her world was a swirl of color and pressure and pain.

Then crazy amusement-park-ride pull of centrifugal forces stopped as abruptly as it had started.

Her eyes were squeezed tightly shut. This was all so familiar.

She'd been through this before—the same sounds, the same

sensations. Just like when she was in the explosion in Lebanon, she simply needed to give her brain a second to identify what was going on.

Back at the hospital under sedation. Red had dreamed about the two women. She dreamed she was sent on a wild ride up and down. As Red walked through the desert following Simone, Red thought that that dream had been a premonition.

And at the end of that dream, Red now remembered, had been a car accident.

Back at the hospital, Red couldn't feel her legs but had decided that was the effect of sedation.

But this…they were the same sensations as in the dream.

In the dream, someone had been beside her; she'd reached out.

There had been blood.

"Are you okay?" Red had asked in the dream.

Holding very still, her eyes closed, Red forced her lips to move. "Nomad, are you okay?" When he didn't answer, she managed to reach a hand toward him. "Are you okay?"

EPILOGUE

Two years later

THE WOMAN BEHIND THE DESK AT THE FRONT OF THE ANKARA Embassy's private offices stood and walked around to the entrance. "Madame Ambassador, what a pleasure it is to welcome you." She held out her hand. "I'm Mrs. Serife. And Leeland." She put her hand to her chest. "My apologies, Mr. Kesling."

"Leeland. Or Nomad. It's so good to see you again, Mrs. Serife," Nomad smiled.

"I received your letter after your last visit to the embassy. I am so grateful that you solved that puzzle for me. You were so familiar, but I simply couldn't put my finger on it." She turned to Anaïs. "I knew your husband when he was a five-year-old boy. Just the sweetest, gentlest child. He loved soft things, so I'd bring my Angora rabbit for him to sit and play with on rainy days. They were very good friends." She focused on Nomad's face. "The eyepatch is new. And somehow dashing."

"My wife and I were in an automobile accident in Morocco." He put his hand on the back of Anaiis's wheelchair. "It was the compass needle that turned our life around one-eighty."

Mrs. Serife nodded gravely. "You had to leave the military?"

"I chose to," Nomad said. "I could have stayed in and worked out of the Pentagon, but it's not a good fit for me. And, of course, Anaïs, after she was healthy and wanted to be back in this region that she loves so much, was offered the ambassadorship—a well-deserved gesture of gratitude from our administration—and she decided to accept the position."

"Well, I can't tell you how delighted I am," Mrs. Serife said. "At your request, we've asked the introductions be put on hold until tomorrow. Your visitors have arrived already, Ambassador Rousseau. A Ms. Johnna White and a Mr. John Green."

"Thank you," Anaïs said. "But while they were my colleagues, they came to speak with my husband. Nomad works for the State Department now, just as his father did back in the day."

Look for new Iniquus titles coming soon.

The next book in Iniquus World Chronology is:

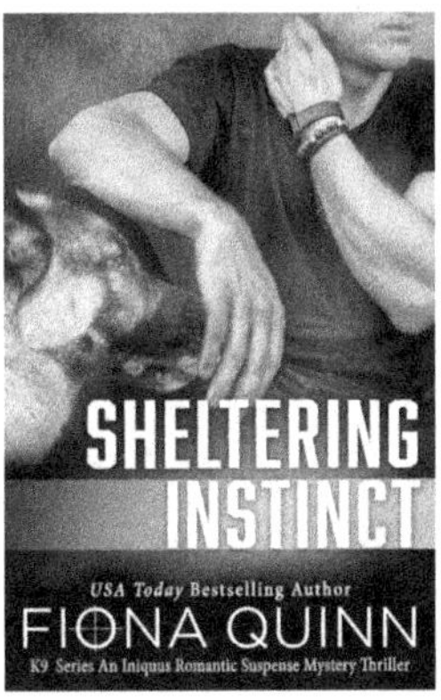

DID YOU KNOW THAT

SHELTERING INSTINCT IS BOOK THIRTY-FIVE IN THE WORLD OF INIQUUS!

**Sheltering Instinct
(Cerberus Tactical K9 Team Charlie Book 2)
Is scheduled for release in January 2025**

Meet the newest member of Iniquus' Cerberus Tactical K9 Team Charlie.

While on a close protection assignment, Levi travels to Namibia to test a tactical K9 to see if they'd be a good match. Close protection? Close call is more like it. It's not only Levi's life on the line but his heart as well.

If you're new to Iniquus, ***turn two pages*** to read chapter one of
WEAKEST LYNX .

At the end of the Weakest Lynx chapter, for your convenience,
you will find

THE WORLD of INIQUUS in chronological order.

READERS

I hope you enjoyed getting to know Red, and Nomad. If you had fun reading **Red Line**, I'd appreciate it if you'd help others enjoy it, too.

Recommend it: A few words to your friends, book groups, and social networks would be fantastic.

Review it: Please tell your fellow readers what you liked about my book by writing a quick reviewing.

Discuss it!: In **Fiona Quinn's SPOILER group** on Facebook.

WEAKEST LYNX
CHAPTER ONE

THE BLACK BMW POWERED STRAIGHT TOWARD ME. HEART pounding, I stomped my brake pedal flush to the floorboard. My chest slammed into the seat belt, snapping my head forward. There wasn't time to blast the horn, but the scream from my tires was deafening. I gasped in a breath as the BMW idiot threw me a nonchalant wave—his right hand off the wheel— with his left hand pressed to his ear, still chatting on his cell phone. Diplomatic license plates. *Figures.*

Yeah, I didn't really need an extra shot of adrenaline—like a caffeine IV running straight to my artery—I was already amped.

"Focus, Lexi," I whispered under my breath, pressing down on the gas. "Follow the plan. Give the letter to Dave. Let him figure this out." I sent a quick glance down to my purse where a corner of the cream-colored envelope jutted out, then veered my Camry back into the noonday DC gridlock, weaving past the graffitied storefronts. I recognized that the near-miss with the BMW guy probably wasn't his fault. I couldn't remember the last ten minutes of drive time.

I watched my review mirror as a bike messenger laced between the moving cars on his mission to get the parcel in his bag to the right guy at the right time. Once he handed over his package, he'd be done—lucky him. Even though I was handing my letter off to Dave, the truth was that wouldn't be my endpoint. I wasn't clear about what an endpoint would even look like. Safe. It might look like I was safe, that I had my feet back under me. But that thought seemed like it was far out on the horizon, and right now, I was just looking for something to grab on to, to keep me afloat.

When I finally parked in front of Dave Murphy's mid-century brick row house, I sat for a minute, trying to regain my composure. I'd pushed this whole mess to the back burner for as long as I could but after last night's nightmare… Well, better to get a detective's opinion. Dave had handled enough crackpots over his time with the DCPD that he'd have a better grasp of the threat level. Right now, even with all my training, I was scared out of my mind.

I glanced down at my hands. The tremor in them sent the afternoon sunlight dancing off my brand-new engagement and wedding rings. I felt like an imposter wearing them—like a little girl dressed up in her mother's clothes. *I'm too young to be dealing with all this crap,* I thought as I shoved my keys into my purse. I pulled my hair into a quick ponytail and stepped out into the February cold. Casting anxious glances up and down the street, I jogged up the stairs to bang on Dave's front door.

The screen squeaked open almost immediately as if he'd been standing there waiting for my knock. "Hey, Baby Girl," he said, stepping out of the way to let me in. Dave had been calling me Baby Girl since I was born because my parents couldn't decide on my name, and that was how I was listed on my hospital ankle tag.

"Glad I found you at home." I walked in and plopped down on the blue gingham couch. It had been here since I could remember. The fabric was threadbare and juice stained by his five-year-old twins. On a cop's salary, fine furnishings ranked low in priority. Right now—edgy and confused—I appreciated the comfort of familiarity.

Dave shifted into detective mode—hands on hips, eyes scanning me. "Long time, no see."

"Where are Cathy and the kids?" I asked.

"They've got dentist appointments. Did you come to tell us your news?" He lifted his chin to indicate my left hand and settled at the other end of the couch, swiveling until we were face to face.

"Uhm, no." I twisted my rings, suddenly feeling drained and bereft. What wouldn't I give to have my husband Angel here? The corners of my mouth tugged down. I willed myself to stay focused on the reason for the visit. My immediate safety had to take priority over my grief.

Dave raised a questioning brow, waiting for me to continue.

"Angel and I got married Wednesday. I'm Lexi Sobado now." My voice hitched, and tears pressed against my lids. I lowered my lashes, so Dave wouldn't see. But his eyes had locked onto mine, and he never missed much.

"Married? At your age? No introduction? No wedding invitation? Why isn't he here with you now?" Dave angled his head to the side and crossed his arms over his middle-aged paunch. "I'd like to meet the guy," he all but snarled.

Dave probably thought I'd come here because my husband screwed things up already. I pulled the pillow from behind my back and hugged it to me like a shield. "I'm sorry. I should have let you and Cathy know what was going on—I was caught up, and I just..." I stopped to clear my throat. "Angel and I got married at the courthouse, and no one came with us. Not even Abuela Rosa."

"Angel Sobado. He's kin to Rosa, then?"

I gave the slightest tip of a nod. "Angel is her great-nephew.

I couldn't bring him with me today because he deployed with the Rangers to the Middle East Thursday. That's why everything happened so fast. He was leaving." The last word stuck in my throat and choked me.

Dave leaned forward to rest his elbows on his knees. Lacing his fingers, he tapped his thumbs together. "Huh. That's a helluva short honeymoon. Married Wednesday. Gone Thursday." Dave's tone had dropped an octave and gained a fringe of fatherly concern.

His compassion gave me permission to break down. But those Angel-emotions were mine. Private. Right now, I needed to hold myself in check long enough to get through my mission of handing off the letter. I shifted my feet back and forth over the rug as I glared at my purse.

"Might even explain the expression on your face," Dave said, narrowing his eyes. He slouched against the arm of the overstuffed couch.

Stalling wasn't going to make this any easier. I reached a hesitant hand into my bag, pulled out a plastic Zip-loc holding the envelope, and held it up for Dave. "The expression is because of this," I said.

Dave took the bag. After a brief glance, he hefted himself to his feet. Over at his desk, he pulled on a pair of Nitrile gloves, then carefully removed the letter.

Dearest India Alexis,

O my Luve's like the melodie
That's sweetly play'd in tune!
As fair thou art, my bonnie lass,
So deep in love, am I:
And I will love thee still, my dear,
Till a' your bones are white and dry:

Till a' your veins gang dry, my dear,
And your skin melt with the sun;
I will luve thee until your heart is still my dear
When the sands of your life shall no more run.
And fare thee weel, my only Luve,
And fare thee weel a while!
And I will come again, my Luve, so I can watch you die.

Dave read the words aloud then stared at me hard; his brows pulled in tight enough that the skin on his forehead accordioned. "What the—"

"Someone shoved the poem under the door to my room, and it's scaring the bejeezus out of me." I gripped the pillow tighter.

Dave peered over the top of his reading glasses. "Last night? This morning?"

"Wednesday morning." I braced when I said it, knowing it would tick Dave off that I didn't bring this to him immediately. Ever since my dad died, his buddies had stepped in and tried to take over the fathering job, even though I'd be turning twenty in a few days.

True to my expectations, Dave was red-faced and bellowing. "*Wednesday?* You waited two whole days to tell me you've gotten a friggin death threat?"

Yup, this was exactly the response Dad would have given me.

Dave jumped up, pacing across the room. Obviously, he didn't think this was someone's idea of a joke. Fear tightened my chest at his confirmation. I had hoped he'd say, "No worries —someone is having fun pranking you," and then I could go on about my life without the major case of heebie-jeebies that tingled my skin and made me want to run and hide.

"It was our wedding day." I worked to modulate my voice to

sound soft and reasonable. "I only had a few short hours before Angel had to take off. So yeah, I decided to focus on us instead of this." I motioned toward the paper in his hand.

Dave took in a deep breath, making his nostrils flare. "Okay." I could almost see his brain shifting gears. "When you first picked up the letter, did you get any vibes?"

"You mean, ESP-wise?"

He nodded stiffly, his eyes hard on me.

Vibes. That wasn't the word I would have chosen to explain my sensations. "I didn't hear anything. It was more like an oily substance oozing over me." I tucked my nose into the soft cloth of the pillow and breathed in the scent of cinnamon fabric freshener. "I vomited." My voice dropped to a whisper. "It felt like evil and craziness, and I can still smell that stench." A shiver raced down my spine.

Dave's lips sealed tightly; he was probably trying to hold back a litany of expletives. Finally, he asked, "That's all?"

"Yes."

"Did any of your neighbors notice anyone unusual lurking around? Did you check with management and run through the security tapes?"

"Dave, didn't you hear? My apartment building burned to the ground three weeks ago. I assumed you knew. It was on the news."

Dave's eyebrows shot straight up.

"I've been living in a motel the Red Cross rented out for all the families displaced by the fire. But to answer your question, no, nobody saw anything, and there were no cameras trained on my motel corridor." I curled my lips in to keep them from trembling. I was used to holding my emotions in check. I trained myself to present a sweet exterior, a costume of sorts, but right now, I was filled to overflowing, and my mask kept slipping out of place.

"Shit." Dave ran a hand over his face. "I had no idea. I'm letting your parents down. Apartment burned, married, husband gone, and now a death threat." His eyes narrowed on me. "Do you think that about covers all of your surprises for me today?"

I paused for a beat. "Yeah, Dave, I think that's it for today." Okay, even if he was like family, the way Dave was talking pissed me off. I was frightened. I wanted a hug and his reassurance. What I was getting was... Dave's brand of love. He wouldn't be this red-faced and agitated if he wasn't worried about me. Tears prickled behind my eyelids, blurring my vision.

"Hey, now. Stop. We'll get to the bottom of this. Did you already let Spyder McGraw know what's going on?"

I wiped my nose with the back of my wrist. "Spyder's still off-grid. I have no idea when he'll get home."

"Were you assigned a different partner while he's gone?"

"No, sir. I only ever worked for Spyder—he sort of wanted to keep me a secret." I still couldn't believe Mom had sat Dave down and told him all about my apprenticeship with Spyder McGraw. Under Spyder's tutelage, I was following my dream of becoming an Intelligence Officer, learning to out-think and out-maneuver the bad guys trying to hurt American interests. And like anyone heading toward a life in the intelligence community, my skills needed to go under the radar. Now that my mom had died, only four people—Spyder, the Millers, and Dave—knew that side of my life. I would prefer Dave didn't know.

"Still, did you consider bringing this to Spyder's commander? Iniquus would probably give him a heads up. Get a message to him."

"Iniquus is my last resort. Sure, Spyder told me to talk to them if I ever found myself in trouble." I sucked in a deep breath of air. "Bottom line? He never wanted them to know I worked for him, well, for them. Safety in anonymity and all that." My fingers kneaded the stuffing in the pillow. "Besides, I guess I was hoping this would all just go away."

Dave's eyes were hard on me. "You know better. Once some psycho's caught you on his radar, you're stuck there until someone wins."

"Okay, so I make sure it's me who wins."

"Exactly right." He considered me for a minute before he asked, "You've kept up with your martial arts training?"

"I have a sparring partner who's pretty good. We rent time at a Do Jang twice a week."

Dave lowered his head to read over the poem again. He put the letter and envelope back in the Zip-loc and placed it on his mantle. Pulling off his gloves with a snap, he looked down at them. "I hate these things. They give me a rash. Look, I'm going to take this down to the station and open a file. If you get anything else, I want you to bring it to me right away. Understood?"

"Yes, sir."

"This is the only poem, letter, communication of any kind you've gotten?"

I nodded. For the first time since I walked into Dave's house, I became aware of sounds other than our conversation and the thrumming blood behind my eardrums. A football game played on TV. I glanced over as the announcer yelled some gibberish about a first down, then moved my gaze back to Dave. "You must have taken graveyard shift last night," I said.

He picked up a remote, zapped off the TV, and sent me a raised eyebrow.

"It doesn't take a psychic. You look like an unmade bed."

Dave ran a hand over his dark hair, thick on the sides, sparse on top. He hadn't used a comb today or bothered to shave. He was hanging-out-at-home comfy in jeans and beat-to-hell tennis shoes. It looked like the only thing I was interrupting was the game re-run.

"Double homicide. Turned into a long night up to my ankles in sewage."

"Yum." I tried on a smile, but it was plastic and contrived.

Dave narrowed his eyes. "We need to move you. Pronto. It's priority one. You need to be someplace secure where I can keep better tabs on you."

"I've been looking since the fire, but I haven't found anything."

"Would you consider buying?" he asked.

"Yes, actually—I'm looking for a low-cost fixer-upper I can work on to help me get through this year without Angel." I followed Dave into the hallway. "Diversion, and all that."

"How about here, in my neighborhood? I could keep a better eye on you—and you won't be showing up at my door with a suitcase full of surprises." He grabbed his coat from the

closet and shrugged it on. "I'm taking you over to meet my neighbor. She has the other half of her duplex on the market." He looked over his shoulder at me. "You shouldn't be running around without a jacket." He handed me an oversized wool parka that smelled like raking leaves. He kicked a Tonka truck out of the way, and we moved out the front door.

On the front porch, I slid into the shadows and took in the length of the road—no cars, no barking dogs, everything quiet.

Dave glanced back. "Coast is clear."

I tucked the coat hood up over my ponytail. Screened by Dave's broad back, I started across the street. Down the road, a car motor revved. I reached under my shirt and pulled out my gun.

I hope you enjoyed this sample. Find Weakest Lynx at retail stores in eBook, Paperback, Hardback, and Audiobook formats.

THE WORLD of INIQUUS

Chronological Order

Ubicumque, Quoties. Quidquid

Weakest Lynx (Lynx Series)

Missing Lynx (Lynx Series)

Chain Lynx (Lynx Series)

Cuff Lynx (Lynx Series)

WASP (Uncommon Enemies)

In Too DEEP (Strike Force)

Relic (Uncommon Enemies)

Mine (Kate Hamilton Mystery)

Jack Be Quick (Strike Force)

Deadlock (Uncommon Enemies)

Instigator (Strike Force)

Yours (Kate Hamilton Mystery)

Gulf Lynx (Lynx Series)

Open Secret (FBI Joint Task Force)

Thorn (Uncommon Enemies)
Ours (Kate Hamilton Mysteries)
Cold Red (FBI Joint Task Force)
Even Odds (FBI Joint Task Force)
Survival Instinct - (Cerberus Tactical K9 Team Alpha)
Protective Instinct - (Cerberus Tactical K9 Team Alpha)
Defender's Instinct - (Cerberus Tactical K9 Team Alpha)
Danger Signs - (Delta Force Echo)
Hyper Lynx - (Lynx Series)
Danger Zone - (Delta Force Echo)
Danger Close - (Delta Force Echo)
Fear the REAPER – (Strike Force)
Warrior's Instinct - (Cerberus Tactical K9 Team Bravo)
Rescue Instinct - (Cerberus Tactical K9 Team Bravo)
Heroes Instinct - (Cerberus Tactical K9 Team Bravo)
Striker (Striker Force)
Marriage Lynx (Lynx Series)
A Family of the Heart Cookbook
Guardian's Instinct - (Cerberus Tactical K9 Team Charlie)
Beowulf - (Certified Cerberus Tactical K9)
Red Line (CIA Color Code)
Sheltering Instinct (Cerberus Tactical K9 Team Charlie)

With more Iniquus novels to follow!

For the most up to date list go to FionaQuinnBooks.com
This list was created in 2024.

ACKNOWLEDGMENTS
MY GREAT APPRECIATION

To my publicist, **Margaret Daly**
To my cover artist, **Melody Simmons**
To my editor, **Rossana Tarantini**

To my Street Force, who support me and my writing with such enthusiasm and kindness.

To all the professionals who shared their knowledge of working K9s especially the various Virginia search and rescue teams.

To all the wonderful professionals whom I called on to get the details right as I conducted my research, especially **B. Boswell** and **M. Carlon** for their medical expertise.

To **Janelle Axton** for her kindness, her companionship, and all our glamping and Medina adventures, especially our visit to the Mouassine Hammam.

To **Jason Leonard**: At 6' 6", Jason threw me over his shoulder and let me try to escape, which, admittedly, only resulted in his booming laughter. I could not, in fact, escape. But I appreciated his suggestion that as Nomad put Red back on her feet that she "Spaz out like a cat." The scene in the Amsterdam streets was the result of our improv. Thanks for being such a good sport, Jason.

Please note: This is a work of fiction, and while I always try my best to get all the details correct, there are times when it serves the story to go slightly to the left or right of perfection.

Please understand that any mistakes or discrepancies are my authorial decision-making alone and sit squarely on my shoulders.

Thank you to my family for your love and support.

I send my love to my husband. T thank you for the help with the diamond information, a font of knowledge. You are my treasure.

And, of course, thank YOU for reading my stories. I always smile joyfully as I type this sentence.
I so appreciate you!

ABOUT THE AUTHOR

Fiona Quinn is a USA Today bestselling author, a Kindle Scout winner, Amazon Top 40, and an Amazon All-Star.

Quinn writes suspense in her Iniquus World of books, including Lynx, Strike Force, Uncommon Enemies, Kate Hamilton Mysteries, FBI Joint Task Force, Cerberus Tactical K9 Series: Alpha, Bravo, Charlie, and Certified Cerberus Tactical K9, the Delta Force Echo series, CIA Color Code Action Adventure, and now, an Iniquus cookbook!

She writes urban fantasy as Fiona Angelica Quinn for her Elemental Witches Series.

And, just for fun, she writes the Badge Bunny Booze Mystery Collection with her dear friend, Tina Glasneck, as Quinn Glasneck.

Quinn is rooted in the Old Dominion, where she lives with her husband. There, she pops chocolates, devours books, and taps continuously on her laptop.

Visit www.FionaQuinnBooks.com

COPYRIGHT

Red Line is a work of fiction. Names, characters, places, and incidents either are the product of the author's imagination or are used fictitiously, and any resemblance to actual persons, living or dead, business establishments, events, or locales is entirely coincidental.